5-16-11

Book one of

The Atonement Trilogy

The Spirit of Revenge

Written by

Bryan Gifford

All rights reserved. No part of this book shall be reproduced or transmitted in any form or by any means, electronic, mechanical, magnetic, photographic including photocopying, recording or by any information storage and retrieval system, without prior written permission of the publisher. No patent liability is assumed with respect to the use of the information contained herein. Although every precaution has been taken in the preparation of this book, the publisher and author assume no responsibility for errors or omissions. Neither is any liability assumed for damages resulting from the use of the information contained herein.

Copyright © 2011 by Bryan Gifford

ISBN 0-7414-6470-5 Paperback
ISBN 0-7414-6471-3 Hardcover

Printed in the United States of America

This is a work of fiction. Names, characters, places, and incidents either are the product of the author's imagination or are used fictitiously. Any resemblance to actual events or locales or persons, living or dead, is entirely coincidental.

Published May 2011

INFINITY PUBLISHING
1094 New DeHaven Street, Suite 100
West Conshohocken, PA 19428-2713
Toll-free (877) BUY BOOK
Local Phone (610) 941-9999
Fax (610) 941-9959
Info@buybooksontheweb.com
www.buybooksontheweb.com

**** ****

This book is dedicated to all my friends and family,
without whom this dream would never
have become a reality.

**** ****

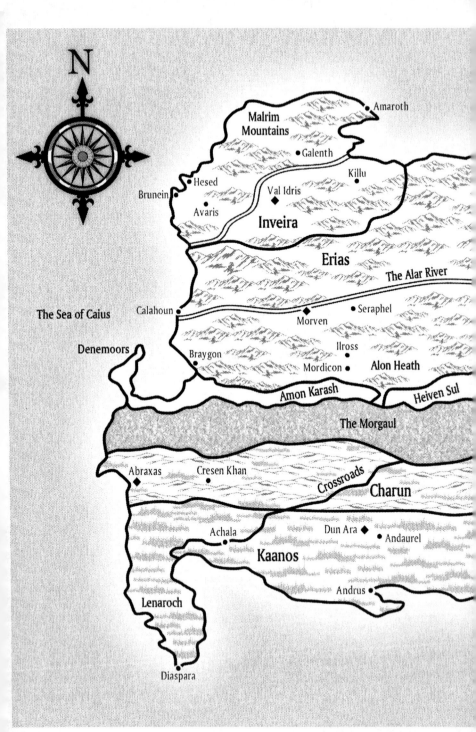

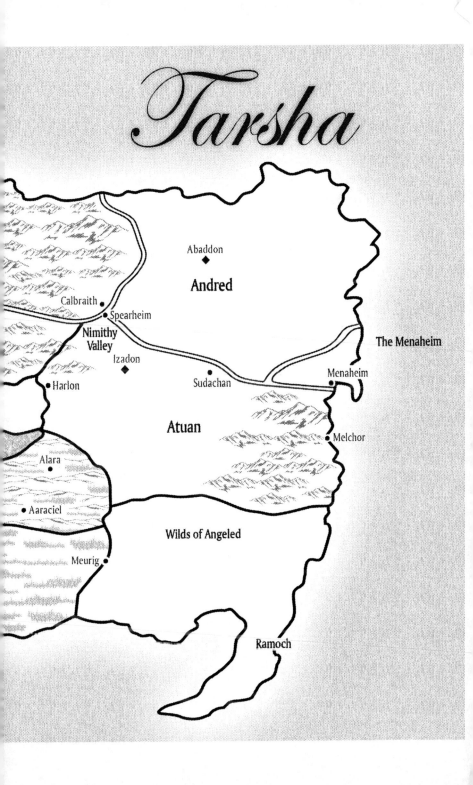

CONTENTS

CONTENTS

The Spirit of Revenge

"Revenge is but a confession of pain."

–Latin proverb

A Promise Undone

Dust rose high off the plains as fifty riders galloped over the countryside of Kaanos. An autumn wind blew from the north, sending ripples through the blonde grass. It was near sunset, the skies stained scarlet with the blood of the dying day. Their horses were flecked with foam and sweat, yet the soldiers did not cease their fierce gallop until their leader threw up a hand. At once, the riders slowed to a standstill at the crest of a hill.

Below them lay a city swathed in sunlight, its thatched roofs glistening bullions in the dusk. The soldiers whipped their reins and guided their mounts down the hill. They soon reached the cobble road that split the town in half and followed it deeper into the sea of buildings. The crowds of people split as the riders tore through the city and came to a stop at the town square.

Hundreds gathered around them, quickly filling the court. An old man pushed through the crowds and approached the beleaguered soldiers. "What is it, Cain?" He asked.

"The Arzecs," the man at the head of the column replied, "They're here…" With this, the crowd was instantly silenced.

"This cannot be." The old man's brow furled, sending wrinkles cascading over his dark seamed face.

"I'm afraid so," Cain continued, "over a thousand troops march upon us as we speak. They'll be here by sunrise."

"Are we to receive any aid?"

The soldier closed his eyes behind his helmet. "These are the Arzecs we have been tracking for weeks. They have been on the march to the capital until now, and in his fear, the King has ordered all troops to the capital. We are alone in this fight."

The old man shook his head. "Then we have little time." He turned and raised his arms to the crowd of silent onlookers.

"Behold, people of Andaurel, the Arzecs descend upon us! For four hundred years, the world has fought against the tyrant Abaddon! We have battled his armies for four centuries, seeking freedom from his ruthless genocide! We have sacrificed too many lives and shed too much blood! This ends now!" The crowds cheered.

"We have the chance to do so within these next few hours! All able-bodied men gather your arms and await further instruction at the north road. Citizens, leave behind all you do not need and wait for an armed escort to the capital, Dun Ara. Tonight we fight for our very survival, unaided and alone…"

**** ****

The courtyard was now empty. The crowds had long since left, unwilling to leave their homes behind and even more unwilling to face what lay before them.

The soldier named Cain removed his helmet. He was tall and strongly built. He had clearly been in the sun so long that his skin was baked nearly as dark as his eyes. He wore heavy leather armor and a brown fauld that swayed about his knees as he walked.

The old man approached him. He stopped at Cain's side and clapped him on the shoulder. He gazed off through the buildings and brushed the mane of silver hair from his eyes before speaking. "This war against Abaddon has been dragging on for over four hundred years. I have fought its battles since I was your age. I was certain I would see its end. But now…I'm not so sure."

Cain ran a hand through his sweat-drenched hair. "I'm not so sure even I will, Grend. I don't even understand half of what's going on."

Grend fingered his graying beard in thought. "You will come to understand soon enough. I take leave of you now; I must prepare our men for the fight at hand. Go and speak with your wife, I'm sure she is eager to see you."

"Aye," Cain replied. He shook Grend's hand and walked across the court before turning down a side road. He weaved his way through the crowds of panicked citizens and wagons piled high with possessions.

He soon came to a stop at one of the many windowless daub homes and stepped inside. The warmth of a hearth's fire quickly met him as he stepped into the main room. Shelves covered with pottery and cookware lined the walls, and a large table filled most of the room.

A woman in dark linens was packing a rucksack, her back to him. He closed the door and she turned, eyes lit with surprise. She bound across the room and embraced him firmly.

"Cain! I've missed you so much…" She said near tears.

Cain kissed her warmly on the forehead and brushed the russet hair from her face. "I missed you too, Eileen."

"You've been gone for six months, fighting. I was beginning to think you'd never come back…or worse."

Cain kissed her again and turned from her. He unbuckled a long sword from his belt and set it beside his bow on the table.

"Alas, it's the war that brings me back. Some of Abaddon's forces we've been tracking have begun a march for Andaurel. They will be here by nightfall."

His wife nodded. "So I've heard. You promised you would set aside the sword when our baby is born…"

"How is our child?" He reached forward and rested a hand on her swollen stomach.

"He kicks. He has his father's strength."

"And hopefully his mother's brains," Cain laughed. "You think it's a boy?"

"I know it is," she smiled softly.

Cain stepped toward her and held her arms firmly. He looked deep into her vivid eyes, struggling to form his next words. "This war has taken everything from me, my parents, my childhood, my sanity. This war against Abaddon has lasted for four centuries, and I do not see its end in sight. I am tired of fighting when it matters not in the end. Every day I long to feel your hand in mine, but only the warmth of spilt blood do I find in them. I promise you, Eileen, that when our son is born, I will leave this path of bloodshed and take your hand forever in mine."

**** ****

Two hundred and fifty soldiers, fully clad in the garb of war, quietly waited by the crude spear walls that had been hastily thrown together to make a meager defense for the north section of the town.

The rasp of sharpening steel rang out in the crisp dusk air. The last of the sun's light dipped beneath the horizon and dark tendrils of twilight began their conquest of the skies.

Tension filled the air and permeated all around them. Silence enveloped the town of Andaurel, a shroud of ambiguity burying men among their thoughts.

Cain sat among the front ranks of the militia, leaning wearily against the palisade walls. A man weaved his way through the soldiers and stopped before Cain.

"There you are," the man said with a grin. He wore tattered black clothes over his spindly frame. Deep emerald eyes smiled at him from behind a curtain of sable hair. "I've been looking for you."

"Sorry, Aaron. I've been with Eileen."

The man named Aaron sheathed his saber in its scabbard before sitting down beside his friend. "I've been your friend for many years; I can tell when something's bothering you."

Cain smiled despite himself. "When the Arzecs killed my parents, I vowed to avenge their deaths. I have been fighting Abaddon's Arzecs for fifteen years now, and it seems so fruitless. Eileen wants me to quite fighting and leave it to others. But fighting is all I've ever known."

"Ah, women," a gruff voice said from beside them. They turned and saw two men standing near them. One was nearly a head taller than any other and extremely bulky, not all of which was muscle.

His hair was relentlessly shaven and polished steel armor covered nearly every inch of the vast canvas of his flesh.

The second man was shaven as well and adorned in a steel cuirass and fauld.

"Good to see you again, Joshua," Cain nodded to the taller man, "and you as well, Silas."

Joshua and Silas sat down beside them. "How is she?" Joshua asked.

"I don't know," Cain replied, "I haven't seen her in six months, and now that I have, I have to be here fighting...yet again."

"Don't beat yourself up about it," Silas said. "You'll get out of this scrap alive and end up happily ever after like all those other bullshit stories."

Cain laughed, "Thanks...but that's not what's really bothering me. This war has been going on for four hundred years against the same man, Abaddon. How has one man managed to bring war to all the countries of Tarsha, let alone live for four centuries...it doesn't make any sense."

"Aye," Joshua replied as he fingered his scraggly beard, "we've all heard the stories. They say humanity was blessed, loved and nurtured by their creator. But they grew corrupt and wicked, blinded by their arrogance." He paused for effect, clearly having recited this speech in his head prior.

"They began to worship themselves and turned their back on their god. In his anger, he gave them Abaddon, as punishment for their transgressions.

'In exchange for limitless power and immortality, Abaddon has since followed the will of the Forgotten who seeks to eradicate all of his errant creations."

Silas snorted, "That's nothing more than legend."

Joshua nodded, "Probably so, but I believe the stories. They make more sense than anything I can think of."

"How can you possibly believe that?" Silas inquired. Joshua merely shrugged and returned his gaze to the fields before them.

"All we have are legends," Aaron said, "not yet a single fact. We are muddled in the middle. But we will know the truth soon enough, before we see an end to it all."

"If we live to see an end," Silas retorted.

Cain shook his head. "Either way, I still want to know why the Arzecs we've been tracking all these weeks turned from their path of attack on Dun Ara to Andaurel. They had our capital in their sights, yet they chose to attack Andaurel, why?"

"Who knows?" Silas shrugged. "Our home is nothing but a small, isolated trade town. It's an easy target for the Arzecs. Their whole mindset in these four centuries of war has been nothing but kill as many of us as possible. Maybe they're just here for a bit of fun..."

Aaron rolled his saber slowly in his hand and dragged the tip through the sand. "But the Arzecs attacked Andaurel twenty two years ago remember?"

They knew this all too well. Their parents were killed in the attack, and as children, they were forced to evacuate before the enemy razed the city. And now, over twenty years later, they lay in wait to defend their home against

Abaddon's forces, just as their fathers had done on that fateful day. A cold weight sunk in their hearts at this thought.

"This isn't random," Aaron continued, the first to recover from this sinking feeling. "There's a reason the Arzecs are marching for Andaurel, I know it."

"Well whatever their reason," Silas replied, "I'm ready for the bastards." He reached over his shoulder and pulled a long staff from the sling at his back. It was over six feet in length and four vicious blades curved out of either end. "My Sitar will show them what hatred can do."

"And you're not alone, my brother," Joshua said as he picked up the massive double bladed axe he had set in the dirt.

The group soon fell quiet. Cain ran a hand through his auburn hair and lay back in the grass, gazing out over the starlit skies. Thin wisps of clouds floated across the starry heavens, mere silhouettes in the sky. The plains around them rippled like an ocean of gold beneath the glow of the full moon.

A nervous, pensive, look glazed over every soldier that lay in wait, awaiting that imminent black wave to pour over the hills. The hours dragged on as every second seemed a lifetime, every minute, an eternity.

Silas and Joshua sat playing cards beside the others, tossing coins into a pile, betting against each other to pass the time. Joshua cried out in elation as he threw down a hand of cards and dove for the pile of coins. Silas punched the ground and cursed at his defeat. Suddenly the coins chattered quietly.

Cain heard the noise and looked down at the pile. The small coins shook slightly and chattered again, then nothing. They then shook with abrupt force before tumbling from the pile one at a time.

Aaron turned to him with the same anxious look. "They're here," he muttered. Together, they jolted up and looked out to the north.

Through the darkness, a black line poured slowly over the hills. The coins at their feet scattered across the ground, a thousand thunderous footfalls jarring them apart.

"They're here!" Cain shouted as he tore his sword from its sheath. The soldiers stumbled from their thoughts and jumped up to gaze out over the ramparts.

Grend tore his way through the soldiers and ran toward the front lines, stopping beside the spear walls at the sight of the advancing enemy.

He turned to face his men and paced a moment before stopping beside Cain's company. "My fellow countrymen! We are abandoned by the very country we fight for! But do not despair! Do not dare let your wrathful flames be doused!" Grend thrust his sword in the air.

"Fight with me on this day of war! Fight for your families, fight for your homes, fight for your country! Show me what is worth fighting for; show me what's to die for! Live for vengeance, die for honor, but on this night, let your swords ring and the blood flow. Bask in the blood of your enemies!"

The soldiers of Kaanos let out an ear-piercing scream, two hundred and fifty fists thrust defiantly into the air. They were ready for death.

"Bows at the ready!" Grend yelled over the fierce wind. A sharp rasp of wood followed his command, arrows notched and strings pulled taught. The archers aimed down their arrow shafts at the oncoming tide of Arzecs.

The Arzecs were but a mockery of life, an insult to the very word. They were of human figure with gray and blackened skin drawn taught over bone. Their eyes gleamed a brilliant gold and their mouths spread wide in a grin of amber fangs.

Black scaled armor covered their hulking frames. A crimson serpent adorned their blackened chest plates, the war crest of Abaddon. They bore large, hide-covered round shields in their left hands and cruelly forged scimitars or pikes in the other.

The soft orange glow of several hundred torches flickered among the masses; glaives piercing the night sky as they marched down the hill toward their virtually defenseless prey.

As they crept closer towards Andaurel, a sharp metallic ring pierced the air and resounded through the night. Soon the ringing turned to a deep drumming of metal as the Arzecs began pounding their swords against their shields.

"Keep your sights on the bastards!" Grend shouted over the fierce clamor of the enemy. The black tide of Arzecs crawled into range of the town, barely visible in the night.

"Steady!" Grend's hand shot up in the air. "Fire!" His arm shot forward and arrows rushed past him in a massive volley of deadly projectiles.

The arrows arced over the gap, slicing through the darkness before descending upon the enemy. Arrows crashed down into their ranks in a thick rain of death as bodies fell from the formation, tumbling under the thundering masses.

Shouts of death pierced the air as arrows ripped their uniform ranks asunder and sent scores of bodies falling under a relentless barrage. The squall of arrows died off and the Arzecs drew their bows in retaliation.

They raised their black horn bows into the skies, arrowheads glinting in the torchlight. A volley of arrows disgorged from the sea of Arzecs, a single black cloud descending over Andaurel.

"Shields!" Grend screamed over his shoulder to the defenders.

Cain ducked behind a wall of shields as the soldiers cried out in surprise and threw their shields up in defense. The clinking of arrows rang loudly in Cain's ears as he knelt behind a soldier. At last, the clinking of the ineffectual arrows ceased and he stood up from behind his comrades.

The soldiers peered out from behind their shields as the ring of arrows died in the air, thousands of the deadly projectiles hanging limp from their shields like a thicket of thorns. Not a single man dead, Cain thought.

The roar of approaching Arzecs shook his thoughts and he tore his gaze over the ramparts to the enemy before them. The sea of Arzecs cascaded towards Andaurel, weapons raised in a bloodthirsty war cry.

"They're going to hit the wall!" a soldier shouted.

"Brace yourselves!" Cain cried out.

The wave of Arzecs slammed into the weak wooden palisades like a great ocean's swell. Timber flew in a shower of dust and earth as the walls barely withstood the powerful blow. The Arzecs concentrated all their power into a small area of the wall, tackling and battering down the timber ramparts with unrelenting might.

The palisades began cracking drastically as the violent battery continued, shards flying with every blow endured. They could not see their enemy, but the defenders knew what lay ahead.

Weapons at the ready!" Grend commanded over the din of Arzecs. The chime of drawn swords rang out as the defenders thrust their swords and spears before them. "Let us show them true vengeance!" The militia let out a fierce cry, their shouts barely heard over the roar of the enemy assault.

The palisades suddenly gave way with one final stroke in an explosion of timber and earth. Debris rained over the defenders and dust filled the air.

The hordes of Arzecs poured over the rubble and sprinted towards the steel-fisted bastion of soldiers before them.

The two factions collided and the roar of battle instantly filled the city, weapons ringing in a deafening clash as the front ranks of Arzecs were torn asunder by the defenders. Bodies hurled back into the Arzec lines, blood and entrails flying in a haze of death.

The stalemate dragged on as the two masses fought on with bloody retribution. Bodies fell like endless rain, cries of death and anguish filling the night air.

Cain charged forward from the defending soldiers, several men following close behind as they tore through the enemy ranks like an iron spearhead.

He swiftly dodged the first row of Arzecs and brought his sword down on one. Its head shot off in a fount of blood as another ran forward to take its place.

Cain ducked and blocked the thrust of its spear. He quickly pulled its wielder forward and threw the Arzec over his shoulder, sending it tumbling over him as it slammed into the ground. He spun his sword and thrust the blade downward, piercing the Arzec's throat. It cried out in muffled pain, blood gushing about him as he wrenched the sword from its body. He raised the bloodied weapon to his side and charged head on into the sea of Arzecs.

He leapt into the air at an oncoming Arzec and thrust his sword forward, plunging it through the Arzec's face. He landed beside the body and tossed his sword at a second. The blade ripped through the Arzec's spine and dropped it to its knees.

Cain sprinted towards the body and evaded several sword strikes. He pulled his sword from its victim and ran toward an unsuspecting Arzec. He jumped toward it and bound off its shield, flipping over the Arzec. He sliced its head off as he spun over it, and landed to a knee behind the body as it collapsed in a torrent of blood.

He swung his sword at a wall of onrushing Arzecs, hewing their legs off. A final Arzec fell upon him, and he shot up from the ground and thrust his sword through the Arzec's neck. The tip exploded out the top of the Arzec's skull and with a violent pull on his sword, the blade ripped through the Arzec's face. Its skull erupted in two with a blast of brain and blood that splattered over Cain.

Suddenly Silas dashed past him and crashed down on his enemies with a murderous scream.

He swung his Sitar full force into the Arzecs. Bodies flew as the huge weapon slammed into them and sent them flying with every swing. The vicious blades disemboweled its victims, ripping entrails from bodies in an inexorable bloodbath.

He thrust the bloody weapon forward and ripped the head off an Arzec before throwing it at a passing Arzec, knocking it off its feet as Silas laughed.

Cain ran up to his side and the two of them thrust their weapons into the chest of an Arzec. "Have you seen Aaron?" Cain shouted to his friend over the din of battle.

"No, why?" Silas replied before spinning and bringing his Sitar over the head of an Arzec, crushing its skull with a loud crack and burst of blood.

Cain left his friend and tore through his enemies, searching the battlefield for Aaron. "Aaron!" He called for him, but his shout died quickly in the chaos of battle. He looked around the battlefield through the blurs of struggling combatants to the road that led to the southern half of the town.

"I'll go without him then..." He muttered as an Arzec ran toward him, axe raised. He ducked swiftly and swung his sword at the Arzec's leg, hewing it off in a spray of blood. He grabbed its shield as it fell to the ground and he bashed its face in, blood spewing across the sand as he threw it off its foot.

He quickly ran towards the south end of the fighting, taking no care to avoid trampling the Arzec he had just slain. He fought his way out of the battle and stumbled out onto the road moments later.

He stood there a moment and took in the sudden flare of cool air. He looked down the road towards the town square, barely visible through the sea of daub buildings.

He sprinted away from the fighting and ran towards the square. Dirt kicked up from his heels, his breathing labored from the fighting.

As he reached the courtyard, he noticed the ruddy glow of a fire. Suddenly a scream broke out and echoed through the still night.

Cain cursed under his breath and sprinted towards the town square. He reached the outer buildings at last and hid in their shadow for a moment. He gazed out from behind the wall and his eyes lit up in horror.

The citizens of Andaurel had been waiting for an armed escort to lead them safely to the sanctity of Dun Ara. However, the few soldiers Grend could spare lay slaughtered in the town square.

Arzecs dashed across the court, butchering the defenseless civilians. Fire consumed their wagons and belongings and the entire court was now ablaze.

The screams of women and children pierced the air as Arzecs chased them down and brought them to their knees. They massacred the innocent, hacking off limbs and heads and sinking their fangs into every inch of flesh.

In the confusion, one woman tried to escape down the north road towards the fight. An Arzec noticed her and jumped on her back, thrusting its teeth into her neck. Her eyes rolled back into her head and she collapsed near Cain.

He pressed himself against the wall as the Arzec stood up from her corpse, blood running down its chin.

Cain raised his sword and stepped forward to kill it before he was pulled back into the shadows.

The Arzec raised its sword and brought it over the woman's neck, severing her spine with a sickening crunch of bone as if to make sure she was properly dead. It looked around for a moment and licked its bloodied lips before returning to the town square. Cain wrenched free and spun around to see who had stopped him.

Aaron shook his head. He pointed to the town square and threw a finger to his lips in an indication of silence. Cain spoke as loudly as he dared. "Eileen's in there! We've got to help them!"

"That's exactly what we're going to do." He pulled his saber from his belt and ran to the opposite side of the building. They gazed around the wall and saw the same chaotic scene.

"I thought Grend already sent them to Dun Ara?" Aaron whispered to his friend.

"I don't care, Eileen's somewhere in there, I'm going in…" He left the safety of the shadows and sprinted towards the town square, screaming to draw the Arzecs' attention.

The Arzecs turned from their victims and faced their newest prey. They raised their weapons and bared their fangs at the prospect of fresh blood.

Cain and Aaron charged over the fallen bodies and past the flames, colliding head on into the mass of Arzecs. A ring of steel broke out as they tackled through the wall of enemies and threw themselves into the waiting arms of death.

With the well-timed arrival of their saviors, the few remaining townspeople slipped away and faded off into the night with nothing but their blood-soaked clothes.

Cain pulled his sword from the last of the Arzecs and wiped the blade on his fauld. He looked around at the carnage, breathing heavy with exertion. Hundreds of bodies littered the courtyard, all victims to the Arzec's brutality.

Then, through the fire and smoke, he saw his wife. She lay limp in the sand, blood pooled around her. Cain let out a frantic cry and rushed toward her.

She was dead, still as stone in her own blood. Her clothes were mere shreds on her bloodied body. A massive gash was hewn across her stomach, spilt entrails spread out before her. And from her severed stomach, a baby's hand hung limp. Blood ran along its arm and dripped down its tiny fingers.

Cain crumpled beside his dead wife and child. He stared forward with disbelief, refusing to accept what he was seeing. He bent over his wife and brushed her blood-drenched hair.

"Eileen..." He muttered as tears brimmed in his eyes. "Eileen." He looked over the ghastly scene and closed his eyes at the sight of his wife's entrails. He gently turned her over and wrapped a finger around his child's hand. Tears poured down his face.

"Why was it you who had to die? I deserve this, not you!" Cain cradled his head in his hands, the blood of his family staining his face. He wept uncontrollably, cursing the skies to end his sorrow. Tears streamed down his cheeks as he pounded the earth with his fists, weeping and bellowing with anger.

Aaron approached him and rested a hand on his friend's heaving shoulder. "The Arzecs...there's more of them." Aaron turned and raised his saber as a wall of Arzecs slowly approached.

Cain remained at his wife's side, cradling her head as he wept. "Cain..." Aaron pleaded as he backed up slowly. "They're coming...help me!"

Cain rose to his feet and turned to face a wall of one hundred Arzecs, every one of them grinning at his sorrow.

Cain picked his sword off the ground and wiped the blood and tears from his face. "They killed my wife...my child..." He suddenly shot forward and sprinted straight at the Arzecs. "I'll kill every last one of them!"

With a vengeful cry, he lurched forward and tossed his sword, the blade impaling itself through the face of an Arzec. He continued forward and tackled into it, ripping his sword from its body before letting loose his rage.

He jumped sideways, hewing the head off an Arzec before plunging his sword through the chest of another. He pulled it out and stabbed it into the gut of another Arzec, wrenching the shield from its arm.

He spun around and slammed the steel shield into an Arzec before crashing it over the face of another, tossing bodies about him with every powerful swing. He tossed the shield into the tide of Arzecs and grabbed his sword from a body, slaughtering everything within his reach.

He roared with hate as his sword flew like a blur around him, blood, limbs, and bodies flying. Anger burned unbridled in his heart with every thought of his dead wife and child.

He had promised his wife only hours before that he would put aside the sword and live at her side forever in happiness. But now that happiness had been taken from him, and vengeance kindled deep within. He fought on with a mindless ferocity, all reason thrown aside for bitter hatred.

Yet, despite his efforts, the two men were soon surrounded and found themselves standing back to back amid an encircling wall of Arzecs. Their enemies formed a large circle around them and stood in silence, weapons raised to finish them off.

Time seemed to freeze as they stared into the eyes of their foes. The sixty pairs of amber eyes seemed to bore into Cain and Aaron as they stood heaving from the exertion of the fight, sweat trickling down their brows, the bodies of the fallen littering the ground about their feet.

The circle parted and a large Arzec walked through the gap. He stood a head taller than the others and several times as muscular. His skin was pure ebony, teeth a dull brown and eyes a bloody crimson. He carried an enormous scimitar in one hand and his body bulged beneath a burdensome set of black and scarlet armor.

A blood red tattoo of a snake wound its way across nearly all of his dark flesh. The serpent's head was curved over the Arzec's brow, its grimacing fangs stretched over his face as the body wound its way down the back of his neck and spine, the tail finally ending at his closed palm.

The enormous Arzec stepped out from the circle and faced his prey. "You're a bold one," he spoke in a hoarse, throaty voice.

Cain stared up into his bloodied eyes. "You killed my family..." He raised his weapon at him and glared down its edge, seething with hate.

The Arzec twirled his scimitar and turned his gaze back to the two men. He suddenly lurched forward and charged towards his opponents.

The tremendous force of the scimitar hit Cain's sword like a hammer, sending him stumbling back in an explosion of sparks. Before he could recover from the blow, the captain descended upon him.

Cain spun and swung his blade. The captain jumped around his opponent and grabbed Cain's arm as his weapon sailed by. The Arzec hurled him through the air, sending him crashing into the dirt, weapon flying from his hands.

Aaron ran towards the captain and jumped into the air, saber raised to strike down his foe. The Arzec threw his scimitar up before his face. Aaron's sword crashed into the Arzec's and this time it was the captain's turn to stumble back.

Aaron and the captain exchanged a fierce maelstrom of steel, weapons flying in a flurry of sparks, their swords shimmering in the roar of the enclosing flames.

Aaron ducked under a swing to the head and rolled to the side as the Arzec pulled his weapon back for a second strike. The sword sailed overhead as Aaron fell on his back and threw himself backwards before flipping up and landing smoothly on his feet.

The captain charged forward and swung his sword into his foe. Aaron's saber was nearly torn from his hands, the massive scimitar pinning his blade to the ground. The Arzec threw his body sideways and sent his armored boot colliding into Aaron's chest with tremendous force.

Aaron was thrown back several feet, a cry of pain on his lips as he rolled to a stop in the sand.

Suddenly several Arzecs jumped from the circle and threw themselves at the downed men.

"No!" The captain let out a fierce bellow as he swung his sword into the masses, lobbing off several heads. "They're mine!" His soldiers cowered in fear, immediately disinclined to his wrath.

The men rose to their feet, swords raised warily before them. The captain stepped back, eyeing them searchingly. The two men looked at each other and charged their foe.

The Arzec stood firm and raised his sword, effortlessly deflecting their attacks. He pulled his sword from the lock and flicked it side to side. With inhuman speed, he tossed their swords about and battered both men into the earth.

He knocked Aaron's sword away and swung his scimitar, slamming the side of it into Aaron's face. The blow sent Aaron tumbling back, falling heavily to the ground before rolling to a stop motionless.

Cain watched his friend sail across the court, stricken by the strength of his opponent. The Arzec lunged at him and unleashed a fearsome barrage. Cain parried several repeated blows, slowly faltering under his ruthless advance.

Cain blocked a strike to his side, sliding over the sand before jumping into the air towards his foe. He spun and threw out his leg, kicking the Arzec in the side of the skull. The captain staggered under the force of the blow as Cain landed beside him and threw his sword down for a fatal strike.

The captain jumped back and grabbed the weapon. His bare hand wrapped around the blade, pulling weapon and wielder forward before thrusting his armored knee into Cain's gut. He lurched forward in pain as the Arzec then picked him up by his tunic and tossed him to the ground.

"This is a true battle," the captain muttered, a malevolent gleam in his deathly eyes. "Only, a sad thing...you, wanted dead. Taste the last bitter dregs of your life; fear the wrath that is Abaddon."

Cain rose painfully to his feet, Aaron unconscious yards away. Cain turned to look at his opponent, shifting nervously as the Arzec spoke. A gust of wind blew across the court and flames danced about them.

"What do you mean?" he asked, eyeing the captain cautiously.

"Abaddon is searching for Cain Taran. You are him, are you not?" The captain blinked, his red eyes bloody beacons in the night.

"Why me? I don't understand…"

The Arzec shook his head. "I don't have time for your questions. We are here to kill you…embrace your fate, Cain Taran."

Cain raised his sword, the bloody steel glistening in the firelight. "Then back your words and end this!"

The Arzec stepped toward the burning wreckage of a wagon and kicked a woman's body aside.

With an unflinching hand, he plunged his arm into the fires and pulled out an enormous length of wood from the bottom of the ashes. He stabbed his scimitar into the sand and grabbed the flaming timber with both hands. He turned and faced Cain, his massive frame silhouetted against the inferno.

Cain rushed toward Aaron and shook his friend fervently, struggling to wake him. Aaron remained limp in his arms. Cain gave up and rose to his feet, weapon held uselessly before him.

The Arzec charged forward and effortlessly swung the flaming timber, forcing Cain to jump back to avoid it. The captain swung again, narrowly missing his target. He continued throwing it about as Cain darted back and forth, each swing of the flaming weapon narrowly brushing past him.

As the flames whipped by, Cain rolled to the ground before bounding to his feet. He leapt toward his opponent and thrust his sword against the armored chest of the Arzec.

The captain stumbled back from the blow, surprise lit across his face. The two stood in silence, eyes locked. They raised their weapons and charged.

As they met, Cain tackled the timber aside and in one fluid movement, leapt onto the flaming debris, ran up its length and bound off.

He leapt over the Arzec and swung his sword as he frontflipped. The blade tore the Arzec's skull open with a gush of blood, brain exploding from the chasm. He landed behind the Arzec and twirled around, thrusting his weapon through the back of the captain.

The Arzec's body slipped down the blade with a sickening crunch. His sword glistened with blood as it carved through the spine of the Arzec.

The captain stood frozen in shock, not a sound escaping his cloven skull. His body gradually lurched forward, taking the sword still embedded in his spine.

The Arzec turned around to face him, blood cascading from his open skull. He raised his scimitar and slowly walked toward his killer. Cain stepped back in surprise as the Arzec staggered towards him.

The captain halted and his lips flew open, a gleaming saber protruding from his gaping maw. Aaron stepped out from behind the dying Arzec and pulled the sword from the back of his neck with a revolting squelch.

The Arzec shuddered violently and fell to his knees. He gazed up at Cain, blood sloshing from his eviscerated face.

Cain stepped forward, pulled his weapon from the Arzec's back and swung the sword. The captain's head flew from his body in an explosion of blood. The men watched as the headless corpse dropped in a pool of blood.

They looked up from the body and saw the Arzecs circled around them, staring forward in disbelief. The head of their captain landed at their feet and they looked up at his killers. They surged forward, weapons raised and screaming with vengeance.

Cain and Aaron once again stood side by side, weapons at the ready. The Arzecs reached them in moments and surrounded them like a black ocean's swell.

Cain ducked as the front lines of Arzecs surged over them. He struck several soldiers and sent them to the ground in a bloody mist, parting them of their legs. Aaron ran forward and jumped over Cain. He crashed down into the wall of flesh and swung his sword, ripping the heads off several of the beasts.

He opened a pathway for his friend and Cain fought mercilessly towards him.

They stood back to back fending off the hordes of Arzecs, bodies falling under a torrent of blood, the dead quickly piling at their feet.

Suddenly the Arzecs swung around to face the edges of the town square.

Through the fires, a wave of horsemen poured forth. The Arzecs threw down their arms and turned from the fight, fleeing for their lives.

The riders galloped across the court and collided into the backs of their enemies with one harmonic cry. They plowed through their ranks like a spearhead, decimating everything that stood in their way.

They surrounded the Arzecs from all sides, bodies falling like flies to the hoof and blade of their assailants. The riders mowed down the remaining hapless Arzecs in seconds.

The soldiers then reined their horses around the bodies in a tight circle, shouting in victory. The column turned and rode across the court, galloping through the smoke and fire toward the southern edge of the city.

Two of the horses broke from the formation and galloped towards Cain and Aaron. A hand reached out to Cain and he grabbed it as the horse shot past, swinging himself into the saddle.

Cain looked back towards the town square as it slowly disappeared over the hill, fighting back his tears. Aaron and Joshua rode close behind them, continuing down the south road.

"Looks like I saved your ass again, eh?" Silas's voice broke out from the thundering hooves of their mounts. He looked back at his friend in the saddle and laughed. Cain remained silent.

"Our men were surrounded and overwhelmed. We lost most of our force once the Arzecs gained the higher ground. They've…taken the city."

The soldiers continued to follow the main road that led them away from the town and into the endless expanse of surrounding plains.

Through the cloudy night and meager starlight, they barely made out a wooden building in the distance, its thatched roof softly glowing in the moonlight. They galloped down the long stretch of road and soon reached the open doors of the building.

Once safe within the building, they dismounted and several others greeted them warmly.

Forty men now stood inside the stables, awaiting whatever came next, an uneasy tension filling the room.

"This is all that survived?" Aaron asked Silas. The two men looked over the small group of bloodstained and battle scarred men.

Silas lowered his head. "Aye, only forty of the two hundred and fifty."

Joshua cursed sharply and spit on the hay-littered floor. "Took those bastards a four to one odd to defeat us." He wrapped his hands around his head, struggling to hold back his anger.

"We're not defeated yet. Where is Grend?" Aaron inquired. "He would know what to do." The room was quiet once more.

Silas's face fell grave. "He didn't make it; he was pulled down in the retreat. He's dead..."

The soldiers hung their heads at this. The room fell to deathly silence as they waited for Aaron's response.

"They're burning Andaurel!" A soldier cried out, breaking the grim unease. Everyone in the stables rushed for the windows, silence crushed under foot. They crowded around the windows and peered out over the plains to their home.

A brilliant glow rose from the outline of the town. Black smoke climbed into the sky in thick pillars of ember and ash, blotting out the starlight. The whole city was ablaze and drowning in flame before their eyes.

"Damn them!" The soldiers cursed. They screamed in rage and hissed with disdain.

Cain rested his head against the wall and pounded the planking with agony. "They killed my wife and child...they killed everyone I tried to protect. Now they raze my home..."

"We have to retreat," a soldier cried, "the city is done for, we are done for!"

Cain turned to the man. "There is no retreat! I will not rest until every one of their heads lie wrenched upon a spear! We will face our enemy as one, or I alone!"

He walked forward and the crowd split, leaving a clear path to his horse. "Cain," Aaron said as he grabbed his friend's arm. "I understand your pain. I know you are angry, we all are...but don't be stupid. There are hundreds of Arzecs out there. We have to call the retreat..."

Cain simply glared back and pulled his arm from Aaron's grip. He jumped onto his horse and grabbed hold of the reins. He looked over the last of his soldiers and Andaurel's militia.

His fellow soldiers followed suit and mounted their horses. Cain's friends rode up to his side and soon all were saddled and facing the open stable doors.

Aaron returned Cain's gaze and smiled lightly. "If you're willing to face certain end, then I won't let you face death alone."

"And I wouldn't have it any other way…" he turned to face his men.

"The Arzecs have slaughtered our families and friends. They butchered our brethren, burned down our homes, our city, our livelihoods…and now they want us."

Cain drew his sword with a ring of steel and the remaining soldiers drew their weapons in turn.

"And we will give them that, with sword and shield."

He looked to his fellow soldiers, the men he had known his entire life, to meet the enemy who had taken everything from them. He looked at them solemnly for the last time and tore his gaze back to the dying town.

Without a word, he reined his horse forward and began riding down the path. His friends followed, and behind them, the soldiers in formation. There was nothing left to say. Only one thing remained, to paint the streets with the blood of their enemies.

As they approached the town, they saw what was left of the Arzec force. Six hundred now remained in their way. They formed a solid line of sword, shield, and pike at the edge of the town, the burning buildings of Andaurel at their backs. Their only hope of escape, the main road, was now entirely barred off.

The soldiers continued their death march toward the pyre of Andaurel, undaunted by the sheer number of enemies before them. Disbelief fell on the faces of the Arzecs at the sight of the forty soldiers who still dared oppose them.

Cain raised his sword and let out a fearsome scream. His soldiers followed his lead and spurred their horses towards the city.

The Arzecs hesitated for a fleeting moment as the riders galloped up the hill and charged straight for them. This hesitation led to the only weak spot in their defense, the only hope of escape for Andaurel's defenders and the only hope they needed.

The small wave of horses crashed down upon the Arzecs and plowed head first into a sea of steel.

The riders shot through their formation, struggling to keep their horses galloping amid the overwhelming masses. Bodies fell from their ranks, crushed under hoof and torn asunder by the blades of their enraged enemies.

The soldiers continued hacking through endless waves of Arzecs, blood and bodies flying, screams filling the air. The riders trampled anything that stood in their way, pushing on toward certain death.

They at last reached the streets of Andaurel. An ocean of fire instantly engulfed them, hell arisen to disembowel the fated city.

The riders embraced the flames and leapt into its abyss, a mass of Arzecs close behind.

The city fell to its knees, every brick and stone of its structures trembling to the earth, every building crashing about them.

They rode on through the damned city, the fire on both sides of the road now encompassing them, flames engorging the streets below.

They crossed the town square, almost entirely consumed in fire. Buildings tumbled to the earth and plummeted around the soldiers, explosions of flame and debris shaking the very air.

Fireballs fell from the buildings and crashed down around the soldiers as they jerked their horses aside in an attempt to escape the explosions. Several met their mark and fell upon screaming men, crushing horse and rider under instant death.

The soldiers rode desperately onward, leaving behind their fallen brethren. Hordes of Arzecs still chased after them, heedless of the peril.

A firestorm rained down upon them. Buildings tumbled into the masses, tossing scores of burning bodies with every collapsing structure. The Arzecs pushed on through the hellfire, bloodlust red as the flames in their eyes.

The militia rode on in a desperate struggle to shake off their enemy. A large two-story building collapsed before them and crashed with a great explosion of debris. The debris shot through their formation and tore men from their mounts in a flash of fire.

Cain and his friends spurred their horses into the fire and jumped over the burning rubble.

The flames licked at their feet as they sailed overhead. Their horses cleared the fire and descended over the street, landing heavily in a cloud of ash. The few remaining soldiers continued through the flames and left the blazing building behind.

At last, they burst out from the mouth of hell and came out into an unfamiliar world, devoid of flame and death, the endless plains stretching out before them under a silver veil of starlight.

Andaurel withered and collapsed. Its final moments were crushed beneath the weight of every falling building. The cries of hundreds of Arzecs pierced the night as flame and debris descended over them, snuffing their bodies in the sand. The last of Andaurel's buildings toppled to the ground and nothing remained now save a great pyre that seemingly bound across all the earth.

The failed defenders of Andaurel tore their gaze from their home and flicked their reins. They rode away from the town that had consumed so many lives, yet somehow spared theirs.

They had survived the battle and escaped with their lives, but they would live on with more than a few scars to haunt their lives forever.

Their town was destroyed, nearly all of their fellow citizens put to the sword, their families and friends forever lost. Their blood now stained the streets of that which they died to save. They had given their lives in defense of their homes, but in the end, they lost both.

**** ****

The Warrior's Code

The sun crept slowly over the distant horizon, at last breaking the feeble dregs of night. The shadows fell from the lofty heavens and the sun's rays blared down on the backs of thirty men.

They rode throughout the night, no reprieve to ease their fatigue. The night's ride and hours of fighting had taken its toll on the beleaguered soldiers. The men hung weary in their saddles, blood encrusted skin soaked with the sweat of the long ride.

Cain and his friends whispered amongst themselves at the head of the formation, hesitant to break the grave silence. "How much longer?" Silas asked Aaron as loudly as he dared.

"Dun Ara should be over the next few hills," Aaron retorted.

Silas looked out over the flat expanse of grass stretching out as far as they could see. "Uh, right," he muttered to himself, "Over the next few hills…got it."

Silas turned to Joshua after a long silence and the two began whispering heatedly, their muffled voices breaking the hushed air. It was obvious to anyone within earshot of the two men to grasp what they were saying.

A fierce exchange of whispered curses and threats, the Arzecs…killing their fellows, destroying Andaurel, and of course their master, Abaddon, he who ordered the assault on their town. They would not forget who was behind their suffering.

The soldiers were not sure of their fears, but they knew they rode now on the winds of a storm, a storm of something far larger, and of far worse consequence.

They rode now to the capital of Kaanos, Dun Ara, capital of more than just their country, the capital of information, and what better way to find out what was going on than to travel to where the information was? All this ran through Cain's mind as he stared out over the dancing fields before them.

Why an attack on Andaurel, he thought to himself. All of Kaanos lay open to Abaddon's wrath, yet he attacks Andaurel? What does it benefit him in destroying such an insignificant town? Yet, it mattered little to him. His parents were taken from him in his youth by Abaddon, and now his wife and unborn child. Anger flooded his soul, and he vowed it to vengeance.

His thoughts trailed off as Aaron's voice broke the long silence, "We're here!" The riders shook themselves from their thoughts and peered out over the plains. In the distance over a stretch of swaying grass, loomed the shadow of Dun Ara.

The soldiers spurred their horses forward and galloped towards the city. As they reached the capital, the shadow's hold over Dun Ara fell, at last revealing the city.

A lofty wall of sharpened timber poles encompassed a vast network of cobble causeways. A web of roads stretched across the capital city, intertwining with one another to connect the city's many homes and buildings.

A main road led from the wooden front gate and over the crest of a hill, splitting the city in halves. The hill upon which the city was constructed was not large in girth but instead incredibly long, stretching across the plains like the spine of a great slumbering beast.

The soldiers at last approached the city's front gate as four sentries peered over the causeway.

"Hold, riders!" One of the guards cried out.

Cain gazed up at the men and called back in return. "I am Cain Taran, captain of the Kaanos Outriders. Let us pass."

The men nodded before disappearing from sight. Soon the iron locks of the gate were released and the gates were slowly pushed outward, beckoning the riders inside. Cain flicked his reins and led the company through the open gates.

They came out into a large, open court of stone. As they rode across the entrance yard, a large granite statue loomed in the middle.

It was an armored soldier atop a bucking horse, the standard of Kaanos in its left hand and a spear in the other. It stood fifteen feet over the court, casting a shadow over the company as they rode around it.

The soldiers left the courtyard behind and approached the main road. Buildings of standard Kaanos construction surrounded them; all built of timber, rock, and thatched roofs of grass.

The street overflowed with people. An overwhelming wave of smells hit them as they approached the market road. Raw meats, spices, breads, human stench, and ale reached their nostrils in a barrage of the senses.

Stalls of all kinds lined the street. Men sold their wares of tanned hides and clothing, tack, silks, dies, foods, armor and weapons, ales, barley and spices, anything that would fit in their wagons.

The air was filled with the voices of thousands of people, a roaring clamor that drowned out all else. Few people noticed the men on horseback; an indifferent crowd barring their way as they slowly gained distance in the overcrowded street.

Emaciated dogs roamed the streets as they scrounged for oddments of waste. They chased after the riders, barking incessantly before losing them in the crowd.

The soldiers guided their horses down the winding road and pushed through the hundreds of venders. Men cursed at the riders as they were shoved aside, further adding to the deafening confusion.

Eventually the soldiers fought their way out of the crowds. The main road continued winding up the hill at a gradual slope, rounding the corner before disappearing behind distant buildings.

They spurred their mounts down the main road, leaving behind the chaos of the markets before stepping into the heart of the city. The buildings on both sides of the road halted and the main road merged with a central square.

A twin statue of the one at the entrance stood in the middle of the courtyard. This courtyard was barren, devoid of buildings on either side to encompass its emptiness. A great stone building stood on the other end of the court.

Cain reined his horse forward and led the others across the court and around the statue. The riders reached a flight of stairs and dismounted at the foot of the steps.

With Cain and his group in the lead, they made their way up the stairs and came to the building. Several stone columns lined its front, leading towards a gilded door at the far end. Several guards formed a wall of spears, blocking the entrance.

A large man stepped in front of them, spear held loosely at his side.

"I am Cain Taran," Cain informed him as the group approached. "These men are what remain of my company and the Andaurel militia. The city is lost…"

"We feared as much," the guard replied, "the King wishes to speak to your leader."

The soldiers fidgeted anxiously at this before Cain replied, "He was killed during the assault…we have no leader now."

"I am sorry for your loss. But the King requires an audience, if you are the next leader, then step forward." Everyone stepped back, leaving Cain and his friends remaining. A hollow laugh escaped the guard. He then opened the door and beckoned them inside.

Cain sighed and followed him through the open doors, his friends close behind. They came to a long throne room, sparsely and humbly decorated. The guard closed the door behind them and led them down the hall.

A large wooden and gold trimmed throne sat on the other end of a stretch of oiled mahogany. Long walls of wooden planking stretched into the palace, leading to a room that shouldered the throne. The guard led them across the throne room to this archway.

They came to another near barren room and the guard led them through one of the several arches that lined its walls. They followed a congested hallway until they came to a large, circular study.

Wooden bookcases lined its stone walls and nearly every inch of its shelves were brimming with volumes of velar books and scrolls. Several windows lit up the study, the morning sunlight giving the room a soft glow. Several brass globes sat around the foot of a window and beside them was a desk piled high with scrolls and parchment.

A man sat beside this desk with a book in hand, his back turned to them. The man stood up at the sound of their footsteps.

He stood very tall, a warm facade etched across his face. His bright straw hair fell to his shoulders and parted to reveal his slightly rumpled brow.

He wore a fustian blue tunic and dark leggings. A thick ringlet of pewter wrapped around his forehead, set gently over the locks of his hair. His light blue eyes gleamed as he approached his guests; arms extended in an inviting flourish.

"Welcome friends!" He greeted them, shaking hands with each of the men. "I am Ethebriel, king of our blessed country. Please, sit down." He gestured to several plush chairs that lined the walls of the room. Cain and his friends took their seats as their king returned to his.

You may be excused," he offered the guard. The soldier nodded and bowed before leaving the room. The King turned his attention to the remaining men, tapping his fingers on a book as if deep in thought.

"You do me great honor in coming here," he said after a long moment.

Cain nodded, "The honor is ours."

Ethebriel smiled at this. "I wish to become more acquainted with all of you, but there are matters that need attending. I assume Andaurel has fallen, for I receive her survivors. I must ask your forgiveness for not sending troops to your aid. My soldiers were spread too thin and I could not risk the garrison of Dun Ara. But that is no excuse…I cannot imagine the horrors you have endured." Cain's company remained silent. "My scouts have reported to me of many rumors, but I must ask, why would they attack Andaurel?"

Cain hung his head and muttered, "We know not why they attacked Andaurel. Only that hundreds of our people lay dead in her ashes."

Ethebriel's face darkened as he fingered his goatee in habitual thought. "Abaddon has kept his forces out of Kaanos for the most part, until now. We have fought this war mainly on foreign fronts alongside our allies yet with this attack on your city, Abaddon brings the war to our front door. The battalion of Arzecs you fought is only a small portion of the force he has sent into Kaanos.

'We need to withdraw our people in and keep them safe in our walls. I will send warning to the rest of the country of this looming threat." Ethebriel's fists clenched white as he continued.

"I do not need more blood on my conscience; I cannot bear the thought of more of my people dying when I could have prevented it. If I had foreseen an attack on Andaurel then I could have prevented all of this…alas, I am but a fool."

He cradled his head in his hands for a moment. "What plagues my mind is why, out of all the places he could have caught off guard, why choose Andaurel as his target? Even after four hundred years, Abaddon's methods are still a mystery."

He stood up from his chair, a forced calm and collected look on his face. "I do not know much, but I am King, and I bear the fate of thousands on my shoulders. I know not the state of the rest of Tarsha, but right now, the throngs of Abaddon lay at our doorstep. We must not succumb. We must not surrender. This fight we will not lose. This time...the blood will pour on their side."

**** ****

Cain and his friends left the company of Ethebriel and followed the escort back through the palace, soon returning to the throne room.

The guard turned to the men as they reached the door. "The King has opened his arms for you and your soldiers, he has several rooms for all of you in our finest inn, you may stay as long as you deem fit...the inn is across the courtyard and near the arena...just follow the road off to the right. We dropped your horses off at the stables near the palace." They nodded and the escort turned back into the palace.

Cain opened the palace doors and came out onto the columned terrace. The guards turned and saluted as they descended the steps to the open courtyard. The other soldiers had already left the court, eager to enjoy the comforts of a warm meal and hearth.

The four men crossed the courtyard and followed a cobble road that branched off the main road. They followed the street, towering brick buildings casting shadows over the men below.

A large inn lay not far down the street, a nearly identical building among hundreds. They approached the inn where a soldier stood beside the door, waiting silently for them to approach.

The man nodded at them with a slight bow. "So, how did it go?" He asked as he turned and opened the door for them.

"He wanted to know what happened to us at Andaurel," Cain replied simply and followed him into the building.

The inn was large and spacious, the walls and floor made of tarnished wood. Several windows let in the morning sun, the golden rays of which shone over the numerous tables that dotted the room. A large bar surrounded by stools took up most of the right side of the tavern, racks of ale and spirits covering the wall behind it above stacks of barreled rum.

The Kaanos Outriders sat around several of the tables, drinking and eating heartily, conversing merrily among themselves. They raised their hands and waved for the new arrivals to join them.

"Where's the militia?" Cain asked his fellow soldier as the other three approached the table.

"They lost their homes, their families, everything…it's a safe guess to say they're grieving." Cain sighed heavily at this. He had grown up in Andaurel, he knew most of these men his entire life. To know they grieved with the same agony that clenched his own heart only exacerbated it.

"Andrew!" one of the soldiers called out, "bring these men some drinks!" The four men pulled up some chairs and joined their friends at a table. One of the men set a silver platter of mugs on their table and sat down before splitting a deck of cards and passing them around.

Joshua looked at his cards and paused. "So, what do we do now? What can we do?" The soldiers fell silent for a moment, eyeing their cards.

"The palace guards said the King wishes to speak with you four tomorrow," one of them said, "they said it would be important." He pushed the platter of ale towards the four men. "Drink up friends; you're going to need it."

The men took their tankards and Silas and Joshua leaned back, chugging the frothy liquid. Joshua slammed his mug on the tabletop and laughed as his brother coughed.

Aaron sipped his mug in thoughtful silence. He glanced at Cain who stared absentmindedly at the cards in his hand.

"I'm going to the room," Cain said as he set his cards down. He stood up and left the room, leaving his untouched ale behind.

"Damn," Silas snorted as Cain left, "what's up his ass?"

Aaron turned to him. "His wife is dead."

Silas lowered his glass from his lips and stared at Aaron with disbelief. "Eileen's...dead?" Aaron remained quiet, but his eyes answered the question. Silas and Joshua's gaze fell.

The nearby soldiers heard this grave news and bowed their heads. Many of them had fought beside Cain in the army and as Outriders for half their lives and never before had they seen their friend in such anguish.

"To Eileen," Silas said as he raised his tankard. The soldiers raised theirs in unison.

"And to Cain," Joshua added. The soldiers repeated the toast and lifted their mugs to their lips.

**** ****

The sun's rays refracted through the room's only window and shimmered brilliant against the wooden walls. Cain and his friends were scattered around their room in various positions, sleep still heavy on their eyes.

Several beds lined the wall and faced a stone hearth. A table piled high with food stood in the middle of the room. Goblets of watered wine littered the tabletop. Several of them, having been drained of their contents, were discarded and abandoned on the floor.

Cain propped his feet up on the edge of the table and knocked back the last of the wine. He dropped the goblet to the ground where an impressive pile of emptied goblets was accumulating.

Silas and Joshua sat at the foot of a bed, polishing their armor that lay in a heap beside the door. Aaron sat beside the hearth and stared intently into the smoldering embers.

He stood up, put on his hauberk, and walked towards the door. "Where are you going?" Silas asked him.

"To get some actual food," Aaron said with a smirk as he gestured towards the table.

He reached for the door handle when his boot fell with a light crunch. He paused a moment and lifted his foot to see what it fell on. A sealed piece of parchment lay halfway under the door, as if slid through the crack in haste.

He quickly opened the door and glanced around the empty hallway. He shook his head and slowly closed the door and picked up the letter. The others rose and circled around him as he turned the parchment over.

"Open it, Aaron," Silas commanded impatiently. Aaron pulled out his knife and split the wax seal. The parchment fell open smoothly, revealing the left-handed scrawl of Ethebriel. He read the letter aloud.

"I am pleased to have had the honor of meeting with all of you despite the circumstances that have brought us together. I understand your pain and I sympathize greatly for your loss. However, time will not allow us to finish what we had begun.

'Tarsha has fought this war against Abaddon for four centuries, and Kaanos has done her part to protect her. We have aided our allies as best we could, giving our blood to defend our freedoms. Each country fights their battles alone, unable to assist their allies. We fight disbanded and without hope. Tarsha will soon collapse due to its own folly, broken by the detriments of war.

'Alone we fall, but together we may stand firm against the armies of Abaddon. We must form a united front if we are to survive. One would assume that amid the chaos,

Tarsha would unite as we have in days long past, yet we do not, for pride and distrust burns unbridled.

'Abaddon has realized this and he holds the probability of defeating us, one by one, to fight our own losing battles. This I believe is Abaddon's design to change the tide of this dragging war to his favor. He will pick us apart, one at a time.

'I however must do something to protect my country and keep Tarsha alive. Those of us who wish to do something about this war and unite the countries are few, but over time, we hope to rebuild the Alliance of old and stand firm against the might of Abaddon.

'Lord Darius, King of Erias, is at the head of this reformation, gathering his armies and calling for aid to assist us in our struggle.

'Several others have also agreed to assist in the reformation, including my dear friend Verin, King of Charun, as well as the country of Atuan in the eastern deserts.

'In order to turn the tide of this war, we have decided that the only way to rebuild the Alliance of old is to send a group of warriors to the other countries of Tarsha, assist them in their struggles and unite them under the banners of Alliance.

'As you might have guessed by now, I have chosen the four of you for this task. Abaddon's forces run rampant and unhindered within our borders, preventing us from contacting the other countries and cutting off our trade routes, further adding to our need of a small group that can slip past their blockades.

'Our lack of communication in this time of confusion has dealt us a fatal blow. We are now cut off and alone, we are ready to break. There is no way we can continue fighting if we remain isolated and cut off by the enemy that now swarms our lands. This is where you come in my friends.

'Each of you is filled with a driving spirit of revenge that will push you to the very end, and that is exactly the motivational force required for this precise and difficult task. You are a very tight group of friends and have fought together in this war for many years.

'You are bound to one another by friendship since your youths, and once again, that type of unique brotherhood is exactly what we need for this task. I beg of you not just as your king but also as your friend and fellow, to consider this task of un-paralleled importance.

'If you wish to inquire more before you make your decision, I have asked a friend to meet with you at the arena. Please consider this task, my friends; it is of the absolute necessity. Tarsha needs you.

Ethebriel."

Aaron finished reading aloud and folded the parchment, looking at his friends in contemplation. "Well," he asked the others, "Should we meet with his friend? This is a heavy burden he wishes to place on us." The others remained stolid.

Aaron fidgeted with the letter for a moment as Cain looked the group over slowly, "Let's at least hear them out before we make our decision, and I have questions... questions that need to be answered." He fastened his sword to his belt and opened the door. "Besides," he continued, "he may even talk us into it. It's not like we have anything more to lose."

"Way to stay positive," Joshua replied.

**** ****

Cain's company left the inn and followed the road for several minutes before reaching the end of the street and the foot of a large hill. They climbed it, and at the other side of the hill loomed the arena.

The four men approached the great stone building, its towering walls casting them in shadow.

They crossed under the massive archway that served as its entrance and came out into the expansive interior of the arena, awestruck at the size and splendor of the coliseum.

Several flights of stairs lined the arena, cut into the walls of stone for seating. In the middle of the arena was a large pit of sand, dug into the ground and surrounded by high walls that protected the spectators.

Cain's company descended the stairs and sat near the wall on one of the steps. The entire arena was completely empty, not a single spectator to fill its seats. They leaned back against the steps and watched over the sand pit. They noticed a large stable attached to the south wall of the pit.

A faint noise filled their ears and suddenly the doors of the stable burst open. Several soldiers rushed out and dashed across the sand.

A horse then exploded out of the doors and thrashed frenetically about as the group of men held onto their ropes helplessly, struggling to tame the beast.

The horse kicked a soldier in the chest and sent him off his feet where he crashed unconscious in the sand several feet away. The horse bucked again and tossed its head into a man, sending him tumbling to the earth.

The soldiers eventually beat the wild animal into submission and strapped on a saddle and bridle, a look of fear in its once wild eyes.

They led the horse back into the stables and the wounded men were picked up and carried away.

"It's always a shame," a voice said from behind them. Cain's company turned to face the source of the voice.

A man with brown, gray-flecked hair stood on the stairs above them. Lackluster eyes looked over them thoughtfully. He wore a set of Kaanos plate armor, its dull shades of brown and red glinting in the noon sun.

"To sap a horse of its will, to strip it of its freedom, to crush its wild spirit, that is always the result of breaking a horse to serve our needs." The man stepped fluidly down the steps towards them.

"Yet it must be done to keep our lives mobile and efficient, to keep our country alive, because without the subservient horse, our nation would crumble. You see, they sacrifice for us.

'Sacrifices must be made for the greater good, for the common interests of humanity. They must be made if we are to hold onto what is good in this world and make it a place worth fighting for.

'That is the Warrior's Code, a code worth living by and a code worth living for. It calls for you, my friends, to make sacrifices of your own."

The man stopped before them and held out his hand. "I am the mercenary, Armeth, Ethebriel's friend. It is a pleasure to meet you."

They shook his hand firmly in turn and gave him their names. Armeth sat down beside them and sighed. He looked out over the arena for a long while before speaking.

"Well, Warriors, I have been sent here to persuade you to accept the task called upon you. You do not know how desperately Kaanos need you, how desperately Tarsha needs you. I plead for you to listen to what I have to say in the hopes that you may understand all there is to know and join our cause." The Warriors nodded, gesturing for him to continue.

"Very well then. We are in the midst of a long and dark shadow. Four centuries ago, Abaddon began his war against Tarsha. Ever since his rise to power, he has been killing us off whether we fight back or not.

'We have been forced to fight in order to keep our very lives, but now we grow haggard. Against an immortal enemy, we cannot win. Few question not why we must fight this war, why Abaddon hates humanity so, why we must suffer such a needless war. Yet, one question persists and is asked by all. How can a mere human live all these centuries? That is where the stories intertwine, where truth becomes lies and facts become myths." He fingered the hand and a half at his side before continuing.

"The story of Abaddon has been hazy since its beginning, and even now, over four hundred years since its birth, the stories are still cloaked in mystery. How is a man able to live for over four centuries?

'Some say he is not even of physical form, for none of us have even seen him. Some say a forgotten deity granted him immortality and boundless power in return for wiping out humanity for their sins. That would seem to explain why he so relentlessly pursues our deaths." Joshua nodded to Silas as the mercenary continued.

"He fights not to conquer, he fights not for riches. He fights for our very demise. Let us not ponder these questions, for it seems fate will never deem us an answer.

'One question we can answer however is his origins. Everyone has a beginning no matter how great you are, and he has tried every means to stamp out his past, and he has succeeded in this for few know of the truth. Yet, it has survived and has passed down throughout the generations.

'I am one of the few who has been blessed and cursed with this knowledge, the knowledge of the very thing he fears, his own mortal past. This is the one weapon we have that we can use against him, the one thing that can help us end this war.

'His story began nearly five hundred years ago in the grandest city of Tarsha, Morven. Abaddon's true name is lost to history, but what we do know is he was a well-known and highly honored captain of the Citadel Guard, respected by all for his bravery and loyalty.

'It came to pass that he loved the King's daughter, Jocelyn Fallon, and she returned his love with equal passion.

42

Her father however, wanted her to marry the prince of Atuan.

'Jocelyn refused her father's commands, and in his rage, the King banished the young captain from the country on pain of death, forcing him to wander the wilderness until starvation and loneliness finish him. The captain was arrested violently before Jocelyn's eyes and thrown from the city…and into the bitter winter of Erias." Armeth paused for a moment. His weathered face drew gaunt before continuing.

"The captain wandered the wilds of Tarsha, crossing the barren ice wastes of what is now Andred. He roamed the Eastern Desert of Atuan, the wild regions of Heiven Sul and Amon Karash, even over the distant Denemoors.

'He wandered the wilderness for two years, carrying with him the weight of shame and hatred on his darkened shoulders. He vowed to one day avenge his suffering; he vowed to one day rid himself of the source of his pain, the father of Jocelyn.

'He eventually wandered into the Barrows of Alon Heath, the sacred burial grounds of the kings of Erias. On that fateful autumn night, everything would change.

'The stories say that a massive pillar of light poured down on him from the heavens and filled the night with an ivory light. No one knows what it was or why it came to him alone, but the light birthed the demon, Abaddon, and he would use his newfound powers to reap death, to sow chaos, and lay the seeds of human demise.

'The light forged for him a sword, a sword that would be at the very heart of his genocide. It granted him utter power and immortality, creating a god among men. But that story is for another time.

'At this point, the young captain had the lust for one man's blood, and he set out to finish what had been started.

'He set off across Tarsha, each step bringing him closer to his revenge. On a crisp winter evening was the setting that the lore of old detailed, an evening that would leave all others pale in comparison.

'He crossed the Alar River and came upon Morven. The guards failed to recognize him for who he was, for he had changed much in the light of Alon Heath. The guards let him through the gates, a fatal mistake. The vengeful captain struck them down and entered the city.

'He ascended the main road and ran for the heart of the city. Several soldiers threw themselves at him to bar his way, but every man that hindered his path only fueled his wrath. The captain tore their ranks apart, leaving behind a bloody wake as he chased after the crowds of fleeing bystanders. The berserk captain hacked his way through unarmed men and women, callous of discerning between the two.

'Remorse and pity were left far behind; nothing now remained but the cold shell of a heart. He worked his way deeper into the city, murdering hundreds in cold blood.

'He at last arrived at the palace he had once held guard over. One hundred of the finest soldiers of Erias, the Citadel Guard, formed a wall of steel before their captain.

'The rampaging captain charged toward his former brothers-at-arms, a murderous cry on his lips. The Guards held their ground, confident in their numbers. Their confidence would prove their bane, for they underestimated the strength of their attacker.

'A fell flame rushed from his blade, ripping flesh from bone and consuming them alive. The flames could not reach all of them however, and the few men left alive threw themselves at him.

'Soldier after soldier charged foolishly forward, and one by one, he cast them aside. The captain slaughtered all of his former brothers that night, not a hint of guilt to gnaw at his blackened heart. He was far beyond compassion.

'The captain left behind the butchery and threw the palace doors open. He crossed the threshold and entered into darkness. He fought his way through the palace and soon came to the King's quarters, bursting into the room. Several men surrounded the bed, guarding their king who was deathly ill.

'The captain threw forth his hand and sent four of the men flying across the room, falling to the ground in a dead heap. Only two soldiers remained to stand in the way of his revenge.

'As he approached them, they dropped their swords and turned, jumping through the windows in a shower of glass. They tumbled from the top floor of the palace, their screams soon silenced by the stone below.

'The satisfied captain turned and approached the King in his bed. The father of Jocelyn, maker of his sorrows, laid sickly pale beneath the sheets. The captain raised his sword.

'Suddenly, a shout broke out from behind him. He turned and barely blocked a would-be-deathblow. He swung his sword and slit the throat of his attacker.

'The body fell into the moonlight, revealing the face of his defeated assailant. The captain's eyes lit up in shock as he knelt beside the body.

'Jocelyn stared up at him dying. She convulsed and heaved violently, blood spewing across the floor. He cradled her head and watched as she slowly died in his arms. She soon fell still and lay back dead in his hands.

'He stared for a moment into the face of his love, cradling the bloodied corpse in his arms. He slowly closed her eyes. He stood up and turned from her, his sorrow now buried beneath rage.

'He stood over the bed and looked at the King a moment. The King slowly opened his eyes and gazed up at his killer. The captain raised his sword, ready to bring it down through the old man's chest.

'Before he could end his life, the King's head fell back and he died. The captain stood in disbelief. He could not find his revenge, to release its hold over him.

'Then out of the corner of his eye, he saw the King's only son, Ivandar, enter the bedroom. He came upon a scene of four dead soldiers, his murdered sister, and the man who caused it all, standing over the body of his father.

'The captain stepped away from the bed, turned his back to the prince, and jumped through the window.

'Ivandar reached the window in time to watch the captain run off across the courtyard, soon disappearing from view.

'Thousands of soldiers remained to challenge him, yet none dared, afraid to meet the fate of the hundreds who did. He left Morven, leaving behind him a trail of death."

Armeth paused to let his words take their full effect. The men sat in contemplation, attempting to drink in every word.

"Why did he kill her?" Aaron asked; the first to recover from the narrative.

The mercenary shook his head and replied, "He did not mean to, I'm sure if he had known it was her he would have stayed his hand. If he had known it was her...then maybe this war would have been avoided. But alas, who knows how things could have been..." His voice trailed off as he finished speaking.

"Why didn't he kill Ivandar?" Silas asked.

Armeth smirked at this, "Yes, you would think he would have. Yet he did not, and this simple action puzzles me immensely. I think maybe there was a small sliver of pity left in his callous heart."

"Earlier you spoke of a sword given to him?" Cain asked, "What is that about?"

"Ah, Ceerocai," Armeth replied, "perhaps the greatest legend of all. That is a story for another time, my friend.

Nevertheless, the story of Abaddon is not over yet, for this was just the beginning.

'The captain escaped through the wilderness, avoiding the wrath of the Erias army. He fled into the icy wastes of what is now Andred and stopped running, and began working.

'No one knows what drove him to do what he did next, but what he did is truly unimaginable. The rogue captain crossed back over the borders into Erias and invaded several small towns, stealing into their graveyards. He spent many years doing this, stealing the bodies of the long since dead. He soon came to find that his transcendent powers knew no limits. His strength was endless.

'What he accomplished was beyond anything ever heard of, breathing life back into the long dead, if you could even call it life.

'He had brought the dead back to the realm of the living, yet their souls were not of their own. He had defiled their minds and contorted every aspect of them into his acerbic will. He had reproduced a false life, a heartless being peering through the eyes of a hollow shell. He called them the Andreds, named after the empire he would soon make for himself.

'The resurrected dead followed every whim of their master and creator. His sleepless soldiers built a city for him, and as it grew, so too did his territory.

'Soon his country began to rival that of its neighbors, taking control of the eastern wilds that no one laid claim to. His forges swelled, hungering for the forests' timbers and sapping the land of its beauty.

'The terrain slowly morphed from a land of forests and snow, to a land dead and barren, the face of the very earth scarred and pitted with the years of its tainted inhabitants.

'Abaddon soon sent his creations into Tarsha, terrorizing every country, every village, killing thousands and pillaging every last flake of wheat and trace of gold. In months, Tarsha was severely crippled. The ruler of Andred saw how easy it was to destroy his enemies and soon began to send out his armies, to kill and to slaughter.

'He eventually gained the title of Abaddon, The Destroyer, for all of Tarsha would soon fall to oblivion. And since then, we have been fighting against him...to little avail."

Aaron turned to Armeth and asked, "So Abaddon was given his powers? By who? Why?"

Armeth sighed at this. "No one knows, we can only speculate. One day...you will know the truth of it all...but for now, do not worry yourselves with such questions."

"What about Ivandar?" Aaron inquired again. "What about the rest of the story?"

"You will know the full story soon enough. It is not my place to tell you. This is not story time. I am here to make you realize your importance to Tarsha. You must concern yourselves with the here and now; everything else will fall into place. Abaddon seeks to crush us. We must fight back if we are to survive.

'At one time, we had an alliance, and we were strong in our unity. But, after years of fighting, we disbanded, and now we are weak against Abaddon's wrath.

'If we unite, then we may end this war against Abaddon at last. Our country needs you, our people need you, Tarsha needs you." Armeth's voice faded and he looked at them patiently, waiting for an answer.

Cain looked at his friends as they sat in silence, contemplating what Armeth was asking of them. Slowly, one by one they looked up and nodded to him. Cain turned and said to Armeth, "We will go."

The mercenary stood up, a look of elation on his face. However, his smile soon turned grave. "Thank you deeply for offering yourselves, no one else would dare such a task as the one the King has proposed. Tarsha is forever in your debt." Armeth shook their hands and a broad smile parted his lips.

48

"Only one thing," Cain said as Armeth shook his hand. "Why us? There are thousands of others you could have chosen for this."

Armeth scratched his beard before replying, "Because a thousand other souls do not thirst for revenge like yours do. All of you have lost your families, your homes; you have nothing left. Abaddon has torn your worlds apart.

You are the only ones who will dare reach out across Tarsha and do whatever it takes to repair the threads of a broken Alliance. Your hatred for the enemy will drive you to the end. We need men like you with such a drive to help us win this war."

Cain nodded meekly, satisfied with the answer. "So, what's next then?"

"I will talk to Ethebriel and let him know that you have accepted. You and your friends may return to the inn. I will meet you there at sundown."

He grinned and thanked them once again and left the arena with a wave.

Cain walked away from his friends and stopped at the foot of the stairs. He ran his fingers through his hair and sighed. "I hope we're doing the right thing," he muttered.

His friends approached him and Aaron rested a hand on his shoulder. "I know we are."

The Warriors

The sun's setting rays shone through their inn room windows, hues of amber that danced across the timber walls. Cain and the others stood around a large table in the middle of the room and listened tentatively to Armeth as he spoke. The mercenary had carried in an enormous bag and set it down on the table. As he spoke, he pulled out its contents.

Rope, tinder, flint and steel, mats, blankets, cookware, water skins, and several other items were strewn across the table. He had brought in large packs for each of them and he began to pack the equipment into each of these. He pulled out several smaller bags of rawhide and set them on the table.

"This is your tack and bridle gear. And here is…" he fell quiet for a moment as he pulled out several more identical bags, "Your food. It should supply you for a few weeks if you ration it sparingly. Everything is dried and salted so it should keep fine."

The bags were soon packed to the brim, bulging with equipment for a trip that no one knew how long would take.

"Ah yes," Armeth said as he clapped his hands together, "before I forget, I have one more thing for you." He walked out of the room and moments later entered with another man.

The man dragged behind him wooden poles with limbs branching off at various points. Pieces of armor were hanging off these limbs, glistening dimly in the evening light.

Armeth smiled as he saw their expressions and said cheerfully, "This is Locke, the master smith of Kaanos. He has graciously made these fine works of art for you on his behalf..." He grinned and nudged the smith in the side, "Right?"

The man jolted as if Armeth had awoken him and looked at him with exasperation. "Uh, yes...right," he looked away from everyone in the room until his eye caught an attractive knot on the wall.

The benefactors of the armor walked toward them and admired the handicraft. Every piece was made of folded steel, polished and gleaming from hours of devoted care. They removed the armor from the poles as the smith glared at them, taking no care to mask his disdain.

Cain strapped on his armor one at a time, each piece fitting securely around him as if measured precisely beforehand. He clamped on a set of large leather vambraces, a long leather fauld, lastly slipping into a lightweight but sturdy hauberk of cloth, chain mail and leather.

Aaron took the second set of armor, putting on a set of steel greaves and arm guards before strapping on a black leather and chain mail jerkin.

Silas took a set of plated armor and eyed it with a trained eye. He clamped on the breastplate, admiring the large pauldron that protected the left side of his neck. He fastened a short, scaled steel fauld around his waist and let it rest about his thighs. He slipped his hands through a pair of vambraces and nodded, impressed with the smith's skills.

He turned to his brother and helped Joshua into the largest set of armor, clamping piece after piece to his bulky frame until it nearly buried his entire brother beneath a sea of shimmering steel.

The four men stood beside their rucksacks, fully ar-mored and admiring the skills of the man that had given them such a gift. They thanked the smith but he merely grunted and walked out of the room, muttering inaudibly under his breath. Armeth watched his friend leave the room and slam the door behind him.

"Ah, Locke, always the talker...anyway, I'm glad you like the armor, it will come in useful later on I can guarantee. I take my leave of you for now." He turned and opened the door.

"Wait!" Cain called out to him.

Armeth stopped and eyed him curiously. "What is it?"

"I need to ask you something." Cain followed him out of the room and into the hallway.

The light of the setting sun faintly skimmed through the window beside them, casting their faces in gold and flicking shadows as they talked.

"What's on your mind?" Armeth asked softly, waiting for Cain to gather his thoughts.

Moments later, Cain replied. "Something has been plaguing me since I left Andaurel. I have hoped to make sense of it, but I cannot. No one would know the answer to what I ask, but after hearing how much you know, maybe you might." He paused a moment before continuing.

"At Andaurel I fought and killed the captain of the Arzecs, he who murdered my family...." Cain's gaze fell for a moment. "Before I killed him, he spoke strange words to me. At the time, I pushed them aside, but now they fester in my mind. He said that Abaddon wants me dead. That they attacked Andaurel in order to lure me to my home and kill me."

Armeth's eyes lit up. "Are you certain of this?" Cain nodded. "This cannot be." He turned and gripped his forehead as if deep in thought. "This would explain many things..."

"What are you talking about?"

Armeth looked at Cain and grabbed his arm firmly. "Look, my friend, I cannot explain it...you wouldn't understand."

"Try me."

"Alas," Armeth shook his head, "I cannot. I can barely make sense of it myself. However, if it is what I think, then things will soon change. This war will take a turn for the worse and you, Cain, will be in the midst of it all."

**** ****

Cain slowly opened his eyes and glanced around their room, eyes heavy with sleep. The others were still sound asleep, unaware of the noise that had awoken him. He threw his sheets aside and stepped out of the bed and stretched stiffly.

He walked towards the table and took a loaf of bread and a goblet from the platter of food on the table. He walked over to the window and gazed out of the paned glass, eating pensively in silence.

The sun had yet to rise above the horizon, the dull azure light of the early morn cast over Dun Ara. The countless homes and buildings were slowly appearing through the darkness, softly lit in the dawn. The city's market street, normally overflowing with people in the day, was now barren and quiet. The city was still and silent as if frozen by the night.

A metallic click rang out and Cain turned his gaze from the window. Aaron was sitting beside the hearth, prodding the embers of a dying fire. He looked up at Cain as he walked over and sat down beside him.

Cain broke the loaf of bread in two and handed one of the halves to his friend. Aaron bowed his head in appreciation and they sat in silence, gazing into the ashes of the hearth.

"It makes me wonder," Aaron said after a long moment. Cain looked at him questioningly. "What can four men do to save Tarsha from its fate? What if we deserve this war? What if we deserve everything that has happened over these four hundred years? Who are we to say Tarsha doesn't deserve it."

Cain glared at the smoldering ashes. "Tarsha reels in her agony. She burns, she bleeds, she suffocates in the reek of her dead. Who are you to say Tarsha deserves this fate?"

"I'm not saying that. I'm just saying we need to be realistic..."

"I am being realistic. Every second people are dying. Every second the Andreds and Arzecs slaughter another innocent and burn another home. Lives are forever torn and broken. People are left behind in the wake of such destruction. People like me..."

"Eileen? Is that what this is about?" Aaron shook his head. "Are you telling me you accepted the King's offer out of revenge? Cain, as your friend, I've seen you take things too hard, I've seen what damage you can do to yourself. If you do not learn how to move on from her death then it will consume you. You have to do what is best for your sanity. That's what she would want."

"You don't know what she would want. Until you lose a wife and child then you will never know what I feel. Abaddon took them from me and I vow with all my soul to avenge their deaths and find justice for my sorrows."

"Revenge isn't everything, Cain."

"Yes...it is. How do you not want justice for the pain we have endured? Our parents were killed, our homes have been burned down twice now, and everyone we have every loved or cared about is dead! How do you not want revenge?"

Aaron returned his fiery gaze with an unremitting cool. "I do want justice...with all of my heart. But I'm not willing to sell my soul for it like you." Cain turned to the ashes and mulled over his words.

"Sounds like a shitty existence to me," Joshua said as he rose from his sheets. He sat wearily on the edge of his bed and shook his head at Cain. "You think what little we have left, we have to give up for a suicidal chance at revenge that won't even matter in the end? I don't care what happens to us now. We have nothing to live for…we might as well die for something." He stood up and approached his brother's bed, waking Silas from his sleep.

"We need to leave, Armeth will be expecting us," Aaron said, unsure of a proper response to this.

The group ate swiftly and donned their armor. They pulled their cloaks from the backs of their chairs and threw them over their shoulders. They shouldered their packs and adjusted the straps.

"Well," Cain said curtly as he strapped his bow and quiver to his pack, "are we ready then?" The others nodded and followed him out the door. He led them down the hall and crossed the tavern.

"You're leaving us?" a voice called out to them from the tables. One of their fellow soldiers sat at a nearby table, his beard soaked with ale and restless eyes red. The men stared at him in silence.

"I know what you're going to do…we all do," he muttered slowly. The four said nothing. "We wish you luck…go now and avenge our brothers."

Cain nodded solemnly at this and rested a hand on the door's handle. "Revenge…that is all we have left." He threw the door open and led them out into the empty street.

They made swift progress through the barren city and arrived at the mouth of the main road in minutes. They soon reached the entrance yard and crossed the court and approached a figure beside the gates.

Armeth waved at them as they approached. He clapped them on the backs and greeted each of them with a warm grin. They noticed him glance over to his side and they turned to follow his gaze. A man crossed the courtyard with a swift gait.

"Ethebriel wishes to see all of you off…" Armeth explained as the King stopped before them. The five men bowed humbly at his presence.

"I trust Armeth has fitted you with everything you need for the journey?" their king asked. The others nodded in confirmation. "Very well…" he continued, "I need to speak with you a moment before you leave." The King held out a large scroll and unraveled the twine that held it. He unfurled it and revealed a large map of Tarsha.

It was incredibly detailed, the intricate physical features and political boundaries distinctly visible across the tarnished velar. Ethebriel handed it to Cain and the others crowded around him to get a view of the map.

The King pointed to Dun Ara on the map. "You'll travel north after you leave our gates and continue until you cross over into Charun. Once you leave our borders, stay on a northwest bearing until you come across the Crossroads." He pointed to a large river system that ran through the middle of Charun. He dragged his finger in a small circle around a point on the rivers.

"The Crossroads are a large system of gullies and ravines that wind through and around the rivers. You will easily become disoriented; however, the Crossroads are one of the only places you can safely cross the rivers. Keep your head straight in there and you should be fine. After that, you will travel due west until you reach the capital stronghold of Charun, Abraxas.

I have already sent word to Charun's king, Verin, that you are the ones leading the unification of our countries. He awaits you in Abraxas, go there and serve him well. If you help in raising his armies, then they may have the chance to open their borders and send aid to the rest of Tarsha. If you do this, then we will be one step closer to uniting our broken countries and reforming the Old Alliance."

"What of our country?" Cain asked their king. "You send us to Charun to save them? Are we to do nothing but watch our own country fall to ruin under the Arzecs?" The group fell silent as the men stared at the King, awaiting his reply.

"Abaddon may have dispensed many of his forces into the south, but his elite soldiers, the Andreds, rape and slaughter the rest of Tarsha. They need you far more than we do. Kaanos and Charun have not bore the brunt of this war as Erias, Atuan, and Inveira have. They can fend for themselves for the time being, but Charun is wilting under the Arzec invasion. We need them alive, for they are an important piece in the reconstruction of the Alliance.

After you aid them, then we can focus our attention to the North where the true war lies. As for Kaanos, sacrifices must be made, my friend. You will come to understand that soon enough…may the blessings of Tarsha be upon you."

With that, he turned and waved them off with a smile, walking up the main road and disappearing behind the buildings.

The group turned their attention back to Armeth who walked forward and threw up his hands dramatically. "Ah! Your horses!" They glanced over their shoulders and saw several young farriers leading their horses down the road.

Their horses were brushed and trimmed, their manes neatly cut. Large, comfortable saddles were strapped onto their backs by a network of straps and buckles. The stable hands bowed to the horses' owners and handed them the reins.

"Well, best get to it my friends; I can delay you no more," Armeth finished with a smile.

The group strapped their rucksacks to their horses and shook hands with the mercenary. They saddled their horses and reined them towards the gate.

Armeth removed the planking that braced the doors and leaned into them. The doors slowly swung out and he stopped once they were fully open. He turned and looked each of them over.

"You will face many foes and fight many fights my friends. Follow the Warrior's Code that I have given you, for it will guide you well. But remember, you must guide yourselves before you can lead others. Lead your souls down the right path, your feet will follow." He gestured towards the open gate and they reined their mounts through the doors. "Farewell, Warriors."

They rode past him and bid farewell, waving as they began their journey.

With a proud solute, he turned from view and the gates of Dun Ara shut behind him.

The four of Andaurel spurred their horses down the steep hill and maneuvered them carefully through the rough terrain. They reached the foot of the hill and followed the road into the rising sun.

They looked over their shoulders at the city one last time as it slowly faded into the distance. The sun cast its bullion rays over the capital, now nothing more than a golden gleam at their backs.

They soon reached a fork in the road, one traveling east, the other branching off to the north. They reined their horses to a stop and faced the eastern road. Their home was only miles away, or rather, what remained of it.

A shared sense of loneliness suddenly fell over them. With the fading shadow of Dun Ara at their backs and the ashes of Andaurel before them, sorrow fell like a weight upon their conscience.

The gravity of their situation finally set in. They had no families, no friends, no home. They had only themselves, and a shared sense of vengeance. They were but soldiers, like millions before them, yet all of Tarsha had placed their hopes on these four men of Andaurel. They knew not what lay ahead or how difficult their mission would be. However, they were now indentured to the Alliance cause, and they could not disappoint.

They turned from the east road, knowing they would never return to their homes. Cain continued gazing out toward Andaurel. The endless plains swayed before him, shimmering in the mounting sunlight. "Goodbye, Eileen..."

He muttered. He tore his gaze from the plains and followed his friends down the northern road.

They continued in silence, lost in thought. The monotonous crunching of their horses' hooves in the smooth sand and pebbles of the road filled the quiet.

"Armeth called us Warriors," Joshua murmured as if to himself, "I like the sound of that."

Cain looked at him and smiled. "The Warriors...I could get used to that." The others nodded in agreement.

"Everything has changed..." Aaron muttered after a while. Everyone looked at him curiously.

"Just think," he continued as they listened tentatively. "Only three days ago our entire world was turned around. How do things change the way they do? Why did it have to end this way? You start to ask yourself..."

"Why us," Cain finished for him.

"Aye," Aaron nodded. "Why us..."

**** ****

The following day, the Warriors continued through the lifeless plains of Kaanos. Clusters of trees spread sparse across the rolling countryside, little green to please the eye in a world of lackluster fields.

They passed few travelers on the road and even fewer villages. They were alone in their near silent journey, save the occasional song of a morning bird.

A raven flew overhead, eyeing them intently and screeching into the noonday sun.

Cain turned his attention back to the ground and unlatched a saddlebag near his knee. He took out a bundle of dried meats wrapped in wax. He removed the twine that bound it firmly together and separated the food, tossing a handful to each of his friends.

He then removed the map of Tarsha that Ethebriel had given him. He unrolled the parchment and found the small dot labeled Dun Ara.

He scanned the map for a moment before reporting to his friends, "Dun Ara is south of Charun's border by a three days ride. We should be seeing hills by tomorrow."

**** ****

The Warriors urged their mounts up a ridge of hills. Their horses ascended the steep slope, hooves fumbling on the loose shale. After several minutes of labored climbing, they reached the crest of the hillocks.

Large hills stretched across the land as far as the eye could see, intertwined and laced together to provide a complicated series of channels before them. They stood on a large ridge of hills opposite a seemingly identical ridge.

Below them was a steep slope leading into the bottom of a valley. Trees spread thin across the valley, their thorny limbs baking in the afternoon sun.

They had lived in the plains of Kaanos their entire lives and had never seen anything as green as the distant lands before them.

"Charun..."Aaron whispered to himself, awestruck by the view. The others absorbed the striking scene from their vantage point as Cain reined his horse ahead of them.

"We will follow the valley to the west," he pointed to the gorge below and traced an imaginary line through the canyon with his finger. "We'll see how far we can go before we set camp, but...I doubt we'll get very far in this terrain." They nodded tiredly and followed their friend.

Cain led them through a cluster of trees and down a small rocky path that cut through the steep hillside.

They followed the trail down the valley wall towards the gully and picked a path through the rocks with care. They eventually reached the bottom of the path and came under the shade of several trees.

The valley was far more daunting once they were in its depths than at its towering crest. The walls of the valley loomed several hundred feet above them. The sun peered down on the travelers from between the hilltops, the midday heat blaring directly on top of them.

They looked around the valley for a moment as Cain searched for a path through the western end of the gully. He gestured for his friends to follow and reined his horse forward.

They rode close to the opposite side of the valley, the high walls scarcely shielding them from the heat of the noon sun. The rocks under their hooves seared in the heat and their horses struggled onward with every step.

After several hours of riding, they stopped under a large cluster of trees where gnarled limbs hung low over the ground. The group dismounted and threw themselves under the shade. They drew out their water skins and gulped down the warm water.

"You're sure this is the right way, Cain?" Silas asked him.

"We're going northwest aren't we?" he replied, "The gorge we are following stays mostly on a straight path. It should take us to the Crossroads if we follow it. I will get us to Abraxas safely...I hope."

**** ****

The next day, they followed the valley system deeper into Charun, the hours passing away with every tired step.

As the sun hung low in the sky, they finally came to the end of the valley. They saw through the dimming light that the gorge narrowed drastically ahead of them.

They entered the tapering ravine and followed it up a gradually ascending slope. Soon they came out at the crest of the valley and emerged into an open expanse.

They stood on a large terrace that loomed out over a labyrinth of valleys. The plateau was flat and barren at its northern end and behind the Warriors and to their sides was a thick line of thorny trees.

They climbed off their horses and tethered them to the trees, and after giving them a drink, crossed the plateau. As they neared the cliff's edge, they noticed that it extended out over a rocky path below.

The foot of the terrace melded into a slope that extended out ahead for several yards. At the end of the path, a series of hills stretched as far as they could see. The setting sun gilded the skies with a vibrant orange, its warm glow now resting atop the shoulders of the hills.

"At least it's not more valleys..." Joshua remarked as they stood staring over the hundreds of hills dotted across endless fields. A warm breeze whipped across the plateau as they walked back to their horses.

Cain stayed at the head of the plateau and scanned the hills for a course to follow. After a few minutes, he turned and walked towards the others.

"I found a trail leading down into the hills; I think we could get to the bottom from here."

The men saddled their horses, confident in their friend's abilities. They followed him through the trees and came to a small dirt path that extended out from the tree line.

They followed the trail that wound its way down the side of the plateau. The path was narrow and hugged closely to the cliff face. Below them was a steep rock wall that stood a hundred feet or so above the floor of the ravine.

They eyed the edge of the trail, imagining themselves impaled on the jagged rocks below. They avoided the edge and followed the precarious path down into the plateau.

Eventually, the trail leveled out and they followed it for several minutes. The pathway abruptly ended and they came to the base of a small knoll.

They ascended the hill and then dismounted. All around them were hundreds of knolls in varying stature, strewn across the vast landscape. They removed their horses' saddles and let them graze on the grassy prominence.

They soon lit a small fire and passed several strips of dried meat among themselves. They lay down on their mats and stared up at the hues of a dying sun, gnawing halfheartedly on their paltry rations.

"What I wouldn't give for an actual bed right now," Joshua muttered as he tossed away a rock hidden under his mat. "How long until we get to Abraxas anyway?"

"By looking at the map…" Cain replied wearily, "I'd say probably a week until we get to the Crossroads and another four or five days after that…if we continue at the rate we're going that is."

"And how fast would that be?" Silas asked.

Cain laughed lightly, "Not fast enough…"

The Ivory Arrow

For the next few days, The Warriors crossed the endless knolls and valleys of Charun, riding ever west towards Abraxas. The sun rose and set, an endless and perpetual course across the heavens.

As noon came and passed, they rode around the side of a hill and came to a river. Its waters flowed swift and rapid, broken here and there by jutting rocks. A vast expanse of green field stretched before them.

A complicated series of gullies cut through the hills at the other end of the expanse. Several small rivers flowed over fields afar and converged in the maze of gullies. The rivers merged as one at the heart of the ravines, crashing into each other like a great storm. It formed a mighty whirlpool, its roar heard even miles away.

Cain scanned the Crossroads, searching desperately for a path to follow, but every ravine either lead to a dead end or merely merged into another. For several minutes, he sought frantically for a path through the labyrinth, but found none.

He sat back in his saddle and ran a hand through his hair. The others looked at him fretfully, if he could not find a way through the Crossroads, then none of them would. They sat for several minutes in silence and gazed out over the gullies, the river beside them rumbling past.

Cain turned to his friends and informed them, "It looks like this river here flows into the middle of the Crossroads. If we can follow it, it should be able to get us at least halfway through those gullies. But if we do follow it, there's a chance there might not even be a riverbank in those narrow channels."

"We can give it a try," Aaron replied, "it would get us at least halfway through." The others nodded in agreement.

"All right then, we'll try it." Cain spurred his horse forward and led the others down the hill and across the grassy expanse.

They soon reached the Crossroads and gazed up at the walls of rock looming before them. The ravine trailed off into the distance before merging into hundreds of smaller gullies.

They sighed heavily and guided their horses into the narrow gully. Shadows immediately enveloped them.

The roar of the river reverberated off the walls and echoed loudly in the narrow channel. The waters flowed violently through the gullies, throwing sprays of cool vapor in the air that rained down on the travelers. The entrance to the Crossroads disappeared in the distance as they continued deeper into the ravine.

Silas stared over the whitewater that rushed swiftly by. He soon noticed a dark shadow appear on its surface. The swift flow of the river and rocks it broke upon morphed its shape and soon it disappeared. After a moment, he noticed a movement in the corner of his eye.

He let out a startled cry as a figure fell from the cliff top above and crashed into him. The figure tackled into him and tossed him from his saddle.

The others swerved their horses around and drew their swords at this sudden attack. Silas rolled to a stop near the river's edge and his attacker leapt on him, clawing and biting with blind ferocity. The figure drooled over his face, revealing the foul fangs of an Arzec.

The two struggled across the grass, the Arzec near throwing him into the churning waters. The Arzec raised a sword, the tip pricking Silas's neck as he cursed with disdain. With a desperate heave, he tossed his attacker off and ripped the sword from its owner before thrusting the blade through its chest.

Silas jumped to his feet, soaked with frigid water and panting from exertion. He kicked the body over, cruel fangs grinning up at him through gushing blood. "Why's an Arzec-"

The shrill note of a horn rang ominous in their ears. The Warriors drew their weapons and formed a tight cluster with their horses, uncertain as to what awaited them.

A group of Arzecs appeared on the cliff top above, leering down at the soldiers. "Get ready to fight," Cain ordered as they raised their weapons.

Then, from the entrance, a great roar arose. The Warriors turned in the direction of the noise that grew ever louder until it echoed like a godly thunder in the ravines.

From the entrance a great tide swelled, a single, black mass that blotted out the rising sun beyond. Like a looming shadow, the tide poured into the ravine, the roar now booming in the chests of the four men.

Arrows suddenly shot from the masses, whipping around the Warriors. "Oh shit! Arzecs!" Silas screamed in the thunderous din.

"Run!" Cain shouted as he lashed his horse's reins, sending it in an instant gallop into the Crossroads.

The Arzecs atop the cliff jumped over them, and the Warriors swerved to avoid the crashing Arzecs. They broke into a fierce gallop, the river near a blur beside them as they raced into the heart of the Crossroads. Behind them, thousands upon thousands of Arzecs merged and began sprinting after their fleeing prey.

Arrows lashed past their faces as they turned a bend in the ravine, following the cutting course of the river to whatever end awaited. Arzecs continued to pour into the Crossroads, and like a great flowing beast, the black tides pursued.

"Where the hell are we going?" Silas screamed as they galloped around another bend.

"I don't know!" Cain replied, "Just keep riding!"

Driven by desperation, the Warriors swiftly wound their way through the maze of ravines, galloping for their very lives. Yet despite their efforts, several Arzecs reached them.

An Arzec leapt onto the back of Silas's horse, and Silas turned and stabbed his Sitar through its face. The Arzec tumbled to the ground, blood spurting from its skull.

He leaned back and tossed his weapon through the air, sending it sailing several yards before tearing through the back of an Arzec close on Cain's heel. Silas rolled in his saddle as he galloped past its body, tearing his Sitar free and chasing after the others.

Cain turned in his saddle and notched an arrow. With a trained eye, he plunged it through the throat of an Arzec. He notched a second arrow and embedded its broad head in the face of another. He began a fearsome barrage, lobbing frantic arrows into the crowds.

Bodies tumbled under the hailstorm, yet the Arzecs pushed on vehemently. The Arzecs chased after their frightened prey, arrows whipping around the men as they fought to escape.

Several Arzecs dropped from the cliffs before them and rushed down the hill towards their now hemmed in quarry.

Joshua spurred his horse forward, and with a mighty swing of his axe, rent the chest of an Arzec in half. The body launched violently into the air and shot back toward Cain.

Cain pitched back in the saddle, spine level with the saddle as the body soared over him, near inches from his face. The corpse crashed into the pursuing hordes and threw several Arzecs off their feet.

Cain smirked with content and turned toward the others that by now were several yards ahead. An Arzec then tackled into him and tossed him off his saddle. He rolled to a painful stop, sword abandoned in the distant grass. The Arzec rushed toward him, spear raised to finish its disoriented prey.

Suddenly, the Arzec rolled to the earth dead, an ivory arrow embedded in the back of its skull. The Arzec fell on top of Cain, blood running over his face as he pushed the body off. He stumbled towards his sword and jumped to his feet, weapon raised to the oncoming swell.

A volley of arrows shot down into the ravine, felling several Arzecs instantly. A shadow leapt from the cliff, a final arrow loosed as the figure descended into the ravine.

With a gleam of steel, the figure landed atop an Arzec, sword plunged through its chest as it crumpled beneath the weight of its attacker. The figure spun, blonde hair flashing as a sword sliced through the gut of an Arzec.

The figure spun again and hacked the head off an Arzec before hurling the sword. The sword spun over itself and shot into the face of a third Arzec, knocking it violently off its feet.

The figure rushed forward, evaded the swing of a sword, and tumble rolled, pulling the weapon free before bounding off the ground. With a fearsome cry, the figure leapt through the air and thrust the bloody sword through the chest of an Arzec.

The figure landed, straddling the body of the last Arzec. The figure turned, revealing the fair face of a woman. Cain stood speechless as the woman ran towards him.

"You have to get out of here now! The Crossroads are swarming with Arzecs, you'll be overrun!"

"Where the hell are we supposed to go?" He called back to her as he saddled his horse.

From around the bend, a great tide of Arzecs poured. "Anywhere!" She screamed as she leapt through the air and threw herself in the saddle behind Cain.

Cain whipped his reins and sent his horse in a brutal gallop up the hillside. The others appeared over the crest, riding towards him.

"Go! Go! Go!" Cain yelled over the roar of the thunderous footfalls. The others reined their horses in a sharp bend around Cain and followed after their captain.

The Crossroads grew black with Arzecs, swallowed whole by the sheer depth of the enemy. Twenty thousand Arzecs swelled over the ravines, chasing after their defenseless prey.

Cain and the woman at his back turned in the saddle and unleashed a vicious barrage into the oncoming hordes. Bodies tumbled every second, arrows plunging into their tightly packed ranks and sowing discord. Bodies plummeted to the ground, trampled underfoot as Arzecs fumbled past, bloodlust driving them ever on.

The army descended upon them and they now shot blindly into the enclosing Arzecs. Cain drew his sword and hacked madly at the Arzecs that fought to tear him from his saddle.

The girl at his back elbowed an Arzec off their horse and kicked another in the face, lobbing an arrow through its mouth as it stumbled back.

The Warriors followed the ravine until it led them down a sharp turn. They rounded the bend and soon came to a vast maze of gullies. Every ravine that formed its capillaries merged now at the heart of the Crossroads.

Countless gullies carved their way through the rolling landscape, disgorging their waters into the heart of these. A mighty whirlpool formed the middle of it all, violently churning the many rivers into one.

The Warriors descended the hill and galloped along the closest river. The whirlpool thrashed its waters fiercely about, tossing chilling water into the air that crashed down upon them. They rode undeterred through the numbing torrent, coming out the other side to yet another river.

With the Arzecs close on their heels, and arrows lashing about them, the Warriors came to the end of the ravine.

"What now?" Cain cried out to the girl as he eyed the swift approaching bank of a river.

"Just cross it!"

Cain inhaled deeply and threw his horse over the edge, instantly swept up by the churning waters. The Warriors fought to maintain control as they struggled to cross the river, whitewater flogging their sides. Their horses held their heads above the tossing water, fighting for their very lives.

The Arzec hordes stopped at the river's edge and howled with rage as their prey escaped. They watched as the Warriors floated down the river, beating their weapons and shields against their breasts in loathing.

The Warriors fought to keep their horses above water. Mind-numbing water lashed about them, soaking every fiber of their clothes. Arrows shot from the incensed masses, narrowly avoiding their targets before disappearing in the torrential waves.

The river swept the Warriors around a bend in the ravine and at last, the Arzecs slipped from view. The river's current gradually settled as it left the fury of the whirlpool.

Eventually, the Warriors managed to cross over into more shallow water, giving their horses a much-needed rest. A hundred yards ahead of them, the riverbank widened and formed a strip of rocky land at the foot of lofty cliffs.

The Warriors carved through the waters and eventually reached the riverbank. They clambered onto dry land, dripping wet and numb with cold. They sat for several minutes, panting with exhaustion. Cain laid his head on his horse's neck and patted it fondly.

"We can't stay here." The girl pointed to a narrow path barely visible through a cluster of trees. "We'll follow that channel up into the hills, it leads to higher ground. From there we can cross the gullies safely."

Cain turned to the woman. "Who are you?"

"Not now," was her reply.

Cain shrugged and led the others across the rocky riverbank. They rode through the encroaching trees before reaching a narrow channel that sloped up a ridge of hills. Their horses picked their way carefully through the shale, hooves sopping wet.

The channel abruptly ended after several minutes and left them atop a series of flat hills.

"We can rest here for now," the woman suggested. They slowed their horses to a standstill and dismounted. After unsaddling their horses and removing their saddlebags, they sat down in the grass and drained the water from their boots and cloaks.

Once they were finished, the girl stood still for once, allowing them to get a good look at her.

She stood a head shorter than the men but looked to be scarcely younger than them at most. Pallid blonde tresses rolled over her smooth shoulders. Deep sapphire eyes looked over them with a questioning gaze.

A flexible leather and white linen top adorned her thin frame. She wore large leather vambraces that protected the entirety of her forearms. Her upper arms and some of her thighs were exposed, revealing her smooth skin. Gray leather boots rose to her knees beneath a small cloth and leather fauld.

"We didn't expect to come across the Arzecs so soon," Cain muttered as he took another sip of his water skin.

"You couldn't even tell you were under the noses of the Arzecs, and yet you call yourself a soldier? What the hell were you thinking anyways? Going into the Crossroads! They could have killed you!"

"We didn't know the Crossroads were so dangerous-"

Joshua cut him short. "Don't defend yourself to this girl. Who are you anyways?" She crossed her arms and simply blinked.

"Fine, don't say anything. I could care less." Joshua turned and removed the rucksacks from his saddle and shook them of water. "Let's get out of here, we're losing daylight and the Arzecs are sure to be looking for us."

Aaron and Silas stepped towards their horses and grabbed their reins. "I'm staying with you," the girl informed them.

Silas snorted at this. "Bullshit you are." He looked at his brother who nodded with a smirk.

The girl stepped forward and looked up into Silas's icy eyes. "Charun is swarming with Arzecs. Around every corner, in every shadow they lay in wait, waiting for an unsuspecting fool like you to wander by. If it wasn't for me you'd already be dead...Arzecs...gnawing on your bones." Silas blinked with unease.

"She's right, Silas," Cain added. "She saved our lives. She can at least guide us through Charun."

Silas lowered his gaze. Joshua shook his head and slammed his axe in the dirt. He grabbed a satchel of food and walked away from the group.

"Don't mind him," Cain said to the girl.

"I'm not." She wiped her ornate, bloody sword in the grass and returned to the horses. "We need to get out of here; the Arzecs will be looking for you. You will be safe with me. For now at least," she finished with a grin.

**** ****

The Warriors sat in the shadow of a barren oak tree, night long since protracted. Distant stars flickered like heavenly torches, barely lighting the food that the travelers now keenly devoured. A chill breeze blew through the still autumn night, calling the Warriors to the fact that they had never fully dried.

They huddled inside their cloaks for little warmth. The naked branches above them clattered and danced in the stirring winds, the only sound daring to break the apprehensive silence.

The woman sat several yards away on the edge of a prominence, ashen longbow lain across her lap and ivory quiver held ready at a moment's call. She stared ever intent on the wilderness beyond, scanning the night for signs of life.

Cain looked to her back. He wanted to talk to her, but he knew it would do no good; she would not talk unless she wanted to.

"Wish we could have a damn fire," Silas muttered after they finished eating a ration of slightly sodden bread.

"So cold…" Aaron stuttered through chattering teeth.

Joshua grunted and removed a boot, shaking water from it before throwing it aside. "This is her fault," he said as he bored holes in the woman's back with leering eyes. "We wouldn't be in this situation if it wasn't for her."

"How is this her fault?" Cain asked. "She saved my life in the Crossroads and probably all of yours as well."

"Cain's right," Aaron added, "if anything it is our fault. We've been soldiers for over ten years and yet we failed to notice we were being tracked by thousands of Arzecs…we had what was coming. If it wasn't for her, well they'd probably be gnawing on our bones right now like she said." Joshua grunted in response and continued leering at the woman.

Silas leaned back against the tree and began stabbing his knife into a root in habitual thought. "Why were there so many Arzecs in the first place?"

In the heat of the moment, this fact had gone unnoticed to them. Yet as they pondered the question, they realized the peculiarity of it.

Arzecs have been in Kaanos and Charun for over four hundred years. They have always fought the Arzecs, yet never in such large numbers.

"They're marching for Abraxas…" Aaron muttered with sudden realization. The greatest amassing of Arzecs any of them had ever witnessed could only mean this.

Abaddon intended to finally crush the capital of Charun and lay waste to the resistance of the South. If Abraxas falls, so too would Charun, and without the aid of Charun then Kaanos would fall as well. The Warriors returned each other's gaze with widened eyes.

The woman on the edge of the camp suddenly stood up and notched an arrow. In the silent of the night, her stable breaths were easily heard. A faint plume of mist rose from her lips as the bowstring strained in her fingers.

With a slow release of her fingers, the scarcely visible projectile pierced the night and met its unseen target with a thud. A dying gasp reached their ears as the body of an Arzec fell dead to the earth.

**** ****

The next morning the Warriors rose from their mats, eyes red with little sleep.

They ate a small ration of dried mutton and packed their rucksacks. As they prepared their horses for another day of riding, the girl walked over to them, having been gone since they had awoken.

"I found a trail that will lead us back to the river, but we will have to stay on higher ground for now." The others nodded fervently in agreement, keen to avoid the Arzecs.

Cain saddled his horse and held his hand down for the girl. She smirked and jumped nimbly into the saddle behind him, his hand still extended in rejection. He pulled his arm back and shrugged lightly before flicking his horse's reins, leading the group across the knoll.

The travelers followed a small path that ran down a steep hillside before leading them to a stream. They crossed the brook, their hooves plodding through its shallow waters.

They soon rode into a wooded dell. Their steps were instantly stifled in the moist forest floor. The earth around them was covered in a thick blanket of fallen autumn leaves.

Brilliant hues of orange, yellows, and scarlet painted across the forest floor as if a great brush had swept them across the canvas of this early dawn.

Surrounding them were the skeletal remnants of trees, long since made victims of the shifting seasons. Dew clung to their overhanging branches, raining down on the travelers as they rode.

"So," Cain said to the girl as they guided their horses through the trees. "Why are you still with us? You already saved our lives. That should be enough."

She thought for a moment. "Why not? Always being lost, chased by Arzecs, constantly cheating death…you're too much fun. Besides, I was told to find you and stay with you."

"By who?" He asked with raised brow.

"You ask a lot of questions…" She answered in return. He opened his mouth to comment but shrugged off her newfound revelation.

"Well why don't you talk to us?" He began anew.

She smiled at this. "I'm talking to you now aren't I?"

"Aye…"

"You seem sad. Why is that?" Cain shook his head and reined his horse around the last of the trees. "I'm beginning to wish I didn't save your lives…"

The travelers came to a rise in the road, and through the barren branches of the trees, they saw a ridge of hills looming in the distance.

"We'll follow this path to those hills there, we'll be safer on higher ground. The Arzecs have no choice but to follow the ravines."

They followed her command and continued down the leaf-strewn path. The barren trees rained mist upon the riders that softly kissed their skin. Leaves sailed the wisps of cool wind that trickled into the gully, vivid shades of autumn brushing past. After following the dell for several minutes, it began sloping upwards at a steeper angle.

Their horses began fighting to ascend the slippery slope as mud clawed about their hooves. After several minutes of labored climbing, they reached the crest of the hills.

A vast stretch of rolling knolls splayed before them and rolled over the horizons. A sea of grass danced in the morning gale, waves of emerald rippling across the rolling landscape. A large river poured from the mouth of the Crossroads on their right, its waters now flowing calm and languid into the north.

"Three more days of riding will put us at Abraxas. The Arzecs we had the misfortune of meeting are certainly marching for the capital. We have to warn them in time."

"You know of our destination?"

"I know a lot of things, Cain Taran," she replied.

His eyes lit up at this, befitting the reaction she anticipated. "How do you know my name?"

"Again, you ask too many questions," she curtly retorted. Cain tore his gaze from her, struck with the same blunt edge for the second time. The girl laughed and said, "We need to get moving. We have a country to save."

**** ****

Cain threw each of his friends a strip of salted venison and sat down on his saddlebag. The five of them stretched dramatically, weary from another day of riding.

They had traveled several leagues in short work, riding west over the ever-changing countryside of Charun. The wilderness encompassed them for hundreds of miles, not a village to be seen.

The four of Andaurel had long since tired of this constant force of solitude, ever present and forever indomitable. It seemed beneath the stars and silver clouds that they were alone in their endeavors. What they felt beneath those stars that night was not too far from truth.

The woman approached the group. "Mind if I sit?" Cain shook his head and she stabbed her sword in the ground before sitting down beside him. She crossed her arms, unable to mask the unease in her eyes.

"You ready to talk?" He asked her.

The girl nodded and looked at each of them in turn. "My name is Adriel Ivanne…I was sent out to guide and protect you on your way to Abraxas."

"We don't need protection," Joshua retorted.

"Oh really!" Adriel chided with a denouncing cry. "I think since you-"

"Calm down, both of you!" Cain ordered, cutting her reproach short. The group fell silent.

Aaron turned to the girl and bowed his head. "I think what our friend here means to say is that it's nice to meet you, Adriel." She smiled in return.

"Continue," Cain urged.

She glared at Joshua a moment before continuing. "I was informed that you were traveling to Abraxas," she began. "I was told nothing more than that…only that you needed a guide to cross Charun safely. So I set out to find you. I've been tracking you since."

Cain looked at her curiously. "Who told you this?"

"My father," she replied. Cain returned her gaze as if gesturing for elaboration. "Ethebriel, the king of Kaanos." The Warriors stared at her in bewilderment.

"Ethebriel is your father?" Silas asked.

"I just told you that didn't I?" Adriel replied sharply. "The day you left Dun Ara, he said I needed to follow you and guide your way so you can do whatever the hell it is you're doing."

Joshua glowered at her and grunted with discontent, "We've been soldiers for over ten years; none of this is new to us. We don't need your help, girl, you'll only get yourself killed." Adriel opened her mouth to comment but Cain interrupted her.

"Yes Joshua, I think we do need her. She saved our lives once already. She guided us through the Crossroads and she has kept us from the Arzecs this far. She may prove invaluable." A cautious smile pulled at her lips as he finished.

"If we can trust her..." Silas added.

"Trust is hard to find," Aaron finished, "need is the only thing we have, and we need a guide."

Cain nodded at him. Silas shrugged his acceptance at this and Joshua tossed his hand, relenting.

"Good, now that that's settled," Adriel said after a tense silence. "Now you have to talk."

Cain glanced at his friends before replying, "I'm sure Ethebriel has his reasons for not telling you what we're doing."

"I knew you would say that," Adriel replied airily. "All right...well, I will see you in the morning," she said as she stood up. "Good night." She walked away and stopped at the edge of the hill. She pulled her cloak close and lay down in the grass.

The others lay down on their mats with a wearied sigh. Cain passed a hand through his hair and glanced over at the girl before returning to his bed.

**** ****

The next morning they woke to Adriel shaking them violently from their sleep. "We need to get moving," she ordered as they stood up and stretched with displeasure. "We're about two days from Abraxas. We have to get there before the Arzecs."

Joshua ignored her plea for urgency and dug through his rucksack. "Dried food again..." He muttered as he stuffed a slice of crusty bread between his portly cheeks. Silas glanced at him and blinked tiredly at his food, stretching dramatically for a moment before tossing the bread over his shoulder.

As the sun rose over the horizon, they packed their rucksacks and loaded them onto their saddles before mounting their horses.

Cain held out his hand for Adriel and she looked at him for a moment and slowly accepted his hand. He lifted her into the saddle behind him, her long legs whipping over his back. He nodded at her and spurred his horse away from their camp. They descended the knoll and guided their horses around a series of hills.

"Ethebriel told me much about you," Adriel whispered into his ear as they rode on through the morning.

"And what did he say?"

She paused a moment before replying. "He said you were very pigheaded." Cain laughed at this. "He was always able to look at someone and know who they really are…but he said you're a hard man to figure out. If even my father cannot make sense of you, then you must be a very complicated man indeed."

"Well if I'm complicated, then you're impossible," he jested. She glared at him with crossed arms and fought a smile.

"What else did he say?" He asked after a while.

"He said you are filled with hate…and that if you continue on the path you have set for yourself, revenge will surely destroy you." Cain's smile quickly faded. He turned from her and looked up at the cloudless sky. The thing was; he could see the truth in that.

**** ****

The sun slowly fell to the horizon, painting its bloody rays across a mural of opaque clouds. The travelers came to a small cluster of tree-covered hills and rode through them. As the light of day faded, they reined their horses to a stop and dismounted.

They led their horses over to the foot of the largest hill and removed their saddles. After tethering their horses to a tree, they climbed the hill.

They came atop the breadth of a great hillock, its far splayed crown stretching for hundreds of yards over flat fields. Miles of open countryside lay before them, endless hills, trees, and plains stretching far beyond the fading horizon.

They dropped their rucksacks and crumpled exhausted to the ground. Joshua passed a handful of biscuit between them and they finished this pitiable ration with a handful of dried fruits. They lay back on their mats with a flourish.

Adriel removed her armor and tossed it aside. A silk tunic and long skirt rippled in the breeze like fresh fallen snow. She sat down in the grass and removed her knee-high boots.

A discomfited silence enveloped them as they searched for something to break the lapse in conversation.

"My uncle told me what happened to all of you at Andaurel...I'm deeply sorry." They looked up at her angrily. She immediately fell quiet, aware of what she had done.

"All right...remind me to never bring that one up again," she noted under her breath.

The men slowly shook off the memories and fell quiet for several lengthy minutes. "Is there anything I can say that's right?" The men continued to ignore her. "Come on...I'm trying here. First you're mad because I won't talk and now you're mad that I am." She fell silent, plucking her bowstring with tense fingers. She lifted her knees from the dirt and laid an arm over them, resting her cheek against it.

After a while, she lifted her head up and looked at them. "So what did all of you do before...this?" They acknowledged her continuous effort to communicate. They shrugged at each other and decided in their minds that it was a harmless question.

"Well," Aaron began, "I was a farrier, for a time. My mother died in childbirth so I never knew her. My father, Sable Hayden, was always ill. I took up his carpentry practice but I could not afford to take care of him. Silas helped me get through between pay however..." He finished and glanced over at his friend.

"My brother," Silas gestured toward Joshua, "and I never knew our parents. They deserted us when we were young, and Cain's parents helped us through our rough childhood. We were Andaurel's only blacksmiths, we made everything and anything for our people...I found a value in these skills and took an interest in fashioning weapons. I even made Joshua's axe." He picked up his Sitar from beside him. Its four pronged blades glistened in the starlight. "I made this as well. It took me several months to construct it but it is one-of-a-kind, an invention of my own."

Adriel nodded and turned to Cain curiously. "And what of you?"

He looked back at her austerely. "I've always been a soldier, fighting this war is all I've known."

"Surely there's more?" Adriel asked with a blunt push of words.

Cain replied, "Aaron's father and my parents were killed twenty two years ago in an attack on Andaurel. All the children, including the four of us, were evacuated. Our city was lost. I vowed to avenge my family's deaths and when I came of age, I joined the Army to fight against Abaddon's injustices.

'My friends here joined a few years after I did. They were a part of the Andrus Defense Brigade and I was eventually transferred and put in charge of their battalion.

'Circumstances later forced us to join the Kaanos Out-riders. We have traveled our country for the last five years, defending her people and scouting for enemy forces. We have killed many Arzecs and lost many men, all in the name of this senseless war. I have always fought her battles with little self-doubt, but after this last attack on Andaurel...I couldn't handle the loss."

"What happened?" Adriel asked; curiosity now peaked.

Aaron shook his head hurriedly. "It's best not to bring that up..."

"Why not?" She asked, perplexed.

"Don't you take a hint?" Joshua snapped.

Adriel's gaze fell, stricken by this fierce and sudden reprimand. The group drew quiet again. A constant breeze blew across the hilltop, grass rippling in the whispers of wind. They drew their cloaks closer, desperate for warmth in the bitter winter's night.

Cain eventually stood up and left the group. "Cain..." Adriel started as he crossed the hilltop.

Cain turned and looked the girl over. "Look, none of us need you, we don't even know you. We never asked for you to stay." He stepped over the hill's shoulder, the night engulfing him.

**** ****

Cain stood amid a cluster of trees, cradled in the dark of night. He leered down the shaft of an arrow, bow trained on the knot of a nearby tree. His calculated breaths rose as a mist before him, carried softly away by a cold draft.

The cloth of his fingerless gloves tensed as he pulled his bowstring back to his cheek, and with a final exhale, he released the arrow. The projectile shot just shy of its target, embedding its broad head in the soft underbelly of the oak.

The rustle of leaves reached his ears and Cain turned to see Adriel approaching. He turned his attention back to the knotted tree and notched another arrow. He pulled the string back quickly, breaths now hastened. He released this second arrow, again missing its target.

Adriel appeared beside him, bow raised and ivory arrow pulled back to its neck. The girl flicked her fingers and sent the arrow center of its mark. She turned to Cain and smiled.

"Come to show off…" He asked as he began walking towards the tree.

"No," she replied and followed him. "I wanted to apologize. I didn't mean to pry."

"Of course not."

"Honest. I let my curiosity best me. I'm sorry."

Cain nodded and stopped before the tree, pulling an arrow from its breast before returning it to its quiver.

"Do you always shoot defenseless trees in your spare time?"

"Only when I need to think," he answered as he pulled the second arrow free with a grunt. "And you can see where that gets me."

Adriel laughed at this and retrieved her arrow. The two began weaving through the trees, walking silently through the still night.

"Did you mean what you said back on the hill?"

Cain thought for a moment. "No, no I didn't. I don't know anything about you of course, but regardless, we need you."

Adriel nodded in satisfaction and returned her gaze to the moonlit trees before them. "Whatever happened to you in Andaurel must have been heartbreaking…"

Cain remained silent. Together, they left the trees and ascended the hill to their camp. As they reached the top, a brilliant glow awaited them.

Joshua and Silas sat around a campfire, bantering loudly at the other. Silas tossed a bundle of brushwood into the fire, its flames leaping up to engulf the fresh fodder. Joshua held a strip of venison over the flames, quickly burning his hand. He dropped his meal in the fire with a yelp and clenched his hand.

"What the hell are you doing?" Adriel screamed.

"Not freezing my ass off for once, that's what!" Joshua replied.

"You idiots!" scolded Adriel as she kicked the fire, dispersing the burning wood. She began frantically stamping out the fire.

"I tried to stop them!" Aaron cried as he rushed over and poured his water skin over the blaze.

A distant horn suddenly rang in the night. Its strident note echoed over the hills, stopping the Warriors in their tracks.

Joshua lurched over the fire and grabbed the girl's leg as she struggled to stamp out the fire's remains. "Get off me!" The girl demanded.

The distant horn blew again, this time much closer. The Warriors could no longer ignore its presence. They dove to the earth as a great light appeared on the horizon.

"What is that?" Silas whispered.

Aaron turned to him with graven unease. "Torches…"

Through the darkness, thousands upon thousands of torches poured over the fields. Their radiant, ruddy lights amassed like the sun confound in darkness. Twenty thousand Arzecs marched across the plains, the earth bemoaning a mournful cry beneath the weight of so great a punishment.

The horn blew again as the Arzecs spotted the distant glow of the Warrior's fire. Like a beacon in the night, it flashed atop the tallest of hills.

"We have to get out of here!" Adriel screamed over the now fierce blowing horn.

The Warriors bound to their feet and hastily threw on their packs, sprinting down the hill to their horses.

"I didn't know they were so close!" Silas cried as he shakily untied the knot to his horse's lead. "We were a day ahead of them!"

"It doesn't matter now," Adriel explained as she climbed onto the horse after Cain, "Abraxas won't be expecting an attack of this magnitude. We have to warn them!"

The Warriors whipped their reins and broke into a swift gallop, the mass of Arzecs not far behind.

**** ****

They rode throughout the night, the hours quickly waning by. The landscape around them soon began to change from endless knolls of heather and grass to furrow fields of blackened earth.

They rode through the morphing terrain, ash and stone flying, a gray pillar of dust billowing forth from their horses' hooves. "We're getting close!" Adriel screamed out to the others over the rush of wind. They lashed their horses' reins, urging them forward with every ounce of their strength.

The ground ahead of them stopped and disappeared over the edge of a cliff. They let out a cry and pulled on their reins in alarm. Their horses skidded to a stop before the edge of the cliff.

"Keep riding!" Adriel yelled in Cain's ear.

"Are you insane?" He cried back.

She kicked their horse in its sides in response. Their horse cried out and jumped over the edge, falling onto the steep sloping cliff face. The others peered over the edge after them and watched as they came to a stop at the foot of the precipice.

They looked at each other with unease and hesitantly ushered their mounts over the edge. They landed on the rocky slope and began sliding down the steep cliff. The slope gradually leveled out and they soon came to a stop, breathless with exertion.

Adriel laughed as they rode up beside her. "We're here." The others looked up, awestruck at the sight before them.

They stood in the basin of a great crater, two hundred foot cliffs circling all around them. The steep walls blocked out most of the sun, bathing them in shadow. At the base of this crater was the capital stronghold of Charun.

Abraxas stood in the middle of the basin, its back wall merging into the immense cliff face behind it. Large gray stones formed its walls, worn with countless years. The front corners of the stronghold appeared like the heads of arrows, their triangular structures designed for maximum liberty within a limited space.

A great gorge stretched across the front of the fortress, one end tapering off and melding into the right corner of the stronghold. The other end of the chasm followed the walls of the fortress and disappeared around the farthest end of the keep.

One narrow bridge of stonework stretched across the gap, forcing the travelers to ride across single file. They carefully traversed it and came out into a small, rocky area that separated the gorge behind them and the fortress walls ahead by only a few yards.

A large gate stood before them, its solid iron face gleaming dully in the morning light. They stopped in the shadow of the fortress and peered up at its towering walls. Several archers roamed the causeways, gazing out over the crater's edge.

Several guards noticed the travelers and peered down at them.

"You there!" Adriel cried out to them, "Open the gate!"

"Lady Ivanne! Of course!" A soldier replied. "But who are these that travel with you?"

"We are the soldiers Ethebriel sends to your aid! We are the Warriors!" Cain called up to the man. The guards stared at them a moment before ripping their gaze away, talking quietly amongst themselves.

"Are you going to open the gate or not?" Adriel shouted with agitation.

"Yes, right away!" The sentry replied before hurrying off. The guards below removed the gate's bracer and pulled the doors slowly open. The Warriors reined their horses forward and guided them towards the fortress

"They called you Lady Ivanne," Cain said as they crossed under the gateway. "They know you?" Adriel hid her eyes behind his back. Cain led the group into the first floor of the fortress.

Several yards ahead of them was a large stone wall that blocked off the upper floor from the first. They stood now in the middle of a long road that stretched to the left and right of them.

Hundreds of soldiers ran mindlessly through the first floor, barking orders and passing armfuls of supplies through their ranks.

The Warriors flicked their reins and guided their horses to the right. They followed the road and picked their way through the mass of soldiers.

The road came to a rather thin tower that jutted out from the causeway and loomed over the first floor.

They continued down the road until they came to a wide staircase on their left. They ushered their horses up the steep flight of steps and came out onto the second floor of the fortress.

The Warriors urged their horses into the droves of soldiers. Men darted madly about, passing weapons, armor and barrels of arrows every which way. Every man wore the armor of Charun, simple steel and iron embellished with leather, yet hardy as the men who bore them.

The smell of burnt metal reached their noses and they turned to see a large forge barely visible through the sea of heads. Smoke billowed from the building's many arches, rising like a cloud in the morning sky.

Several smock adorned men labored around the furnace, pulling rods of red-hot steel from its depths before plunging them in troughs of saltwater. Their sooty faces grimaced with each blow of their mallets, molding sheets of iron into armor and tossing them into piles at a blinding rate.

Through the thick smoke of the forges, the Warriors could barely make out several barracks that lined the road.

Men burst from these buildings, frantically throwing on their armor and joining the confusion.

The streets between the barracks bristled with soldiers, men dashing about sporadically like a host of schizophrenics. The Warriors continued through the fortress and fought through the sea of men.

After several laborious minutes, they left the barracks and came out into an open courtyard. Directly across from them was a great bowl carved into the heart of the fortress. Several steps led down into its basin, where a stone building awaited.

As the Warriors crossed the open area, they noticed an armory on their left that lay hidden in the shadow of several buildings.

Hundreds of soldiers crowded around the armory, shouting into the open doors. Several men passed armor and weapons to the soldiers closest to them, nearly crushed under the tide of men.

Soldiers fought their way to the front of the group, a near brawl ensuing as they battled for the few remaining supplies.

The Warriors continued unnoticed by all as they reined their horses carefully down the flight of stairs.

A tall stone building stood in the middle of the basin. Seven rows of columns stood at its front, bracing a large and decorative terrace above. Numerous standards of Charun flapped in the breeze, their bullion colors shimmering with every wave.

A statue of a soldier, twice the size of a man, stood in front of the columned building. It was fashioned entirely of iron and held a huge standard in its right hand. A sword stabbed into the iron dais upon which it knelt. The soldier's face contorted with shame and sorrow, his brow furled with despair. Its left hand cradled its face as it wept, iron tears streaming through its fingers.

The Warriors rode past the statue and gazed up at it curiously, fighting off the sadness it seemed to divulge. They rode through the rows of columns and approached a large door that lay in the darkness of the terrace above. Ten soldiers guarded the entrance to the building. The travelers quickly dismounted their horses and led them towards the guards.

The soldiers wore weighty hauberks of chain mail. Long swords were fastened to their belts. They bore short spears and stood with a portentous air, unperturbed as the riders approached.

Without a word, two of the guards opened the building's heavy brass doors.

Half of the guards stepped forward, took their reins from them, and led the tired horses to a nearby stable. The remaining guards gestured for the Warriors to enter the building.

The Warriors walked through the doors and entered the building. The guards closed the doors behind them.

The Great Hall had but one extremely long room. Elegantly carved columns lined its walls, crafted solely with pretentiousness in mind. They were flecked with silver, gilded with gold, and seeming held together by supple cords of velvet. Numerous stain glass windows lined the room's walls and between each was mounted a lushly woven tapestry.

A single wooden table stood in the middle, stretching along the entire length of the room. Long benches of the same reddish wood were pushed under it as if in a hurry.

Numerous tin plates and goblets littered the table's surface. Traces of breakfast still encrusted the plates and the dregs of wine lay stagnant in the bottoms of many goblets.

Two men stood beside the table on the far end of the room, pouring over a large piece of parchment that sprawled across the tabletop. The Warriors approached the men who remained deep in conversation, dragging their fingers across the parchment.

One of the men glanced up from the map and noticed the Warriors. He whispered something inaudible to the other and threw a hood over his face. He then left the man's side and walked toward the Warriors.

He stared curiously at them through the shadows of his hood, his black fur cloak brushing past. He crossed the room and threw the doors open, soon disappearing from sight. The man who remained rolled up the parchment and approached.

A heavy crown of platinum sat atop a nest of crimped, sable hair. Its many jewels glistened at the Warriors as they approached. A rather prominent nose stuck out from his smooth shaven face. He wore elegant clothes of black silk and linen that gave off a vibrant sheen. He bore a heavily ornate sword at his side, its gold handle and hilt encrusted with the finest jewels.

"Welcome to Abraxas, travelers," he greeted them with a hoarse, slightly nasally voice. "Ethebriel could not have sent you at a more perfect time." He opened his mouth to say something else but closed it for a moment before speaking again.

"Ah yes, I forgot to introduce myself. I am Lord Verin, King of Charun." He held out his ringed hand for them to shake.

He shook Aaron's hand and bowed lightly. "Aaron Hayden, the keenest of minds."

He stepped sideways and shook the brothers' hands. "Silas and Joshua Valfalas, the bravest defenders of Andrus. Relentless pursuers of the enemy. It is an honor."

He came to Cain and extended a hand. Cain lowered his gaze as the man shook his hand. "And Cain Taran...I have heard many things about you." He continued with a strange air as if having solicited this speech in his head prior. "You are destined for greatness. Do not sway from the path you follow." Cain returned this casual praise with a questioning gaze.

Verin extended a hand to Adriel and stood for a moment in disbelief. "Adriel? Ethebriel told me nothing of you in his letter…"

The girl shrugged and replied, "It was a last minute decision. They needed a guide through Charun."

Verin shook his head with incredulity. "I see the reasoning behind it…but there will be blood spilt by tonight I can assure you. You should not be exposed to the ugly face of war. You have been through enough as it is."

"You honestly think it's up to you to make that decision for me?" Adriel replied defensively. "You always thought you could. Ethebriel did everything for me, and yet you were the one to say you played his part. You're such a-"

Cain threw a hand over her mouth, cutting her short. "What can we do to help, my lord?" He asked, desperate to ease the tension.

"Ethebriel informed me of your many talents, Cain Taran. He failed to mention you knew when to stay tongues." He glared at Adriel a moment before continuing.

"I will put each of you in command of a regiment, each at different positions of the stronghold. You will lead an archer battalion atop the gate section. That is where we need our forces focused most if we are to fend off the enemy's assault.

'Joshua and Silas, you two will lead individual battalions on the first floor near the entrance to slow the enemy if they manage to breach our gates.

'Aaron Hayden, you will lead a battalion on the north stairway leading to the second floor. If the enemy manages to push past your regiments, then there will be little we can do to stave off their advance. Hopefully they will not be able to push through that far, Abraxas' defenses are nigh impenetrable.

'You must go now; there is much to do before the Arzecs arrive. Matthew will take you from here."

A soldier walked towards them from the end of the room and bowed before the King. "Lead them to the regiments I showed you earlier…and make sure everyone has an assignment, we need to be prepared long before the enemy steps foot inside this crater."

With that, Verin picked up his parchment and stepped forward to leave the room.

He passed Adriel and paused for a moment. He slowly lifted his hand and raised it as if to strike her. Adriel lowered her head.

"You, my girl," he began, "would do well to stifle your impudence…" He turned his palm to face the ground and flicked it. Adriel closed her eyes and slowly leaned forward, her soft lips kissing the rings on his hand.

The King smirked in satisfaction. "Do not forget your place." He turned and left the room.

Adriel wiped a tear from her face and glared after him as he walked away, a quiet jeer on her face. The man named Matthew gestured for them to follow.

"Verin said crater?" Aaron asked the soldier, the first to recover from the strange scene.

The soldier led the group out of the hall and across the columned court, leading them towards the stairway. "What exactly is all this?"

Matthew glanced over at the group and replied, "This crater is actually an extinct volcano that has remained dormant for several hundred years. Its past eruptions have morphed the landscape and destroyed our soil, causing the earth to become infertile and unfit for tilling. Despite its drawbacks, this area of Charun was perfect for a military position, because we could literally see for miles from here," he pointed to an enormous tower behind the Great Hall.

"Abraxas was actually built during the early years of the war as a last line of defense, used mostly for supply purposes. However as the war dragged on, the fortress became a prime target for the Andreds. It expanded over time and eventually it became our primary stronghold. We have actually fought several..."

Cain let the group continue their walk across the court and up the stairs. He stepped beside Adriel who had lagged behind, eyes locked solely on the stone at her feet. Soldiers dashed about her, nearly trampling her as she indifferently split the crowds.

"What's wrong?" Cain asked her.

She inhaled deeply and raised her head. "Nothing." She quickened her pace and hurried after the others.

"What was that in there?"

"Nothing, Cain. Stop prodding your nose into every-thing you deem fit."

Cain shook off her comment and looked over his shoul-der to the Great Hall. "Something's off with that man..."

Adriel snorted and attempted a laugh through teary eyes. "You're telling me."

**** ****

As the sun climbed gradually through the sky and the day dragged on, the defenders of Abraxas continued their preparations for battle. The Warriors were scattered across the fortress, preparing their regiments.

"So what happened this morning?" Adriel inquired of a soldier as she heaved a barrel of arrows onto her narrow shoulder. "We came to warn Abraxas of the enemy, but you already knew?"

"A scout arrived during breakfast," the man replied, "he saw the Arzec hordes marching west across the hills; it's only a matter of time now before they descend upon us. We had contemplated such a move, but they have not attacked Abraxas in years. Since the scout's arrival, we have been working without end. Only until the Arzecs arrive will we be able to stop, but when that time comes, we'd wish we never had..."

Adriel laughed nervously at his remark. "Where are the nearest reinforcements? Were we not prepared for this?"

"Alas we were not," the soldier answered, "Abaddon has focused his attention on the North for centuries; Kaanos and Charun have felt only the taste of war on their tongues. Only now does he let the hammer fall on us. The attacks come from all around, our villages fall like flies to the enemy. We have been focused on aiding our villages and we have sent out many of the garrison that was once here. We are only half our number..."

"How many Arzecs were sighted?" Adriel asked as the soldiers began carting their supplies away from the armory.

"Our scout said he could not search for a number; there is no end to the black tides. They will be here by to-night...our time left on this earth dwindles with each passing hour." The soldier fell silent and Adriel stared at him with sudden realization.

Now that she saw the dying light in these men's eyes, now that she saw hope die before her, she saw the truth in these men.

They were trapped in a pit with no hope of escape. An army of unimaginable number marched upon them, seeking to crush any hope remaining to the outnumbered and beleaguered soldiers. An endless tide of blood would soon befall them.

Charun was not ready for such a sudden and fierce invasion. They were ready to fall.

She had pushed aside the reality of the war when she was safe in the halls of Ethebriel.

Yet now the garnishments of war fell before her, revealing the truth of it all and stealing away her naivety.

Charun shared the same fate as Kaanos. The Arzecs of Abaddon now pushed relentlessly through the countryside, slaughtering and burning everything in sight. Thousands lay dead in the grave of innocence.

She had heard the sighs of Ethebriel as he received yet another letter from Verin, writing that yet another village had fallen, that more souls were extinguished, that more blood was being spilt. She heard his sorrow and saw his misery, but until now, she had never understood it.

The gravity of their situation finally set in, that the armies of Andred were descending upon them, seeking to snuff out the final resistance of the feeble South.

A soldier's voice broke Adriel's thoughts. "That statue embodies all that Charun has ever been," he said as he gestured towards the grieving statue before the Great Hall. "Our country has fought many long and bloody battles. It represents the blood we have spilt and the tears we have shed…are we to die today, are we to fall now after all these years of fighting? We are a proud people; the dogs of Andred will not destroy us. We will seek our revenge on Abaddon for all he has done to us."

"Speak for yourself…" a nearby soldier muttered.

The Art of War

The soldiers of Charun had been at work for countless hours, struggling against time and fate to prepare for the inevitable. They now filled the first floor of the stronghold, awaiting the end.

The Warriors stood behind the last line of soldiers on the second floor. They donned the last of their armor and strapped on their weapons, a sinking feeling in their hearts as they armed for battle.

"I feel…" Aaron muttered, "I feel as if fate has sealed us to this path…this path of destruction that we have chased for so many years. We will surely meet our end if we continue like this." He glanced over at Cain. "We were destined to war, destined for bloodshed…this path will only destroy us."

Cain looked at his friend and replied strongly, "Our way is war and we are destined to follow it. The same Arzecs that took everything from us now marches for Abraxas to take the only thing we have left, our lives. And we will give them that. We will fight for revenge, for every spilt drop of our families' blood and every ash of Andaurel."

"Can we continue this though?" Aaron replied, "If we follow this path of revenge, it will lead only to ruin. Will it continue to fester in our hearts until we turn like animals, seeking blood to sate our urges? When the blood dries and there is none left to spill…what then will we fight for?" The group fell silent, unable to give an answer.

Grim faced and heavy hearted, the Warriors left each other's company and went to their separate regiments. Only

Adriel and Cain remained, gazing out over the fortress before them.

Cain could not heed the sobering words of his friend now; he had to fight for the injustice against his wife and child. He must fight to avenge their deaths and appease his thirst for revenge at whatever cost. He shook his head, struggling to stave off the thoughts that swirled within.

He looked to Adriel who still remained at his side. "What happened earlier between you and Verin?" He asked her. Adriel looked at him and sighed deeply.

"Verin is my uncle…I told you Ethebriel was my father so I could gain your trust…and save myself from your incessant inquiry." She glanced at him with a slight smirk.

"Before you ask, Verin was my mother's brother, and I have had to deal with the hardships of my relation to him. He is a pathetic excuse for a man. He believes himself to be superior to anything that draws breath, especially those of his own blood as he showed earlier today…"

Cain looked at the girl with new understanding. "Even kings are human," he said after a moment, "but he is your uncle, you cannot hate him forever." He fell silent and looked out over the sea of heads to the setting sun beyond.

"Watch me. You don't know him like I do; if you did then you would think the same."

"Enlighten me then."

"Very well," Adriel replied, accepting the offer. "I grew up in the village of Alara, near Charun's eastern border with Atuan.

'My mother loved me dearly and never failed to sacrifice for me.

'My father was a nobleman but used his power and wealth in all the wrong ways. He was a drunkard and a gambler. He spent his days drinking away his sanity and his nights by beating my mother and I.

'The years passed and my father eventually fell victim to his vices and took his own life. However, his wealth went to

Verin, for the snake seized the money from under us and used it to furnish his many palaces. We lived in poverty for months with little food, for who would provide for a helpless widow and her daughter?

'Driven by need, we went to Verin and pleaded for mercy. Instead of mercy, we received a miracle. We met his friend, Ethebriel. He was the miracle we were searching for. He ignored our plight and fell in love with my mother for who she was. He provided for us and loved me like the father I never had. He eventually proposed to my mother and I had never been happier than to move to Dun Ara and start a new life.

'It was too good to be true. My mother fell ill a year after their marriage...and eventually it claimed her life. Ethebriel and I were heartbroken from the loss, but I think that common ground between us only drew us closer. Ethebriel was the father I never had.

I lived with him in Dun Ara for a few years, where he and a man named Armeth taught me all I know. They even made me this bow," she gestured to the ivory longbow at her back.

She fell silent and left Cain to contemplate her words. The light of day slowly dwindled. Night veiled the sky at last. Dark clouds hung heavy in the sky, blotting out the stars.

"I'm sorry for all that," Cain said after a while. "I didn't know."

"It's in the past...speaking of the bastard, where is he anyways?"

The two looked around for a moment and locked eyes. "Come on," Adriel gestured. She led him across the second floor, passing the barracks and armory.

They descended the steps to the Great Hall and approached its doors. "I'm sure he's in here," she muttered as she pushed the doors open with a loud creak. They walked into the hall that now glowed with the light of several torches.

Verin stood alone at the far end of the hall with his back to the door. The two approached him and eyed what was occupying his attention.

A mural extended from one corner of the wall and stretched across until it ended halfway to the opposing corner. Adriel and Cain had failed to notice it in the daylight but now it glowed brilliant in the torchlight.

The painting was of two clashing armies as if frozen in time and captured in all their glory. Spears and swords were plunged through screaming soldiers, lips frozen in silent suffering, blood pouring from their wounds and falling about their feet.

White light encircled the battle and varying shades of black clawed at the shins of the soldiers below. Verin stood at the end, detailing the face of a soldier.

"Two clashing armies," Verin murmured, his back still to them. "Both former brothers-in-arms until a great treason split their ties. Countrymen killing countrymen, brother killing brother. All of this bloodshed is the result of betrayal, treason of the highest degree. It will be a new reign among the people, a new reign of Tarsha..."

The torchlight cast dark seams across his face as he turned and smirked at them. He swirled his brush in a cluster of white paint and began dabbing it onto the wall, lining it up with the white already on the mural.

With a keen artist's hand, he extended the white farther across the wall, inching his way toward completion.

"I have been working on this painting for several months. I have seen the things that are to come, and it is a grim and hopeless future. War will plague Tarsha eternal, purging all the world until but death remains. One will rise among many, one who holds the hearts of men and knows this world beyond any. He will destroy Abaddon and bring about the Iscara Turganoth. The future of humanity grows ever the bleaker…and I will paint its story on these walls before it is too late."

Cain raised a brow, intrigued by this. "What are you talking about?"

The King could not respond however, his portend ending abruptly as Adriel stepped forward and screamed at her uncle. "Our country is about to throw itself into the most important battle it has yet to fight! We must win this fight if we are to survive! If we lose, then our country will fall to Abaddon's genocide and Kaanos will only follow! Yet here you are, painting in cowardice behind the backs of greater men! You're a disgrace!"

Verin's hand fell from the mural and he turned to glare at his niece, hand raised to strike her.

Suddenly the blaring of a distant horn split the air, redirecting his attention. They fell silent and listened for the noise. The horn blared again, a deep and rasping note that resounded in the walls of the crater.

"They're here," Verin whispered. He bolted from the Great Hall, threw the doors open, and sprinted across the platform.

Cain and Adriel looked at each other a moment and drew their weapons. They ran after him and came to the front of the fortress. Verin pranced up the steps beside the gate and Cain and Adriel followed suit.

The fortress was utterly silent. Every soldier's eyes were locked on the outer rim of the crater. The distant horn blew again, this time much closer. Then from over the crater's edge, poured forth the Arzecs.

A black and crimson tide crawled over the crater's rim like a river of blood and converged at the foot of the cliff face. A never-ending flood of soldiers continued to cascade into the crater until a solid mass of twenty thousand Arzecs marched upon Abraxas, soon filling the entire basin.

"Men of Charun!" Verin cried out over the roar of the approaching army.

"Abaddon has oppressed us for far too long! He has held us in the cruel chains of war for four hundred years, darkening our lands with his shadow! We must fight back and end this cycle of death and destruction! The fortunes of us all rest upon your shoulders, for on this night, you are the makers of fate!"

His screams faded in the silent fortress, trampled beneath the roar of the enemy's approach. He looked to each of his soldiers, standing solemn before the death awaiting.

"Draw your weapons men!" Verin ordered.

The soldiers drew their weapons, but remained silent and unmoved by their king's inspiring words. Despair and loss filled every man's heart, each unwilling to face their certain demise.

"For freedom!" Verin shouted as he thrust his sword in the air. His soldiers remained quiet and many let out a halfhearted scream.

Verin looked over the fortress of despairing men, the roar of the enemy getting louder with every passing moment.

"For death!" Every soldier raised their weapons to the sky at this and bellowed in the face of their ruin.

The mass of Arzecs raised their weapons in response. Their cries boomed in the crater, rattling in the chests of their enemies. With a final note of their war horns, the Arzecs broke formation and charged frenetic towards the stronghold.

The archers along the causeways drew their arrows at a signal from their king and aimed their broad heads into the oncoming tide.

"To the glorious death!" Verin screamed as a wave of arrows shot past. The volley rained down into the Arzecs, instantly felling hundreds. The Arzecs continued undeterred, trampling over their fallen comrades. A second volley shot down, soon followed by a third. Hundreds of Arzecs fell with every barrage until they raised their own bows and fired back in retaliation.

A massive cloud of arrows rose in the air and arced gracefully over the fortress. The defending soldiers raised their round shields above their heads as the arrows crashed down upon them.

The ringing of thousands of arrows filled their ears as the ineffectual projectiles deflected off their shields. Men fell from the causeways above as several met their mark, their bodies falling into the groups of soldiers below with dying screams.

The Arzecs reached the gorge that stretched across the front of the fortress and the narrow bridge forced them to a stop.

Arrows poured down from the walls, shooting into the front line of Arzecs. Bodies dropped like stones, toppling into the depths of the gorge below and engulfed instantly in blackness.

Their front ranks split to reveal several long ladders. Hundreds of Arzecs carried them toward the gorge and tossed them over the gap. They began to climb onto their makeshift bridges and inched their way across the gorge.

The archers on the walls loosed a constant stream of arrows into the crossing soldiers, bodies tumbling into the depthless maw of the gorge. Their cries echoed in the chasm, at last stifled against the rocks below.

Despite a fierce opposition, their front lines managed to cross the chasm. They fired their horned bows into the fortress, dropping archers from the walls and smashing their bodies against the shale rock. More and more Arzecs managed to make the perilous journey across the gorge, their endless ranks gradually gaining ground.

On the other side of the chasm, several Arzecs brought forth mighty ballistae. The Arzecs rolled them to the edge of the gorge and loaded long metal spears into them. Then with tremendous force, the projectiles rocketed into the fortress.

The iron javelins exploded through the ranks of archers along the walls, ripping bodies in half and sending showers of blood into the men below. Several spears skewered scores of men at a time and embedded their bodies into the walls behind the causeway with a spray of blood and entrails.

A tide of Arzecs now streamed across the gorge, almost completely unhindered by the few surviving archers. Thousands of Arzecs rushed towards the stronghold and crashed into its walls.

The Arzecs began pounding their weapons against the gate, eager for the blood orgy that awaited them. Their eyes gleamed gold in the night, baring their vicious fangs at the terrified men above.

From the midst of the army, a horde of Arzecs carried forth a massive battering ram.

Hundreds of the defending soldiers ascended the steps to the causeways and gathered above the gates. The defenders threw stones and spears into the Arzecs' ranks, anything to slow the crawling advance of the battering ram. Their feeble attempts did little to hinder the ram, and soon it bore down on the iron gates.

The steel-capped ram shook the gates with a violent thud. The defending soldiers threw down a hopeless barrage of spears over the ram as its wielders drew back for another strike. As the Arzecs who wielded it were struck down however, others rose instantly to take their place.

The snake-headed ram thrust forward again into the gates, this time a weaker blow as the defenders threw themselves against the doors to dampen the impact of the mighty beast.

They fought desperately to fend off the ruthless attack. Bodies soon piled around the feet of the ram. A never-ending cycle of bodies falling and others to take their place repeated itself as the ram shot forward a third time and slammed into the gate with thunderous force. The doors shuttered fiercely and sent debris cascading. The ram collided into the doors repeatedly, shaking them to their foundations.

Great javelins continued to sow havoc among the despairing defenders, impaling scores of men and skewering them against the fortress walls. Men blasted through the air, torn violently in half, limbs and entrails painting the skies as their dying screams filled the chaos of the night.

Beneath the destruction, the ram drew back a final time and collided with the gates under a hailstorm of stones and spears.

The doors rocketed open with tremendous force, throwing a shower of stones into the defenders. Scores of men were blown apart as the debris rent their ranks asunder.

With a deafening roar, the Arzecs thundered through the broken gateway.

The two armies collided with a mighty clash. A fount of scarlet stained the air, painting the fortress red with every stroke of steel. Bodies tumbled; shield and sword rang shrill. Shouts of death pierced the air, ringing in men's ears as they fought for their very lives. Blood soon pooled at the feet of the combatants, limbs, entrails, and bodies littering the fortress floor.

Cain and Adriel threw their bows aside and drew their swords. Without a word, they jumped off the causeway, swords poised as they plunged into the masses below.

They landed in an ocean of Arzecs, bodies dropping about them with every blind swing in the cramped quarters of battle.

The hordes of Arzecs swarmed the entrance to the stronghold, their sheer numbers pressing back the defenders who fought fiercely to stave them off. Wave after wave of Arzecs poured into the fortress, cutting down the defenders left and right and hacking through their ranks by the hundreds.

The defenders soon staggered back as swarms of Arzecs continued their unrelenting push through the keep, crushing all that stood in their way.

"Fall back!" Verin cried out over the chaos. The call for retreat filled their unwilling ears, and reluctantly the defenders surrendered the first floor and turned their backs on the enemy.

The soldiers sprinted across the first floor towards the stairways, the enemy swift on their heels.

The Arzecs soon reached the last lines of retreating soldiers and leapt onto their backs, sinking their fangs into their faces and breaking their necks with vicious snaps. Any retreating soldier that fell from their lines were pulled instantly to the ground and stabbed repeatedly, bodies mangled and mutilated beneath a crushing squall of enemies. The Arzecs ripped apart the still living men, throwing limbs in the air as they disemboweled their helpless victims. Entrails shot from the masses, blood gushing as the Arzecs reveled in their bloodlust.

Adriel tripped over a body in the midst of the retreat. She cradled her head, struggling to avoid being trampled as men rushed over her. She turned and looked down the stairs where hundreds of Arzecs raced towards her with fangs bared.

Adriel cried out in terror and rushed up the stairs towards a man calling her name, arm outstretched to pull her to safety.

As she reached for him, a ballistae's javelin shot through his chest, ripping his body in half and sending his torso flying over the stairs. She let out a panicked scream and stumbled through his blood, the Arzecs close behind.

Cain rushed down the steps towards her, screaming her name. He rushed past her and swung his sword into the front lines of Arzecs. Fending off the encircling enemy, he grabbed Adriel by the arm and retreated up the stairs with her, the Arzecs close behind.

The surviving soldiers ushered them up to the second level. The defending army then converged around the stairway, shields and weapons drawn to face the oncoming tide.

The Arzecs rushed up the steps and threw themselves mercilessly into the spear and sword of their enemy.

The two armies clashed once again, blood flying and weapons blazing in the hellish din of battle. Arzecs continued to surge through the shattered gates, filling the entire first floor.

The cramped stairway began hemming in the Arzecs and the defenders saw their chance. They thrust their weapons deep into the enemy lines, impaling their fetid flesh against avid spears. Bodies tumbled down the steps, engulfed in the sea of onrushing Arzecs. Screams of the dying filled the blood-soaked air as the two armies fought on in a bitter maelstrom.

The Arzecs tackled into each other, pushing themselves recklessly against the shield wall of the enemy. The defenders bashed their shields into the ensuing tides, thrusting sword and spear deep into the Arzec's ranks. Bodies piled high around the defenders as Arzecs continued throwing themselves recklessly up the stairs.

Nevertheless, the Arzecs began slowly pushing back the defenders through sheer weight of numbers. Now it was their turn to wither.

Their ranks receded under the crushing weight of the Arzecs, and the bodies of men now dropped under the slow advance of their enemy. Suddenly they heaved forward, a wall of flesh and steel finally ascending the crest of the stairs.

Thousands of Arzecs met the defenders with full force, hacking deep into their formations. The defending lines thinned by the second.

Cain and Adriel fought desperately at the front lines, struggling to hold their ground as long as possible. The other Warriors ran towards the battle leading hundreds of panicked soldiers.

"The north stairs have fallen!" Aaron shouted over the chaos, "We're surrounded!" From behind them, hundreds of Arzecs charged.

"Retreat!" Their king shouted, but his command came far too late. The defenders spun around as the Arzecs slammed into them like an ocean swell. Hundreds of Arzecs collided into their left flank and tore through their lines, pinning them against the fortress walls. They were now surrounded.

"We're being overrun!" Verin shouted, "Fall back! Fall back!"

The defenders battled madly to escape the ever-tightening noose of the enemy. They slowly pushed through the encircling enemy, allowing a decant of soldiers to escape towards the third floor, running for their lives.

The noose of the enemy was shortly broken and hundreds of men escaped their fates, but many were not as fortunate. Bodies tumbled to the earth as the defending ranks were ripped apart by a relentless foe.

The Warriors fell back and followed their frightened soldiers across the second floor.

Hundreds upon hundreds of Arzecs now climbed onto the second level, filling half the fortress as they closed in on the retreating soldiers. Arzecs swarmed around the Warriors as they ran, forcing them to fight once again.

Cain ran slightly behind the others, and soon the Arzecs surrounded him. He twirled his sword and hacked down any who dare guard his way. He spun frantically, sword flashing in a blaze of steel and sparks, slashing his way through countless enemies.

Several Arzecs lunged at him from behind as he turned to run and dragged him to the ground. His sword flew from his hands and he fell to the earth, drawn into their ranks. The Arzecs stood over him and pinned him to the ground as he fought to escape their grasp.

Their amber eyes stared greedily down at him and their lips parted, dripping blood on their terrified prey. They bent over him and bellowed into his face, their rancid breath stealing the air from his lungs.

A sword ripped through the face of an Arzec, blood and brain spraying the air as the steel ripped through the side of its skull. The body collapsed beside Cain and the Arzecs turned to face Adriel.

Cain pulled his hands free from his opponents' grip and reached up towards the closest Arzec.

He pulled its face forward and thrust his knee into its chin, snapping its neck with a loud crack. He threw the body aside and managed to crawl away from the Arzecs as Adriel fought them off.

Cain reached his sword and spun around on his knee as the Arzecs charged at him. He swung his sword and sliced the legs off several Arzecs, tossing their bodies into the air with a gush of blood.

He bolted from the ground and twirled his sword in mid air. He plunged his sword through the chest of an Arzec and landed as it collapsed in a spurt of blood. A second Arzec lunged at him with a spear and he jumped aside before kicking the spear and pinning it to the ground.

He slammed his boot down and broke the pike in half. He then grabbed the bladed end and swung it, slitting the throat of its owner. The Arzec dropped, and as it fell, another charged at Cain.

Cain bounced the spearhead in his hand and tossed it at the Arzec, throwing it off its feet in a spray of blood.

Silas jumped in front of him and stabbed his Sitar into the oncoming Arzecs. The massive weapon met its mark, slicing the head off an Arzec.

Can't let you have all the fun now, can I?" He jested as he lifted his Sitar before Cain's face, the glaring head of an Arzec cradled in its blades. Cain smirked and struck the weapon aside.

Silas jumped back and dodged a sword strike before lunging forward, tossing the head at an oncoming Arzec and knocking it off its feet. "That never gets old!" Silas cackled before impaling his Sitar through several shrieking Arzecs.

Cain wrenched his sword from the body of an Arzec and looked through the crowds of battling soldiers.

"Aaron!" Cain cried out to his friend barely visible through the sea of ebony. "We have to fall back! We'll be overrun if we stay here!" Aaron nodded in confirmation and fought to reach him. Together, they hacked a path through the surrounding Arzecs and reached the others who fought to keep an open route through the enemy.

Cain and Aaron darted past them. "Run!" The others looked back as hundreds of Arzecs rushed straight towards them. The Warriors turned and sprinted after their friends, the Arzec hordes swift on their heels.

They bolted across the second floor, buildings near a blur as they sprinted past. Fear gnawed at their hearts as Arzecs clawed at their backs, mere feet separating them from certain death.

They noticed a large group of defending soldiers at the other end of the road, spears and shields braced for the oncoming swell.

"Run!" Cain screamed. The line of soldiers split as the Warriors reached them, allowing them through towards the third level. The Warriors rushed by them, calling the retreat.

Cain stopped running and turned back to look at the group, his friends following likewise. The group continued to stand in a uniform formation, staring resolute into the eyes of the Arzecs.

"Fall back!" Cain cried out to the soldiers.

One of the soldiers looked back at his leader and replied forcefully, "Go!"

The man turned just as the Arzecs reached them. They were instantly swallowed in the sea of blackness. The Warriors looked on helplessly as the soldiers fought for their lives, slowly crushed under the weight of their enemy. The men continued to hack at the front lines of the Arzecs, fighting on to the last man.

"Go!" The same soldier ordered again as the Warriors stared on in horror at the massacre. They finally ripped their gaze from the fight and continued running towards the third level.

"Come on!" Adriel screamed as she pulled on Cain's arm. "We've got to get out of here!" He slowly turned as the Arzecs cut down the remaining men and crushed them underfoot.

The Arzecs climbed over the bodies of their freshly slain, swift on the heels of their prey. The platform of the third level came into view as they sprinted past the last of the barracks.

They dashed down the stairway, the defending soldiers beckoning them forward. At last, they reached the bottom of the basin. The remaining soldiers circled the front of the Great Hall, weapons held forward to meet the onrushing Arzecs.

The enemy appeared over the crest of the stairs. A vast wave poured down the steps as hundreds of Arzecs encircled the despairing men. A great roar filled the basin as the hordes descended upon them, sounding ruin in every lamenting ear. The Arzecs exploded down the stairs and crashed into the defenders. Spears flashed and swords flew as the two armies battled once again.

The defenders refused to lose the last floor, for this would mean the end, and they were determined to fight to the last breath.

The Arzecs slowly pushed up the steps, throwing themselves recklessly into the spears of their foes.

Corpses toppled around the feet of the living as they continued to toss themselves frenziedly at the defenders.

Blood flowed in the deep of the basin like a churning eddy, a torrent that rushed over the bodies of hundreds of

Arzecs. A bloodbath ensued as hundreds of Arzecs were slaughtered in their relentless push for the final floor and the destruction of their enemy.

However, against the steel wall of Charun's finest, the Arzecs crumbled. A horn suddenly blew, sounding defeat in the ears of the Arzecs. Their shouts of battle instantly turned to panic and they fell at last from the fighting and ran.

"Let us end them!" Verin shouted before leading his men up the steps. This time, they would be the ones to do the chasing. They chased after the Arzecs, close behind their fleeing prey.

The defenders' spears stretched long and ripped through the backs of their victims. They pursued the fearful beasts through the fortress, bounding over countless corpses and slipping through rivers of blood.

The few remaining Arzecs retreated through the gates and came out into the open and darted across the bridge for their lives. The defenders hurled their spears at the retreating Arzecs, who had escaped their fates for a few precious moments.

The spears descended over the Arzecs and shot clean through their spines. They tumbled into the gorge and were instantly swallowed in darkness, their cries sounding victory for the men of Charun.

The Second Calling

Clouds of vultures circled Abraxas, blotting out the afternoon sun. The black clouds descended and filled their gullets with the flesh of the bloated dead.

Soldiers roamed the carnage, tears shed as they knelt beside the bodies of friends and brothers. They screamed in anguish and cursed the heavens at their sorrow.

The Warriors walked among the dead, the heavy weight of grief on their hearts. They walked like ghosts over the thousands of bodies, stumbling through the smoke of funeral pyres. The stench of burning flesh filled their nostrils, fetid death clawing at their lungs.

Soldiers cast the bodies of the Arzecs into the gorge to rot in the depths of the chasm. They took the weapons from their dead brethren in an almost ceremonial fashion and returned them to the armory of the stronghold in solemn procession.

War is all the country of Charun had ever known, all any of them had ever known. The history of Tarsha was written in blood and Charun was no different. Their history was written across the graves of their fallen, of those who had died to defend it. The men at Abraxas were no different from their ancestors, willing to die for the next bloody page. Many had died the prior night, and many more would follow in the war that held no end.

The day slowly waned to evening. The sky above was stained a deep red as if all the blood of the dead were smeared across the heavens. The Warriors stopped walking and stood frozen, gazing over the destruction.

**** ****

"To a magnificent victory," Verin muttered as he raised a mug of ale above his head.

The survivors of the battle raised their mugs after their king and replied in unison, "Victory!"

Verin lowered his mug and put it to his lips a moment before finishing, "And to our dead…who found a lasting victory."

**** ****

The strong smell of ale hung heavy in the Great Hall. Men conversed merrily among themselves, their laughter reverberating against the walls. Frothy ale poured from the taps of barrels. Men danced euphorically around the tables, their boots churning through puddles of alcohol. Coins chattered, laughter rang, and talk echoed in the cramped quarters of the hall.

The Warriors sat in the midst of this mirth. Joshua cried out gleefully and slammed a group of cards onto the table, throwing his burly hands around yet another pile of coins as his friends and several others looked on helplessly.

"You can't beat this one!" Silas shouted as he threw down his cards. Joshua glanced down at them and grinned before revealing his hand. Silas's smirk fell from his face as he stared down in horror at yet another victorious hand. Joshua grinned and pulled another group of coins toward his ever-growing pile.

"Damn it! You said I had the perfect hand!" Silas cursed at the soldier beside him. The soldier laughed and shrugged in reply. Silas cursed again and stabbed his knife into the tabletop.

"Don't do that!" Matthew cried out from across the table.

"Do what?" Silas retorted.

Matthew lunged at Silas from across the table. "That's ancient mahogany! You're damaging its priceless surface!"

Silas pulled his knife from the table and waved it at the soldier. "I'll damage your priceless surface if you're not out of my face by the time I'm done yelling!" The soldier jumped from his seat and dove into the crowd. The Warriors laughed as Silas sat smoldering in anger, attempting to quench it with a flood of ale.

The night sped by as the ale poured, coins flew and laughter filled the air. The Warriors downed several more mugs of ale, recalling their tales in the Army from ages seeming long past.

"It was my third year in the Army," Joshua said as he paced before a large group of curious soldiers. "We were stationed in Andrus for going on two years when an army of Arzecs attacked us. They soon breached the gates and stormed the city. Thousands of unarmed innocent and soldier alike died that night.

'I lost my sword in the fight, and to my dread came an Arzec, a head taller than even I! In the struggle to come, I found the brace of a wagon, and in one swing," he took his axe from its sling and slammed it into the bench beside a soldier, "Took the head from his shoulders!"

The soldiers remained awestruck, wide-eyed as Silas lifted his leg and rested his boot on the axe handle. "It's true. I saw it with my own eyes!"

Joshua smirked and looked the group over, continuing with a sudden, graven air. "We lost the city...but if it wasn't for Cain Taran we would not be here today. He is the true hero of Andrus; no better soldier has graced our homeland."

Cain approached the group, balancing a tray laden with mugs. "Drink up!" He cried before slamming the tray on the table beside them. The group remained silent, watching Cain with newfound respect as he began his way through a malted ale.

Verin approached them, a sober look in his eyes. "I need to speak with you four," he said as he glanced at each of the Warriors in turn, ignoring Adriel. "It's urgent." The four of Andaurel rose and stood before the King.

"Not me?" Adriel asked her uncle as he led the Warriors away.

"No," Verin answered over his shoulder, "not you." He split the crowd of soldiers and led the Warriors towards the door.

Cain stopped for a moment and looked back at Adriel who sat down and slouched over the now empty table, sighing heavily.

She glanced up for a moment and locked eyes with him. Cain quickly looked away and ran a hand through his hair before following after the others.

Verin led the four men out of the Great Hall. The sky was black with night. Thousands of stars now dotted the heavens. A chill autumn wind tickled across their skin as they walked, sating the alcohol that raged inside them.

The King led them up the basin steps and across the second floor. He stopped as he reached the stairs to the lower level. He approached the wall above the first floor and rested his arms wearily against the cold stone. The Warriors waited for him to begin.

"I received a letter from Ethebriel only moments ago. His messenger rode for several days to deliver this to me as swiftly as possible." He held out a badly stained scrap of parchment. "He asked for you and only you to do what is written in this letter."

"What does it say?" Cain asked.

Verin paused and looked at each of them. "It is as we have feared. Abaddon's sudden and fierce attack on the South was only a diversion. The attacks on Kaanos, the invasion of Charun, the assault on Abraxas, all of it was only a ruse to distract us from his true intentions. His eyes were on the North this whole time. Since the war started, his focus has been almost solely on them. We should have seen this for what it was, but alas, we did not.

'While we turned our focus on ourselves, Abaddon's elite forces, the Andreds, have begun a fierce campaign throughout Inveira, Erias, and Atuan. The North has been weakened by the loss of our support and troops, and the Andreds now roam free through the countryside, slaughtering and butchering as they march on to some apparent objective.

'Ethebriel has also informed me that the king of Erias believes that the capital of his country, Morven, is the target of the enemy.

'Morven is the largest city ever built and its domination over trade and transport make it a primary attractant. It is heavily defended and beyond impenetrable. It will take hundreds of thousands of troops to even leave a scratch on Morven, but this I fear is exactly what the enemy is planning.

'The enemy has never before dared undertake such a siege, but Abaddon has become emboldened as of late. Something has spurred him into drastic action and forced him to play a risky hand. We do not know what that something is, but it may have helped us. We are confident that Abaddon intends to destroy Morven.

'Tarsha cannot afford to lose this valuable city; it is the lifeline of the resistance and the very lifeblood of Tarsha herself. If we ever lost Morven…then Tarsha would surely fall to the will of Andred.

'The northern countries are now under heavy assault. Their scattered villages are being burned to ash while every man, woman, and child is put to the sword. Their military is spread far too thin and is forced to fight their own isolated battles.

'With Charun and Kaanos now free of the Arzec threat, Ethebriel and I have decided that we must concentrate on Erias, to soften the Andreds' ruthless advance and protect the heart of Tarsha from the blades that seek to pierce it. We have called the pieces together and have made our move. If we can crush the armies of Andred in Erias and at Morven, then Abaddon will receive a crippling, if not fatal blow. This leads us to several complications however.

'With the Arzec threat gone from our lands, we are now free to act. We have to feed and supply thousands of troops while we move them to Morven by route of sea. This will be an extremely slow process as well as difficult.

'Secondly, the North has been broken since the fall of the Old Alliance and uniting them will be an almost impossible task. Nevertheless, we require unity if we are to win against Abaddon. That is where you come in.

'Ethebriel is highly confident in your abilities, and I vouch for his confidence after seeing you lead my men in battle. Ethebriel and I ask far too much of you, but we desperately require your help. If we do not have someone to unite the countries of Tarsha and salve their needs in battle, then we will lose the North...and the war. We need you to travel to Morven and unite the country and its people-" Verin opened his mouth to continue but Cain interrupted him with a pointed retort.

"For fifteen years I have fought this endless war. My reasons for fighting may have changed, but what you ask is beyond the sacrifices any man should make. You are asking us to travel across the entire world, fight Erias's battles for her and risk our very lives in a foreign land when after all we do it won't even matter in the end."

Cain stepped back from the group. "I have seen so much senseless loss; I have seen so much suffering. I have fought for so long...and I have seen nothing come of it but pain.

Tarsha's war will burn forever, and we shall be consumed by its flames. I have done enough for kings, they ask too much of mere men. Give me my revenge. Give me my justice. No more will I be used by bickering kings and broken countries." He turned to walk away but Verin's voice stopped him in his tracks.

"You have no home Cain. You have no family. You have nothing...you are nothing." A frigid wind blew across the fortress, buffeting the group of men in their perturbed silence. Verin paused a moment before continuing.

"The only thing you have left is your life and you have no choice now but to give that up for a greater purpose. We are all willing to sacrifice whatever it takes to win this war, and if you say you want to keep your life and everything you have left, then tell that to the five thousand men we burned to ash." He fell silent and let Cain absorb his sharp words.

"You're afraid, Cain," Verin continued. "And you should be. War is no game; it will not relent. War will only take and take until there is nothing left, and once it reaches that point, it will take the only thing left to you, your life. Open your eyes and see what war will do to us." Verin pointed out over the fortress where thousands of bodies lay smoldering. Cain hung his head.

"You are a soldier of Kaanos, a captain of men. You have fought for half of your life and have seen nothing come from your suffering. We are all the same. Men have come and gone centuries before us who have fought this war and hoped to see its end. Only suffering did they find, just as you have. You are not alone, for we all have suffered. Nevertheless, we must fight, for the survival of us all depends on our will to do so.

The outcome of this war will be decided by the choices made here tonight. You know what is right, Cain." Silence enveloped them. A shrill wind blew. Cain's friends looked at him with quiet earnest.

"Listen to him," Aaron urged.

Cain turned and faced the King. "We will go to Morven. But know this…I do so for justice and justice only. I will not rest until my sorrows are repaid with blood…only then may my losses be atoned." The wind died as quickly as it had come.

Verin shook his head. "A fool never learns." He sighed before drawing out a large map from the depths of his tunic.

The Warriors gathered around him as he unfurled the velum scroll. Cain sighed and gazed around the fortress for a moment before stepping into the group.

Verin laid the map across the top of the wall they stood beside and pinned its edges to the stone. They noticed the map was the same that Ethebriel had displayed on the wall of his study.

It was extremely ancient, weathered from countless years of use. Faded lines of ink separated the countries, each one labeled in elegant writing. The country of Erias filled the middle of Tarsha and stretched across half the parchment. The country was covered with sketched mountains and rivers of ink that flowed through endless forests.

"Morven is here," Verin said as he pointed to a large blot in the middle of Erias. The city sat on the end of a mountain range that spanned from the western border of Andred to the heart of Erias. A large river snaked through the mountain range and through Morven, continuing until it reached the western Sea of Caius.

Verin moved his hand and pointed to a speck labeled Abraxas on the western edge of Charun. "I would propose your route by sea but we cannot spare any transports, and your small group by land will go more easily unnoticed to the enemy. Therefore, your only option is by land.

It is extremely difficult to enter Erias from Charun. If you follow my instructions however, you should be fine." He slowly dragged his finger across the country until he reached its northern border.

A large band of trees stretched across the majority of Charun's northern border. "Cross Charun on a northeast bearing until you reach our northern border...the forest of Morgaul," Verin muttered as he rested a finger on the thick line of trees.

"It is a dark and unmapped region. The few who dare enter its forests say that many strange things happen among its shadows. Be prepared for the worst. It will be extremely difficult to navigate its terrain, but if you can conquer it and come out its other end, then you should be...somewhat safe for the remainder of your journey."

Verin slid his finger across the forest and stopped as he reached a small area directly above the left half of the forest. "These are the Gullies of Amon Karash. It is a vast and lifeless land, scarred with endless chasms. It is also the breeding ground of Arzecs, who thrive in this lifeless region. Under any circumstances are you to enter the Amon Karash; you will not come out alive.

Also bordering the Morgaul is a region known as Heiven Sul. It is a parched and arid band of active volcanoes. Rivers of fire weave across this wasteland. Very few creatures can live in this unforgiving climate, and those who do are beyond rational comprehension. A massive breed of beast lives in Heiven Sul, known as the Gehet to most. They are extremely dangerous creatures. It is best to stay away from the Heiven Sul as well.

Thus, the only remaining way to cross both regions into Erias is a very thin strand of life-sustaining land that splits the two regions, the Knife Ridge. You must be very careful to navigate through the Morgaul if you are to reach it. If you do not enter out into the Knife Ridge then you will find yourself in either of these regions, and in immediate peril. However, if you manage to enter into the Ridge, then it is almost a perfect shot to Morven.

You must hold your friends close and your blades closer. The armies of Andred run rampant and nigh ndered across Erias, they will not relent in the ruination of man.

It will be an extremely long and difficult task, but that is why Ethebriel chose you four, because only you have what it takes to endure. Ethebriel could not have chosen better men. I know you will succeed in aiding the North against the shadow of Andred." Verin carefully rolled up the map and drew a small clamp around it. "The fate of us all now rests on your shoulders, Warriors."

Joshua sighed heavily as Verin handed the map to Cain. "No pressure then…"

**** ****

The Warriors entered the Great Hall as the first rays of dawn lit the skies. Empty mugs and scattered cards littered the table. Broken glass laid bathing in pools of ale and vomit. Men covered the tables and floor, splayed out in various painful positions. Only one person remained sobered and awake, sitting on the tabletop among the refuse of food and discarded mugs.

Adriel looked up as they entered the hall, the creaking of the iron doors echoing loudly in the silence.

"I'm going to find a bed," said Aaron after scanning the scene before them. He turned and disappeared across the court, his silhouette a mere outline against the sea of azure dawn.

Joshua walked forward and threw his bulky frame to the ground and rested his back against the legs of the table. "We're going to the barracks," Silas informed him, "you could just sleep there?"

"Try something different for a change, mate," he replied as he grabbed a half-filled mug from the hand of a sleeping soldier that lay sprawled out on the tabletop above. "Besides," he took a swig, "everyone else is doing it." He

121

rested his head on the table legs with a belch and closed his eyes.

Silas shrugged and lay down on the floor beside his brother. Joshua handed him the mug and Silas drew it to his lips.

Cain shook his head at them before approaching Adriel who sat on a table, head held in her hands.

"May I sit?" He asked. She looked up at him and nodded lightly. He threw himself up beside her.

"What did Verin want?" she asked as she brushed the hair from her eyes.

"He received a letter from Ethebriel," Cain replied, "It appears that we've only been fighting a diversion."

"A diversion?" Adriel asked with lifted brows.

"Aye, Abaddon sent the Arzec hosts into Kaanos and Charun to distract us and cut us off while his armies launched a full-scale invasion behind our backs. His troops march across the North, killing the innocent. The king of Erias fears they march for Morven."

Adriel's eyes lit up at this. "Morven! Abaddon has never been bold enough to attack such a mighty city. If we lose it…then everything is lost."

Cain nodded and replied, "Yes, I know. That's why Verin wants us to go to Morven and assist in the war effort."

Adriel fell silent. "You mean…you're leaving?" She asked quietly, her eyes fixated on the wall before her.

Cain nodded. "The Alliance needs us there…and we have gone too far to turn back now." Adriel made no remark. "We're leaving tomorrow."

"What about me?" She asked.

"I'm not sure. None of them…want you with us."

"What about you?" She raised a brow at him. "What do you want?"

Cain ran a hand through his hair at this. "You've saved our lives once, and mine again in the battle. We could use you."

"And that's your only reason?"

This time it was Cain's turn to raise a brow. "What reasons would you even have in going with us?"

Adriel's gaze fell and she shook her head. "I have my reasons, but if none of you want me to come then forget it." She stood up and left the Great Hall. Cain watched her leave, confused at her response.

"Well played, my friend," Joshua said from somewhere under the table.

**** ****

The Warriors tore through the mound of equipment piled high in the armory and pulled their packs from its dark recesses.

They returned to the barracks and packed their rucksacks quickly and in pensive silence, each of them burdened with the weight of their thoughts. They had no idea when they would ever see their country again, or for that matter their homes, or what was left of them.

Each of them longed to have a family once again, to go back to the untroubled days of their youth. They had nothing now in life but war, loss, and certain death to come. They longed for peace; but all that remained to them was a false sense of justice, the vengeance they sought to obtain.

They threw their heads back, weary with little sleep. They were in the only room of their barrack, circled around a table that was heavy laden with their swollen packs. They lay their heads back against the walls of stone. Rays of the midday sun peered in through the arrow thin windows.

Cain sharpened his sword as the others rested in silence, the small stone in his hand moving along the blade with methodic precision. He had sharpened its edge so often that it had become habitual, a daily routine to appease his shaking hands since the day they left Andaurel.

Utter silence enveloped the barracks as the slow and systematic rasp of grinding steel echoed in the room.

Cain stayed his hand and raised it before him. His scarred hands shook slightly despite his opposition.

"Has anyone seen Adriel?" He asked, breaking the heavy silence. His friends shook their heads apathetically.

"Oh..." He muttered and leaned back in his chair, shortly forgetting his compulsive habit. "I think she should come with us."

Joshua looked up at him from one of the beds. "Why would we need her? She'd only get in the way."

"I'd have to agree with him on that one, Cain," Silas offered.

"She saved our lives once already and mine again in battle," Cain argued as he sheathed his sword. "We need all the help we can get. Besides, we need a guide."

Aaron shook his head. "Look, you know it, we all know it, she's not going to come with us. Why would she? Besides, you barely even know her. The only thing any of us really know about her is she's thickly stubborn, and that's all I need to know."

Cain nodded distantly and replied, "We need her a lot more than you think we do. She'll come."

Aaron shook his head as his friend began sharpening his sword once more. "Just as stubborn as you," he sighed under the rasp of steel.

**** ****

The following morning brought with it a heavy fog that fell thick over Abraxas. The sun had yet to reach the sky, but the Warriors were already in the stables, weary with little sleep once again.

They jadedly tied their bags to their saddles and mounted their horses. They guided them out of the stables and entered out into a sea of fog. They blindly rode through the mist and worked their way across the fortress until they reached the front gates.

Verin stood beside the open doors and gestured them forward. "Winter has reached us at last," the King muttered, "A heavy fog sets upon the hills."

"Just our luck," Joshua murmured.

Verin reached down and picked up a large bundle of cloth. "You will need these," he tossed each of them a cloak of black wool, extremely warm to the touch. "They will protect you from our bitter winter."

"Thank you for your generosity," Cain replied as he set the cloak on the saddle behind him.

"Go now, Morven needs you," Verin extended his open palm toward the gateway, "Tarsha needs you. Bring unity to our world in this dark hour." The Warriors nodded and followed him out of the fortress. "May grace be with you."

With that, he turned from them and retreated behind the closing gate of Abraxas, slamming the doors shut behind him.

"You ever get the feeling we're being used?" Silas asked his friends as they reined their horses forward.

Cain looked at him and laughed, "Not even the slightest."

They rode across the bridge and came out into the crater. The fog hung thick about them. They rode through the mists and began picking their way across the loose shale rock.

Around their horses' feet, bodies split the chill mists, dead eyes gazing up at them. Blood caked dry on the earth and the reek of it all tore at their lungs.

Ghoulish hands reached for them through the mists. The eyes of thousands of Arzecs pierced the veil, as if each were a torch emblazoned in dismal forgot. The silence hung like a millstone in the winter's morn as if the land itself conveyed its sorrow for so great a loss as this.

"Shit," Aaron muttered as his horse stepped on the body of an Arzec. Bones snapped and punctured out of its rotting flesh, spewing forth a stream of bloody pus. They weaved through the thousands of bodies, blood squelching beneath their horses. Carrion fowls flew about them, fleeting shadows amid the fog. Several vultures flew over their heads and cawed angrily as they sped by, soon disappearing in the mist profound.

The crater wall appeared through the fog and the Warriors forced their mounts to a stop. Their horses reluctantly halted and their riders led them carefully up the steep slope. They eventually reached the top of the crater and glanced around anxiously.

An impenetrable wall of ivory surrounded them, blocking out their vision entirely.

As they urged their horses into the mist, a cry broke out behind them. They turned around to see someone tearing through the fog.

The mist swirled and Adriel sprinted out of its grasp, panting with exertion. She leaned heavily against Cain's horse, struggling to catch her breath.

"You're going to leave without saying goodbye?" She eventually asked Cain.

He looked down at her, puzzled, yet fighting a smile. "You stormed off the other night; I assumed you didn't want to come with us."

"You assumed wrong then," she replied, "you need me whether you realize it or not." Cain smirked at this and glanced at Aaron.

"Someone please kill me," he said as he reined his horse forward.

"I can help you with that, Aaron," Silas called out to him.

"I was joking!" Aaron cried out in panic. Silas and Joshua rode into the fog after him, followed by several screams from Aaron.

"Besides," Adriel said as she grabbed Cain's outstretched hand and pulled herself into the saddle behind him, "What would the Warriors be without me?"

Cain shrugged at her and laughed, "Probably a lot better off."

**** ****

They continued riding throughout the day, leaving the volcanic earth of Abraxas behind them. Hundreds of hills now encircled them, barely indiscernible through the fog.

Streaks of ice rained down and was carried through the hills by a wind that clawed like frozen nails. A thin blanket of ice covered the grass at their feet and their horses' hooves crunched loudly in the frost.

"Winter in Kaanos was never this bad," Joshua muttered as he adjusted his cloak.

Adriel replied, "It's always this bad. Many travelers die in our winters."

"Good to know," Joshua retorted.

They rode on for hours without track of time. The sun was somewhere behind the mists, but where they could never tell.

They continued ever east across the endless hills and fields of hoarfrost.

After hours of silent riding, Adriel broke its spell. "I know what you're thinking," she muttered in Cain's ear.

"And what might that be?" He asked with raised brow.

"The others have followed you for years without question, but now you begin to question yourself. You have no idea where you are at right now, and I am willing to bet you're hoping for a miracle to guide you so you don't look like a fool. Am I right?"

Cain turned to look at her. "You're never wrong."

"I will not lead you astray," she replied, "I have lived in Charun for many years and I know what is required to survive our winters."

"How do you know the land so well? Most people never even leave the village they are born in."

Adriel thought for a moment before replying, "I used to run away from home all the time when I lived with my father. To me it was better to starve in the wilderness than live with the likes of him. No one knows this land better than I, you are in good hands."

Cain smiled. "I'm glad you came with us." Adriel smiled back at him and the two fell quiet. They continued for hours without rest.

Evening came at last, dismal as the early morn. Ice swirled about the travelers, clinging to their wool cloaks and stinging against their skin. They rode on in deathly silence save the crunch of their horses' hooves.

They guided their mounts around the outlines of hills, continuing into the night in a blind stupor. As the veiled skies filled with black and stars rose beyond its depths, the fog began to clear. Through the parting wisps of fog, the Warriors could clearly see the sky for the first time that day.

Thousands of stars flickered in the heavens, cradled in the soft embrace of clouds. The thin brim of a crescent moon hung overhead. Its pale light cast over the hills as far as they could see, gilding the earth in boundless silver.

Adriel gazed up at the night sky, her eyes filled with the glow of the moonlight.

"It's beautiful…" She muttered in awe. "Look," she pointed to a constellation in the skies, their lights brighter than that of any around them. "Seraphel."

"Seraphel?" Cain asked.

"The brightest stars in our skies. Look, can you see her wings and sword?"

Cain squinted and searched the stars. "All I see are dots…"

Adriel sighed and shook her head. "She used to never show her face. They say if Seraphel shows herself, then those who seek her find heaven's fortune when all else has abandoned them."

Cain glanced over his shoulder at her. "Then let us hope those are more than just dots."

**** ****

Cain plunged his foot into the smoldering ashes of their campfire and stamped out the last of its embers. He pulled his boot from the smoke and looked around, wiping his eyes with exhaustion.

They were in the dried remains of a riverbed, towering cliff walls encompassing them. Fog clung to the valley like dew to the trees. Dawn's azure light barely pierced the mist.

Cain could hear the breath leave his lips; see its warm vapors swirling before him. His heart beat loud against his ribs, a sounding drum in absolute silence.

He looked to a nearby tree and saw the others sleeping soundly encased in their cloaks. Joshua snored once again, astonishing Cain that he had ever managed to sleep through it. He walked over to his friends and shook them from their sleep.

They stood up and brushed their cloaks of ice. Cain tossed each of them a biscuit and some dried fruit from his saddlebag. They mounted their horses with little conversation, unwilling to leave behind the comfort of sleep for another day of riding.

They followed the riverbed for several hours. Eventually the valley walls spread forth and released them into a wall of mist. "This way," Adriel said as she pointed to the right.

They guided their horses down a slender path that snaked its way down the side of a wooded knoll. The trail slowly leveled out and they tore their way through a bed of overgrowth. They noticed a large stone protruding from the earth before them.

"What's this?" Cain asked Adriel as they approached it.

Large cracks wove along the face of the stone, distorting the once intricate carvings that covered it. Moss clung to the rock and flowering weeds protruded from its base.

"It is a testament to our forefathers..." Adriel said with a whisper. The others watched it curiously as they rode around it. The group soon dismounted and tethered their horses to the trees at the base of a hill.

They began to climb the slope, and after several minutes, reached its crest and emerged from the fog.

Ahead of them was a mighty ring of earth, seven hills rising like giants beyond the trees. They could barely make out several chunks of stone strewn across the hilltops, almost entirely buried in grass.

"This was once the capital of Charun, Cresen Khan. Now, it is nothing more than a testament to our once glorious past.

'It was built over two thousand years ago. It was one of the first built in Charun and one of the largest since. However, its glory would eventually become its ruin.

'Three hundred years ago, Abaddon led his armies into the South and crushed the resistance there, sending them retreating to their final hope, Cresen Khan. In forty nights, he besieged the city alongside his armies. He eventually breached their defenses and entered the city.

'Blood flowed like a river in its streets. Every man, woman and child was put to the sword. They demolished every building and wiped out all traces of the once great citadel.

'The few who managed to escape Abaddon's wrath retreated to Abraxas, where it eventually became our country's present capital.

'Abaddon made a grave mistake however in overlooking Abraxas to the west as without threat, for it was naught but an outpost at the time. He left the city with his armies and turned his attention back to the North, leaving Charun to wither. After three hundred years, we never forgot Cresen Khan and its demise."

The Warriors picked their way through the ruins. The remains of walls, towers, and buildings lay forever abandoned beneath a bed of wildflowers. An otherworldly silence seemed to fill the hills, setting heavy on the mists.

They passed several moss-covered columns and approached a massive head that seemed to gasp for life above its earthen grave. Its stone flesh was blackened with the tongues of an ancient fire. The face stared stolid into the skies above with cracked and pitted eyes.

Around the head was a hood of stone that hid a crown set atop its brow. The rest of its body was destroyed, nothing remained save its forlorn face.

A strong wind suddenly picked up and tore across the hilltop with force. The head let out a tremendous crackling before toppling over and crashing into the grass with a spray of dirt. The Warriors watched it fall, eyes wide.

"That's not a good omen..." Joshua muttered.

"Wait...do you smell that?" Aaron asked the others.

They raised their noses to the wind. Silas grimaced. "Smells like smoke?"

Adriel's eyes lit up and she bolted from the group.

"Where are you going?" Cain called after her. She disappeared into the mist.

The men looked at each other anxiously before chasing after her. They followed her through the trees and around Cresen Khan, eventually coming out into the open. Adriel stood on the edge of a small precipice, her back to them.

"Are you all right?" Cain asked as they approached. She remained frozen. They followed her wide-eyed stare to a field before them.

At the bottom of the hill they stood upon was a large village, a hundred or so wooden homes spread across the hilly terrain. Through the fog, hundreds of bodies lay sprawled across the village.

Men, women, children, every villager lay dead in a lake of blood. Infants were impaled on bloody lances; their tiny bodies limp in the wind. Blood covered all the earth, near illuminating the dead with a vivid crimson hue. Flocks of vultures covered the deceased, filling their beaks with rotting flesh. Several homes still smoldered in their ashes, billowing forth great plumes of smoke. The Warriors stood in horror at the sight, anger mounting in their hearts.

"Damn the Arzecs..." Silas growled.

Adriel bowed her head. "This isn't the only village...and it won't be the last."

**** ****

A man ran a scarred hand through a pile of ashes, the remnants of a campfire several days since extinguished. He stood up and held out his hand, letting the ashes sift through his fingers before drifting away in the breeze.

He turned and approached his chestnut horse.

The man readjusted a massive bow that hung on his back beside a silver quiver of arrows and climbed into his horse's saddle with skillful grace. He pulled the black wolf furs of his cloak closer to his broad frame, and with a flick of his reins, guided his mount towards a narrow valley chain, the setting sun at his back.

Shadows of the Self

For several days, the Warriors rode through Charun, following the river Setlon towards the Morgaul. Days of bitter chill and blinding fog fought to tear them down, seeking to lay waste to their morale.

Cain looked over his shoulder at Adriel who had fallen asleep, her head lying against his back. The mist had relented since noon and he could see her hands held limply around his waist, her hair falling around his back and shimmering gold in the sunlight. He opened his mouth to say something to her but quickly closed it, instead running a hand through his hair.

The movement shook her from her sleep and she sat up.

"Oh, I'm sorry, Cain," she apologized when she realized she had slept on him.

"It's fine," he replied.

Adriel shook her head and stretched vigorously for a moment. They grew quiet, listening to their horses trudge through the thick undergrowth. Cain turned to the girl after a while and said, "Where the hell is this Morgaul? We've been riding for over a week."

"Well you don't have to worry any longer."

Cain looked at her curiously. "What do you mean?"

"Because we're already here," she said as she pointed ahead of them. Cain turned and followed her gaze.

A line of trees stood dark and defiant before them, towering over the landscape. Fog swirled around their feet, captive mists in their thorny grasp.

Cain reined his horse to a stop and the others followed suit. They halted a few feet before the tree line and stared up into the darkness beyond.

The trees loomed high above them, their thick trunks clustered closely together to form an impenetrable blackness. They stared wide eyed into the forest, their minds lost in the shadows, lost for words.

Cain sighed and exchanged a nervous glance with each of them. "Well…"

"I have a feeling," Aaron replied, "that if we go in there, we can't turn back."

"So this is it then," Cain said to them, "there is no turning back. There will be no going home…"

Silas's gaze fell. "We have no home to go back to…"

Aaron looked his friends over and returned his eyes to the trees before them. "On the other side of that forest, open war awaits us."

Cain turned and stared into the ominous trees. "Then let us embrace it." He reined his horse forward and rode towards the Morgaul; his friends following close behind.

Fog and blackness engulfed them as they crossed through the tree line and stepped into near absolute darkness.

The trees around them had spiny bark of an unnatural, sickly hue. Their roots protruded from the earth, bounding through the dark land like worms delighting in fleshly fodder.

Leaves of glossy ebony covered these unearthly beings, as if they fed off the very darkness pervading. The ground all around them seemed chiseled by an enormous blade, hewn and butchered into a violently twisting landscape. Deep fissures snaked across the forest floor, where it seemed more than just shadows crept from their depths.

The Warriors glanced around the Morgaul, drinking in the surrounding malevolence.

"We'll need some torches." Cain dismounted and began to fumble through his rucksack. He pulled out a hatchet moments later and approached the nearest tree.

He grabbed a low-hanging branch and swung his axe. The hatchet reverberated off the tree limb harmlessly. He swung again and the hatchet deflected off the branch before slipping out of his hand.

"Move aside," Joshua said as he stepped forward, swinging his massive battle-axe at the tree. The axe bound uselessly off the branch. "What the…what's going on?"

Cain picked up his hatchet and saddled his horse. "I don't know, but let's not find out. Everything about this place feels wrong."

They reined their horses forward without a word and cautiously began weaving their way through the maze of trees. Slowly they descended a steep hill, roots clawing underfoot as if seeking to ensnare the travelers in their depths.

Fog swirled in thin beads about them, mere threads of silver in the dim light. They fought to gain any noticeable distance, forced to a slow and grueling pace by the unremitting terrain of the Morgaul.

Branches hung low over the path, whipping at their faces as they rode by. The air was cold and musty, stale from thousands of dark and silent years.

They passed several hills covered in a vast cocoon of roots. They followed the trail through these hills, mist swirling at their horses' feet. All was deathly quiet. Not a sound dared grace their ears. They rode overwrought, shadows closing in around them.

The leaves of every tree began to rustle as if lifted by the fondling of wind. But no noise reached the travelers' ears, no wind met their skin. The leaves seemed to dance with a life of their own, and from the shadows they divulged, a form arose. It appeared as sorrow, guilt, without flesh to see or touch.

THE SPIRIT OF REVENGE

Cain felt its heavy gaze bore into his back and he spun around in his saddle. A blur flashed across the mist and disappeared among the shadows.

He opened his mouth to say something, but no words fled his lips. He drew his sword as the shadow disappeared through the fog a second time.

"There's something out there..." He muttered to the group. He spun around and scanned the encircling trees, fighting for a glimpse of the shadow.

It left as swiftly as it had come, leaving a qualm expression on his face.

"What is it?" Silas asked, his hand slowly reaching for the Sitar strapped on his back.

Cain raised his head and suddenly the shadow appeared directly in front of them. The entire group pulled their weapons out with a ring of steel at this apparent threat. The figure suddenly retreated through the fog.

"What the hell was that?" Silas asked them as he held his weapon warily before him.

"I don't know," Joshua replied, "but whatever it was...there better not be more of them." The others stared at him in trepidation. There very well could be more.

**** ****

The fog swirled dense around Cain as he awoke from his sleep. He shook his head and stood up from his mat. Something had awoken him, but he knew not what. He looked around his surroundings and struggled to see through the dark trees. The distant howl of wolves echoed eerily around him. A light breeze brushed across his face.

Then through the night, a figure approached. Cain jumped for his sword and unsheathed it. A young child stepped out into the moonlight, his vivid green eyes smiling warmly at Cain.

Cain lowered his weapon as the boy approached. He then noticed the pendant around the boy's neck. It was Eileen's, and this was his son. Cain dropped to his knees in disbelief, tears brimming in his eyes. Cain tossed his sword and knelt before his son, embracing him firmly.

"I thought I'd lost you..." The boy said nothing as Cain buried his fingers in his son's hair. "Do you have a name?"

The boy pulled himself away from Cain's embrace. "You never named me..."

Cain's gaze fell. "I'm so sorry...it's my fault you're dead...and your mother. I couldn't save her."

His son reached out and brushed a tear from his father's cheek. "It's not your fault."

"I wish I could believe you..."

"One day you will, Dad," he said as he began combing his father's hair with tiny fingers.

"This...this is just a dream. Isn't it?"

The boy nodded in reply. Cain sighed and stood up, resting a hand on his son's head. "So you really are dead?"

"And mother too..." The boy wiped a tear from his eye.

Where is she?" Cain asked.

His son pointed to a nearby tree. Cain followed the imaginary line of the little finger to a silhouette lying in the grass. Eileen lay in a bloody mess; stomach ripped apart, her entrails spewing forth. Her eyes stared cold and lifeless at her husband, lips silently pleading to end her suffering.

His son suddenly disappeared from his side and an infants arm reached to him from within its mother's womb.

That horrid memory of a night long since past swelled within Cain's mind, releasing the flood of pain and despair that he had so bravely held at bay.

Fires rose behind Eileen and engulfed all the forest as Andaurel rose from the shadows, glowing in the light of its pyre.

Cain's eyes flew open and he leapt from his mat, screaming in agony. The leaves around him danced by an unseen sinew that gave them motion. They whispered with the softest words of wind, casting shadows over Cain as he roared with despair.

His dream had become a nightmare, what once had warmed his heart now blackened his mind. He had fought so hard to bury that memory lest it consume him with despair, but now it swelled within him, clawing its way out.

He howled at the pain of this memory, stabbing his sword repeatedly into the ground. His friends awoke to his madness and threw themselves over him.

Cain screamed and lashed out at them, cutting Silas on the arm with his sword.

"Sorry, mate," Joshua said as he reeled back and punched him in the face.

**** ****

Cain rose from the grass, head searing with pain. His friends gathered around him, a scared and confused look etched on their faces.

"What?" He asked as he gripped his forehead.

"Sorry about that," Joshua said. He leaned forward and pulled Cain's hand away from the bruise above his eye. "You went mad, I had to stop you."

"That's bullshit," Silas muttered as he wrapped a cloth around the gash in his arm. "What the hell's the matter with you anyways?"

Cain groaned and shook his head. "Nothing...just a dream."

"Well get your head together," Silas replied as he stood up. "We don't need you going crazy."

Cain rose to his feet and picked up his rucksack that they had already packed. "Aye, sorry about your arm."

Silas shook his head and saddled his horse. "Just a scratch."

The group reined their mounts back into the forest and down a hill riddled with roots.

They crossed a large patch of black mushrooms, taking little care to avoid trampling them. Soon they came to an extensive network of crevices.

They picked their way slowly and cautiously across the chasms, forcing their horses to jump over the larger ones. They wound their way through the endless expanse of trees, fighting to maintain a straight course ever north.

Cain closed his eyes as they rode, breathing heavily to calm his racing mind. He knew it was just a dream, but even so, it felt too real. He could still feel his son's hand in his; feel his young heart beating louder than his own.

He had managed to lock the events of that night within the recesses of his mind for the pain of it was too much to bear. It was as if the Morgaul released it, unlocking every painful memory and beating them senseless against the walls of his mind.

With every glance at the surrounding trees, he could see only his son's face. However, as he would close his eyes and open them again, the images of his son would be gone. Cain knew he was only plaguing himself, for his son was as dead as his father's happiness.

"Cain?" Adriel's voice called out quietly from behind him. He looked over his shoulder, shaken from his thoughts.

"I'm fine," he replied.

"No you're not," she stated, unimpressed with his halfhearted lie.

He turned and fidgeted with the straps of a saddlebag. "You're right," he muttered to himself, "I'm just going insane."

**** ****

Morning brought little fog on the third day, letting thin strands of sunlight pierce the canopy veil. The Warriors downed the morning's rations and saddled their horses for another day of riding, spurring them onward through the thick sea of trees.

They left behind the small patch of fallen leaves that they had made camp on the night before and followed a narrow path that twisted sporadically through the hills.

Roots hung low from the sides of the path and dangled over their heads as they rode. They continued through the beams of sunlight that pierced the canopy, allowing for precious bursts of vision. The path ahead made a smooth curve to the right and disappeared behind a hill.

The trees around them seemed to whisper, as if bemoaning the presence of still-beating hearts. Their leaves began to fester with unrest, condemning shadows to the mist with hands begot of normalcy.

With the rustle of leaves, an all too familiar ring of steel echoed in their ears. The Warriors whipped their reins and tore down the path, searching desperately for the battle at hand.

They soon came to a dark vale split in half by a stream of murky, stagnant water. Standing atop the brook, a small group of soldiers stood with shields raised and eyes locked on the trees before them. Their translucent forms shimmered in the sunlight, utter quiet as their mouths opened to voice silent screams.

A man at the back of the formation turned to the Warriors. His mouth screamed for them to go, but his cry was silent.

The Warriors looked on awestruck as the men began thrusting their spears blindly into the trees before them, cries of pain and battle on their lips. However, their voices remained silent, deaf cries to the ears of the living.

An invisible force began brutally hacking down every man as they fought desperately for their lives. Spears flashed with undying rage. Yet despite their efforts, their ranks faltered.

Go, the same man cried out to them despairingly. The formation suddenly fell apart and the men were hacked down. Their bodies tumbled to the earth and were instantly trampled by an unseen force.

Go, the man screamed a final plea before turning to face his death. His translucent body fell to the earth with a silent, dying curse.

All these shadows of men fell to the ground, their rotten flesh torn asunder. Their corpses lay immobile in the leaves, bodies piled tall in a pool of blood.

Then with a flash of light, they stood once more. The men reformed their tight ranks and began wildly flailing their spears.

Go, the man at the back cried out to them. The men were slowly cut down again, their formation falling apart as the invisible force crashed over them once more.

The Warriors stared on in disbelief and fear. Eventually they turned and whipped their reins. They tore their gaze from the horrors of their past and galloped through the forest as fast as their horses could carry them.

Wind tore at their faces and the trees of the forest blurred by as they dashed down the path, oblivious to everything but the fear that pushed them onward.

"I'm tired of this shit!" Joshua cried out to the others as branches lashed at their faces.

What seemed a lifetime later, they finally came to a stop. Aaron panted heavily as he pondered over what they had witnessed. "This forest is some kind of record of our past...these trees have a strange gift. I wonder if it's like this for everyone who enters."

"Gift?" Joshua asked. "More like curse. Who in their right mind would enter a hellhole like this?"

"We would," answered Silas.

**** ****

The following day, the Warriors crossed a brook, their horses' hooves splashing across its murky waters.

Fewer beams of sunlight pierced the treetops overhead, the canopies even more dense than the days before. They followed a trail that took them down a steep hillside and worked their way across the treacherous terrain.

They reached the bottom and came to a crossway. Four paths extended off in every direction from a central point before them. They leaned back disheartened in their saddles, confused as to which way to follow.

The group glanced at Cain who sat scratching his chin in contemplation. After a moment, he shrugged with defeat and left the others sighing in bemusement.

A faint noise then came from the canopy above and they looked up into the leaves. A black raven swooped out of the trees and circled over them twice. It then alighted on the branch of a dead tree beside the second path on their left and cawed incessantly at Cain.

Cain glanced over his shoulder at Adriel who nodded slowly.

His friends looked at Cain with disbelief as he reined his horse forward and rode towards the path.

"I can't believe I'm about to follow a bird," he murmured. His friends shrugged at each other and followed him.

The raven dove from the branch and flew over the narrow path, sailing through the treetops with impressive ease. They eventually caught up with it as it landed on a tree that hung over the end of the path. The trail stopped at a dead end before them.

The bird landed on a tree near a washout that would have gone unnoticed to the Warriors. The raven began crying profusely and jumped with glee. It bound from the tree and spun gracefully in the air, gliding down the washout trail before disappearing into the shadows.

The Warriors hesitated a moment before reining their horses down this second path. The raven sailed down the length of the trail for several minutes. The travelers cantered after it as it turned and followed a third path.

They cautiously followed it, but soon the bird slipped from view and disappeared into the shadows.

The travelers looked at each other with surprise that they had followed a bird for directions.

As day fell and night darkened the shielded skies above, they dismounted their horses. They removed their saddles and equipment and spread out their mats in a tight circle.

"Now that's more like it," Silas said as he lay down under a tree and stabbed his knife into the sallow dirt.

"No dead people today. That has to be a record," Joshua sighed as he sat down beside his brother.

"Don't entice them. They may change their minds," Aaron warned. He threw his saddle down in the leaves before glancing into the encircling trees.

He carted his bags over to them and unclasped the metal loops that held them together, removing several handfuls of dried meats and bread from its depths. "Let's just forget about it," he said as he tossed each of them a portion.

"Forget about it?" Cain asked as he leaned forward from the relative comfort of a root. "How can we forget about it? The visions I see, the memories they bring, they're eating me alive...I have to get out of this forest."

Aaron sat down on his mat across from him. "Do you think it's this place? Or is it just you?"

**** ****

Cain's eyes ripped open with a gasp of air. He sat up in his mat, shaking from the shadows that haunted his sleep. Images of his past swarmed his crowded head, thoughts racing as his heart beat profusely.

He wiped the sweat from his brow and stood up from his mat, pulling his cloak closer to his body as a chill wind blew across his skin.

He bent down and picked up his water skin, taking several gulps of the cool water.

He looked around the campfire at his friends who lay deep in sleep. He noticed a figure standing off in the outskirts of their encampment.

Cain stepped over Silas and walked towards the figure. As he crossed the small glade, his boots crunched loudly in the leaves.

Adriel turned around to look at him as he approached. He walked up and stood beside her.

A few feet before them was the edge of an overhang. Over the cliff was an enormous expanse of trees that stretched far into the distance. On the horizon were the faint outlines of distant mountains, sulking giants in the black of night.

The mountains spanned across the entire horizon, stretching off to the very ends of the earth. The night sky lay exposed above them, unhindered by the forests of Morgaul.

Thousands of stars dotted the skies, flickering zealously in their own right. The moon hung low in the heavens, full and grand, an overbearing radiance amid the deepest black.

The moon illuminated the forests and mountains below, drowning the world in a sea of light.

Adriel turned and smiled at Cain. The sapphire pools of her eyes shimmered in the starlight, her hair dancing in the breeze.

"It's a beautiful night," she said in awe as she gazed out over the trees bathed in ivory.

"It is…"

They stood in silence for several minutes, engrossed in the beauty before them.

"I feel a tension in the air," Cain whispered.

Adriel tilted her chin to the wind, letting her hair blow back in the cool breeze. "I feel it too." They looked at each other for a moment before breaking their gaze.

"It's the winds of war," Cain continued, taking a step towards the edge of the outcropping. Adriel followed likewise and looked at him for a moment. "I can feel the cries of the innocent, the blood that is spilt across the North. It is as if their pain sails these winds. War descends upon us..."

Adriel looked at Cain, worry masked beneath the radiance of the moon. "Cain...what happened to you in Andaurel?"

He looked out over the grandeur before him, pain and greater sorrow a weight in his throat.

"Cain...please tell me. Maybe...maybe I can help you."

Cain shook his head. "What happened is in the past."

"Obviously not. You still carry it with you. I see the pain it brings. The others may not see it, but I do."

"It's nothing but a memory now. Maybe it haunts me to make me stronger. Maybe it haunts me to make me a weaker man; unfit for the task I have been given. Tarsha places all of its hopes on me, and I long to do what is right. As long as my past, my memories, and my regrets guide me toward my vengeance, than I don't care what end awaits me..."

The Guiding Hand

The next day the Warriors mounted their horses well before the break of dawn, eating a handful of their rations as they rode through the fading darkness. The sun gradually rose in an unseen sky, bringing with it a warmth welcomed by the travelers.

The riders twisted their way through the trees of the forest that had long since begun to thin out. Thick, thorny vines clawed about them as they followed a narrow washout through the heart of the Morgaul.

For several hours, they traversed the winding paths that snaked their way across the undulating landscape. Noon came to pass and they guided their horses over knotted hills of root and stone, soon coming out into yet another trail.

As they crossed onto the pathway, the same raven screeched at them from its perch overhead, barely visible among the black-leafed trees. It swooped down and circled over them before flying down the path, screaming incessantly as it glided into the shadows.

Cain led the group down the path, following their strange companion. The raven led them through a sea of trees and hills, working their way through the never-ending labyrinth of trails.

The Warriors rode throughout the day, riding on with little rest, more than ready to leave the Morgaul.

As the hours slowly passed, they sighted the bird again. The raven flew in a continuous circle over a path that branched off to their left. They reined their mounts toward this trail with reluctant compliance.

The bird floated ahead of them and quickly disappeared into the shadows. The travelers followed this path and soon came to the top of a prominence. As they reached the end, the treetops above suddenly split.

A blinding wall of sunlight struck them and they blinked rapidly. Once their eyes had adjusted to the light, they noticed the trail continued ahead for several hundred yards. The wide path split the Morgaul and left the ebony trees to wither in the blazing sun.

The Morgaul's power waned as the Warriors grinned, realizing the end lay ahead. The travelers flicked their reins and sent their horses into a swift trot. The black trees of the Morgaul whipped past as they sped down the path.

Suddenly they burst out of the trees, leaving the forest in their wake. They pulled their reins and came to a halt as a blast of fresh air brushed over them. They sighed with relief and looked around at their new surroundings.

They stood now in a long pathway that gradually ascended the slope of a hill. Tall walls of rock loomed over them from both sides of the ravine and cast the edges of the path in shadow.

Thick clusters of oak trees spread across the wilderness. All was barren and forlorn with the cycles of the seasons. Even then, these trees were a welcome sight after the surreal Morgaul. Patches of snow covered the leafy ground in various areas, masking the jagged rocks of the ravine.

"This must be the Knife Ridge Verin told us about," Aaron said to the group as they absorbed their newest surroundings.

Cain turned to Adriel and informed her, "It cuts between the Amon Karash and Heiven Sul. Now all we have to do is follow this ridge for a few miles until it puts us safely past both."

"Easier said than done," a voice called out to them. A figure appeared over the crest of the hill before them, looking down on the travelers.

Cain looked up at the figure and cried, "Who are you?" The man said nothing but held out his hand in silent response.

The raven they had followed through the forest glided toward the man and landed lightly on his outstretched arm.

"I see she led you safely through the Morgaul," he said to them as he stroked the bird's head. The man began to walk down the path towards them and Cain instinctively wrapped a hand around his sword.

"Peace, friend," the man said to him. "I wish you no harm." He stopped a few yards before them.

He was nearly the same build as Cain and just as tall. Disheveled sable hair rose from his forehead before curving lightly around his brow and over his shoulders. He was thin and toned, his strong arms covered with the sleeves of a black tunic. He wore tattered black clothes and a cloak of gray wool. A small leather quiver rested against his back beside a white longbow.

The man looked at each of the travelers with intense sapphire eyes.

"Who are you?" Cain repeated the inquiry once more.

"Who am I?" The man replied, "Who are you should be the question. I will tell you who you are. You are Cain Taran, one of the Warriors sent by Ethebriel of Kaanos." The Warriors stared back in surprise at the man who simply smirked at their response. Cain opened his mouth to reply but the man finished the question for him.

"And how do I know that, you were about to ask...word travels fast, my friends, faster than your horses ever will. Ethebriel sent word of you to the King a few weeks before you even began your ride for Morven."

"And how do you know the business of kings?" Cain asked.

The man locked eyes with him a moment before replying. "I am a drifter...I wander Tarsha and learn many things, Cain Taran, including the business of kings. Secrets sail the winds," he said as he raised a hand in the air, "Waiting to be broken."

He clenched his fist fiercely. "I have been waiting here for three days now, waiting for you to show yourselves. I was beginning to wonder if you would even survive the clutches of Morgaul."

Cain looked at him curiously. "You were waiting for us?"

The man nodded and smiled again. "I was looking for you, yes. If it were not for me, you would still be wandering aimlessly to your deaths in those trees. You are the ones the people have set their hopes upon, hoping that their heroes would arrive and sweep them off their feet to unite the broken countries.

But that fairytale is nothing more than a fool's hope, for it falls dead with the fact that you could not even find your way out of a few trees, let alone find your way to Morven."

"We know how to get there," Cain retorted defensively. "And we're not heroes...we are far from it."

The man raised a brow at this. "I can see that." He took a few steps forward and raised a hand. "I have been a drifter for most of my life; I know the countries of Tarsha and their terrain better than any alive. Ever since I heard of the people placing their hopes on the shoulders of four foreigners, I knew I could not let anything happen to you. I have made it my personal duty to find you and guide you safely to Morven, to protect the fragile hopes of Tarsha's people."

"We don't need your help," Joshua retorted.

The man nodded at him. "You will find you will need me before the end. Whether you like it or not, you will receive my assistance."

Cain held up his hand to silence his friend. "What is your name?" He asked the man.

"I am Malecai," he replied with a curt bow.

"Well, Malecai, we have been following the directions given to us by the King of Charun," Cain said. "But if you can lead us to the capital, then you are welcome to join us."

Malecai nodded and threw his arm up, sending the raven flying into the sunlight. "I will lead you safely across Erias. You will not be disappointed, my friends." He turned and began walking up the path, beckoning them to follow.

"Are you sure about this?" Joshua asked Cain as they rode after the man.

"No, but we need all the help we can get. We have a heavy burden on our shoulders; we would be foolish not to accept aid when freely given." Joshua nodded and stared into the man's back.

"Aye, you're probably right," he sighed with a great heave of his shoulders. The Warriors followed the man up the hill and as they reached the top, they noticed the path extended far ahead of them.

The man walked over to the trees that lined the path and approached a russet horse tethered to a tree. Beside the horse was an enormous sword stabbed into the rocks.

The weapon was three hands wide and nearly an inch thick. Malecai walked over to the sword and pulled it from the ground, swinging it onto his shoulder with one fluid motion.

The sword was over five feet long and made of sturdy yet lightweight steel. The blade curved fiercely near the end, turning to a sharp point at its tip. Its handle was extremely long, able to fit nearly six fists around its black leather grip.

The sword had no hilt for it needed none since the blade's wide bottom provided a hand guard in of itself. A large steel pommel was fashioned at the base of the handle where a white jewel rested in its curved prongs.

Cain rode up beside the man as he began tying his bow and quiver to the horse's saddle. "You said Ethebriel sent word of us to the King of Erias?"

"Yes, I did," Malecai replied as he fastened his sword to a baldric that wrapped diagonal across his back.

"How do you know this? Ethebriel could not have sent word of us to Erias, he did not even know of the looming attack on Morven until a few weeks ago. Even then, we were already in Charun."

"You are a soldier; you follow your orders with blind obedience. You think you know all there is to know, but you know so little. As long as there are those willing to do the work of lesser men, then the gears of war will never cease." He untied his horse and guided it over to the Warriors.

"There is one thing you should know, however," he said as he saddled his horse. He turned and began leading the Warriors down the path. "A group of Iscara Knights are guarding the path a few miles north from here. We cannot risk following the Knife Ridge, it will lead us straight to them. We will have to follow the edge of Heiven Sul."

"Wait, what do you mean Iscara Knights?" Cain asked as he rode up beside him. Malecai turned and looked up the path ahead. "I am sure you will see soon enough."

**** ****

The man named Malecai led the Warriors through the Knife Ridge. They worked their way through endless trees and followed the large rock walls that choked the path on either side.

"We are only a few miles from the western border of Heiven Sul," Malecai informed the group. They descended the path that twisted down a large, rocky hill.

"Verin gave us direct orders not to step foot into that place, it's suicide to enter Heiven Sul," Cain replied but Malecai cut him off.

"We are not going to enter Heiven Sul. But I wish we were...it is far less dangerous than crossing the path of the Iscara."

Cain turned to him and asked, "How could they possibly be more dangerous than the Gehets?"

Malecai glanced over at Cain with mild annoyance. "Because Abaddon wants you dead, Cain. His Knights are looking for you and they will not relent until they kill every last one of you...that is how."

"That's reason enough for me," Joshua remarked.

Cain fell silent and glanced nervously at Aaron who rode close at his side. The two nodded slowly as their eyes locked, remembering the words of the Arzec captain. His words that night still rang clear in their minds.

"How do you know all of this anyway?" Cain asked as he tore himself from his thoughts.

A smile pulled at Malecai's lips. "You ask a lot of questions...does he do this a lot?" He asked Adriel.

"He doesn't know when to stop," she laughed.

Malecai chuckled for a moment and glanced up at the sky. "It will be dark soon; we will set up camp on the border." He ushered his horse off the trail as the rock walls enclosing their path extended down a gradual slope and stretched deeper into the trees.

"They were five miles or so up the path from here," Malecai said as he pointed back up the slope. "Hopefully we will be safe for the night."

He led them through the trees and crossed over a stream, following a straight path to the east.

"Through the trees ahead is a small cave under an outcropping," Malecai informed them, "we can spend the night there."

They rode through the trees and came to a large rock formation that protruded from the treetops, towering above the forests as it stretched off into the shadows of the growing dusk.

As they approached it, they noticed the foot of the prominence curved inward, providing several feet of open space within the rock face.

They guided their horses towards the cave-like shelter and dismounted, tying them to the trees that lined the walls of earth and stone.

Darkness fell across the skies and blackened the heavens, the stars spreading their light across the forest. There was no moon tonight.

The travelers climbed into the cave and threw down their rucksacks. They pulled out their mats and lay down wearily.

Malecai pulled a satchel from his rucksack and poured its contents out on a piece of cloth before them. Several hunks of meat fell from the bag and he sighed at the cold slabs.

"I have fresh venison, but we cannot risk making a fire tonight." Instead, he returned them to his bag and handed each of them a strip of salted lamb.

They broke a loaf of hardened bread and finished it off with watered wine from his wineskin.

"I apologize for coming across as I did," Malecai said to Cain as the group began to fall asleep one by one. Cain nodded at this.

"It was not the time for inquiries, I needed you to leave the Knife Ridge quickly...I could not afford another encounter."

"Another encounter?" Cain asked with a raised brow, "You've encountered these men before?"

"I arrived at the Knife Ridge several days ago to search for you, but I was not alone. There were fifteen Iscara waiting for you as well. I rode right into their camp...I killed six of their number, but I barely escape with my life."

He raised his right hand and flicked his sleeve, revealing blackened bandages that wrapped tightly around his entire arm.

"They burned most of the flesh from my arm. It is not a pretty sight."

He removed his cloak and laid it at his side before lifting his tunic, revealing a massive scar that stretched from his shoulder to nearly his hip. Blackened flesh surrounded the wound, as if burned and charred, a massive lesion that revealed bone, flesh, and bloody muscle beneath.

Cain cringed as Malecai dropped his tunic. "My only regret…I could not kill more of them," he ended solemnly.

Cain shook his head and replied, "Well then why couldn't we just do what you did, fight them to escape. I have been a soldier for fifteen years, I can hold my own. If what you said was true, then there are only nine of them left, which more than evens the odds."

Malecai smiled vaguely at this. "You underestimate their power, my friend. These men would rip you apart."

"Then what makes you so qualified to kill that which we cannot?" Cain snapped back.

"I have trained in the 'finer' aspects of combat. You may have survived the clutches of Abaddon through Charun and Kaanos, but you have yet to be tested against true power. You have only fought the dogs of the Destroyer's army, the lowest on the ladder.

The Arzecs are pathetic; they are mere animals of the earth, wallowing away in their breeding grounds of Amon Karash. Their true use lies only in their numbers and brutality, and even then, these uses are few.

The Andreds are a much stronger force, hollow shells of their once former beings. They fight only to spill the blood of their master's enemies. That, my friend, is their sole purpose, mere puppets of their creator.

However, the Knights of Iscara are the true might of his army. They may be far fewer in number, but they are more powerful than anything you can imagine."

"How do you know so much about them?" Cain asked, lying back against his mat.

"I have devoted my life to studying ways to expose their weakness. Every man is weak. To cover it is strength, yet to reveal it in your enemy is true power. It is survival of the fittest and I intend for us to win."

"You say you've studied the ways of these Knights for your entire life, but how is that possible if you're scarce older than I?"

Malecai laughed lightly. "Cain, there are many things you do not understand. But know this, that things always happen for a reason. You must reach out yourself to find the answers to it all. All of your questions will one day be revealed to you, you just have to know what to look for."

Desecration

Cain's eyes snapped open, waking up to Malecai kneeling beside him. Malecai slapped him lightly on the face and stood up. "Saddle up, we have a long road ahead of us." Together, they woke the rest of the group and ate sparingly. They then packed their bags and saddled their horses.

Malecai flicked his reins and led the group away from the cave and into the surrounding trees. They followed a path that snaked down a steep slope and cut deeper into the forests.

The travelers continued east for several minutes before branching off north from the path. They stepped into the trees and were forced to spread out.

"How far-" Joshua began to ask but was cut short.

"You would do well to quiet yourself," Malecai said, "the Iscara may be anywhere. We ride in silence."

The Warriors heeded his words and continued in silence. The sun rose atop the trees, filling the forest with light. Snow trickled around them. A cool, gentle breeze tickled across their skin.

The company continued throughout the day, the sun slowly creeping across the skies. They rode along the foot of a hill that atop it must have been the Knife Ridge. They ate a quick meal and continued through noon, the sun now falling fast from the sky.

The travelers rode for hours, the miles quickly slipping by. The sun at last fell behind the treetops and its light began to dwindle.

They rode into the dusk and soon into night, bound eternal in silence. Darkness fell and the cold of night closed over them.

They pulled their cloaks closer for warmth and continued through the now thinning forest.

The sky above was cradled in clouds, their dark masses blotting out any glint of light from the moon and stars. The night grew darker until they could see nothing but the reins in their hands. The silence of the night was eerie, almost supernatural.

The Warriors blindly stumbled out of the forests and into a field of shrubbery. Every tree around them was dead, barren and rotting in the chill air. Weeds and dead grass stretched far off into the breadth of a distant hill.

Their horses crossed through the thick undergrowth, weaving through hundreds of dead trees. Malecai turned and informed the others, "This should have put us well around the Knights; I doubt they would be this far around the Knife Ridge."

They blindly reined their horses through the trees, struggling to find a path in the darkness. "We are close now," Malecai muttered, "there is something ahead I wish to show you."

They continued for several minutes through the dense overgrowth until they came to a large formation that towered far above them. It was a massive hill, a lone silhouette in the night.

"We are here..." Malecai whispered as quietly as he dared. He dismounted and gestured for the others to do likewise. They jumped off their horses and tethered them to a rotten tree.

Malecai approached the foot of the hill, the Warriors close behind. He halted and closed his eyes.

"What are you doing?" Cain asked as he walked past him.

Malecai threw his hand in front of Cain's chest, stopping him in mid stride.

"Keeping us alive." He held his palms out, his elbows bent slightly as a feeble wind picked up and blew across the grass.

He muttered inaudibly and held his hands out farther in front of him. He began to gradually push forward as if leaning into a wall of stone. He continued to murmur, his face wrought with concentration.

He stepped forward and leaned into a sudden gale of wind. After a short struggle, he then walked forward again and pulled his hands to the sides as if to part the air before them. He then dropped his arms and the wind died instantly, leaving the air still and unperturbed; falling thick around them once again.

"What did you just do?" Cain asked with a raised brow.

"This land is protected with the consecrations of holy men, if you pass over them..." He laughed a moment, "Well, it is best not to find out."

He began to climb the steep hill and the others followed close behind. They soon reached the top and looked around.

They could scarcely discern through the darkness that they stood now upon a flat hilltop. Several other hills encircled them, towering far above the dead and wilted lands.

"Welcome to the Barrows of Alon Heath, my friends. The ancient burial grounds of the kings of Erias." He held his arms up in a flourish and stepped forward.

The group began to cross the hilltop, turning slowly as they walked to soak in the grandeur of the Barrows.

Malecai continued to speak to the awestruck Warriors, his quiet words sailing the shadows before being stifled against the mighty hills. "These Barrows are hallowed ground, sacred to the peoples of Erias. Only the Tongueless of Helika were allowed to enter this sacred ground.

The Tongueless were men who devoted their entire lives to their religion, their dedication to their one god. They believed in ultimate piety, and went to extreme lengths in their attempt to reach a higher calling.

They severed their tongues upon completion of their studies, believing that in doing so would prevent slander and sin, a needless way of remaining pure.

The Tongueless performed their morbid tasks, burying their kings for over four thousand years.

However, their ancient and sacred religion was thrown aside by the people of Tarsha, who over the course of history grew comfortable in that which their god provided. They fell to sin and began to worship themselves, turning their backs on their one god, their creator and provider.

The stories say that Tarsha's god grew angry with his children, and saw his answer in the callous heart of the young Abaddon. He lured him into these lands and bestowed a great gift upon him, immortality and limitless power.

In return for this endowment, Abaddon follows the will of the Forgotten, to eradicate all of humanity for turning their backs on him. We have fought this war ever since…"

"I told you the stories were true," Joshua said as he turned to his brother.

Silas retorted, "I can't believe you think this shit is real. It's just a story."

"Think what you want, but I know what's right. There is a reason we're fighting this war. There has to be."

The group fell silent and Malecai began to speak again. "The stories are indeed true. How else could a mere man live for four centuries? As far as the Barrows are concerned, the last devout followers of the Forgotten sealed the tombs, forming the barrier we passed over.

Since then, no one has dared enter Alon Heath. You are the first to set your eyes upon the holiest site in the world…"

Cain wrapped his fingers slowly around the handle of his sword and eyed the encompassing darkness with angst.

"Why did you bring us here?" he asked Malecai angrily as they reached the top of a second hill.

Malecai smirked and replied, "Why not?"

Cain glared at him, his glossed words dying in the weight of the silence. He turned his attention from the man, his eye shortly caught with fascination as they crossed the hill.

Looming hillocks rose around them and stretched off afar. Wildflowers and shrubbery adorned their brows.

Colossal stones and pillars lay barely visible beneath thick blankets of undergrowth, cracked and weathered over the centuries.

Statues of robed men stood lofty and pompous on every hilltop, their crowned heads bowed in reverence, hands folded in eternal prayer.

The Warriors walked across the hill toward three statues that stood in the middle of the mound.

They were at least twenty feet in height, each standing defiant against the crippling hands of time. They were fashioned entirely of ivory stone and swathed in chiseled robes. Great cracks wove across their faces and garments, marring the once shimmering and brilliant.

The middle statue's hands extended from its robes, palms rose to the night sky as if it once held something of prominence.

"They're beautiful," Adriel said in awe, delicately touching the stone robes of the middle statue. A heavy raindrop fell from the sky and ran down the statue's cheek. Soon, a soft rain fell over the Barrows, pattering with a whisper in the grass.

The air hung profoundly stifling around them, filled with an unbreakable tension. The earth seemed to inhale deeply, engulfing all life as it held its breath.

Then, through the rhythm of the rain, the Warriors heard a faint rasp of steel behind them. They spun around and peered anxiously through the drizzling rain.

A large ball of blue light formed at the base of the first hill and spread its rays through the darkness. The Warriors stepped back as the beams sprawled forth over the crest, revealing them among the darkness.

The light blinded the Warriors instantly and they stepped back helplessly, shielding their eyes.

"There they are!" A voice shouted through the rain.

Suddenly, the skies above Alon Heath lit up in a flash, turning the night sky into instant day. An intense sea of ivory light poured forth from the clouded skies, blinding the Warriors once again.

Two men ran through the light straight for the Warriors, swords raised to strike down their unsuspecting prey. "No!" a man's voice cried out from behind them.

The air pulsated in violent waves that rippled through the grass. The ground then shook violently, ripping massive chunks of earth from the hills that then began to float strangely into the air. The light collected as a mighty pillar of light and then fell swift from the heavens, colliding into the two running men and stopping them in mid stride.

They instantly dropped to their knees, screaming in pain as if suddenly engulfed in fire. They tossed their blades and tore wildly at their faces. Blood began pouring from their mouths and steam billowed from their eye sockets. They clawed madly at the ground and writhed in agony, their god-forsaken screams piercing the air. They shook violently and their chests suddenly erupted, blood and entrails exploding forth and spraying over the ground.

Then as quickly as it had come, the ray of light disappeared and withdrew back into the clouds. With a last deafening boom, rain and darkness returned to the barrows.

The Warriors stood in amazement, attempting to make sense of the horrors they just witnessed. Malecai, the first to recover, held his weapon warily before him and stared into the ball of light that reappeared at the foot of the hill.

The wind that encircled the base of the mound died and the light began to ascend the hill.

"Hold your ground," Malecai whispered to the others. "Do not let them near." The light advanced and the sound of footsteps grew louder.

"Who are they?" Aaron whispered to the group. Malecai glared at him through rain-drenched hair, a sharp retort silencing him immediately.

The light passed over the eviscerated remains of the dead men and came to a stop several yards before the Warriors. The Warriors could vaguely discern a group of seven men behind the blinding ball of light.

They each wore full sets of body armor painted black as the surrounding night. In the middle of each cuirass was a snake wrapped around a sword, the entire crest painted like a splattered bloodstain across their breasts. The men looked them over through long, dark hair.

Silas let out a shout and rushed at the men. Malecai threw out his arm and grabbed Silas's Sitar as he ran past. He pulled him back into the group and stepped towards the men. One of them stepped forward and the light died in his clenched fist.

Malecai and the man now stood several yards away from their respective groups, glaring at each other in searing hate. A heavy rain now fell down on the Barrows, clinking loudly on the men's armor in the apprehensive silence.

"Did you honestly think you could escape?" The man muttered after a moment. His voice was lucid and strangely chilling, nearly a whisper amid the rainfall.

"Long enough to lure you here..." Malecai replied, smirking at Cain over his shoulder. The Warriors' eyes lit up in surprise, shocked by his words.

"You killed six of my men," the man said, "returning the favor is long overdue, Malecai."

"My only regret, Elijah, is that I could not kill you." Malecai held up his sword, ready for any sudden attack from the man.

Elijah laughed, the chill notes echoing in the hills. "Humor me. You were always weak, Malecai. You cannot keep us from them forever. Abaddon's reach is vast, if he wants them dead, then dead they will be. However, he thirsts for the blood of Taran especially...is that him there?" He looked at Cain for a moment. "Not much of a threat if you ask me, but who am I to question the wish of the Destroyer."

"I know he is wanted. But I will keep him from Abaddon's grasp, unto my death if need be."

The men beside Elijah stepped forward and drew their swords. The Warriors held their weapons out defensively, ready for an imminent attack.

"Very well," Elijah replied, "then I have no choice but to kill him, Abaddon does not need him alive." Elijah glanced at Cain, "Sorry friend, nothing personal."

He suddenly thrust his sword at Malecai, sending a surge of lightning from the blade. Malecai thrust his palm out and the blast crashed harmlessly into an invisible wall before him.

Elijah ran forward and thrust his hand out, sending a blast of black light shooting from his palm and racing towards Malecai.

Malecai brought his sword close to his body as the blast slammed into him. The light struck with full force into the sword's broad face, sending him slowly backwards as it pushed relentlessly at him. With a cry, he spun and sent the light shooting past him.

He threw out his hand and massive bolts of black lightning surged forth and crashed into his enemy. The web of lightning shot into his face, clawing through his eyes and mouth. Screaming with agony, Elijah dropped his sword and stepped back as the tendrils continued to drill through his skull. The lightning blasted through his eyes and mouth, clawing into his head with a sickening squelch of boiling blood. With a final cry, Elijah collapsed to the ground.

The other Knights looked up in horror at Malecai, their leader lay slain at their feet. They threw their swords up and with a cry of vengeance, charged toward the Warriors.

The Warriors raised their weapons and Malecai led them sprinting towards the Knights.

One of the Knights shot a column of fire at him and he rushed forward undeterred, and at the last moment threw his hand up, sending an invisible force crashing into the inferno. The two forces clashed and sent a clap of air across the hilltop.

The Knight threw a burst of ivory lightning that seared through the air towards its target. Malecai struck the oncoming light and tore through it, sprinting toward his opponent. He slammed his blade into the Iscara, lightning flying from the collision. They held their swords in a lock for a moment and pushed against the other.

They broke their block and jumped backwards before slashing at each other, their blades ripping through the rain. Steel flew as a blur, the two men darting about and striking at the other with inhuman speed.

Cain rushed towards one of the Knights and evaded a surge of wind. He leapt forward and swung his sword with full strength.

The Knight dodged the strike and jumped forward, spinning clear over Cain. The Knight twirled and slashed at Cain. Cain barely threw his sword up in time to block the surprise attack, stumbling back before catching himself.

The Knight landed before Cain and threw his arm out, sending a blast of air that tackled into him and shot him over the hill.

Adriel notched an arrow and let loose a well-aimed volley at one of the men. The arrows sped through the rain and shattered into pieces before the Knight. Adriel's eyes lit up in shock as the Knight rushed forward unhindered, sword raised to strike her down.

She quickly spun as the man tumbled past her. She pulled her sword from its sheath as she twirled and thrust it blindly at the man. The blade rebound off his thick armor and as she recovered from the failed blow, he strafed and swung at her.

Adriel dashed to the side, barely evading the strike. She then jumped and double kicked, pushing off his chest before back flipping.

He recovered from the blow and sent her flying with a powerful burst of wind. He jumped to his feet and raised his hands in the air before slamming them to the ground with a cry.

The muddy ground around him flew into the air, a wide area of stone and earth rising from the hilltop. He jumped into the air, the massive chunks of earth shooting about him. He flew several yards over the Barrows before throwing down the debris at his opponent.

Adriel nimbly evaded the earth and rubble as she sprinted through the gauntlet. She jumped and landed on a broken column before bounding off. She landed on another as it flew through the air, and leaping off, she descended over her opponent.

The Knight deflected her sword and grabbed her by the arm and spun, tossing her across the hill. She crashed in a pile of rubble and her sword flew from her hand, imbedding itself in the foot of a statue beside her.

Aaron twirled his saber above his head as one of the Knights charged at him.

Their swords met and they collided into each other, swords ringing viciously as they twirled their swords from the block and swung again.

The Knight blocked a blow to the head and threw the recoiling blade towards Aaron's stomach. Aaron jumped back to evade the strike and the sword narrowly missed his gut.

The man thrust his hand forward as his blade missed its mark, sending a plume of ivory flames bursting from his hand. Aaron fell to his knees and tumbled through the mud, evading the inferno. He jumped up from the roll and pushed off the ground with tremendous momentum, flying towards the Knight.

The man brought his sword up and swiped Aaron's blade aside in mid air. Both of their swords flew to the side from the powerful strike, now both of them weaponless.

As his blade left his hands, the man jumped backwards, dodging Aaron's mid air tackle. The man back flipped and landed lightly as Aaron crashed heavily into the mud.

The man threw his arm to the side and their swords flew straight at him. He grabbed both of the weapons and held them to his sides.

Suddenly, a torrent of ivory flames arose and swirled fierce about him as he charged at his downed opponent.

Joshua lumbered towards one of the Knights, their weapons soon crashing with a shrill ring of steel. Their weapons danced with violent speed, sparks searing from every powerful blow. They exchanged blow after blow, struggling to overpower the other.

The Knight staggered under an overhead strike, and as Joshua swung again, the man sent him shooting back with a surge of wind.

He sprinted toward Joshua and leapt into the air. He swung his sword and the blade recoiled uselessly off Joshua's helmet. Joshua slammed heavily into the mud; his helmet now lying beyond his reach.

Silas rushed past Joshua and stabbed his Sitar into the ground, and using the momentum, threw himself straight into an astonished Knight.

The man jumped back and Silas missed his mark, the Sitar's blades tearing through the mud. The Knight lurched forward and sent forth great waves of light from the blurs of his hands.

Silas weaved about in place, swiping the lethal darts from the air with swift spinning blades.

The man then fell over him, his sword colliding into the hardwood handle of the Sitar.

Silas pushed back as the Iscara fought to overpower him, the two locked in a stalemate. Silas broke the lock and swung his Sitar, sending the man jumping back to evade the four pronged blades.

He thrust his weapon forward and the Knight retaliated with an overhead strike. Their blades met and the sword caught instantly in the Sitar's curved blades.

Silas swung his weapon and tossed the sword across the hill. He swung again and the man jumped back, sliding through the mud now unarmed. The Knight thrust his hand out and a blast of lightning shot from his open palm.

Silas stabbed his weapon forward and the Sitar's blades wrapped around the blast. He tossed the lightning over his shoulder, dissipating in the air as he smirked at his opponent.

The Knight sent a blast of air flying towards him, and Silas raised his Sitar above his head and slammed the flare of wind into the earth. The force of the recoil sent him sailing into the air as the surprised Knight then threw a second wave of wind at his opponent.

Silas swung his weapon again and sent the gale rebounding into its caster. The wind crashed into the Knight and tossed him into the air.

Silas landed lightly in the mud and the Knight flailed helplessly above as he descended directly over his opponent. Silas thrust his Sitar over his head and the man fell over the weapon, impaled on its mighty blades.

The Iscara howled in anguish as the blades wrenched their way through his back and out his chest, a geyser of blood exploding from his skewered body.

Silas held him over his head a moment before slamming the man into the ground. He pulled the Sitar out and brought the weapon down to finish him, screaming with murderous triumph.

Malecai ripped his sword from the ground and swung it into his opponent. Their blades met with a flash of steel and the two began a skillful pirouette of steel.

Malecai jumped back to dodge a lunge from his enemy and he glided across the mud away from his opponent.

He threw out a hand and the man was suddenly pulled towards him, levitating swiftly over the ground against his will. Malecai then jumped through the air and slammed a booted foot into the man's face. The man shot back and landed on his feet.

The man swung his sword, a blade of light sent lashing from the weapon. Malecai turned and ran up the length of a statue as the blast whipped by below him. As he reached the statue's chest, he bound off and swung his sword at it. With a blast of light, the statue split in half.

He then swung around the statue and threw out a hand, imploding it with an earsplitting boom. Thousands of stone chunks flew at the alarmed Knight.

The man charged forward and jumped into the air, leaping deftly off the stones. Swiftly ascending, he bound off stone after stone before shooting into the air at Malecai.

Malecai grabbed his broadsword with both hands and held it over his head, and with a vicious cry, slammed it down on the Knight. The man rocketed back from the blow, slamming painfully into the earth yards below.

Malecai dropped from the air and landed amid the rubble as it crashed into the mud. He scanned the shadows with apprehension.

The man then leapt at him from the shadows. He stabbed his blade forward and Malecai barely threw his sword up in time to defend himself from the strike. He deflected the blade and rounded it for a second blow.

The man disappeared in a plume of smoke and his sword missed its target. Malecai lowered his head and stood still. The rain pelted his face, cold and stinging against his skin. He closed his eyes and breathed slowly, listening to the faint breath that parted his lips.

The Knight suddenly appeared behind him with a swirl of shadows.

Malecai spun as the man lunged from behind. He threw out his hand and grabbed the man's sword. The sword's steel edge cut fruitlessly into his clenched palm. He tightened his grip around the weapon as the man began to panic, fighting desperately to pull it free.

Malecai leered and reached forward, resting a hand against the man's chest. With unnatural ease, he pushed and sent the man shooting back.

He then clenched his fist and pulled it back before throwing the Knight into the air.

Malecai jumped and flew into the air, the rain needles against his skin. He flew over the man and unclenched his fist, throwing his palm forward.

The man was sent tumbling across the hilltop before slamming over a downed column. A spray of debris flew as he landed on his back with a sickening crunch of bone.

Malecai descended over his downed opponent and stabbed his broadsword into the man with a murderous scream.

The massive sword tore through his entire body and stabbed violently into the stone face of the column beneath. A torrent of blood spewed forth and sprayed Malecai red with death.

Aaron jumped up from the ground, weaponless. He pulled a knife from his belt and held it desperately before him. He inhaled deeply and charged forward, plunging through the flames surrounding his opponent.

He came out the other side unharmed and tackled the Knight, knocking him off his feet. The knife flew from his hand as he slid to a stop in the mud beside his opponent.

The flames around the Iscara faded as he picked his swords off the ground and jumped to his feet.

Aaron clawed through the mud and dove over an overturned column. The Knight rushed towards him and swung a sword at him as Aaron climbed over the rubble.

The sword smashed into the column and Aaron slammed his boot into the man's arm, knocking him away from his sword. He kicked the man in the face and jumped over him.

He crashed into the man and in one fluid movement, plunged his knife into his opponent's face. The Iscara roared with pain, blood spewing from his skull. Aaron pulled the knife out and stabbed him several more times, blood spraying with every relentless thrust. The man's body collapsed to the mud, soaked in its own blood.

Cain stood up in time as his opponent bore down on him. Their swords clashed with a shower of sparks. They spun and struck again, both weapons flying as they threw countless blows at the other.

The man jumped back and thrust his arms out, sending forth a massive wall of wind. The blast ripped earth and mud from the hill and crashed into Cain, sending him sailing through the air. As he landed, he stabbed his sword into the mud and the momentum swung him to his feet.

He pulled his sword from the ground and slid in a large ark around his opponent. The Knight charged at him and as Cain continued to slide around his opponent, he saw his opening.

He swung his sword low and struck the man in the legs, sending him off balance. Cain then slowed to a stop and approached the downed Knight. He spun his sword in his hand, pommel facing outward. He stepped beside the man and plunged his sword deep into the man's back, the blade cutting through his spine. With a crack of bone, he pulled his weapon out.

He grabbed the lip of the man's helmet and pulled it off before dropping it at his feet. The man looked up at him, blood dripping from his open mouth.

Cain grabbed the man by the hair and rested his sword against his neck. He looked helplessly up at his killer as Cain slit his throat. Blood gushed from the man's neck as his body collapsed in the mud, twitching uncontrollably before falling dead in silence.

The remaining Knights saw their comrades fall one by one, almost simultaneously at the hands of their enemies. They reluctantly turned their backs on the Warriors and ran for their lives, disappearing into the night. The Warriors ran after them as they retreated down the hill, screaming with rage.

"Let them go," Malecai called out to them. They stopped at the edge of the hilltop and looked down the slope as the three survivors slipped into the surrounding forests.

"We cannot allow their filth to desecrate this hallowed place."

The body of Elijah suddenly let out a gasp. He raised a hand to the skies, weakly crying out for help.

Malecai walked over to Elijah and looked down his sword at the defenseless man. He pulled on Elijah's body with his boot until he rested on his back, forced to look at Malecai.

"Have mercy..." Elijah whispered, barely discernable through the blood that gushed from his mouth.

Malecai lifted his sword. "Mercy..." He said before thrusting his sword straight into Elijah's chest, the huge blade impaling itself through his body. Elijah lurched forward and let out a final breath before falling back to the earth, dead.

Malecai closed his eyes and inhaled deeply before pulling the sword out with a crunch of bone. "Mercy is for the deserving."

He walked away from the Warriors and descended the hill. The others stared after him and sheathed their weapons. They followed him and left behind the bodies of the Iscara and the Barrows of Alon Heath.

The Valley of Death

The Warriors descended the hill and came to where their horses were tethered. "Where are the horses?" Joshua asked.

Cain knelt down and picked up the broken leather strap of a horse's bridle. "The light must have startled them…"

Malecai cursed and punched a rotting tree. The tree fell to the ground with a shower of dirt.

"Damn it," Joshua cursed, "they have all of our equipment!"

"Don't you think we know that?" Adriel shouted at him. "What are we going to do? We have no food or water now…"

"Let me think," Malecai said as he sat down at the base of the tree. He rested his right arm across his knee and raised his sleeve.

The black bandages wrapped around his arm were soaked with blood and badly torn. He grimaced as he began unwinding them from around his arm. As the bandages fell from his skin, they noticed the badly burned and blackened flesh, exposing the bloody muscle and sinew beneath. The Warriors cringed.

Malecai dropped the bandages in the mud and pulled a fresh roll from his cloak. "Do not worry, I received this injury the last time I came across Elijah. But he is dead now." He finished wrapping his arm and pulled the bandages tightly before standing up again.

Aaron wiped his knife clean of blood and asked, "What was all that?"

Malecai raised a brow. "Pardon?"

"The fire, the wind, the shadows, those men fought in such strange ways, I've never seen anything like it."

"Ah," Malecai replied, "I would not expect you to know what that was. Only those who truly devote their souls to darkness can attain the powers of which the Iscara have demonstrated. With a soul as black as theirs, strength has no bounds."

The rain had now since subsided and the clouds above slowly parted, revealing small gaps of starlight. The group sat on a cluster of rocks, exhausted from the fighting.

"What was that light?" Cain asked Malecai after minutes had passed.

Malecai shook his head. "I do not know...but whatever it was probably saved our lives."

"Aye," Cain agreed. "Elijah said Abaddon wants me dead. The Arzec that led the attack on Andaurel said the same. What would he want of me?"

"I am sorry, Cain, but I know little more than you. I can only speculate. Whatever the reason, I am here to protect you, all of you."

"Thank you for all that you've done, Malecai," Aaron replied, "we owe you greatly."

Malecai smiled coolly. "You owe me nothing, you are the only hope the Alliance has, and I do my part in protecting it. Now...as for the situation at hand, we are without supplies. We cannot get very far without water, so making it to Morven will be impossible. The closest city where we can buy provisions is Ilross. If we can make it the three days to Ilross, then we should be fine."

"Sounds like a plan," Silas said.

"Easier said than done," Joshua retorted. "I'm already hungry..."

"Either way," Malecai said, "we need to try it, it is our only option."

Cain tossed the broken strap in his hand and stood up. "Then let's go."

The Warriors began trudging through the dense undergrowth, working their way through the rotting trees of Alon Heath. They eventually crossed the borders of the Barrows as dawn crept across the skies. They walked for hours without rest, fighting to gain as much possible distance.

Sleep deprived, drenched from the rain, and exhausted from the fight, they marched on with little morale and with the weight of their situation heavy on their minds.

"Let us hope more of the Iscara do not roam these southern borders," Malecai said, breaking the hours of heavy-eyed silence. "We will not be as lucky if we come upon any more of them." They nodded in accordance.

"There are more of them?" Cain asked.

"Much more…however, the full hordes of the Andred army is sweeping across the country. It is much more likely we will come across the Andreds than any more of the Iscara. Keep your weapons close…the open country of Erias lies not far ahead."

The sun at last peered over the distant horizon and spread its rays across the dead forests below, a welcome sight to the beleaguered travelers.

The Warriors trudged through a slurry of mud. The trees about them were quickly thinning and soon stretched sporadically across the open turf before them.

They stepped out of the trees and came to a massive wall of snow-covered rock. The cliff spanned from north to south, disappearing into the trees far into the distance. It loomed high above them, shielding the borders of Alon Heath from the outside world.

They approached a small archway that was cut through the breadth of the cliff and braced for whatever awaited them on the other side.

They crossed under the gap and shadow instantly immersed them. They stumbled blindly through the narrow tunnel until a light appeared at the end. They stepped into the sunlight and crossed out into the country of Erias.

They stood at the edge of a sea of snow that spanned for miles in every direction. Massive pines dotted across the snow-laden earth, an endless forest of life in a lifeless winter. An undulating terrain lay hidden beneath a marring mask of stone and snow.

A bitter cold befell them, bringing with it the full brunt of winter's fury upon unsuspecting travelers.

Malecai laughed as they buried themselves in their cloaks, frozen in place. He stepped between them and rested his hands on Cain and Aaron's shoulders. "This country is unforgiving to outsiders. But you are in safe hands, my friends."

He beckoned them to follow and took the first step into Erias. "I will guide you safely to the capital; try not to die till we get there."

The Warriors began to trudge slowly through the thick blankets of snow, leaving the surreal Barrows behind them.

"How far is it to Ilross?" Silas asked as they fought through the snow.

"Three days," Malecai answered, "that is if we do not run into any more… complications."

The travelers soon came to a fast-flowing stream, slightly iced by winter. They knelt by the brook and filled their water skins.

The day slowly passed them by as they continued deeper into the heart of Erias.

Cain hurried towards the front of their silent procession and came to a stop beside Malecai.

"What is it?" He asked Cain with a raised brow. The group came to a halt.

"I need to know some things, Malecai."

Malecai glanced at the others and beckoned them to follow. "Then let us carry on, the day is dying."

"Not until you answer me."

Malecai paused and glanced at him questioningly. "Very well," he said after a moment.

Cain blinked with satisfaction and asked, "Who are you?"

"Pardon?"

"You know what I mean. It's time we get some answers." Malecai's smirk died at this. "You come out of nowhere and expect us to follow your every word with no questions asked. You could have been one of the Iscara for all we know! You say the Knife Ridge is not safe and take us on a senseless detour to avoid the Iscara, only to walk right into their hands.

You led us right into a damn trap and nearly got us killed because of it! I don't know what happened to those two men, but that could very well have been us! You're the one who got us knee-deep in this shit, and it's time you start answering our questions!" The group held their breath and awaited Malecai's reply.

"I came to provide the security you need to get to Morven alive. I led the Knights to us because I knew the light would protect us. I knew that we could kill them and end their pursuit. I did what was necessary to keep all of you alive. Yes, it was risky, but you are all alive, are you not? After everything I have done for you, this is how you repay me? With doubt?"

He turned from Cain and walked away from the group, leaving them behind in the shadow of a pine.

**** ****

"Wake up," Malecai said as he shook Cain firmly. Cain slowly opened his eyes, weary with exhaustion. He looked around and shook his head of sleep.

177

Snow had fallen heavily during the night, covering every inch of earth beneath winter's vestige.

"We need to get moving, we are losing daylight," Malecai said as he helped Cain to his feet. They brushed snow and ice from their clothes and drew their wool cloaks closer. Plumes of warm mist rose from their mouths with every breath they took, dissipating quickly in the numbing air.

"Malecai..." Cain said as Malecai kicked snow over the remnants of their fire. "I apologize for yesterday."

Malecai strapped his broadsword to his back and shouldered his quiver. "I understand. You lead these four as more than a friend; you lead them as the captain you were born to be. I understand your concerns with me and I know you have your questions. However, I have my secrets. Trust is all that will get us through this war together. If you learn to trust me, then we can do great things for each other." Malecai extended a hand to him.

Cain reached forward and shook it firmly. "Very well, I'll trust you."

Malecai grinned and replied, "And I, you. I will not let you down, my friend."

The two men turned and woke the others, and soon they stood on the fringe of their camp, the open wilds of Erias before them.

Malecai stepped into the trees and led them on a straight path northwest, following a mental bearing to the distant city of Ilross.

They drew their sodden cloaks closer and trudged on through the snow at a grueling pace, weak with lack of food. The limbs of trees were covered with glistening sheets of ivory like silken sails. The air was bitterly cold, icy talons clawing at their skin.

The Warriors climbed a hill and turned the bend, panting heavily with exertion. The forest suddenly ended ahead of them.

A large field lay before them, stretching for miles afar. Deep drifts of snow protected the fallow expanse. On the far side of the meadow was a band of pines that stretched over the horizon and into distant mountains. The mountains of Erias stood tall and domineering over the landscape; dark clouds perched ominously atop their shoulders.

Malecai looked to the others and informed them, "A snowstorm is blowing in from the north. We might be able to cross this field before then."

"How do you know there's a storm coming?" Aaron asked him.

Malecai smirked in reply. "Just wait."

**** ****

Darkness veiled the earth as the sun fell swift over the western peaks. The skies were eerily black, not a trace of starlight amidst the sea of clouds that now rolled over them.

The Warriors huddled around a fire, the cold of night lashing at their backs. Joshua was fast asleep, snoring contentedly. Aaron lay down on his mat and rested his head against the root of a tree. Malecai sat staring pensively into the fire, his face dancing in shadows. Silas sat beside Cain, carving a piece of wood with his knife. Adriel sat slightly away from the group, staring over the field they had crossed.

Cain unsheathed his sword and leaned against a tree. He held his weapon before him and rolled it in his hands.

The firelight played across the blade, a grinning sadist in the night.

He saw his reflection in the glowing steel, his haggard face staring back with sullen eyes. Those eyes had changed from what they once were. The light of them was long gone, and in their place was an atrocity.

He had killed his first man. After fifteen years of killing, this latest meant uncertainty for Cain. What was he becoming that extolled the killing of a man? And he did it with such a callous heart that now, outside the cloud of battle, it sickened him.

He had once promised Eileen that he would set aside the sword when their child was born. Now that his wife and son are dead, he could never fulfill that promise. He had nothing left in life but the revenge he so desperately hung onto.

Was that what Eileen would want? He looked at his reflection in the sword again. She would not even recognize him. He was so far gone from the man she fell in love with five years ago.

His heart burned now for blood, burned for a false sense of justice. He had changed drastically since the beginning of this journey. He fought for selfish ideas of vengeance and how it all would repay his sorrows in the end. He had forgotten what this war really meant, what was at stake for Tarsha, and humanity.

He could help end this war and put an end to Abaddon's genocide, but his own self-interest was nothing more than a hindrance to their cause. He could not continue like this, he knew he had to change. He knew Eileen would not want to see him like this.

He looked at each of his friends in turn. All of them were changing somehow, into pitiless offspring of war. They were no longer the carefree friends of his youth. They were now killers without regret, living only to appease the spirit of revenge that burned eternal.

And he was the worst of them. He knew where his feet were walking, but his soul was taking a much different path. He knew not where it was going; only that it stumbled every step of the way.

He looked at Adriel; the only one he felt had remained the same through their ordeals.

She glanced over at him, sensing his gaze. She locked eyes with him for a moment and smiled. He struggled to return her grin, but quickly dropped his gaze to the ground.

His sword lay limp in his hand and he gazed once more into its glowing depths. He sighed and stabbed it into the ground before standing up and walking over to Adriel.

"You seem troubled," she said as he sat down beside her. "What's wrong?"

Cain looked at her and turned away, staring out over the glistening field of snow. "I feel too much, and can't make sense of a single thought. I long to do what is right, but I cannot…"

Adriel rested a small hand on his shoulder. "It is better to feel than to have your heart turned cold."

A gust of wind blew through their camp, bringing with it the first breath of a looming storm.

"Too late for that," he jested as the wind whipped around them. Adriel let out a gasp and dove at his chest for warmth. The wind died after a moment and she pulled away from him, laughing lightly.

**** ****

The Warriors slept little through the night's bitter tempest and now rose to a brilliant scene.

Every inch of earth was covered in snow, every tree, limb, and rock. The early morning sun cast the snow in a vibrant light, flooding the world beneath a sea of ivory.

Their fire had long since died during the night and was now buried in a grave of snow.

They were ravenous and exhausted, and wanted nothing more than to stay where they were. Yet they knew they had to carry on. They packed their equipment and left behind their makeshift camp, trudging through the blankets of snow.

"Ilross is another day's walk from here," Malecai informed the group as they tore a path through the forest. The air was calm, not a breath of wind on its lips. It was deathly cold and lifeless, not a whisper of a heartbeat other than their own, nor the songs of birds to grace their ears.

The snow ended and they stumbled out into a barren field. The area was covered with frozen grass and filled with stumps of felled trees. Many of the larger stumps had iron axes imbedded in them as if left there for future use.

"A logging camp," Malecai said as he knelt to pick up a rusted chain. "We must be close to a village."

He stood up and dropped the chain in the snow. He rushed towards the tree line and the Warriors followed suit.

The shadows of the forests once again engulfed them. A narrow path extended from the field and weaved its way through the trees before trailing off into the depths of the pines.

Malecai beckoned the others to follow as he stepped into the trail. He led them down the path that was deeply scarred from the wheels of wagons.

The cart path led them through the trees and wound its way deeper into the forest. The Warriors followed the path and soon it led them to the edge of a cliff that overlooked a wooded valley below. The trail continued into the northeast, hugging closely to the cliff's edge.

Nearly a hundred buildings were clustered closely together in the gorge. They were all fashioned of timber, skillfully built even atop the jagged terrain.

As the travelers continued along the top of the valley, the remainder of the gorge rolled into view. Suddenly, a foul stench reached them and they peered into the edge of the village.

They noticed bodies scattered and mangled in the snow, barely visible through the thick trees. The Warriors quickly pulled out their weapons at the sight of this and ran to the edge of the cliff.

Malecai knelt down and scanned the trees. "Something is not right," he muttered. He bolted from the group and ran along the path, the others following close behind. They eventually reached a large hill and slid down it.

As they reached the bottom, an overbearing stench welcomed them. The Warriors raised their weapons and charged into the valley entrance.

They came under the shadow of massive rock walls that loomed above a long band of trees and snow that stretched out into the dark maw beyond. However, what they saw beyond the trees was far beyond comprehension.

Bodies littered the valley floor in the tens of thousands, stretching along the entire length of the gorge. Corpses were strewn along every inch of available space, piled on top of each other for several yards. Blood drenched the snow beneath them, forming a stagnant sea of scarlet. The overwhelming reek of death filled the air for miles and seemed as if to sap the very life from the earth.

The Warriors cautiously approached the mountain of dead, weapons held at the ready. They stepped into the trees and weaved their way deeper into the valley. They passed several piles of bodies consumed by fire. Billows of smoke rose into the treetops, filling the air with the reek of burning flesh.

They then heard the voices of men. They came around a pile of bodies and saw a score of soldiers ahead of them. They pulled several carts piled high with bodies. Two men overturned a cart and several others began throwing the bodies onto the mountain of deceased.

The men heard the crunching of the Warriors' boots in the snow and drew their swords. "Who's there?" The man in the middle shouted into the trees. The Warriors stepped into the clearing, weapons raised.

One of the soldiers charged towards them and threw his spear at Malecai. Malecai stepped to the side and grabbed the spear from the air. He spun it and tossed it in his hand before lobbing it back at its owner. The spear's shaft crashed into the man's face, breaking the weapon in half with a resounding crack. The man was thrown off his feet and fell to the snow, bleeding from his skull.

Malecai stepped forward. "We are the Warriors, lower your weapons."

The soldiers' eyes lit up with surprise and they immediately set their weapons down in the snow. They began whispering among themselves, pointing at the Warriors and eyeing them curiously.

"My apologies, Warriors," the middle soldier said, "We didn't know who you were." The Warriors sheathed their weapons and crossed the clearing.

Each soldier was covered head to foot in steel-scaled armor. Swords were belted to their sides and lances were strapped to their backs.

The man in the middle stepped away from the others. He removed the cowl tied around his mouth and bared a toothy smile.

He appeared older than the others, scarce under forty years of age. Hair the color of rotted hay fell around his sweaty brow. A large beard masked his chiseled face. Gray hazel eyes looked them over searchingly.

Flexible steel and leather armor of decorative green and gold adorned his stout frame.

He wore an exceedingly long, leather fauld that fell from his waist to his ankles and steel greaves that protected his legs. On his back was strapped a long spear, nearly nine feet in length, with three sharp blades on one end and a long spike on the other.

Two short swords were sheathed in decorative gold scabbards on his back. They were each several hands long, both identical in appearance. Their blades were fashioned of well-forged steel, the hilts of wrapped silver and the handles of gold-flecked leather.

"I am Isroc Braygon, son of General Hallus and a captain in the Grand Erias Army," the man said as he stopped before them. He held out his right hand where his third finger was missing. The Warriors gave their names and shook his hand in turn. "So travelers, what brings you to the beautiful town of Mordicon?"

"We are passing through," Malecai replied as he returned the man's inquisitive stare.

"Then it is a shame you have to see this," the man named Isroc said. He gestured toward the mountain of corpses beside them.

"What is all this?" Cain asked.

Isroc sighed and lowered his head. "It is the people of Erias. Ever since Abaddon dispensed his full forces into our country, they have been attacking our villages night and day. The people can do little to defend themselves, and this...is the result."

"Can you not defend them?"

"Alas," Isroc replied, "We try, but the armies of Andred are spread vast over Erias, and as a result our military is spread too thin. It's almost as if the Andreds are only after killing the innocent, not in fighting a war." He turned to his men and gestured at the now empty carts. "Take the last load; we'll be done after this."

He knelt down beside the unconscious man as the others disappeared through the trees with their carts. "Damn, he's out cold."

Malecai knelt down beside them and pulled a roll of bandages from his cloak. Together, the two men managed to wake the man and bind his wound. "Get your sorry ass out of my sight, Alec," he chided the man. Alec glared at Malecai and hobbled off after the other soldiers. Eventually they returned with full carts.

"We need to get out of here," Isroc said to them. "They're going to light the fires soon."

They began to walk alongside the mountain of bodies, passing thousands upon thousands of deceased.

Men, women, children and infants were haphazardly thrown together to form the towering heap. Blood and pus gushed from every gap, pouring over the bloated dead.

Maggots covered their rotting skin and vultures gorged themselves on the remains.

Lurid eyes stared at them lifelessly and fetid hands reached for them, lips calling despairingly, silently. Tiny hands of infants still grabbed longingly for their mothers, but love they would never find. It was everything the Warriors could do to hold back their tears.

"This village, Mordicon, was my home, where I grew up as a child," Isroc began. "My father, Hallus, had founded it many years ago, but when he became the General of the Erias Cavalry he left it in my stead. Shortly after, a battalion of Andreds attacked Mordicon and destroyed it. Everyone was killed, except for me. I was too young then, and in my naivety, I fled my own village and doomed my people to their demise. Mordicon has been abandoned ever since, but I had to return last week to finish this morbid task."

"That's awful," Adriel managed to mutter through abated tears.

"Is it?" Isroc retorted, "Or do I deserve this for my sin of cowardice. I may be a captain of men now, but it does not erase my past." .

They came to a small path that snaked its way to the top of the valley. They left the bodies behind and eventually reached the crest of the valley wall.

"Why are you doing this?" Silas asked the man.

"The King needs the people to cling to what little hope they have left if we are to push through this war. The number of our dead grows every day, and we need to hide them from the civilians. If they knew how many were really dying, they would be disheartened…and if that happens, then the enemy has won the war."

Adriel glanced at him questioningly. "The King orders you and your men to keep the truth from Erias's people? That's sick…"

"I don't agree with it either. However, I follow my orders as a soldier. War is no game, we do what we can do win. The King knows this, and if lying to his people will keep their hope alive, then so be it."

The group fell silent at this, contemplating Isroc's words. The skies above began to roar, echoes of thunder reverberating through the mountains. The sky began to darken for several minutes and slowly rain began to fall over the area. The storm grew in power and began drenching the forests, ice and sleet falling around them.

Then, a faint glow appeared in the valley below. Isroc's men appeared through the trees and stood beside the group. The glow began to flicker and flames leapt up around the bodies. The fires slowly consumed the corpses and black smoke began to rise into the skies. The stench of cooking flesh and boiling pus reached their noses.

The fires grew in size until they bound across the entire valley, setting every tree and building aflame. A sea of black smoke rose into the sky, rivers of embers ascending the foul winds. Flames roared and crackled in the dying valley, consuming Erias's fallen and the remains of what was once Mordicon.

Isroc bowed his head and choked back a tear. "Damn the Andreds, damn Abaddon. Such suffering he has brought upon us. And for what? Humanity does not deserve such a fate as this..."

Suffering and Shame

Night brought with it an expected cold. Snow swirled in the air and a fierce wind tore through the forests. The stench of burning flesh and smoke filled the soldiers' campsite as the distant inferno still burned strong. Isroc's men huddled around a large fire for warmth. The Warriors sat with Isroc away from the men, heartily devouring pounds of freshly cooked veal the soldiers had provided.

"I sure needed that," Joshua sighed as he patted his portly stomach. "Thank you, Isroc."

"Anything for you, my friends," the captain said. He leaned forward and struggled to hold back a smile. "I can't believe you went into the Alon Heath. No one has entered there in centuries. And to survive the clutches of the Iscara as well, you are truly astounding. Tarsha has done a great thing in placing its hopes on the six of you."

"Well," Joshua remarked, "not to boast...but aside from the murdering light, the madmen wanting to kill us, and our horses running off with our food, I say we've done a good job."

Silas laughed at him. "As if you have room to talk, you didn't even kill one Iscara. You're about as useful as Isroc's finger, wherever that is." The group laughed at this.

"In all seriousness," Isroc continued after a moment, "I cannot stress how great a thing you are doing for Tarsha. The people need unity, and you will bring it to them through the Alliance. You are truly the hope of Tarsha. You fight for the good of the people and our salvation from Abaddon's relentless genocide; you are truly noble in this cause." The four of Andaurel glanced at each other anxiously. Nothing they have done had been for that.

**** ****

The Warriors stood at the edge of Mordicon, their backs turned to the smoldering dead, smoke still rising into the crisp morn.

The new day's sun rose now at their backs, its light spreading across the heavens, bringing with it much-needed warmth.

Isroc approached the group with a bundle of rucksacks in hand. He dropped them in the snow at their feet and the Warriors thanked him for the supplies.

"It's nothing, my friends," he said, "It is the least I can do." He bowed humbly before them. "May I ask something of you though?" The Warriors nodded.

Isroc paused a moment and fingered his gray-flecked beard in thought. "May I go with you? To Morven that is?"

"What about your men?" Cain asked him.

"They know I wish to retire from the Army soon, I've been a soldier long enough. I have fought for far too long and have endured many a dreadful thing while serving my country. Maybe leaving the Army and traveling with you will be for the best."

"Well," Cain said, "We need every sword we can get."

"Then you have both of mine," Isroc proudly replied. He stepped forward and shook Cain's hand.

From behind them, Isroc's men approached and stopped beside them. Isroc turned and looked solemnly at each of them. They knew what he was going to do.

"Alec," he said to one of them, "I leave you in charge of my men. You will serve them well."

"You can't go now," the bandaged Alec pleaded, "We need you."

"No you don't. I am getting none the younger. It is time for me to leave. The Warriors passing through here was not of chance, it is a sign for me to move on to greater things and join them in their cause."

"But what of Hallus?" The man inquired. "Your father has been missing for three weeks now; you can't give up on him."

"I'm not giving up on him. He may just be at Morven, awaiting my arrival."

One of the men stepped forward. "Even so, we need you, sir," he implored.

"Yet the people of Erias need me more, you would do well not to hinder me. I'm leaving with the Warriors." He rested a hand on Alec's shoulder. "Listen, Alec. There are bigger things than us in this world. We all must learn to follow our fates, to whatever end we are destined. Each of us must accept the fate we are given and play our part."

Alec nodded and saluted his captain with as much respect as he could exhibit. Isroc saluted in return and shook the man's hand firmly.

Cain looked away from the group, struck with the power of this man's words. He struggled to have such faith, such selflessness.

Isroc shook each man's hand and said goodbye to them all. He then turned and faced the Warriors. "I'm ready."

**** ****

The Warriors followed Malecai across the constantly rolling landscape, weaving through the pines and climbing over the ever-changing countryside.

Streaks of snowfall fell from the skies, raining down around the travelers, their boots crunching loudly in the freshly fallen snow.

Malecai led them along the bank of a swift-flowing creek, rushing through the rocks toward some unknown destination. An endless sea of trees surrounded the miniscule travelers, spread dense across the snow painted mountainsides.

The branches of the towering pines stretched out from their trunks like the sails of mighty ships, clawing at their heads as they walked underfoot.

"Why were you going to Morven with your father?" Cain asked Isroc as they crossed the brook.

"My father is the head advisor of the King and leader of the Erias Cavalry. We were going to Morven to aid in its defense in case Morven is indeed the enemy's target. We were at my father's stronghold, Braygon, on the west coast when I received word from the King to...well you saw what I had to do. My father and I agreed we would meet up at Morven, but that was weeks ago, and I haven't heard word of him ever arriving there."

Malecai grunted from the head of the group. "Kings need their advisors, they are hopeless without them. It would be an enormous loss for our side if any one of them were killed. We are weak as it is, we cannot afford those kinds of losses. The enemy knows this and will exploit any advantage they have. Have you ever considered the fact that-"

Isroc suddenly bolted from the middle of the group. He threw a hand around Malecai's neck and pinned him against the trunk of a tree. The group immediately came to a halt, hands instinctively reaching for their weapons at the defense of their friend.

"You would do well not to finish that sentence..."

Malecai nodded at his threat. "Then you know it to be true...you are only in denial."

Isroc glared at him with contempt and slowly released his grasp around Malecai's neck. The two men glowered at the other for several moments.

Isroc clenched his fist and punched Malecai in the face. He slammed his fist into Malecai's jaw, a dull thud echoing through the trees from the impact.

Malecai pulled his head back from the blow and flicked his hair, loudly cracking his jaw as he returned Isroc's stare with indifference.

Isroc's disdain suddenly turned to an impassive mask as he struggled to shield his face from the sadness that fought to divulge.

"I thought as much," Malecai continued, "you cannot hide from the truth. Your father is dead."

Isroc returned his stare for a moment, rubbing his battered knuckles as he managed to regain his composure.

Malecai then turned and walked away from the others, following the bank of the creek and disappearing through the pines.

**** ****

They continued throughout the day, trudging through the knee-deep snow. Malecai led the group through the pines, following his mental bearings as the light of day faded from the skies.

After a while, Malecai threw down his rucksack. "We will arrive at Ilross by tomorrow. We rest for now."

The others sighed with relief and dropped their rucksacks before collapsing beneath a cluster of trees.

"Ill weather will set in soon. Many that travel die once the storms set in, few dare travel long in winter. I will go find firewood."

He brushed his cloak of ice and walked past the group. He stopped and glanced at Isroc who sat staring up at him, silently fingering his bruised and bloody knuckles.

Malecai reached into his cloak and threw a bundle of wrappings onto Isroc's lap. "Clean yourself up," he muttered, "we may need you."

**** ****

The Warriors sat around a large fire, circled together for warmth. Snow swirled around them, the cold clawing at their backs. Dusk had fallen hours prior but they could not find sleep in the growing storm. The fire danced vigorously in the wind, snow and ice whipping painfully across their faces. The Warriors sat encased in their cloaks, struggling to stave off the mind numbing cold.

"I'm sorry for striking you," Isroc muttered through the cowl tied around his mouth for warmth.

"Never apologize," Malecai replied, "It is a sign of weakness."

"Aye…I guess I've just been in denial about it. It is foolish to remain hopeful when your father is surely dead. After all that's happened to me, I guess I just wanted something good to hold on to."

"What happened?" Adriel asked him.

Isroc removed the cowl and stared pensive into the fire. "The death of my daughter, Claire. An Andred raiding party attacked the city we lived in, and she was killed in the struggle. I was with my father in Braygon when it happened. I received a letter a few weeks ago, saying that she was dead. I could have done something…if only I had been there. She was all I had…I've never endured such agony as I did that day, and I still feel its sting even now."

"I'm sorry for your loss," Cain apologized. He knew all too well the pain Isroc was facing.

"Thank you. But I know you four of Andaurel have suffered as much as I have. You have lost your home twice, your parents, your families and friends, yet still you push on for peace in this world. I envy your selflessness. I want to join you in the fight for what we believe in and will gladly die for, the salvation of our people."

**** ****

They woke the following morning to fresh snowfall. The massive pine trees above were heavy laden with jackets of snow, falling like rain as the branches shook from their burden. A light snow drizzled down from the clouds above. The Warriors climbed out of their icy tombs and shook the ice from their clothes.

"Eat quickly," Malecai ordered, "We leave soon."

The Warriors drew out their morning meal, gnawing on the dried lamb in silence as the songs of distant birds filled the trees.

"Damn," Silas cursed. He pulled his boots off and held them upside down. "It's cold as hell. There's snow in my boots." He shook them vigorously and a small shower of snow fell from the openings.

Joshua walked over to him, removed a boot and held it over his brother, snow cascading over his head. "So do I."

He laughed and walked towards his rucksack as Silas shook the snow from his hair, hissing with disdain.

Malecai laughed and turned from the group. He kicked snow over the remains of their fire and slung his broadsword over his shoulder.

The company at last left the cluster of pines behind and trudged through the snow before ascending the side of a hill. They climbed higher and higher, slowly working their way above the forests.

They eventually reached the top and came to a long ridge of rock that formed a kind of bridge towards the foot of a distant mountain. Its peak loomed far above the earth, an avarice hand reaching boundless for the heavens.

Dark clouds swathed its girth, a cloak of shadows draped over its shoulders. They spit snow across the wilderness below, an eternal storm of unremitting fury. The tempest soon blew over the Warriors and swallowed them in its blinding gale. Wind whipped around them, buffeting the travelers with snow and ice. The storm lashed savagely around them as they struggled to see through the sheets of snow.

The hours passed as they battled their way through a dogged storm. As the veiled sun began its arcing descent, the Warriors could scarcely make out the outline of Ilross in the cradle of distant mountains.

They began the slow struggle through the mountains, flogged right and left by ruthless winds. They followed the edge of the peaks and peered through the snow to the cragged gorge below.

The Warriors continued for hours in silence, trudging through the ever-growing snow.

They eventually passed the mountains and descended their treacherous slopes. They soon reached level ground.

A band of green appeared through the snow and the Warriors stepped into this forest, shielded from the storm by mighty pines. They breathed a sigh of relief and continued through the trees, the time wasting away to the crunch of their boots.

The storm eventually subsided, and as the sun finally began to dip its gilded feet over the horizon, they left the forests and came before Ilross.

Through the faint flurry, they could see a large field stretched out before them over a mile in every direction. White capped mountains encircled the field, their jagged peaks clawing at fading sunlight. A city sprawled across the expanse, its stone buildings barely perceived in the growing dark.

"Ilross…" Malecai murmured and gestured for them to follow. They traversed the field and soon their boots met the smooth brick of a road. They followed its straight path towards the town, stepping through the piles of snow that covered the street.

Two guards armed with glaives saluted the Warriors as they walked between the first two buildings of the city. The Warriors nodded curtly at the soldiers as they passed.

They stepped into the town, instantly encompassed by its many buildings. Brick and timber shops and homes lined the streets, their doors and windows all facing inward. Row after row of these structures lined the road, many two or three stories in height.

Columns of smoke rose from the chimneys of many of these, the hearths inside of which were filled with simmering food and crackling fires. The city was silent and somber, as quiet as the snow that fluttered to its streets.

They soon came to a tall building that stood a floor or so above the surrounding buildings. A wooden sign hung above its entrance, rickety in the wind.

Malecai halted under the sign and wrapped his fingers around the door's iron handle. "From here on you are to be cautious. Speak to no one. The Iscara has spies lurking in every rat hole in Erias." With that, he pushed the door open and walked inside.

They came into a large tavern, the floor and ceiling made entirely of dark gray stone and its walls of timber planking. Several round tables were scattered across the room, an inadequate number of wooden chairs surrounding each of them. An over-sized hearth stood opposite of the entrance, a fire burning vivaciously inside its open maw.

A long bar stretched along the wall to their left, stools placed haphazard along its length. Massive kegs lined the bar's wall, lying prostrate on a heavy iron rack. Few people filled the room and even less awake or sober.

The few awake glanced up from their drinks to the door flying open with a burst of frigid wind. Their eyes bore into the Warriors as they walked into the room. The remaining guests of the inn stood up from their tables and quickly left the room.

The Warriors approached a man in dingy gray clothes who stood behind the bar, listlessly wiping the inside of a mug with a soiled cloth. He stared transfixed into the glass, clearly disinterested in the task at hand. "Rooms for seven,"

Malecai muttered to the bartender as he drew a satchel from his cloak.

The man opened his mouth as Malecai took a handful of silver from his coin purse. He placed them onto the bar in front of the man, glancing up as he did so.

The innkeeper opened his mouth again but Malecai dumped half the bag's contents onto the tabletop. The bartender lifted a brow, accepting the offer.

"Speak nothing of our presence here, we go unhindered and unnoticed," he commanded as the man held out a hand to take the coins. "Understood?" He threw his hand over the pile.

"Not a word," the man replied hastily.

Malecai nodded and withdrew his hand, allowing the innkeeper to grab the coins before he could change his mind. "We will take your largest room." He returned his coin purse to the depths of his cloak and walked away from the bar, leading the others towards an arched hallway.

"It must have been a hard loss to accept," a voice said from behind them. The others continued down the hall, unaware of the voice that called to them. Cain turned and searched the entrance room to find the source of the voice. The voice spoke again. "It must have broken you. Andaurel's demise."

Cain suddenly noticed three figures that had previously been overlooked. They sat around a large round table, curiously searching Cain.

The man in the middle was much older than the others, his face worn and haggard. Muddy russet hair fell over his dark eyes. A small, scraggly beard covered his gaunt face and he clenched a pipe between brown teeth.

The man on his right had a young, stalwart face, short black hair, and eyes of glazed emerald. He wore a full set of blackened steel armor over his toned frame. A woman in black cloth and leather sat on the left of them, long auburn hair flowing down her shoulders.

The man in the middle leaned back on his chair's hind legs and propped his boots on the tabletop.

"What? It's none of your concern." Cain turned and began to follow his friends down the hall before the man's voice stopped him in his tracks.

"Ah, but it is," the middle man replied. "All of your concerns are Tarsha's concerns. You are a marked man, Taran. There is no turning back."

Cain stood frozen at this. He glanced over his shoulder at the man, and returned his solemn stare.

"What is it?" Adriel asked as she and the others returned to the archway.

"Warriors," the man called as he noticed the others. "Please, sit with us. Drinks on him," he said as he nudged the man on his right.

The second man laughed and stood up before approaching the bar.

"Please, take a seat," the older man said, "The night is still young." The Warriors warily approached and pulled several chairs up to the table. "I am Jiran, son of Siphus," The man said.

He pulled his boots off the table, sending the front legs of his chair slamming back onto the stone floor.

"This is Shara, daughter of Ismond." He gestured towards the woman.

"And this is Heric, son of Morein," he nodded at the shorthaired man returning to the table with a tray laden with mugs of ale.

The two groups stared uncomfortably at the other for several moments, an uneasy tension filling the room.

"Please...drink," Jiran gestured towards the mugs. Jiran and Heric reached towards the tray and removed mugs of their own. "It must be difficult knowing the Knights of Iscara haunt your every step. Even now, their spies may be watching...but as long as you are in Ilross, we will protect you."

"Who are you?" Malecai asked as the Warriors cautiously took the remaining mugs. The man raised a brow at this. "Who are you, Jiran?" Malecai repeated tersely.

The man chewed on his pipe and pondered the question for a moment before replying. He blew a ring of smoke. "I am a captain of the Vilante. My company has been stationed at Ilross, for the time being at least."

"Vilante?" Isroc asked as he wiped the frothy ale from his beard.

Heric interrupted his superior with sudden enthusiasm. "I'll tell them. The Vilante were a division of the scouting force of Erias, but now we are largely a civilian force, an army of men and women who seek revenge and the blood of our enemies."

"I have heard nothing of you," Isroc replied, suspicion rising in his voice. "I was a captain of the twelfth regiment, I would know of this Vilante if you speak the truth."

Heric shook his head slowly. "The King has separated us from all military amalgamation, we follow a new creed. Our country is in desperate need of a defensive force to protect its dispersed and isolated towns. Millions of our people have been put to the sword in these four centuries of war. In response to the recent influx in enemy troops, the King pulled the Vilante from the Army and dispersed us across the country in hopes of defending our villages against the raiders of Andred."

"So you're a militia?" Isroc questioned the man.

"More or less," Jiran replied, "we take every man and woman who seeks our ranks. With civilians being slaughtered everyday, their friends and family come to find solace by the sword. Our numbers swell daily with the blood drunk and vengeful." Silence followed his words. The group sipped their mugs in thought.

Eventually Isroc broke the silence. "I was sent to my destroyed hometown to dispose of the bodies of our fallen countrymen. Thousands we had to burn…I will never forget such a smell."

Shara nodded at this. "You are not alone. The Andreds will continue to bring death upon Tarsha, destroying and burning as they go. They will not relent. It is the Vilante's solemn duty to defend our countrymen, down to the last man if we must."

Jiran glanced over at the young woman and set his mug down before speaking. "Their attacks will never cease. However, the King; with good reason, senses an attack on Morven. This would be a tremendous undertaking for the enemy.

'Morven is the largest and most heavily defended citadel the world has ever known. A siege on such a mighty bastion will take nearly all of his troops and vast resources. Abaddon has never before dared risk an open siege on Morven; it is a bold and risky play of his cards. However, if he succeeds in crushing Morven, then Tarsha will surely crumble, and the tyrant's genocide will rage unhindered until all are lay to ruin.

'With great reward comes great risk, and Abaddon knows this well. If we defeat him at Morven, then his armies will be severely crippled, and we may very well see an end to this war. Therefore, he must ensure his strength and gather his armies.

'We see before us the eye of the storm. The Andreds have not been sighted in over a week. This can only be the result of their withdrawal. I feel they will soon begin their march for Morven.

'Our capital calls for aid in this lull, but few come from our country, and even fewer from over our borders. Morven's defense is slowly gathering, but at our present strength, we will wither if the enemy chooses to attack."

Cain ran a hand through his hair as he gazed out the glass paned window beside them. "Wait," he asked, "you said genocide…what do you mean?"

Jiran blew a cloud of smoke from his pipe and leaned across the table. "How is it that a man can live for over four hundred years? It is because he is immortal. He is beyond the confines of man. His body never ages, his mind never fails with the changes of the seasons. That is the essence of Abaddon, hardly human, not of death, not of life, always alive but never living. His vengeance never quenched, his anger never appeased.

'I speak of the genocide he has brought upon humanity. At the hands of an angry god, we were cursed for our sins and sacrilege. We turned our backs on faith, and in return, were given Abaddon. He is our curse, our punishment, our destroyer. We may never escape it..."

Shara nodded at this. "You cannot cheat the will of the heavens, if there is indeed anything beyond this hell. If divinity calls for the death of man, then damned we will be. Abaddon is the vessel of heavenly order, and if he is called to purge us of the sins of our forefathers, then through death we meet our just reward."

"Great..." Silas mumbled, "More of this shit."

Heric ignored Silas's remark and looked at Shara questioningly. "You speak as if we fight for nothing."

"Who are we to question anything," she replied, "we fight Abaddon because it is in our nature to do so. If we do not fight, then we die. It's nothing more, nothing less." Cain nodded.

The group soon fell quiet. The power of her words and the weight they carried sunk heavy in the hearts of the Warriors. The sound of rain began to patter against the tavern windows. Shara stood up and walked towards the bar.

"But why us..." Cain asked the Vilante. "Why Andaurel?"

Jiran took a swig of his ale before replying. "To tell you the truth, we don't really know. No one knows why Abaddon so meticulously attacked your homes." The four of Andaurel gazed into the hearth, its light flickering warmly against the inn's walls.

"But do not worry," Shara said as she returned with another tray of mugs. "Someone is sure to find out. The truth is bound to reveal itself to you eventually."

Jiran nodded and leaned over the table. "Everything happens for a reason, Warriors. The attack on Andaurel, no matter what anyone says, was neither blind nor random. It was deliberate.

'Despite your Dun Ara being vulnerable, Abaddon deliberately chose Andaurel as his target, and no such attack could have been conceived without intent. There indeed was a purpose behind it all, but that remains hidden for now."

"But what of the attack on our town twenty two years ago?" Aaron asked Jiran. The Vilante pushed his empty mug forward and grabbed another from the tray.

"You are not the secret hand of kings as you were before. All of Tarsha knows of you and your journey to unite us like the Alliance of Ivandar long ago.

'However, little information has been leaked of your various histories. Very few even know of the assault on Andaurel over two decades ago. I am not the one who has the answers you seek."

"But what do you think?" Aaron asked him.

The man fingered his beard a moment. "I think...that both attacks were not random, they are more than arbitrary links in the chain of events." Silence followed, no sound filled the room save the crackle of the fire.

"Damn it!" Cain cried out suddenly, slamming his mug on the table. "Why! Why has all of this happened to us?" He hung his head low, his hair falling over his face. He shook with repressed anger, suppressed sorrow.

His hand clenched fiercely around the handle of his mug, the other shaking on the table, nails digging into his palms.

"We've lost everything! We have nothing and we fight for nothing! Why us? Why any of us? No one deserves such suffering!" He continued to clench his fist until his knuckles turned white and blood trickled onto the tabletop. "No one deserves such suffering…"

The Final Calling

Cain rose from his bed heaving with exhaustion. Beads of sweat poured down his face. He panted heavily, blinking as he looked around the room.

His friends were asleep, sprawled under the thick wool sheets of their beds. A hearth was cut out of the stone on the opposing wall, a dying fire clinging desperately to life in its iron maw. Cain hung his head and closed his eyes before exhaling deeply.

Flashes of his past ravaged his thoughts. Andaurel's buildings burning, men he had known his entire life dying around him, slaughtered by Abaddon's ruthless puppets. His life narrowly taken in Abraxas, more lives falling forfeit to the wanton hand of death. The Knights of Iscara in Alon Heath who hunted them down like animals. Their lives hung ever on the brink, their sanity, his sanity, stepping one-step closer to the edge with every passing day.

Most of all however, images of his dead wife and son hung like shadows over his eyes, haunting his every thought. Eileen's blood spilt across the earth, her body mutilated, his child reaching lifelessly to its father.

Cain sat up from his bed, tears brimming in his eyes. The moon peered occasionally through the clouds, its faint light filling the room before disappearing behind a shroud of passing clouds. The moonlight faded, darkening the room for a moment before slowly returning. Cain noticed Malecai under the window.

He sat atop his bed, left knee raised, his arm propped against it. His bright eyes gazed out the frosted window, the moon shining against his face.

A large cloud rolled across the sky, shielding the moon for several moments before casting the room in a pearly facade once again.

"Never think you are weak," Malecai muttered in the still room. "Your scars make you stronger, never forget that." Cain stared into the moon swathed face of his friend.

"Ideas lead to action, action leads to character, and a man's character shapes the path he must follow. Yours is that of revenge, a path that reaps naught but death and sorrow; for this you have set upon yourself...and if you are not careful, it will lead only to your downfall."

"I don't understand. What are you talking about?"

The room fell to darkness once again. Malecai's eyes seemed to pierce the very blackness profound. "You will come to understand, before the end of it all."

**** ****

Morning came at last, filling the city of Ilross with the rays of early morn. The sunlight split the skies and the clouds rolled away, bathing the earth in an array of accruing hues.

The Warriors rose grudgingly out of their beds. They walked over towards the table beside the door and stretched with sleep.

A large tray of meats and cheeses sat on the tabletop. A long loaf of bread and a bowl of fat lay beside a pitcher of slightly dirty water.

They donned their armor and ate heartily, emptying the tray of its contents as the room filled with the sun's amber light.

Cain set his empty goblet on the tray. "Let's go." He threw open the door and led the others out of the room.

They walked down the long hall, their boots echoing loudly in the silence. They followed the winding halls and soon came out into the main room.

Several men and women were dotted across the various tables, eating and drinking merrily with the vigor of a new day.

Jiran stood in front of the door, blocking the exit with his tall frame. "You weren't thinking of leaving without a goodbye were you?"

"We must get to Morven as quickly as possible, we dare not tarry," Malecai said as he shouldered his broadsword.

Jiran nodded. "Of course, I wouldn't think to delay you any further than I already have." He stepped aside from the door and unfolded his arms.

"Good luck to all of you. We Vilante wish you well." Suddenly, every man and woman in the room stood up from his or her seat. Silence followed as the Vilante proudly saluted the Warriors.

The Warriors saluted back and turned to Jiran. "Thank you for everything, Jiran," Cain thanked the man.

After shaking his hand, they followed Malecai out the door. "Goodbye Warriors...our paths will cross again someday," Jiran called out after them. "May the good will of Tarsha be with you." He returned to the inn with a final wave and closed the tavern door.

The Warriors left the inn and followed the road north. The tan brick of the main road led them through the middle of Ilross, the tall gray and brown buildings covered in freshly fallen snow.

Men and women roamed the streets, children weaving playfully through the crowds. Soldiers and Vilante patrolled the road, tirelessly protecting this isolated town.

Following the main road, the Warriors soon came to the edge of the town and stopped before a field of snow.

"Morven is about seven days from here," Malecai informed the group. "Our time runs thin."

The seven stepped from the edge of Ilross and left the city behind. They trudged across the field and gradually approached the feet of the surrounding mountains.

As they walked into the shadow of a mountain, they noticed a small path cutting up its side. They began to climb this steep path, their knees sinking into the snowy furrows.

Eventually, they ascended the pathway and came to a long valley-like formation that cut its way through the mountains.

They soon came out of the other end of the gorge, stepping from the shadows as they came out onto a large plateau.

The travelers crossed the rocky plateau and came before the edge. They stood awestruck at what lay before them.

Hundreds of mountains seemed to fill all the earth, dotted across a jagged and twisted landscape. The mountains stood like monolith watchmen over their domain. They stretched far into the clouds, their peaks embellished in sunlight, their cragged forms garnished in robes of ivory. The Warriors stood now before all of Erias, its true face revealed at last.

Malecai glanced at the others as they stood in disbelief at the battle ahead. "Erias…it is beautiful is it not?" The others nodded in reverential silence.

He turned and gazed out over the endless expanse before them. "Seven days…make that a fortnight."

**** ****

For weeks, the Warriors traveled across Erias, slowly crossing the vast wilderness, passing over mountains and endless valley chains, trudging through the snow and ice ever towards the country's capital.

Snowstorms blew across the countryside, striking with crippling winds and blinding snow. The sun rose and fell, its perpetual cycle binding the horizon lines, days blending and nights slipping ever to dreams.

Over two fortnights had passed as the Warriors at last arrived at the doorstep of Morven.

The sun peered over the eastern horizon as they came to a lofty hill. The travelers ascended the slope as it wound its way through the forests. Eventually they came out atop its crest and paused to catch their breath.

An enormous snow-covered expanse stretched for miles ahead of them. Numerous mountains lined the field and a chain of peaks extended from these, stretching southwest across half the field. The Alar River poured from the mouth of these beasts, flowing southwest across the expanse before being swallowed by the surrounding mountains.

The citadel of Morven, capital of Erias and the mighty jewel of Tarsha stood defiant in the middle of the field, its imposing walls stretching for miles in all directions, forming a kind of misshapen oval that encompassed the Icadras Mountains.

The mighty Alar split the citadel in half, running from one side to the other through great sluice gates.

The walls of the city towered far above the surrounding plains, well over twenty yards in height and many in girth, fashioned entirely of white and silver stone.

Every few yards along the causeways were outcroppings that housed immense trebuchets. The great beasts of war eyed the edges of the field, monstrous stones loaded in their nets ready at a moment's command.

Thousands of armored men roamed the causeways, pacing the intricate network of bridges and catwalks that loomed far above the city.

From the Warriors' vantage point, they noticed thousands upon thousands of gray buildings that filled the interior of the city's walls like the sands of a shore. White limestone roads webbed through the city. Two mountains loomed far above the mightiest of buildings, one on the farthest bank of the Alar, the other on the southern half.

"This," Adriel stammered as they stared in disbelief at the majesty before them, "This is amazing…" The group stood in wonder at the gem of Erias shining over them.

"The armies of Andred would be foolish to attack such a city," Aaron muttered after moments of silence.

"Foolish?" Malecai retorted, "Or wise?"

"Either way…" Cain shrugged, "We've got a job to do, let's see that it gets done."

The others nodded in response and the group began the long descent towards the city. They eventually came to the edge of the field, ice thrashing about them as they fought through the endless expanse.

After nearly an hour of walking, their legs numb from cold and bodies haggard, they at last came to the front gates of the city.

Two lofty statues stood on either side of the doors, looming many yards above both gate and wall. They were identical in appearance, made of pure granite to match the surrounding snow.

They were carved in the likeness of kings, armored head to foot and regal swords raised above their heads, blades crossing in midair above the city.

The Warriors approached the gates, their eyes raised to the heavens in awe as they stared up at the statues, the mere toes of which were to their heads.

The gate between the kings nearly reached the top of the walls around it. The doors were fashioned of darkened iron, its edges lined with tempered steel. Murals of clashing armies and winged beasts covered the doors, all ornately fashioned of bronze.

The doors were securely shut and sealed; not a handle or latch to be found on the outside of the seemingly impenetrable gates. These doors formed the only entrance in the endless miles of walls, daunting and forever indomitable.

Several men in steel plate armor peered over the gate, curiously eyeing the distant travelers below.

"We are the Warriors!" Malecai cried up to the guards. "Let us in!"

"We were informed of only four!" one of the guards shouted, "Yet you bring seven!"

"We need all the swords we can get!" Cain replied.

"Very well!" the sentry answered. "Stand back!" The guards left the edge of the causeway. Soon, the grinding of rusted iron rang out across the city as gears cranked in some hidden pocket of the city's wall.

The Warriors stepped back as the doors split, at last coming to a stop with a groan of metal. They approached the gateway and crossed under the arch before entering the capital city of Morven.

A wide road of pearly brick stretched far before them and disappeared far into the distance. Tall buildings of white and gray stone lined the shoulders of the streets in orderly rows.

Thousands of people roamed the streets, filling the wide road from shoulder to shoulder. The crowds flowed unbridled in all directions like a churning sea. The city roared with the talk and shouts of its citizens, an overwhelming din that shook the Warriors where they stood.

The Warriors sighed at the challenge at hand and dove into the crowd, instantly swallowed in the masses.

The noise filled their ears, drowning out all else. A wave of various odors hit them as they entered the crowd, the reek of sewage, sweet aromas of perfumes and oils, strong spices and foods, the stench of animals and the thick stink of human sweat. Steam and smoke rose from the trade stalls that lined the buildings, water boiled, herbs burned, and foods roasted behind droves of eager buyers.

Horses burdened with rider and cargo rushed through the crowds, people scattering to the edges of the road to avoid the aggravated animals and even more irritable drivers.

Weapons, clothes, cookware, foods, spices, boots and sandals, bridles and tack, fishing gear, and virtually every item fashioned by the hand of man or earth filled the hundreds of market stalls.

Clothes hung out to dry were draped over wires above the street. Smoke rose from the stone chimneys of the surrounding homes, and children peered out of the windows down on the streets below, eyeing the Warriors with youthful curiosity.

"I hate markets," Malecai muttered after violently shoving a man aside, forcing him to drop a basketful of fish to scatter in the crowds.

After several minutes, they came to a large stone courtyard that stretched off in all directions for hundreds of yards. They left the market behind and passed a tall five-tiered fountain in the middle of the court.

Water rolled down its stone basins before falling into a large bowl that housed its crystalline water.

A naked statue of a woman bowed over the fount, a jar cradled in her hands from which the water poured. White wings protruded from her back and curled over her breast.

Her beautiful figure however was battered and worn with age, perhaps even physical abuse. Large cracks wove across her ivory skin and one foot was entirely removed.

With a rock-sized hole in the side of her face, it was clear this statue had been through several attempts at removal or destruction. Now it stood abandoned and discarded by the hearts of the people, reduced to a sad state from its once former glory.

The Warriors looked curiously up at the statue as they crossed the court and came to the docks.

Ahead of them was an open area of stone brick and wood planking. Barrels of nets, fishing gear, bait, and assorted freshly caught fish were dotted across the area.

Men hustled across the planks with handfuls of equipment, swarming the docks like bees in frenzy.

The Alar stretched vast before them, wide enough to fit several ships in its girth, stern-to-stern, and long enough to fit endless more.

Massive ships floated languidly in its icy waters, their white sails flapping in the morning breeze. Gangplanks were dropped and men scurried on and off the ships, passing crates and barrels between themselves in an ostensibly erratic fashion.

The Warriors slowly approached the docks, their boots dully thudding on the wooden planks.

Tall machines of timber lined the river, lifting huge crates from the ships with their ox-powered arms.

They weaved through these machines and the endless piles of crates and barrels, dodging men as they crossed the docks. They eventually came to the edge of the riverbank and approached two mighty towers.

Malecai glanced up at the towers and flicked his hand towards the other riverbank. The soldiers atop the closest tower noticed him and nodded in reply.

They then grabbed the arms of a large gearwheel and sent the lever in a slow spin. The guards atop the other tower followed likewise, and as they did so, the wooden drawbridge between the towers began to fall from its chains. Its iron capped end at last reached the opposite riverbank and thudded loudly in the snow.

The Warriors passed under the towers and crossed the drawbridge. They stepped off the bridge, leaving half the city in their wake.

Before them was an empty expanse of dark gray stone that stretched off for half a mile in every direction. They grudgingly stepped forward and began the long walk deeper into the city's abyss.

After a while, the faint outline of buildings rose afar, crawling ever closer with every step they took.

The travelers crossed the court and at last reached the buildings. They came to a single road of brick, entirely encompassed by a sea of bleak stone structures.

Men in polished steel sat outside the barracks, many deep in sleep or talking lightly amongst each other. Coins and cards were tossed between small groups, laughter breaking out occasionally. However, a tense silence seemed to fill the area, every man playing his routine with furtive unease.

The Warriors passed the soldiers, fighting the impulse to return their inquisitive stares.

A few of them muttered inaudibly to their friends, the recipients of the whispered message returning their attention to the passer-bys with newfound interest. Many of them saluted the Warriors, but no word need be said.

The Warriors continued down the road, passing thousands of soldiers in their walk. The barracks stretched on for over a mile, forming an endless sea of building and man that must have engulfed half the city in its girth.

The road climbed ahead at a gradual rate and the Warriors ascended the hill through eerie silence, inquisitive stares and fleeting whispers greeting them around every corner.

A mountain stood about a quarter mile ahead of them, towering far above the infinitesimal buildings that surrounded it.

From the streets below, the Warriors could vaguely make out the blurred outline of a road that wound its way around the edges of the cragged mountain, spiraling its way up to the peak adorned in cloud.

They came to the end of the road and the last of the barracks, immediately encompassed in the shadow of the mountain. They reached the foot of the mount and looked up its slope with widened-eyes.

A hood of clouds cast opaque over its peak, its girth cloaked in dismal mists. It seemed to extend beyond the very heavens, like a great hand clawing for unseen stars.

The road ahead sloped drastically up the mountain's base, forcing its way up the rocky mountainside before disappearing around the opposing side.

The Warriors reluctantly stepped forward, their knees at an instant bend as they took those first steps. They followed the river of bricks up the mountain's edge for several minutes before coming to a small building that sat on the side of the road, its back wall level with the edge of the cliff, the barracks a hundred feet below.

The building was made of solid gray stone, a single window and door facing the road.

A large tower stood on the building's right side, attached to the wall and looming a few yards over the tiled roof.

They walked uneasily past the silent, vacant building, not a trace of life within its lackluster walls. In fact, they had seen no one at all on this side of the river other than soldiers.

The life of the city seemed to reside on the opposing side. It was as if the city was split in two extremes, one of life, the other embraced in silent death. The stillness and utter emptiness of the place hung like a weight of lead over their shoulders.

They continued up the steep road and left the empty watchtower. The road led them in a constant spiral around the mount, ascending ever higher.

They came across several more buildings, each identical in appearance. They peered curiously into the arrow-slit windows for signs of life, but every building was devoid of former inhabitants.

They continued slowly and painfully around the outer rim of the mountain, struggling to reach the distant peak.

The hours dragged slowly on. They left beneath them the earth forlorn and climbed into boundless clouds. A clinging haze embraced them, a bone-chilling cold gnawing at their skin.

They were now far above the city. The buildings below appeared now like the grains of sand on a vast gray shore, the streets like threads of a spider's web.

They turned the curve of the road and came to a life-sized statue of a soldier, sword drawn, the blade's tip stating the road's end before them. They crossed under the statue and followed the path around yet another bend.

A staircase stood a few yards ahead of them, the final stretch of the road. With a thespian sigh, the Warriors began the long ascent.

They finally reached the top of the staircase as evening gave way to the early holds of night, falling over themselves as they reached the top of the stairway. They collapsed on the cold stone, breathing heavily as they felt every inch of their muscles pulse with exertion.

They stood up after several moments and regained their composure before observing their newest surroundings.

They stood now at the edge of the mountain's peak, towering miles above the city and far above the mountain range from which the Alar poured. They were above most of the clouds, hundreds of the light gray masses sailing the lazed winds of dusk below.

The sun now fell over the horizon and crawled behind the crests of Erias's mountains, the last of daylight snuffed beneath darkling skies. A strong breeze blew across the peak, the frozen gale sweeping their breath away.

"No wonder no one's on this damn mountain," Joshua muttered to the group as he leaned on his knees, struggling for breath in the thin air. "It's a bastard to climb." The others laughed, at last breaking the hours of tense silence.

They then noticed several guards mere yards away, eyeing them conspicuously. The ten or so men wore black silk cloaks and bore heavy sets of silver armor that covered the white chain mail and silks beneath.

"The King has been expecting you, Warriors," one of them informed the newcomers as they approached, "welcome to the heart of Morven." The Citadel Guard gestured behind them towards the center of the courtyard that formed the flat peak of the mountain.

Across the silver court stood a large building fashioned of white, gray-flecked marble. The building stood four stories in height, its front supported by columns of ivory that gleamed like the light of Alon Heath.

They accepted the guard's gesture and stepped forward, keen to leave the mountain path.

As they crossed the court, Joshua turned and noticed a man brushing a horse. The horse was fully bridled and tethered to a small wooden cart, surrounded by crates and barrels of food and ales.

He eyed the horse and cart with a raised brow, looking over his shoulder at Silas with a grin. His brother followed his gaze and smirked as he saw the cart. Together they glanced behind them towards the steep mountain road. They laughed lightly and followed after the others, not daring to take their eyes off the now swift-looking cart and its glistening brass wheels. The group soon came to the foot of the building.

Two statues stood on either side of the staircase that led to the front door.

The left statue stood over twenty feet in height and was made of solid marble. It was fashioned in the figure of a man donned in glorious armor, massive wings extending in both directions from its hunched back. In its hand was a spear, the point attached to the dais upon which it stood.

The statue on the right was the same size and structure as the other, its wings curving up gracefully from its back. In her right hand she bore a sword, and in her left, was an ivory rose which she held up to the heavens.

The statues were carved with almost inhuman skill, far beyond the artistry of common man. However, despite the beauty and power from their image alone, they were much like the other winged statue they had passed in the city below. They were broken, cracked, and beaten from more than just the destructive hands of time.

It was obvious they had endured attempts at damage and ruin and they bore proudly the scars of that struggle. Their faces were cracked beyond recognition, their wings broken in several places. Yet they stood defiant in the face of time, as if refusing the very iniquities of the world they stood guard over.

The Warriors eyed the statues inquisitively, more so than the palace before them.

Adriel held her hand out to the statue on the right as they passed, her thin fingers brushing against the cold stone of its wings. The Warriors crossed the statues and reluctantly turned their gaze before them.

The Citadel Guards stopped as they reached the tall, gold doors that served as the main entrance to the palace. Two of the men grabbed the bullion handles and pulled the doors. A wave of warm air issued from the open archway.

The guards gestured inside and the Warriors stepped forward and entered the palace. One of the guards followed after them and the others shut the doors with an echo that reverberated loudly in the entrance room.

They stood now in a circular room, walls of white marble surrounding them from all sides. Torches lined the walls every few feet, their small ruddy lights flickering against the marble backdrop.

The guard led them across the tiled floor towards an archway that stood opposite the entrance. They crossed under it and came out into a long hallway.

The hall was made entirely of pure, shimmering marble. Forty columns lined the hallway, supporting the flawless glass ceiling above. Strange, ornate beasts were attached to every other column, vapors of sweet frankincense rising from their maws.

The Warriors stepped out from the archway and were immediately engulfed in a shadow, and glancing up, they saw a large statue that spanned from the crest of the archway to the ceiling above.

It was carved intricately in the form of a valiant man, adorned in granite armor. Below the statue was carved into the wall, "Ivandar, King of the Advent."

They quickly drew their attention back to the hallway as the guard stepped forward and walked down the black runner towards the middle of the hall.

The Warriors followed close behind, their boots clicking on the marble floor. They passed the golden columns that hid paned windows behind them, the dim light of evening still clinging to their marble sills.

At the end of the hall was a silver throne standing atop a dais. A man sat in its wide seat, the tall back of which was etched in ancient writings of a long forgotten tongue.

The man looked up at the approaching group, his face instantly lit with surprise. He nearly leapt from the throne, cantering swiftly down the dais as he came to a halt before them.

Lifeless auburn hair fell far past his shoulders, set in place by a crown of lustrous white gold. Light blue eyes seemed to smile at them. He had a sharp nose and a shaven face that hid a quick-witted mind.

A black cloak fell from his shoulders and draped down to his ankles, attached around his chest by a silver brooch. He wore a tunic of silver and black silks, dark leggings and polished boots that reflected off the marbled floor.

The Citadel Guard knelt before the man and bowed his head. "Darius, King of Erias and Lord of Morven. Bow before your lord."

Malecai turned to the others as he knelt to the ground and the others followed likewise.

"Rise, soldiers," King Darius commanded with a soft, fluid voice.

They stood up and the King gestured to the guard. "Leave us be, we have many matters to discuss." The guard bowed again, and with a flick of his cloak, turned on his heel and retreated through the archway.

Darius looked over each of the Warriors in turn, his eyes locked with theirs as if searching for the answer to an unasked question. He tilted his head a moment and nodded lightly. He spoke in a breathless whisper.

"All of you have been through a great many trials, but I see a few of you have not been together for long. You must learn to play each other's strengths and weaknesses to your advantage; unity among many is crucial. Individuals fall, but together they may stand firm against the tide.

'That is the philosophy Ivandar set for his newly created Alliance long ago, guiding it until its ruin. His philosophy guided kings, soldiers, and commoners alike against the tyrant of Andred.

'Our countries once flew the flags of unity once upon a time, but now we are separated, divided, and weak. We have been sapped of our will, drained of our energy to fight after so many years of needless war. Tarsha is tired of fighting. We are ready to fall.

'Do you not feel the sorrows of our people; do you not feel their hopelessness? That is why we must unify the countries once more as Ivandar did long ago. In unity, we may overthrow Abaddon at the siege of Morven. With an alliance, victory is imminent.

'I see in your eyes an understanding of this knowledge, but you must feel it, feel it with your heart and soul. Reach out and grasp it, only then will you come to understand."

The Warriors absorbed every powerful word. A short pause followed as he clenched his fists.

"You must truly feel the need for hope, the hope for peace. You must feel it before you can make peace possible. Without fighting for the people, you will not succeed. Erias, Atuan, Inveira, Charun, and your Kaanos, they are more than just borders, they are people, people with hopes and dreams that those like you and I must make possible.

'Every day I long for our countries to be strong again as one, to feel the harmony we have not felt in so many centuries." He fell quiet and stared off through the windows into the coming night.

Darius walked toward his throne and threw himself into the seat. "Enough of that." His body hung low as if suddenly tired. "I received a messenger from Ethebriel of Kaanos last month. It informed me of a group he called the Warriors agreeing to assist in the unification of Tarsha.

'He pulled them from the mass of normalcy, and in-stilled in them the information, desire, and will to perform such a daunting task.

'You hardly realize how painfully the feeble contracts of our Alliance need you. You hardly recognize how much of an impact you have made and will continue to make on the peoples of Tarsha.

'Word of a small group crossing the continent to unite the countries under the Old Alliance has brought much hope, and many believe the end of this war is soon to come, and I am guardedly optimistic alongside them.

'You have traveled far and through many obstacles, and the people are now ready to accept this newly hardened group as their saviors. If you are still dedicated to the people and this new Alliance, we have one more task for you.

'The capital of our country Morven may be, but the very heart and ballast of Tarsha as well. If it were to fall, then all of Tarsha will surely succumb to Abaddon and his genocide, a hopeless end to our suffering.

'We are receiving men-at-arms and fine soldiers daily, but our defenses are still too weak, we will easily crumble if attacked. We expect most, if not all of Abaddon's army to besiege our city, and we need many more troops if we are to have the hope of staving off this assault.

'The council and I have agreed that immediate actions must be taken to receive a large enough influx of troops that we so desperately require. Ethebriel and Verin have sent over half of their forces to Morven thanks to your help, but we can only trust they arrive in time.

'Inveira to the north has always been our uneasy ally, for we have fought many times in our extensive history and now they will not answer my offer in joining the Alliance, preferring instead to fight their own battles.

'However, the kingdom of Atuan lies at our doorstep. My brother, the King of Atuan, has been disinclined to our cause, choosing to defend his country under its own power.

'He has accumulated great forces in defense of his country, but in this lull in fighting, he may come to provide us with the numbers we desperately seek.

'That is where you come in, my friends. If it be under your own power or not, you must travel to the Eastern Deserts and the kingdom of Atuan. The capital of Atuan, Izadon, is where my brother rules.

'You must bolster his faith in the Alliance and encourage him to abandon the defense of his country and aid us in ours. We need as many men as he is able to muster, and if we receive enough support, then we may surely defend our city against the might of Andred. We desperately need your help in this task...do you accept this undertaking?"

The Warriors remained silent. Yet another charge from a king. Yet another assignment with no reward. However, his earlier words echoed in the back of their heads, crying out to them their importance, the very fate of Tarsha seemed to hang on their shoulders. They no longer had the freedom to say no, they were now obligated to their tasks not only for themselves, but also for the people. Their souls were now indentured. They stood in silence, waiting for someone to say the binding words.

"We just got here," Joshua sighed, "can we at least sleep on it?"

"Tarsha cannot afford you to sit by on idle hands. Every moment our people are dying, every moment another village falls. The Andreds ravage our country; there will be nothing left to save by the time you make up your minds."

"My brother is right," Silas stepped forward, "for ten years we have been soldiers fighting in this war, with no end in sight. We lose our families, our friends, our homes, and in return, we are used by kings as nothing more than messengers and hired swords.

We've traveled across all of Tarsha as nothing more than shepherds of men, guiding soldiers to their deaths and risking our lives every passing day. We've endured weeks of travel in constant fear of death and stalked like animals by the Iscara. I would gladly die in defense of my country, but in foreign lands and for so wasteful a cause I will not. None of this matters…we'll never win this war! I'm tired of this shit!" His outburst left the group without words, filling the room in anxious silence.

"No one made us do this…" Cain said to his friend after a moment, "We chose this path, knowing full well how difficult every step would be. We are the architects of our fate, no one else."

Silas rushed at him and grabbed him by the collar. "Don't speak to me like you suddenly found a heart! All you've ever wanted from the start of this was your revenge! You're willing to lead your 'friends' to the death if it meant winning your vengeance! Well vengeance is not good enough for me! I'm looking out for our best interest, and I say we've done enough! Now who's with me?" He glanced around at the group.

Aaron remained silent, returning Silas's gaze with a stolid stare.

Isroc shook his head and said, "Since I could wield a sword, I have fought for my people and Tarsha. A few stones in my path will not sway my mind."

Silas turned to Joshua in despair. Joshua shook his head.

Adriel stepped forward and rested a gentle hand on Silas's arm. She lowered his arm and looked up at him.

"Sometimes, Silas, we have to do what we never wish to, what we never thought we'd have to. But that is our fate. Regardless of our feelings, we must fight through it all for the people we are entrusted to protect. And that, that is what I will fight for, and so should you." Cain lowered his eyes at this and Silas was taken aback by her words. Finally, he relented and turned his back on them.

"We will go," Malecai said after a moment. His voice echoed in the silent hall, little more than a whisper.

Darius nodded, a slight smile pulled at the edge of his mouth as the Warriors looked at Malecai bewilderedly. The tension in the room slowly broke as the King spoke again.

"Very well, Warriors. Tarsha is forever in your debt. You have obligated yourselves to no easy task. You are the vessels of Tarsha's hope, and someday…you may very well be her saviors.

I would propose leaving in the morning, the earlier, the better. I will send summons for a transport to meet you at the docks. They will take you as far into Atuan as they can.

Men, escort our guests to their rooms for the night!" Following the King's sudden command, five guards came out of the archway behind them; running past the Warriors before bowing to their lord.

"Escort our guests to their rooms. They have a long road ahead of them." The guards stood up and beckoned them to follow.

"Warriors," Darius called after them as they turned to follow the guards. "Your sense of duty is admirable. You are doing great good for Tarsha; the sacrifices you have made and will continue to make will always be remembered. Never forget that." The Warriors nodded solemnly before following the escorts back down the hall.

Cain glanced over his shoulder to Darius, who returned to his throne, cradling his head in a hand.

Silas stepped beside Cain and cracked his knuckles in thought. "I apologize, Cain. I'm just pissed off at all this.

We've been friends for far too long for me to say those things."

Cain nodded grimly. "You were right, Silas…that's all I have fought for. That's what has kept me going for this long. You don't need to apologize." Cain clapped his friend on the shoulder and Silas smiled. Together, the two followed the group into the main entrance room.

The guards led them down a small hall on their right and led them deeper into the palace. The hall was narrow and dark, scarcely lit by torch-laden chandeliers that hung from the marbled ceiling.

Cain approached Malecai. "You said you would take us only to Morven. Yet you offer to go with us to Atuan. Why?"

Malecai smirked. "Promises are meant to be broken."

"Then what made you change your mind, you are not obligated to us, to the Alliance…to anyone even."

Malecai looked away for a moment as if searching for an answer. "I have my motives. I said I would guide you safely to Morven, and I did. However, things have changed."

"What things?"

"Elijah's words still ring in my head. Abaddon wants you personally; all of his servants are searching for you and will not rest until you are dead. There are certain things that make you a powerful enemy in his eyes, and invaluable in ours. So I have chosen to stay and protect you."

"I don't need protection, but thanks."

Malecai shook his head. "You may think you do not. You have no idea of the gravity of what is to come. Things will soon take a much darker road, and you Cain, will be in the midst of it all."

"Guard," Isroc called to the closest soldier. The man turned to look over his shoulder at him as they turned a corner and continued down a third hallway.

"Have you seen my father, Hallus?" Isroc asked with slight anxiousness.

The guard pondered the question for a moment before replying, "Hallus Braygon? Can't say I have. Well, he has not been in the palace for over six months; he left for Braygon on the west coast. Can't say if he's been in the city since then either, hard to recognize a face in the crowd. I haven't even seen the city in a while either come to think of it." The other guards laughed with amusement.

"Least you don't forget where your house is," another of the guards joked. They laughed heartedly at this, forgetting Isroc's inquiry. Isroc lowered his head, concealing the disappointment in his eyes.

The Sword of Our Despair

Morning came all too soon. The rapping of knuckles against their bedroom door called the Warriors to the fact that the sun was over the eastern mountains, lighting the city with the early rays of dawn.

Cain, Aaron, and Malecai threw aside the silk covers of their four-post beds and wiped the sleep from their eyes.

They were sore and exhausted from the day before and the weeks of combat and travel prior. They were more than ready to rest with the warmth of silk beds and a hearth. Yet they knew they could not, for they must carry out their final calling. They made promises to the kings of Tarsha, duty bound to the people; promises they could not break.

Above all, Cain had made a promise to himself. He vowed to avenge the deaths of his family, the destruction of his home, and the lives lost at the battle that started it all.

The only way to live out that promise is to follow his calling as a Warrior; for that it seems, is the only way to win his revenge. Perhaps, that was his true reason for accepting this final commission.

Cain, Malecai, and Aaron rose from their beds and donned their armor, strapping their weapons on in silence. They shouldered their rucksacks and opened the door. The three stepped out of the room and walked down the hall, their boots clicking loudly on the marble.

They soon came out into a small dome-like area, similar to the entrance room. A large window formed the entirety of the roof, letting in bright rays of sunlight.

A thick scarlet carpet covered the floor, their boots instantly muffled in the velvet fibers. The walls of the room were draped with curtains and paintings lined the walls.

A large wooden table stood in the middle of the room, piled high with a bouquet of fruits. Dozens of silver trays circled the arrangement, covered in meats, cheeses, breads, fats, and oils. Two small kegs of wine sat under the table beside a basket of goblets.

Several Citadel Guards surrounded the table and conversed merrily as they ate. The other Warriors were already there, talking amongst the soldiers. Cain, Aaron, and Malecai immediately took their trays and joined the others.

"The palace cooks prepare our meals for us," a guard informed Silas and Joshua as they ate ardently. "Each day they put out these lavish servings...it's about the only perk of being a Royal Guard. It's still dull work any way you look at it, they can't ever change that."

Near the table, Isroc was deep in conversation with one of the guards. "I couldn't tell you where Hallus is, mate," the guard said as he rested a hand on Isroc's shoulder. "None of us have seen him since he left for Braygon. I never did approve of him accepting that job as the West Rider's leader, I liked it better when he was our captain...but times have changed I guess."

Isroc nodded absent-mindedly as he gnawed on a slice of bread. "I know he was at Braygon, he sent me a letter a few weeks ago saying he would meet me at Mordicon or Morven at least...yet no one here has seen him for six months. It concerns me."

The soldier nodded, "Aye, that it does, and for good reason. We can only hope he will come home. I am sure he has only been delayed shortly. He would bring the West Riders with him if he comes, we could use another fifteen thousand men."

"Well," Isroc replied, setting down his empty mug. "A delay is what I'm worried about; the Andreds could have something to do with it."

The guard laughed with vexed amusement. "You truly are the son of Hallus, always the worrier. He will be fine and you know it. He's the best damn soldier Erias has ever been graced with."

Isroc nodded slowly, struggling to believe his friend's words. "Well," he said after a long moment, "has word been sent to Braygon?"

"Word of what?"

"Of this," Isroc held his arms out, "of all of this, the gathering of troops, the coming siege of Morven. You said it yourself; Morven could use the West Riders. But where are they?"

His friend gazed up at the glass ceiling, scratching his chin in contemplation. "The Council sent out a messenger to Braygon. Now that you mention it, he's not returned."

Isroc hung his head at this. "Then the West Riders do not know of the impending attack, they will never reach us in time."

Cain overheard their conversation and stepped toward the two, setting his tray on the table as he approached. "You are staying here then?" He asked his friend.

Isroc sighed. "I'm not giving up on my father...but I cannot let my heart get in the way, I am a Warrior now. I made a promise to you and myself, I will follow the Warriors unto the end. That is my calling."

Cain nodded. "It's good to have you at my side."

Isroc smiled at him and the two clapped a firm hand on the other's shoulder. Cain glanced past Isroc and noticed Adriel standing alone before a painting. Isroc saw this and his bushy brow rose with curiosity. "Ah, I see..."

"What?" Cain asked, perplexed.

Isroc chuckled. "You know. Go talk to her."

"I just need to ask her if she's coming with us."

"Sure…but make your move before it's too late, my friend."

Cain shook his head as he stepped around Isroc. "It's not like that."

"Say what you want," Isroc called after him as he walked away, "things have a strange way of working out!"

Cain crossed the room and stopped at Adriel's side. "Good morning," she said to him.

"Isroc and Malecai have made up their minds. What of you, Adriel? You haven't told me of your plans. Or for that matter, why you've even stayed with us through all of this."

Adriel looked at him questioningly and sighed. "I told you before I would lead you to Abraxas, then I said I would lead you safely out of Charun…and yet look where I am now. If I had wanted to leave, then I would have long ago, believe me."

"So you're staying with us?" Cain asked as he ran a hand through his hair.

Adriel laughed. "I never told you this, but I was planning on saying my goodbyes back in Abraxas. However, I hate to say I've grown fond of the lot of you. I have chosen my path; I have burned away any chance of returning to what I had before I found the four of you. So yes, I am staying until the end."

"To the end is a great sacrifice," Cain said, "especially when you don't know how any of this will end."

"None of us know how this all will end. But we fight on for those we care about…"

"I'm glad you're coming with us, Adriel," Cain replied, a smile pulling at his lips.

"How is the meal, men?" Darius's voice boomed from behind them. The King stood in the entrance to the room, his sharp eyes scanning over the soldiers. Every soldier knelt to the ground before their king and the Warriors followed likewise. The King walked towards the table and the kneeling guards rose to their feet.

"I hope the meal is to your liking, Warriors. Are you ready for the task at hand?" He looked them over in turn, as he seemed to have a habit of doing.

Malecai stepped forward, "We are ready."

"Very well," Darius said, "I have called for a transport and crew to await your arrival at the docks. Follow me."

The Warriors left the room with a final glance over their shoulders. Darius led them down another cramped hall towards an archway.

They went down a second hallway and soon a third before reaching the entrance room. They crossed the entrance room and approached the doors. Two guards opened the doors with a slight bow, letting in the winter's chill.

The group crossed through the doorway and came to the stairs, immediately thrashed with a powerful gust of wind as they stepped out into the sun-drenched peak. Darius led them down the steps and stopped at the winged statues.

"The guards will escort you to the ship. I must take my leave, friends. I have much work to do."

The Warriors bowed as he stepped from the group and turned back up the stairs. "Goodbye, Warriors, and good luck," he said over his shoulder. With that, he returned to the warmth of the palace.

The Warriors continued to stare after him, long after the doors had closed. They stood frozen for several moments, unwilling to leave the luxuries of the palace behind. Nevertheless, they knew what they must do.

They turned and crossed the peak, leaving the palace in the distance as they walked down the steps to the mountain road.

Two teams of horses stood a few feet away, harnessed together and tied to two different wagons. Four soldiers stood beside the wagons and gestured for the Warriors to step inside. Malecai climbed into the small interior of one of the wagons, followed by Adriel, Cain, and Aaron.

"We'll meet you there," Silas said as he glanced up at the horse and trade cog that still remained by the steps from the prior day.

**** ****

The sun hung low over the horizon, its light smothered beneath a veil of frosted clouds. Few ships now lingered in the river, men roaming like ants up and down the gangplanks.

One ship awaited the Warriors by the riverbank, a massive transport whose four masts towered above the waters like spires. A swarm of armored men wandered its deck, an apathetic look glazed over their eyes.

The Warriors stirred from their sleep, weary from hours of an uneventful ride. The wagon rolled down the main road and soon crossed over the docks. The soldier atop the wagon pulled his reins, slowing the team of horses before coming to a stop.

A man peered over the ship's edge and quickly descended the gangplank. "Are you the Warriors?" he asked in a warm tenor.

"Aye," Cain replied as he stepped out of the wagon.

"Where are the others?" The man inquired.

Malecai jumped nimbly from the wagon and looked out in the direction they had come. Suddenly, several shrill screams echoed in the quiet evening.

A small blur shot across the court. Devoid of its horse, a small trade cog sped towards the river, three men inside screaming in terror as they gripped the edges of the cart.

The back wheels of the cart fell off as it neared the river, breaking with a snap of wood before flying through the air. The front wheel of the cart then broke in half and rocketed through the air as the cog skidded the last few yards towards the river. The cart slid up to the Warriors and came to a stop beside the other wagon.

The men's fearful screams ceased abruptly as they realized the danger had passed. They remained in the small, half-broken cart and looked at each other, eyes wide with disbelief.

Malecai gestured towards the men, "Our better half."

The cart's third wheel rolled past them and they watched as it wobbled towards the river, and with a small plunk, sank with a spur of bubbles.

The group burst out in laughter for several moments as the three men fumbled out of the cart, chuckling with amusement.

Cain shook his head at the remains of the trade cart. "Should I even ask?"

Joshua approached one of the astonished wagon drivers and handed him a horse's bridle. "Sorry about your cart...and your horse."

**** ****

The transport left the northern sluicegate, leaving the walls of Morven behind. The faint din of the market road and docks faded from their ears as the city gradually dwindled from view.

The ship followed the Alar east, slicing through the languid waters. Its deck was silent and a light breeze rippled through the sails.

Cain leaned against the ship's side and peered over the map Verin had given him weeks before. He gripped the edges of the tarnished parchment and gazed over the faded ink countries, rivers, and roads.

He turned his attention to the land of Atuan and the shadow of Andred to its north. He stared at the black ink drawing of Andred, gazing into its borders with wonder, with hate.

A man walked up to Cain and coughed to state his presence, breaking Cain from his concentration. "We'll take you as close to the capital as we can. Do you see that?" The man pointed to a formation of mountains on Cain's map. "That's Nimithy Valley, a fertile dale along the banks of the Alar. At the east end of Nimithy, the river makes a turn to the north and flows along the southern edge of Andred. We'll be risking too much in staying that close to the enemy, so the closest we can get you is to the end of Nimithy valley. After that, well...you're on your own." Cain nodded in understanding as the man finished.

Footsteps clicked on the wooden deck behind them and they turned to see Malecai approaching. "We are coming to the Peaks of Icadras." He pointed to the bow as a shadow engulfed the ship in blackness. Everyone on the deck lifted their eyes to the skies. Their ship sailed into the mouth of these mountains from whence the Alar seemed to pour.

Great peaks loomed far above them on either side, their snowcapped crowns scraping the clouds. Their steep walls of ice and rock formed a mighty and treacherous ravine.

Several of the soldiers grabbed the rigging that hung from the sails and pulled them tight. They followed the thinning river through the Icadras gorge, guiding ship and sail through the many winding bends.

Snow fell lightly about them, the mountains barely visible in the icy mists. The freezing waters of the Alar lapped against the ship's wooden hull as it tore a path through the thin ice.

Hours passed as day slipped into ever-growing darkness, and through the lofty ceiling of the valley, they could see the light of day falling from the skies. Soldiers lit torches and placed them along the ship's edge, barely lighting their way.

The ship escaped the mountains' clutches at last and came out into a dazzling sea of light.

Hundreds of thousands of stars filled the dark void above, their pallid lights shimmering against fleeting wisps of clouds. A thin sliver of moon hung in a heavenly embrace, its light glistening against the mirror of snow that covered the fields around them for miles in every direction.

The Warriors stood side-by-side, gazing over the beauty before them. They whispered amongst themselves, averse to break the heavy silence that now filled the transport.

"Get some sleep, Warriors," The captain advised as he approached. "You have a long road ahead of you; you will need your strength."

The group descended the flight of stairs leading to the main deck and approached their bags and weapons lying abandoned against the railing.

"I never did like ships..." Joshua muttered as he clenched his gut. He sat down, sighed heavily, and threw his head into the side of his rucksack. "I'd rather have my horse."

Silas smirked at this. "You hate horses too."

Joshua shrugged and closed his eyes. "Point taken..."

**** ****

Several days passed as they followed the Alar, cutting its way through Erias's vast wilderness, snaking through the endless fields, forests, and mountains of the east.

As the sixth night faded into embryonic dawn, snow gradually turned to barren rock, mountains and hills to flattened fields. Another day dragged on as the land continued to morph and the sun slipped beneath distant pearly peaks.

"Warriors," a voice muttered from the darkness, "wake up." The captain nudged them, forcing them from their slumber. They stood up wearily and glanced around the shadowed deck.

Many of the soldiers were sprawled across the transport, a light snore rising from the deck. The soft glow of torches flickered in the darkness, casting their feeble lights over the water. Dark masses encircled the ship on both sides of the river and the Warriors' eyes drew instantly to them.

"We are here," Malecai informed the others. He leaned against the railing and stared intently through the darkness. The torchlight revealed the towering walls of Nimithy Valley.

"The open arms of Atuan welcome you," the captain said to the group.

The surrounding mountains towered over the land, blotting out the lights of the distant stars and moon. The torchlight glowed faintly off the leaves of strange trees, their gray, thorny fronds blanketing the valley walls in thick, clustered masses. Their branches hung low over the water, brushing against the ship's sides as it passed.

"This river valley is one of the only fertile areas in all of Atuan," Malecai informed the group. "Look zealously upon these trees; they are the last you will see for many days."

The captain nodded. "We'll come to the end within the next few hours." At this, he left and returned up the stairs.

Joshua and Silas left the group and walked back to their bags. "Isroc," Silas called, "let's play a hand before we leave." He held up a bundle of tattered cards and waved them enticingly before his friend.

"I don't gamble," Isroc replied with a disinterested glance over his shoulder.

"Trust me, you will." Silas tossed the deck at Isroc. Isroc held out a hand grudgingly and caught the cards. "One hand…" Silas tempted once more.

"One then," Isroc muttered as he looked down at the cards in his hands before following the others towards their bags.

Malecai slouched over the railing and bowed his head.

"You've been to Atuan before haven't you?" Cain asked.

"Aye," he replied with a heavy sigh, "many times…"

"What were you doing here?"

"I am a restless soul...I wander to appease my conscience, my heart and mind. That was what I was doing, nothing...and yet, everything."

"So then what-"

"You ask too many questions...if I wished to answer them, then I already would have."

Adriel laughed with amusement from beside the two men. "Believe me, Malecai, I've told him that many times. It's a lost cause."

Cain hung his head until they finished laughing. They soon fell silent and watched over the orange glow of the torches that rippled in the waters below. Hours passed as the faint laughter and cries of the gambling men filled the silent night.

The mountains parted and the star-studded skies at last fell from the valley's dark hold. The ship continued down the river, the Nimithy Valley falling to darkness behind the churning waters of the transport.

"This is as far as we can go," the captain said as he approached the Warriors. "We'll have to drop you off here. Release the gangplank!"

Several men rushed to the middle of the deck and disappeared down a flight of steps to the inner bowels of the ship, soon reappearing with a long, wooden plank in hand.

The Warriors shouldered their rucksacks and strapped on their armor and weapons as the soldiers dropped the gangplank.

"We will wait for your return at the mouth of the valley," the captain said as he shook their hands and gestured for them to leave the ship. The soldiers saluted as they walked by and stopped at the head of the gangplank.

"Good luck, Warriors," the captain replied with a crisp salute. The Warriors nodded and descended the gangplank. Their boots soon touched down on the sands of the Eastern Desert, sinking into the near fluid-like earth.

"Follow," Malecai ordered and stepped into the cold and silent darkness. The others followed him, leaving the glow of the torches behind. The transport soon slipped into shadow and the Warriors continued into blackness. The Warriors walked in silence. Not a noise graced their ears save the chatter of distant insects and the shifting of the sands beneath their boots.

The starlight revealed to them a world of barren solemnity, an isolated and dismal world, void of life and all compassion. No vegetation, no mountain peaks, nothing but an endless expanse of rock and sand.

The air hung heavy around them, a numbing cold that left their cloaks useless against their skin. The Eastern Desert surrounded them on all sides, an unforgiving and barren wasteland.

"Why would you have ever come here?" Aaron asked Malecai.

"I have my motives...much like we do for being here now."

"Don't bother, he won't answer your questions, Aaron," Cain warned.

"I will when I deem it necessary," Malecai retorted, "but now is not the time. Your focus should be on our task, not inventing questions to gratify your curiosity."

His riposte silenced the group and they continued into the strange world of Atuan.

**** ****

Thin beads of light crept over the distant horizon, illuminating what once was hidden with brilliant azure. The sun soon crawled from the dawn, its warm rays of light reaching fast over the land.

The Warriors continued through the ever-warming sands, the cool air around them snuffed under the potency of the sun.

Malecai flicked his shoulder, sending his cloak off his back before catching it. The Warriors followed likewise and removed the cloaks from their backs.

The air grew warmer with every step they took. Their once cool skin now instantly brought to a sweat as the sun filled the skies. The heat grew and grew, rising ever-in intensity.

They walked on through the heat that now simmered against their skin and set their very armor ablaze. Silas and Joshua began removing their steel encasements.

"You could remove your armor," Malecai said, "but it will do you no good. You will still have to carry it."

"I'll do as I please," Joshua retorted and removed his breastplate. Malecai shrugged at him and turned back to the sands before them. Silas glanced uneasily at the two of them and tightened the strap of his pauldron.

A vast sea of barren sand and stone surrounded them from every side. Hundreds of mountains encompassed the edges of the earth, their lofty spires mere shadows amidst the sea of gold that spread over the earth like a godly parchment. The sun hung high over the desert sands, its fierce heat blaring down on the travelers.

"How far until Izadon?" Cain asked as he raised his water skin to his lips.

"Izadon is a few more days east from this point. I have traveled this route many times; we will be at the capital soon." He fell quiet and gestured for the others to follow.

**** ****

The stars shone bright over the desert sands below, the flowing dunes rippling with a silver intensity. The Warriors were encamped at the foot of a dune, enclosed by a cluster of large stones. They sat in silence around a fire and gnawed on the venison they could finally cook.

Malecai stopped eating and looked into the fire for several moments. He dropped his meal atop his rucksack and stood up.

"I think all of you should know some things..." The group looked up at him questioningly. "Your constant questioning of Abaddon's immortality has led me to believe you are as clueless as the rest of Tarsha."

"And you know something we don't?" Cain asked, slightly irked.

"Yes, I do. But do not worry, most of Tarsha does not know what I am about to tell you. The stories say that Abaddon was granted immortality by the Forgotten. That however, is only half the story."

"There's more to the story?" Aaron asked. "Armeth told us everything."

Malecai sighed at this. "You know so little of the truth. If you are to be the saviors that Tarsha believes you to be, then you must truly know your enemy. You cannot fight an enemy you know nothing about, simply because you are told to do so."

"Sure we can," Joshua grunted, "we've done it for four hundred years."

Isroc nodded. "Joshua's right. No one really knows much about him. No one has even seen him. We fight because if we do not, then we all die. That's all I need to know."

Malecai shook his head. "Death becomes of ignorance. Do not blindly follow where your feet lead."

"Malecai has a point," Aaron said, "and if he knows something about Abaddon that we don't, then I say we hear him out." The group fell quiet and turned to Malecai.

"Very well," Malecai began. "In the light that converted the captain of Erias to the demon, Abaddon, a sword was forged for him. It would come to be known as Ceerocai, the greatest legend ever told. It was a physical means for him to assert his god-given power, and through this sword, his strength was endless.

'He removed his soul from its mortal prison and sealed it within this weapon. In doing so, he cast aside his humanity, the only weakness remaining to him. All emotion, all love, all weakness, all that makes us human…forever lost to him. He was divinity incarnate, and with the sword given to him by the Forgotten, he was a god among men.

'The sword gave him immeasurable power, for he could call upon his soul within the blade, and it would fight alongside him in the form of a great, crimson beast. Of course, this was not the only power the sword could muster. It could release the very bowels of hell upon the earth and reap the souls of wanton men.

'However, his godliness would be short lived, for Ivandar, the son of the slain king of Erias and brother of the famous Jocelyn, would gather the forces of Tarsha under the banner of Alliance. He marched upon the stronghold of Andred, four hundred thousand strong. A great battle ensued, but under the infinite armies of Andred and Abaddon himself, the Alliance was ultimately defeated.

'Before Ivandar retreated with his men, he found the sword of Abaddon that was lost to him in the battle. He took it, unaware of its true power.

'For the rest of his years, he kept it as a trophy in defiance of Abaddon. The sword's power would go unnoticed by Ivandar and all of Tarsha, until it was forever lost to time." Malecai paused and leaned against the side of a boulder.

"As the war progressed and Ivandar found his Alliance slowly crumbling, he led a battalion to Izadon, in hopes of rallying more forces to his banner. Somewhere along the way however, a battalion of Andreds ambushed them. Ivandar's men fended off the attackers in a fierce battle and soon lay waste to the enemy. They may have won the battle, but Ivandar had fallen in the battle, and the last hope of Tarsha died with him.

'Ivandar was the last thorn in Abaddon's back, and with him out of the way, all the world lay open to his wrath. Realizing this, Ivandar's men could not face this grim truth, for it was their fault that all of Tarsha would soon fall to genocide, for they failed to protect their king.

'So...they began to dig a grave for their fallen leader. As the days passed in the heat of the sun and the cold of night, their numbers began to dwindle to hunger and disease. More and more of them died, and the survivors buried their fallen brothers.

'They grew over emulative in the grandeur of their creation, and as the weeks turned to months; the last of them succumbed to death. They at last received their wish, release from this sorrow-filled world.

'They left behind a great catacomb, vast mazes of tombs buried beneath the sands of Atuan and hidden to the rest of the world. Tarsha never knew the whereabouts of these tombs, and soon forgot the legacy Ivandar's men left behind. Eventually the tombs slipped into legend, and now most believe it to be nothing more than myth."

Cain tossed a pile of brushwood onto the fire. "That's great and all but I don't see how that fits into anything we're doing."

"Ah but it does!" Malecai jumped up from the boulder, suddenly filled with enthusiasm. "It has everything to do with you! Ceerocai is buried somewhere beneath these sands with the body of Ivandar!"

"So?" Silas questioned.

"Do you not understand? Abaddon's soul lives on inside that sword. That is how he has lived these four hundred years!" The group fell awestruck as this realization left them at a loss for words. This was the answer to their questions. This was why their enemy was undying. This was why he was so powerful. Ceerocai was the key to it all.

"It's called the Lost Tombs of Atuan for a reason," Isroc said after awhile, "people have searched for it for four hundred years and to no avail, what makes you think we can find it?"

"I do not expect us to find it," Malecai answered, "but if someone does, then we may be able to use it against its master, and in doing so we may kill that which cannot die. If someone finds the lost sword of Abaddon, then we may at last put an end to this war…"

The Death of Love

Three days passed as the Warriors continued through the Eastern Desert. The sun was now atop the horizon and the desert sands glowed with the light of a new day. The sands glistened gold and the shrubs trembled with a whisper of wind as the travelers awoke.

They donned their armor and fastened their weapons and wiped their eyes of sleep. They ate a hastened meal and threw their bags over their shoulders, more than ready to reach the gates of Izadon.

They began walking once again, tearing through the endless sea of sand.

Soon, the all too familiar heat greeted them. Sweat began trickling down their brows and their armor and clothes seared against their skin. They continued through the sifting sands as the sun arced its way across the cloudless skies above.

The travelers marched on for several hours under the scorching sun, time passing to memory with every reluctant step.

They eventually came across a strange, graying tree, its twisting trunk and branches splayed out to catch the sunlight. They passed it and soon came to a large thicket of the thorny foliage.

They crossed under the trees, their long overhanging branches casting shadows over the beleaguered travelers. "We are close," Malecai informed them as he brushed a wall of thorns aside.

They walked on through the trees and eventually came out the other side.

Through the iridescent waves of heat, they could see the distant walls of a city. They sighed with relief at the sight and left the trees, walking with newfound vigor towards the city. The waves of heat slowly dissipated as they neared, allowing the travelers a clear view of Izadon.

The city was cradled in a vast, cragged bowl. The sands flowed like the hills of greener dells, split hither by great gorges and ridges of stone. A lofty wall of mountains formed a crescent around the capital, their sharp peaks emblazoned with crowns of brilliant white.

The outer walls of the city were made of dark russet sandstone, towering thirty feet in height, arrow slits cut intermittently across its stone facade. A gate made entirely of stone served as the only entrance to the southern half of the city.

Several sentries peered over the walls in the direction of the approaching travelers. "We are the Warriors!" Malecai cried out to the guards as they approached. "Open the gates!" The guards made no movement to open the gate and instead stared curiously down at them.

Malecai sighed and looked up at the guards above once more. "I am Ambrosia! Open the gates!" The guards hurried off as if suddenly lashed by an invisible whip. The Warriors walked forward as the gates slowly opened.

Cain looked at Malecai curiously. Malecai saw his expression and smirked as they walked through the shadow of the archway.

The gates slowly slid open as the massive stone doors grinded against the sands of the outside world.

The Warriors crossed under the gates and came out into the city of Izadon. The guards under the gateway saluted to the Warriors and stared curiously after them long after they had left.

They came to a large sand road that sloped gradually upwards, cutting its way through the middle of the city towards the crest of a massive hill at its center.

Tall buildings of sandstone and brick lined both sides of the street. The buildings had flat roofs, and cut out windows revealed the mostly lackluster rooms within.

Few people roamed the streets, solemn and silent. They wore strange robe-like garments, dull colored and roughly woven.

The Warriors left the gateway and approached the main road. Few people glanced at the travelers as they passed, every eye cast to the ground with disinterest, every eye hollow as a grave.

They continued up the gradually ascending road and passed hundreds of buildings, all filled with an oppressed silence, not a noise daring to stir the stillness of the day.

"Is it always like this?" Adriel whispered to the front of the group.

Malecai shook his head. "It is much like the streets of Morven, or your Dun Ara. It has never been like this, this concerns me…" The group walked with apprehension as they approached the crest of the hill.

They reached the hilltop and the road soon leveled out and stretched far ahead. A group of armed men approached them from the other end of the road; weapons ready at a moment's calling. "What men are these to approach the King's quarters?" A soldier questioned as they stopped a few feet before the Warriors.

"I am Ambrosia," Malecai said, "and these are the Warriors. We are to speak to King Creedoc under commission of Lord Darius." The soldiers lowered their glaives and whispered intently among themselves for a moment.

"Follow," One of the soldiers ordered tersely. They turned and led the Warriors down the road. After several minutes, the road turned and sloped steeply up a hill. The guards led the Warriors up the hill until the road narrowed toward a thin stone bridge that spanned over the crest of two hills.

The group crossed the bridge, the edges mere inches from their feet, the sharp rocks of the valley floor looming a hundred feet below. They stepped onto the second hill and noticed a small white building atop its cragged top.

The building was nearly identical to the palace of Morven. It was fashioned of imported ivory marble, a near replica to the jewel of Morven.

"Creedoc is the brother of Darius," Malecai whispered to the others as they followed the road up the hillside and toward the palace. "He had the palace of Izadon reconstructed to look like his home in Morven."

"Where's the statues?" Adriel asked as she eyed the vacant spaces beside the stairs.

Malecai frowned at this. "Let us just say there is no need for them here…"

"Does Creedoc know you, Malecai?" Cain asked.

"You could even say he knows me well."

The guards led them up the flight of stairs towards the door of the palace that lay hidden behind several rows of marbled columns.

The Warriors climbed the stairs and passed the columns. The guards opened the ebony doors and the Warriors stepped through the doorway, coming out into a massive hallway.

Walls of sandstone surrounded them from every side and polished ivory granite covered the floor and roof. In the middle of the hall was a large golden throne with brown furs draped over the seat and arms.

At the other end of the hall behind the throne was a large archway that spanned across the entire wall. Sunlight filled the palace, bounding into the room abreast a scorching wind.

The Warriors walked across the hallway, their boots clicking loudly on the polished marble and leaving behind a trail of sand as they approached the archway. They crossed under it and came out into a small courtyard.

Several sandstone columns lined the sides of the court. There was no roof, but the open skies formed an azure ceiling overhead.

A large pool filled the middle of the court, its surface glistening like crystal, undisturbed and strangely beautiful. The sky above reflected off its mirrorlike surface, and at the bottom of the pool was a thick sheet of pure glass, magnifying the brilliancy of its waters. A strange tree dangled its emerald fronds over the water, casting half the court in shadow. On the opposite side of the court was a thin flight of steps that led up to the second floor of the palace.

"Wait," a soldier commanded. The guards crossed the courtyard and ascended the steps. After several minutes, they returned, leading their king down the stairs.

The King stopped at the foot of the steps and turned to his men. "Leave us." The soldiers bowed obediently and clambered up the stairs.

"Welcome, Warriors," greeted the man as he began walking alongside the pool. "I would have better prepared for your arrival, but I did not know you were coming." The man's voice was much like Darius's, smooth and lucid.

He stood tall and daunting, a dignified air about him. Sandy eyes looked over them wearily. Black, neatly groomed hair flowed down his high-cheeked face and down to the small of his back. A large scarlet cloak fell from his broad shoulders, covering a red tunic and dark leggings. A silver gauntlet covered his entire left hand and forearm. He walked with a pained limp and his left arm hung uselessly at his side.

"It is a pleasure to meet you, Warriors," he said as he stopped before them. "I have heard much of you over the past weeks and the hope you bring to Tarsha's people. It is an honor."

The King bowed and looked over the group. They quickly felt the same scrutinizing gaze his brother often gave.

"Skip the formalities, Creedoc," Malecai replied dryly, "there are matters at hand we must discuss; their outcomes depend upon our immediate action."

Creedoc laughed lightly and extended his right hand to Malecai, "Ah, Malecai, I knew it was only a matter of time before you would join the Warriors. I see you haven't changed, always to the point. It's good to see you again."

Malecai smiled and grasped his outstretched hand. They shook hands for a long moment and Creedoc attempted to pull his hand away but Malecai held it firm. The King looked at him uneasily as his friend eyed the bandages that covered his hand.

"You were hurt," Malecai stated simply.

"What of it?" Creedoc retorted as he pulled his hand away. "When you live the life of a king and a warrior, you put your life at risk to protect your people."

Malecai merely stared at him with sharp, searching eyes. "You would need something to fight to be hurt in this manner...what happened?"

"Come. I will show you," Creedoc relinquished. He turned on his heel and led the Warriors across the court.

They ascended the stairs and came out onto a causeway. A wide walkway of sandstone followed the length of the palace walls and the stairwell they had followed opened out into the bowels of these catwalks.

The sun fell quickly over the horizon before them, staining the skies with the blood of the dying day.

Creedoc pointed over the edge of the causeway to the northwest. "Look." The Warriors slowly approached the wall.

The north section of the city stretched out before them, spanning half a mile before coming to the outer wall of the city. A scene of horror awaited them, pain and anguish tearing instantly at their hearts.

Nearly the entire northwestern wall had been disintegrated, nothing now but an endless mountain of rubble atop a sea of ashes. Where hundreds of buildings once stood, nothing but charred earth and ruins remained. Half the city had been leveled and razed to the ground.

Thousands of bodies littered the rubble, lifeless corpses buried beneath a cloud of festering birds. Bodies lay face down in the ashes as if bemoaning their fates, yet others stared up at the sky with pupils dulled by death, glaring like famished ghouls into an abhorrent abyss.

Corpses piled high in masses across the ashes, mountains of rubble and debris crushing thousands of bloated bodies now mangled beyond recognition. Limbs scattered the bloody sands, gashed, torn, and broken bodies strewn everywhere. The innocent lay dead alongside their defenders, soldiers' mutilated heads, limbs, and entrails littering every inch of the battlefield.

The setting sun cast the city in a bloody light, sky and clouds above painted red with death. Thin plumes of smoke rose from the charred earth as the wind then stole them across the desert.

Soldiers roamed the carnage, dragging corpses from the rubble and picking through the destruction, throwing the dead over ever-growing mounds of corpses before setting them aflame.

Malecai rushed forward from the group and nearly threw himself over the wall in his haste. He stared out over the destruction, lips quivering. He opened them to find words, but none came. He let out a despairing cry and cradled his head in his hands.

"It's all too familiar..." Aaron muttered as the group stared on with horror.

"What...what happened here?" Malecai asked through clenched teeth.

"We were attacked a few days ago..." Creedoc began in a hushed whisper. "It seems that Abaddon decided to kill us off in style. We were told the enemy had withdrawn from our lands and returned to Andred. They did, but not without a parting gift. They attacked at night. They destroyed the wall almost instantly and swept through the city, burning and killing everything in their path.

They slaughtered thousands before we could gather a large enough force for a counter attack, but by then it was too late to save our city...it became every man for himself."

The King paused and gripped his paralyzed arm in thought. "We fought bitterly through the night, fighting for our very lives. We eventually fended off the Andreds' ruthless assault, but we had lost much of our city and many more of our people.

For days, we struggled to stave off the fires that threatened to engulf the last of our city, and we managed to stop the inferno before it reached the palace and the surviving half of the city. We burned the bodies of the Andreds and dug graves for our people, but alas, we have run out of space for the fallen."

"Will you then send your armies to aid Morven?" Cain asked him.

Creedoc nodded slowly, his eyes glazed over in pensive concentration. "I had a feeling that was why my brother sent you. He has long feared an attack on Morven. I will join the Alliance...to avenge the deaths of my people and for the sorrows we have endured. I was foolish to think I could fight this war alone.

I gathered my armies at Izadon to protect my people, hoping I could do something, anything, to salve this endless cycle of death. But I was wrong. I was not prepared. The enemy came like the thunder of Angeled and destroyed us...I will send fifty thousand of my finest men to aid in the siege of Morven and join this final resistance against the shadow of Andred. Abaddon's forces have pulled out of Atuan and the rest of Tarsha; they are surely amassing for the assault on Morven. The final battle is at hand, the final chapter is upon us."

**** ****

Cain stood alone on the causeway, leaning heavily against the palace wall.

Night had proscribed the skies for several hours, its blackness enveloping the heavens above and the infinitesimal world below.

The moon hung low in the sky, its waxing face dominating the abyss over which it held such sway. The small lights of midnight stars flickered above and thin wisps of clouds sailed the night's cool breeze.

Cain stared out over the Andred's ruthless scourge of the city. Smoke continued to billow from the remains of the desecrated. The moonlight shimmered against the skin of the dead, glowing ghouls in the night.

Cain gazed for hours upon the ruination before him, unable to turn his gaze and forget what he had seen. It brought back a flood of memories, memories he long sought to forget.

He saw his wife and child in the faces of every dead and his parents in every lifeless eye. He saw death everywhere; to push it aside was folly. It hurt him that his friends ignored this simple truth. They inflicted their hearts with blindness, refusing to be hurt again; after all they had been through.

He turned and looked at the three men whom he had known his entire life, sleeping contentedly beside the fire. It saddened him to see them turn their backs on the world when it screamed its pain so fiercely. The world was slowly falling to Abaddon's genocide. Every soul screamed now for salvation from the fires that sought to engulf them.

Cain looked over his friends, sadness weighing heavy on his heart. What are they fighting for? The revenge they vowed to attain. The suffering they sought upon their enemies. All they once cherished as a purpose to fight, a reason to live, none of it mattered now. Everything they had fought for, everything they had, all that kept them going, all of it was fruitless.

He finally realized that revenge was nothing but a hollow conviction. Vengeance shall never be appeased. Hate can never fill the void within him. His wife and child were dead, and nothing he could do would change that. Sorrow perched in the recesses of his heart, constantly and indefinitely striking at his conscience with this fact.

He had fought to suppress this pain beneath a false sense of justice, but the vengeance he strived to attain was not of his true self. He was not the man of bloodlust and vengeance as his friends and the world had begun to see him.

He was once a child whose youth was wrongfully stolen. With his parents murdered before his eyes, he vowed his young soul to vengeance. However, as the years buried his horrific past beneath the dusts of time, his rage had sated. He fought as a soldier of Kaanos not for revenge, but to protect his wife and all those he loved.

Yet again, as his love was butchered before his eyes, he vowed to find justice. He had fought since for selfish ideals of retribution in an attempt to mask his pain.

The monster he had become was not the true Cain Taran. The spirit of revenge that burned inside him yearned to surrender and return his heart to its rightful path.

Despite its longing for release, Cain could not relinquish the revenge that had given him such drive. It was a part of him now. He longed to let his revenge go, but only emptiness would fill its place. He felt nothing but fire in his heart.

Suddenly, the echoes of footsteps shook him from his thoughts. Someone approached him from the darkness.

"The darkness befits you tonight, my friend," a voice whispered from the night. Cain glanced over his shoulder at his sleeping friends. Five of them slept soundly beside the fire. He knew immediately who stood behind him.

"You should be asleep," he replied. He had grown used to Malecai's absence at night, his constant restlessness as the sun fell.

"Sleep?" Malecai murmured. "Sleep is a waste of one's time; of one's very life…I refuse its perversion."

Cain turned to see Malecai's face glowing in the fire-light, shadows etched across his stern facade, flickering with light and dark.

"You never sleep?" Cain asked with a raised brow.

His friend nodded slowly, the shadows shifting across his face with every movement. "It is my self-denial, my punishment, my penitence. It has been ten long years since it began, and it shall remain my castigation until death. After all, I still have hell to look forward to.

We are one in the same, my friend. You and I, we feel the pain and hurt of war…we see life for the whore she is, that side which many choose to ignore and all tremble at." He glanced at the Warriors as he said this.

You have asked me many questions about my past. My heart was pained with the constant reminder of the memories I long to forget, yet refuse to live without.

My past is naught but pain and grief. Regret and sorrow forever plague my steps. Come with me and I will tell you…" He stepped back into the shadows, the darkness swallowing him as his footsteps faded away.

Cain stood for a moment, absorbing his words. He glanced over his shoulder at the ruins and shook his head, desperate to rid himself of the image of death now carved in his mind.

He sighed lightly before running after his friend. He crossed the causeway and descended the stairs, soon coming out onto the court.

Small torches lined the courtyard, their ruddy flames flickering in the night. The strange tree spread its fronds through the glowing torchlight, casting waves of trembling shadow over the pool. The heavens reflected brilliantly on the water's flawless surface, thousands of stars shimmering in the crystalline water.

Malecai sat beside the pool, his eyes transfixed upon it. "All of my naivety ended here, and where all my sorrows began." He clenched his fist, his eyes never leaving the water's depths.

"My story began many years ago at the death of my father, killed by the cruel hand of fate. He was a soldier by duty to the king of our country, Inveira. He was a great general of men, and he left behind a legacy that was sure to die along with him.

Alanis, leader of the Knights of Iscara, assassinated him. After his death, I vowed myself to vengeance against his murderer. However, I knew my revenge would go unfulfilled if I did not set my hatred on the true cause of my suffering, Abaddon.

I vowed to find the lost sword of Abaddon, the ancient artifact to which his soul is eternal bound. I thought that if I could find it, then I could destroy it…alas, a foolish thought. Nevertheless, I sought to find it.

I set out across Tarsha and for many weeks I rode until I came upon Izadon, weary with travel.

I knew not where to begin my search so I began at the library, searching for anything in relation to the lost sword. For a year, I combed the shelves. I scanned every inch of the city's texts for any possible location. Nothing. Disappointment surmounted me and I left bitterly frustrated and uncertain as to where to continue my search.

Then one day, I met a woman. I did not know at the time, but it was a life altering moment. I was at the stables, contesting with myself: should I saddle my horse and return home in disgrace, or stay in Izadon until an opportunity presented itself. That morning I found that opportunity.

A woman rode up beside me. Her hair was as black as this night, her eyes wild as the eastern seas, her skin pale as the moon's frail glow. She was beautiful, and I was infatuated.

It was somehow an instant connection; I have never felt anything as sweet as I felt at that moment. Love is too weak a word.

Her name was Raven. She was the daughter-in-law of Creedoc. Her status did not surprise me for her poise and composure screamed of nobility.

I felt a thought rise in the back of my mind. What if I could use her to get to the palace library, they were sure to have the information I sought. I quickly suppressed those thoughts, for I refused to use her. Fate however, played a far larger role that day than ever I intended.

Raven took me to the palace where I met Creedoc, a brilliant and honorable man, more than worthy of his title. As the days passed, I became greatly acquainted with the King and the royal family.

Creedoc had heard of my father and the legacy he had left behind. I informed him of my reasons for being in Atuan and my desire to find the lost sword that had eluded humanity for so long. He immediately offered to show me the palace library with Raven at my side.

Together, the three of us scoured the thousands of tombs scattered among its endless shelves. We searched for over a fortnight, finding almost nothing pertaining to the lost sword. It was as if all records of it had been destroyed, erased from history. I left the library in somber disappointment, my frustration now shared with others.

I then decided to focus my efforts on a more mundane manner, searching the deserts for any entrance to the elusive tombs. I saddled my horse and set across Atuan with Raven at my side.

We roamed the desert for many months, side by side across the eastern stretches of Tarsha, from the Alar to the

Menaheim, from the southern borders of Andred to the Wilds of Angeled. For many days, we traveled, and for many nights, we lay gazing up at the stars. Those days that I spent with her were the last days of my happiness...

Eventually we saw what we both knew to be the truth, that the tombs would forever escape man's reach. We decided to give up my...our, quest. We returned to Izadon in defeat." Malecai paused for a moment as if struggling to continue.

"However, upon my return, I felt an uneasy sentiment stirring in my heart. I endured the shame set upon me by every eye. Everyone I passed knew my failure, my defeat, but shared not my sorrows. The shame was painful, impertinent, and I loathed it.

I could no longer stay in Izadon, no matter how much I told myself otherwise. I followed the shadows that veiled my better judgment, saddled my horse, and left behind the city of Izadon.

Suddenly, I saw a cloud of dust rise behind me. I found myself looking into Raven's eyes. The veil lifted from my eyes as I stared into the light of hers. Her gaze pierced my ignorance; she seemed to read my very soul.

She asked how I could ever leave her. I remember the pain in her voice, the clenching agony growing with every breath she took. Her voice rose not in anger, but in frustration, her head bowed and eyes closed as if to fend off the reality of what was happening.

I looked at her in a way I had never felt before, with a strange shroud of spite, and I hated it. I no longer felt love for her; I no longer felt the warmth and friendship we shared. I felt only shame and disgrace festering within me. I wanted more than anything to leave her. I saw then the suffering I caused her, but I did nothing to stop her tears. She knew I no longer wanted her.

I turned from her without a backwards glance...and she let me go.

I found myself...crying. Crying for what? Nothing it seemed, or so I told myself. I rode for a lifetime, away from my troubles and heartaches. Yet, the problem was not behind me or before me; it was in me.

At last, I arrived home and entered in, only to find an empty feeling within its walls.

A man sat behind my table and revealed himself as Alanis, leader of the Iscara, the man who took everything from me.

Alanis told me he had been waiting for me. I looked at him with confusion and reached for my sword. He remained motionless, his eyes watching me for a while. I remained silent.

He then asked what it was he could take from me, what mattered most to me. I looked up at him, realizing what I truly cherished.

I pulled my sword out and pressed it under his chin, my fingers itching to end his wretched life. He simply laughed and told me to give chase if I was to save Raven from her fate. I looked at him with disbelief and rage. I sheathed my sword and returned to my horse.

Killing his words in my mind, I turned sharply back to the trails. The veil before my eyes fell at last; the words of the Iscara tore me from my darkness. I rediscovered my senses, my feelings, the love I had discarded. I had blinded myself to feeling as a safeguard against pain and disgrace. Now, I once again found myself naked to the truth.

I knew not why Alanis and his Knights rode out to kill Raven, but I had to stop them.

I rode without rest, without ceasing. I rode for redemption. Evening fell on the last day of my desperate ride, and Izadon rose before me.

The sun set behind me as I rode through her gates. I galloped down the main road as fast as my horse could carry me. In my haste, I made a fatal flaw in observation that night.

No one roamed the city's streets, not a soldier guarded her gates. The city was empty and silent, much as this night, a heavy and impenetrable silence. This lapse in my judgment would play the first notes of my guilty song.

I came upon the palace with fear. Through the dark, I perceived two Iscara.

Without hesitation, I rode towards them and leapt from my saddle, bringing them to the earth with my sword. I disposed of them and kicked in the broken palace doors.

Armed men rushed at me from every side as I crossed the hall. I struck down every man that stood in my way, painting the walls red with their blood. I killed and killed, and the more that attacked me, the more I slaughtered. I left none alive, and I would do it again a thousand fold.

I left behind the scarlet halls and crossed the court, but as I came to the stairs, a scream filled my heart with dread. I rushed forward and ascended the steps, coming out into the night.

Five men stood before me with swords drawn. Alanis stood with his back to me, overlooking the city.

'What do you want from me?' I asked.

He told me they had been searching for me for many years, and finally they found the key to bringing me in.

I did not understand what he said, but I raised my sword to kill. Alanis turned to me and stepped aside, revealing a figure limp at his feet. Tears and blood streamed down her face as she stared at me for a long, disbelieving moment.

I knew who it was. She said nothing, but through the darkness, I knew the person behind those eyes.

I cried out her name and rushed forward. Two of the men attempted to stop me but I killed them instantly. The other two rushed at me with raised swords and I quickly deflected both, soon dropping them where they stood.

Alanis drew his sword and we locked eyes for what seemed a lifetime, waiting for the other to make a move. Our blades then met with a flurry of sparks.

We fought with such blinding rage, a fierce cloud of sparks about us. In my bloodlust, I quickly defeated him. I threw his sword over the wall and tried to land the fatal blow, but he threw himself towards Raven.

Time around us slowed to a stand still. I let out a cry, but it fell silent in my ears as I flung myself forward. Flames leapt from his outstretched hands. A scream echoed across the city and through my heart.

I swung my sword and a light shot across the causeway as my blade struck Alanis, sending him tumbling over the wall.

The flames around Raven died as his scream fell silent on the street below. The smell of burning flesh filled my nostrils as I fought to accept what I saw before me.

Raven lay more than dead at my feet, skin melting from her very bones. The light of her eyes had disappeared, her body now little more than smoldering shadow. I knelt down beside her and turned over her limp body. Her clothes were burnt to nothingness, mere ash against her charred skin.

I leaned over her and whispered her name, hoping she still had the life in her to hear my despairing cry. I wrapped my arms around her and carried her down the stairs.

I knelt before the pool we are sitting by now and lowered her into the water, daring to believe it would sooth her pain.

I stepped into the water beside her, letting the blackened shell of her body float weightless before me. The ashes of her skin and clothes fell from her, turning the water a sickly black.

I touched her face, her skin clinging to my hands. Suddenly, her eyes fluttered. Flesh broke apart and she looked up at me. The moon reflected in the white pools of her eyes, beauty, even in death.

I leaned over her, my tears breaking the waters, my love dying in my arms. Her lips parted and a feeble gulp of air struggled to fill her lungs. In a voice fainter than a whisper, she muttered her last words, 'I loved you, Malecai.' The last breath remaining to her died with those words...and she passed from this earth.

I stared at her lifeless body in disbelief, cradling her closely. I begged for her eyes to open once more, but of course, they did not.

Her last words were not I love you... the words of fairy tales and happily-ever-afters. My story was that of shame, a story worthy of a loveless end. I had broken her heart and torn it to pieces to fill her every moment with heartache. She no longer loved me, and it was my fault.

I gently closed her eyes and let her fall from my arms. Her body sank through the ashes and fell beneath the surface, coming to a rest at the bottom. I looked into her burnt face through the depths of the water for as long as I could muster.

I slowly turned and rose from the pool. I picked up my bloodied sword and grimaced with disdain. Nothing ever tasted so bitter.

I tore my gaze from her and ran up the stairs and across the causeway. I rushed over the bodies and climbed atop the wall. I stood on the edge, overlooking the city many yards below.

It would be best, I told myself. It would be the only way. My life had lost its meaning. I once felt love, tasted it. And now it had been taken from me.

I felt the cool embrace of wind on my skin. The moon's light filled my eyes, and somehow...I felt Raven in me, our hearts beating as one.

I looked over the city street below and knew I could not muster that final step.

I climbed off the wall and looked back over the palace. I knew what was right. It was my fault she was dead; I could not save her. I knew the only way I could find atonement for my mistakes was to punish myself.

I vowed myself to pain and sorrow that night, as endless punishment for my mistakes. I had to feel the pain she felt before her death. I had to shed every tear she shed. I had to feel every bit of the pain and agony I had caused her..."

Malecai stopped and gazed pensively into the moonlit pool before them. He paused for a long moment, his shoulders heaving as he fought to speak. Cain remained silent, waiting for his friend to continue.

"Never forget what it is you hold onto most in this world, Cain, because I did...and I lost it."

In Decaying Silence,
a Forgotten Memory

The Warriors stood beside the pool as the morning sun slowly rose, their rucksacks shouldered and weapons in hand. They stood in silence, the court empty of all but them. Soon, footsteps echoed over the stones as several guards approached.

Creedoc passed the pool and stood before them. "I will follow my brother's wishes and send my men to Morven...they should arrive within the fortnight." The Warriors nodded in understanding.

"Do not forget the pledge you have made, Warriors," he continued. "You have vowed to serve the Alliance to whatever end. The battle for Tarsha is upon us, I can feel it. Do not turn from the paths you have chosen...it may be the doom of us all." His gaze descended upon Malecai with a slight frown of his lips.

"We must be on our way," Cain informed the King as he sheathed his long sword.

"Of course, I wish to delay you no further. I bid you farewell, friends. I will be at Morven soon. Send my brother my regards."

The Warriors shook his hand in turn and bowed curtly. With that, the King and his guards turned. Creedoc gave a final wave and ascended the steps to the causeway.

Malecai glanced over his shoulder at the pool, the light of dawn flickering against the water's surface. Cain stopped and looked over his shoulder at him as the others entered the palace.

"I will never see this pool again," He said simply as he approached Cain. Cain stared after him, confused. Malecai left him behind and followed the others out of the palace.

**** ****

The desert sands greeted them. The wind blew an auburn veil across the morning skies, casting over the hazy sun with a kind of strange brilliance. The gates of Izadon slammed shut behind them, the grind of its stone echoing across the desert.

The Warriors stood for a moment, a sigh falling over them as they grudgingly stepped into the awaiting hell.

**** ****

The sun hung frozen in the skies, weightless in a sea of azure. Threads of sand blew across the deserts, biting viciously at the travelers as they left Izadon in the dust of their boots.

"I hear much about this siege of Morven," Aaron muttered as if to himself, breaking the hours of silence under an inuring sun. "But…what is the truth?"

Malecai dropped the cowl around his mouth and looked at him. "Many things are indeed said."

Silas shook his head. "Care to elaborate for a change?"

Malecai walked on in silence, staring out over the russet sands. "If what Creedoc says is true, then the enemy has indeed withdrawn from their advance across Tarsha, retreating as suddenly as they had come back to the gates of Andred. It is doubtful that Abaddon would relent his attacks. He has scattered us and dealt a painful blow. He would not surrender this advantage.

Therefore, I believe Abaddon has called this retreated for but one intent, to gather his forces for one strike at the head of the snake, Morven.

It seems foolish to assault the most impenetrable city ever built, yet that is exactly what the enemy is planning, amassing to deal the final deathblow to Tarsha. And with Morven out of his way, we will not be able to resist, and Abaddon will be able to regain his hold over humanity. We will at last perish to his genocide."

They continued for several moments, the sound of sifting sands filling their ears in the silence. "It would easily take hundreds of thousands to ever have the hope of conquering Morven...and that is exactly what Abaddon intends to do."

**** ****

The days passed as the Warriors continued across the Eastern Desert. The wind struck ceaselessly against their skin, throwing sand and stone in a flurry about them. They threw up their cloaks for protection, shielding themselves from the blistering wind and searing sun.

The sun fell from the skies. Its light slipped behind the horizon and the shadow of night at last crawled across the sands.

With this, they felt an unfamiliar relief. The wind died and the sand that churned the air fell to the ground around them. Malecai threw up his hand, halting the group instantly.

"Why'd we stop?" Cain inquired. Malecai continued to stare forward, his face stolid as he gazed into the shadows that now engulfed them. He began murmuring, hand raised to the west.

A faint roar reached their ears and the sand around their feet rose into the air. Suddenly, a massive wall of black rushed at them from over the horizon, a mighty squall of wind and sand that blotted out every star.

"Take cover!" Malecai screamed. They fell to their knees as the enormous mass crashed down around them.

The tempest of sand slammed into them and its shock-wave threw them violently into the air. The Warriors were tossed into the air and slammed repeatedly into the ground, thrown about as they flailed helplessly, rolling with increasing momentum across the sands.

An infernal roar filled the air, a beast of sand and wind running rampant across the desert, resolute on destruction. It tore the earth apart and disgorged its remnants across the sky, its howl of destruction filling the night with dread.

Cain tossed about helplessly for what seemed a lifetime before he was driven into the earth and slammed into a solid object, his back striking it as a wave of intense pain shot across his body. He was pinned to the object behind him, defenseless to a flogging of sand and rock.

Then as swiftly as it had come, the beast died and its terrible roar faded, leaving its victims far behind in its chaotic wake.

Cain fell to the ground and rolled several feet to a stop. He climbed slowly from the sand and stumbled about in disorientation.

Almost total darkness surrounded him. He struggled to perceive even his hand before his eyes, but the dark's hold was absolute. He could see little more than thin streaks of sand falling like rain around him. He turned and reached out towards the object that had stopped his tumble.

His fingers met a solid form and he ran his hand along it. His fingers crossed over several cracks hewn into a rough, cold surface. Straight lines formed symmetrical outlines in front of him.

He stepped back in surprise and strained through the darkness to see the wall he had felt. His boot struck sand as he stepped back, and he glanced up toward a large slope of sand on his right. He walked towards it and looked up at the top.

A small hole was blown out of the roof at the crest of the slope, leading to the outside world. Cain looked up into the starlight that glowed against his beaten face.

What little light leaked into the room revealed a kind of hallway, one end leading into the shadows on his right, the other end locked behind a wall of sand at his side. The hall fell dark and Cain glanced up to see a figure blocking the hole.

"I cannot believe it," Malecai's voice whispered through the darkness. He crouched and slid down the slope and landed beside Cain in a wave of sand.

Malecai looked around their surroundings as if drinking them in. He held his broadsword before him, the steel glistening dimly in the thin strands of starlight.

"I...this is impossible." He staggered back and leaned feebly against the wall behind them. He reached out and the tips of his fingers caressed the sandstone wall.

"We found it," he muttered, a dumbfounded look on his face.

"Found what?" Cain asked.

"The Tombs of Atuan, Cain. We found it..."

Cain looked at him in amazement, astonishment manifested even in the shadows of his face. The two of them looked around their surroundings, eyes wide with mystified perplexity.

Soon the voices of the others called for them from the outside world. Malecai returned their cries and soon the faces of the other five peered down at them.

"Come down here," Cain ordered as he stepped into the starlight. The group slid down the slope of sand and looked around curiously.

Aaron stepped forward and whispered, "What is this?"

Cain ran a hand through his hair. "We're in the Tombs of Atuan." Aaron stared at him a moment with incredulity, struggling for words.

"The Tombs of Atuan?" Silas asked as he brushed his hand along the walls of the catacomb.

"That's impossible," stammered Joshua, "they've been lost for over four hundred years."

"Impossible?" Malecai stepped forward from the shadows. "See for yourself what is possible." He turned and extended his right arm to the shadows.

A small ivory light gathered at his open hand and spread its radiance throughout the hall to illuminate what once lay masked in shadow.

They stood in a long hallway. Rough-cut bricks of sandstone formed the walls, floor, and roof around them. Deeply hewn cracks weaved like webs across their rough surfaces, casting threads of shadow in the light. Dust-laden bones littered the floor, covered in a blanket of webs. The hallway extended forward for several yards before it opened out into blackness beyond.

"Care to disagree?"

Joshua snorted and looked at the others. "Well, what now?" The group remained quiet.

"I think we should leave," Isroc offered. "We shouldn't be here anyway, there's a good reason no one has found it."

Malecai lowered his arm and the rays of light retracted back into his palm, pitching the group back into darkness. "Then go," he said as he threw his sword over his shoulder. "No one is stopping you. But I am staying, with or without any of you."

With that, he turned and walked out of the starlight, instantly engulfed in shadow, the white light at his hand bobbing as he sauntered down the hall.

"Well, I'm leaving," Isroc said as he picked up his rucksack.

"Isroc," Cain called after him, "you're not leaving."

Isroc stopped and looked over his shoulder. "And why is that?"

"Because the key to our enemy's defeat lies within these tombs," Adriel answered. "Don't you remember what Malecai told us? Abaddon's soul still lives on inside that sword; he has lived all these centuries through it.

All these four hundred years of war has come down to this one moment. You cannot ignore the fate we have been dealt. We can save Tarsha. We can save the lives of millions, avenge the deaths of those before us and make the peace we have never had. If we find the sword and destroy it, Abaddon will finally die and we will be rid of him at last! Is that not reason enough?"

Isroc shook his head. "Fine."

"Good," Cain said, finishing the exchange. He turned and stepped into the shadows, walking towards the light that awaited them at the end of the hall. The others followed behind, the clicking of their boots echoing in the ancient walls.

Malecai bowed curtly to them as they approached. He extended his hand again and the rays of light once more revealed their surroundings.

They stood now at the end of the hallway, a large room before them. The walls of the crypt loomed several yards above, the roof a shadow over the pool of light below. Rows and rows of tombs lined the crypt, shadows playing across their weathered faces.

Malecai gestured for them to follow. He led them away from the hall and began to weave through the countless caskets. Bizarre runes and faded paintings covered every inch of the tombs.

They turned a corner and followed a small hall to a stairway, the crest of which was hidden behind a veil of shadow. Sand, bone, and rock marred their path as they ascended the uneven steps. They eventually reached the top and came out into another hallway.

They continued down the hall in silence, all in quiet save their footfalls that resounded through the catacombs like thunder.

The Warriors eventually turned a sharp corner and entered a third hallway.

"Where are you going?" Aaron asked Malecai as they rounded yet another corner.

"Not entirely sure…but when I see it, then I shall know."

The group continued down the winding hallways for several minutes before coming to a pile of debris that nearly blocked their path. They carefully climbed over the debris and came out the other side.

Malecai again extended his hand, sending tendrils of light shooting forth from his palm. An immense mausoleum lay before them, far larger than any building they had ever seen. Sandstone columns, the width of several men, formed lofty supports to an unseen roof.

Hundreds of rows of tombs covered every available floor space and body-sized cutouts carved into every inch of wall. The Warriors descended a great staircase and came out among the dead.

"What is all this?" Isroc asked as they began the long procession through the graves.

"You know the story of these tombs…" Malecai replied, his voice echoing in the cavern. "Ivandar was killed in an ambush along with most of his men. The survivors soon realized that with the death of Abaddon's last remaining threat, he would be able to rise to absolute power. They saw that the end was near, and all hope was lost.

'They began to dig a grave for their fallen king. Yet when they finished, they were unwilling to leave him. They were indisposed to return to a world they knew was doomed. They chose instead to leave their world and its sorrows behind; they decided to follow their king…to the very death."

The Warriors continued across the crypt, picking their way through human remains and weaving through endless tombs. Thin beams of moonlight trickled into the catacomb from the edges of the roof. The moon's light danced in the dusty air, illuminating the Warriors for a moment before returning them to shadow.

"So they began to dig their own graves. They dug through the heat of the day, the chill of night, through ravenous hunger and crippling disease. Slowly they depleted themselves of strength and life, until all that awaited them was the death they so desperately craved. The living buried the dead, the dead leading the living. Then...all were eased of the pain and despair of this world, thus sealing the fate for all of Tarsha.

'They left behind these tombs, the legacy of their lives. Every man...they all died in the build of these tombs, where nothing but a legend survived. Most believe it to be nothing but a story. It gives hope to those that believe that there is a way to defeat Abaddon, that all is not lost. There is indeed a way that is hidden beneath the sands of Atuan, lost to time, lost to history, lost to the world." Malecai fell quiet, again leaving the group in total silence.

A few of the tombs in this sea of death lay open, their contents exposed to the musty air. The Warriors could not help but peer into their inviting mouths.

Ancient bones lay atop mounds of human ash, every crypt filled with the remains of the long since departed. Rusty swords lay gripped in the curled fingers of the dead, tarnished armor abandoned among the vestiges of their owners. The dark hollows of their skulls peered up at the living, loathsome of their presence.

Silence reigned in the darkness. It was profound and forever absolute. Its hold was inexorable. Through the bitter nights and decay of time, its presence was unquestioned. Silence guarded its treasure for over four hundred years, and to the living, it would not relent.

And so, the Warriors moved with utter quiet, fearing what awaited them in every shadow and behind every tomb. Every step was cautious, every breath subdued.

After several lengthy minutes, the labyrinth of tombs finally ended, nothing before them now but a small stretch of barren stone. Malecai guided the light at his hand ahead of them, revealing the bottom of another staircase.

They ascended the flight of stairs and came atop a large stone dais. A wooden chariot plated with rusted iron lay broken atop the stairs, encased in dust and debris. The Warriors looked past it to a tall door fashioned of sandstone, and human remains.

Malecai flicked his palm and the light encircling his hand grew to illuminate most of the door. He walked forward and rested his head against it, running his hand along the many rough cracks that scarred its face.

"How do we get through?" Cain asked.

"We don't," Isroc answered, "it's sealed for a reason."

Malecai turned and looked at Cain for a moment, disregarding their friend's input. "I will never turn back." He slowly pulled his sword from its baldric.

"Shit!" Isroc cried out as Malecai swung the massive sword straight into the door.

The blade struck the stone with a resounding ring of steel that echoed shrill across the tombs. He pulled the hefty sword from the door, leaving behind a large gash. He grunted and swung the sword again, sending stone flying overhead. He pulled it back and swung it again like a battering ram, hammering the full weight of the blade into the door. With each swing, the doors shuddered, sending rock and dust tumbling.

He mustered a final fearsome blow, and with a tremendous grind of stone, the doors blasted backwards and sent debris showering down on them. Malecai smirked at them through the thick cloud of dust.

Suddenly a gust of air blew over them, at last released from the bowels of the tomb. The reek of death and human decay met them, freezing them in the doorway.

They fought to continue breathing, struggling to escape the claws that bound their lungs. Slowly, the breath of life flowed freely as the fetid air dissipated into the crypts.

They continued their struggle for breath as they squinted through the light at their surroundings.

They stood now in a narrow hallway that led them deeper into the heart of the catacombs. Malecai beckoned them to follow and led them down the hall.

As they followed the winding corridors, they noticed several holes chiseled out of the walls. As they passed these cutouts, they noticed what lay within. Human skeletons, covered in veils of rotten cloth filled every hollow. Boney fingers stirred the dusty air, reaching out to the living.

They walked down the hall for several minutes, following its ever-changing course and passing hundreds of cavities filled with human vestige.

The air reeked of the decayed, a rancid odor that suffocated with every gasp. With every stolen breath, the living came closer to the end of the catacombs, and soon they stood at the foot of a massive staircase.

The Warriors climbed the colossal stairs for several laborious minutes. Soon, they came atop the staircase. They stepped forward and walked across the dais before coming to a stop at a foreboding archway.

Malecai raised the light to illuminate the arch, revealing a strange calligraphy etched across its beautifully carven surface. The Warriors stood in silence for a moment, not a word spoken, not a breath taken. Malecai nodded to his friends, this was it.

They entered through the arch and came out into a circular room. Evenly hewn steps encircled its walls and fourteen arches lined these steps, forming the entrances to different areas of the tombs. Several small slits lined the upper walls that let in thin strands of starlight, casting the room in an eerie film of silver.

In the middle was a large tomb that stood over four feet tall and was fashioned of a dull red stone that glowed strangely in the starlight.

"The tomb of Ivandar..." Malecai whispered in amazement. The light faded from his palm and he dropped his sword, letting it clatter down the steps. He stumbled down the stairs, disbelief in his eyes.

"This is not a good idea," Isroc warned as the others climbed down the steps after him.

Cain and Malecai approached the tomb and stood together beside the King's grave with shared interest, hands caressing the large stone slab that covered its mouth. Mysterious carvings were etched into its surface, depictions of the man within, his life, his legacy, and ultimately his inglorious death.

"Help me with this," Malecai said as he grabbed the edge of the slab. Cain nodded and stepped forward.

Isroc reached out to them. "Don't do it."

"And why not?"

"There could be wards around it," he cautioned as he cast a nervous glance around the room. "Or worse."

"I will take my chances. I have waited many years for this moment, and Tarsha has waited many more. More than fate has brought us to this moment."

"And now it is here," Cain said, "rightfully yours."

"Aye," Malecai replied, "so it would seem..."

The two of them threw their full weight against the slab. With a powerful heave, they managed to push it gradually forward. A deafening grind of stone echoed in the room as it slid away in a cascade of dust.

A putrid stench immediately reached them, but they disregarded it as curiosity surmounted. They encircled the now open tomb and peered into the shadows of what lay hidden for over four hundred years.

Inside the tomb was the remains of Ivandar, his bones brittle and eroding atop a bed of human dust and cobweb. A thick layer of linen stained black with decay was wrapped loose around his remains.

Ornate, rusted armor clung to his corroded bones, a thick sheet of dust forever tarnishing the once noble regalia.

Malecai's eyes caught a glint in the King's remains. "At last..."

He leaned forward and held out his hand, a light forming once again at his open palm. The light slowly grew and revealed what had been hidden in centuries of shadow.

A massive sword was clutched in Ivandar's hands. It was over five feet in length, well over two hands wide and half an inch thick. The blade was made of a strange silver metal, unlike anything they had ever seen. Thin veins of blood were woven like hundreds of capillary fingers across its luminous surface.

A sharpened edge ran along one side of the blade before coming to a graceful arch and forming a vicious, hook-like curve at the sword's tip.

A light steel hilt was fashioned at the base of the blade, the tips of which extended several inches from both sides of the sword before curving gracefully up at the ends. At the base of the blade, scarcely above the hilt, was a large ruby, glistening brilliantly in the light.

Below the hilt was a handle nearly a foot in length, made of hard, black leather. Below that was an intricate, darkened steel claw of a beast, its long talons curling inward as it clasped a massive ruby.

The sword seemed to glow as if newly forged from the light of Alon Heath. The sword boasted no rust, no corrosion. It had somehow escaped the crippling hands of time.

"Ceerocai, the lost sword of Abaddon," Malecai murmured as he reached for it. He wrapped his trembling fingers around its handle and lifted it from the sarcophagus. Dust and ash scattered into the air as the sword was disturbed from its centuries old resting place.

Malecai lifted the massive sword from the tomb. Light danced along the silver blade as he raised it before the Warriors. The group stood in disbelief, amazed at what they were seeing.

"You finally found it, Malecai," Cain grinned as he clapped his friend on the shoulder. Malecai stared in awe at the mighty sword, his eyes wide with wonder. He then nodded, and with a pained sigh, held it before Cain.

"It is yours now." Cain looked at him with astonishment. His mouth opened to say something, yet no words came.

"It is yours," Malecai offered again, holding the sword out to him.

Cain ran a hand through his hair. "Why me?" He managed to stutter, "It's rightfully yours. You searched for years; you gave up everything to find it."

Malecai nodded. "And that is why it is yours. I had given everything to find it and now have nothing left; I wanted it so fiercely that I sacrificed everything dear to me for it. If I keep it, I would be holding onto those painful scars. I have sought forgiveness for my mistakes for ten long years, this…is my atonement. So please take it…for my sake." He offered the sword to his friend. The others looked on with bewilderment.

"You gave your love to find this," Cain gestured to the sword. "She wanted you to find it; she would want you to have it."

Malecai's gaze fell to the ground. "I wanted this sword out of revenge, not for the good of Tarsha. Because of this sword and my greed for it, I lost my love. I have already told you, if I hold onto this sword…then I hold her death ever in my hands, a burden I already bear."

A silence enveloped the group as the two men stared at the other, a pained frown in both their faces. "We need this sword, Cain. The Alliance needs it. We have to hold onto it, and I refuse to. So I pass it onto you, to bear until we may destroy it and put an end to Tarsha's suffering." Malecai offered the sword to Cain again, and he reluctantly reached a hand out to it.

"Don't do it, Cain," Isroc warned. Cain glanced at him with indifference and reached for the weapon. Malecai handed the sword to him and quickly stepped back, gesturing for the others to do the same.

As Cain's fingers wrapped around the handle, a faint light rose from the sword. At its heart, the ruby in the blade seemed to gaze at him with a wild eye. Cain felt a strange warmth rise in his arm as the light of the sword pulsed with every beat of his heart. His friends stepped back in surprise as Malecai simply smirked.

The light and subtle growl of the sword ceased and the crypt returned to its prior dark, silence returning its boundless hold. Cain looked the sword over with newfound interest.

It was massive, yet surprisingly light for its size. It weighed little more than the long sword at his belt, yet several times as large. The entire sword glistened elegantly in the moonlight, a kind of strange, wild beauty.

Cain rolled the sword slowly in his hand. The colossal blade cleft the air, roaring violently in its own self-produced wind. The blade danced gracefully with little effort to its wielder, spinning near a blur about him. He stopped the blade, the wind died, and the roaring faded as he stared in awe at the power of the beast before him.

Malecai unfastened the black leather straps around his back and held it out for him. Cain nodded and unbuckled his sword from his belt and laid the old, battered sword beside the remains of the robbed king.

Cain then took the baldric of leather and rings from his friend and pulled his arm through the straps that crossed diagonal over his chest and back.

Cain lifted the sword, swung it fluidly over his back, and sheathed it through the rings. "Let's go," he said as he looked each of his friends over. "We've got a war to win."

**** ****

Cain leaned against the prow of the transport, staring through the darkness at the moonlit waters of the Alar. Malecai stood beside him, the two men gazing over the river.

They had boarded the ship that morning and upon their arrival, the soldiers greeted them warmly. However, at the sight of the sword of Andred, they fell instantly quiet, eyes wide with fear and astonishment.

Cain and Malecai enlightened the captain and his men of their journey and Creedoc's promise in alleviating Morven. They told of the sandstorm seeming guided by fate that revealed to them the Lost Tombs of Atuan. They told of its wonders and mysteries, and of the sword, every passenger on the ship drinking in every word of their lavish tale.

Cain sagged wearily against the ship's railing, exhausted from hours of talking. Now everyone was asleep and all was in silence save the rhythmic lapping of water against the ship's hull.

Malecai threw his cloak closer around him. "Long day," he muttered curtly.

"We had a lot of questions to answer."

"There will be more of that when we get back to Morven. The inquiries will never end so long as you bear the sword, that I can assure you. It is but a taste of the price you must pay for carrying such a burden."

"I didn't even ask to carry it. I shouldn't have to pay any price. Why can't you carry it?" Cain asked, "And don't say what you already have. The story you told me back in Izadon, I don't even know whether to believe it or not. Everything about you is a mystery."

"Pardon?"

"There's too many holes in your story. How do I know you didn't just tell me all of that to make me feel sorry for you?"

Malecai's gaze fell. "I wish I could tell you I was lying, but alas, it is all true."

"Then explain why the Iscara were after you and Raven."

Malecai shook his head and scanned the waters for a moment. In a solemn whisper he spoke, "They want me dead for the things I have done against them."

Cain raised a brow questioningly at this. "How could you have done anything against the Knights of Iscara? All of Tarsha can scarcely leave a dent in Abaddon's armies, let alone the mightiest of his forces."

"There is much you do not know about me."

"Then why don't you carry the damn thing if you're so high and mighty?" Cain cried out as he thrust the sword before him. "If what you say is true, I don't want to pay any price to carry it. I never asked for this!"

Malecai rested a hand on the sword and lowered it slowly. "We never call for the burdens fate places on us. We never wish to make sacrifices, yet we must. One day, Cain, you will learn that you must make the greatest sacrifice, you, and no one else. You carry that sword because you have what no one else has."

"And that is?"

Malecai turned back to the ship's railing and leaned against it as if deep in thought. "You would not understand if I told you now, but soon you shall know the truth. You will not like it though..."

Cain sneered and slung Ceerocai over his shoulder. He turned his gaze back to the waters, contemplating what Malecai had said.

After a while, Malecai turned to him. "You should at least know more of the burden you bear."

"I already know," Cain replied vehemently.

"You only think you do."

Cain lifted a brow and crossed his arms. "Enlighten me then."

"Very well…you may know it is the sword of Abaddon, forged by the hand of the Forgotten in the light of Alon Heath. It was crafted to give him far greater power than his human body could ever harbor, yet at a price no man should pay.

He gave his life and his humanity in return for godly power. He infused the sword with his soul, extracting his life force and placing it into the newly forged blade. This bequeathed him with the power of the god who gave him his purpose, to eradicate humanity for their transgressions.

In placing his soul inside the sword, he was able to call upon the powerful emotions of the mortality within, which granted him the ability to unleash physical and mental devastation upon his enemies in the form of a great scarlet beast, the very essence of Abaddon himself.

However, when Ivandar managed to take it from him, he knew not the destructive power of the weapon. He wielded the sword in life without understanding, and took it with him into death, condemning it to the mortal grave for over four hundred years.

Nevertheless, word of its power eventually leaked into the outside world. What was revealed to Tarsha was this…the sword was imbued with endless purity, impervious to decay and corrosion.

Abaddon used it as a channel to his mortal soul, calling upon its strengths while retaining the immortality granted him. You hold in your hands Abaddon's living, breathing soul, and as long as it remains on this earth, Abaddon will never die." Cain fidgeted nervously as his friend continued.

"Knowing of this sword's existence has given hope to the people of Tarsha, perhaps the only hope that has endured after all these needless years of suffering. To this day, people believe that if the Tombs of Atuan are revealed, then the sword could be found and destroyed, ending this senseless war at last.

However, they are obdurately naive. They know not the full capacity of the sword's power. The sword is indestructible. The blade is made entirely of the purest form of cerebreum, the strongest and lightest metal ever produced from the bowels of earth.

Cerebreum was mined, forged, and mass-produced in every way imaginable for hundreds of years. But humans cleaned the earth of cerebreum a millennium ago, and now none remains to us, as if it all had vanished, to protect man from their own selfish greed. Few artifacts of cerebreum remain, and now a pound of the precious metal can provide a man's salary for life.

The cerebreum blade is indestructible, easily able to crush diamond as if it were mere salt. The knowledge of how to smelt down and fashion cerebreum has been long lost to history. It is impervious to any of our mundane methods."

Cain stared at Malecai for a moment, struggling to form his next words. "So what you're saying is," he began, "that Ceerocai can never be destroyed. That Abaddon's spirit can never be destroyed. That we will...never win this war?"

Malecai returned his gaze for a long moment. "It would seem so..."

Where the Soul Lies

Thick iron chains rolled up the sluice gates of Morven as the transport sailed into the city. Buildings crawled by as soldier and civilian alike ran to the riverbanks to get a glimpse of the Warriors, their shouts and cheers echoing in the early morning. After several minutes, the ship came to a stop at the docks and the waters settled around them at last.

The soldiers dropped the gangplank and began rolling up the sails as the Warriors shouldered their rucksacks.

The captain approached them. "There's someone here to see you, Warriors," he informed them with a slight bow. They followed him across the deck and down the gangplank.

A large crowd of civilians stood in wait around the docks, cheering as they saw the Warriors descend the gangplank.

Several men and women in brown leather and chain mail stood by the riverbank amidst the crowd, each armed with a longbow, sword, and spear. At the head of the group stood Jiran and Heric, the Vilante of Ilross.

"Well if it isn't the Warriors," Jiran cried out as they approached, "a pleasure to see you again, my friends, it has been a while. I'm surprised you're all alive and in one piece!" He laughed heartily.

"What brings you here?" Cain asked him as they shook hands with the two Vilante.

"The war of course," Jiran replied. His eyes suddenly flew open as he noticed the sword at Cain's back.

The crowds then fell quiet and every man, woman, and child stared at the sword. Jiran quickly leapt forward and threw his cloak around the sword, hiding it from sight. He cursed colorfully and herded Cain away from the river, splitting the now fervently whispering crowds.

**** ****

The Warriors and the Vilante of Ilross stepped out of the fleet of covered wagons and came out into the palace courtyard. The sun hung low over the distant horizon, the mountain peak girdled with clouds.

They walked across the windswept court and approached the palace, passing the winged guardians and ascending the ivory staircase.

The Palace Guards bowed to the Warriors as they passed, and two of them opened the gates to the palace, beckoning them inside. Jiran instructed his men to wait by the door before following the Warriors into the throne room.

King Darius looked up, his eyes wide with surprise as he bound from his throne. "A welcome sight indeed," he said with a jovial grin and shaking their hands warmly. "Good to see you again, friends."

"I trust your journey went well?" A familiar voice said from beside the throne. Ethebriel and Armeth walked towards them, their boots clicking against the marbled floor.

Adriel let out a cry and dove into Ethebriel's arms, the two embracing each other warmly. Ethebriel clasped her head in his hands and kissed her fondly on the forehead.

Armeth walked past them and shook each of the Warriors hands, talking intently with the four of Andaurel as Ethebriel and Adriel approached.

"I've heard many things of the Warriors since last we met," Ethebriel began. "We have much catching up to do," he said to them before turning and smiling at Adriel. "Things have gone well for you. I see you've found a home with these men."

"Reminiscing can wait," Jiran said to the group. He swung Cain's cloak to the side, leaving the sword of Abaddon exposed for all to see.

The group stumbled back in surprise, shouts and curses rising in the throne room.

Darius hastily gestured for the guards to close all the doors. "How did you get it?" Cain explained to everyone how they had stumbled across the Tombs of Atuan.

"A sandstorm?" Armeth questioned. "That bodes ill in my eyes...something is not right."

Ethebriel stepped beside his friend and placed a hand on his shoulder. "It seems more like the winds of fate to me. For four centuries, Tarsha has searched for it and to no avail. And yet, a soldier of Kaanos finds it. Fate it is indeed. The world has great plans for you, Cain Taran."

"Fate or not, the world's not going to tell us what to do with it," Darius retorted. "There are pressing matters at hand. The war is building. Abaddon is gathering his armies and preparing to launch a final assault before we can gather our strength.

'He has pulled all of his forces from our lands, leaving us free for the moment. He has given us the precious time we need to gather our forces as well and defend Morven against the coming assault."

Ethebriel nodded, still eyeing the sword at Cain's back. "We have brought thirty thousand of our finest troops from Kaanos, and we picked up another fifteen thousand of Verin's men as we sailed north. Verin himself could not leave with us, but he assured me another forty thousand would be sent soon."

"And what of my brother?" Darius inquired of the Warriors.

"Fifty thousand will arrive within the week," Cain replied.

Darius nodded earnestly. "That is a worthy force. Two hundred thousand men should be within our walls by the end of the week."

"If we have that much time," Armeth added.

"True, but the gates of Morven have never before been breached; our numbers will swell around our enemy. We will prevail."

"Overconfidence has always proved man's greatest bane," Malecai scoffed, "the enemy is intelligent, powerful, and their numbers are far greater than our own. You would be foolish to disregard rationality for confidence."

The group fell silent for a moment before Armeth broke the tension. "The enemy may be greater in number, but we are greater in power." His eyes locked onto Cain and everyone in the room followed his stare. "We have the sword of Abaddon, Ceerocai..."

Suddenly, a great roar filled the throne room. Jiran and Armeth rushed toward the doors and threw them open, the Warriors chasing after him.

Several guards and the Vilante braced themselves against the doors, fighting desperately against whatever lay beyond. Heric turned to them. "It's the people! They've gone mad!"

Armeth shoved aside the guards and opened the front doors of the palace, letting in a flood of frigid air. Hundreds of people crowded the palace steps and stretched across the entire mountaintop.

A great roar rose from the masses as every man and woman screamed and cursed. Soldiers formed a line along the front of the palace, struggling to push back the tide of enraged citizens.

"What's going on?" Armeth shouted over the clamor.

"They want the sword!" A soldier replied as he shoved a man back. "They want to destroy it!"

At the sight of Cain, the crowds grew incensed. Curses and death threats filled the air as the roar rose to an unprecedented scale. Once the warm eyes of those that had placed their hopes on Cain, now grew cold and insufferable, seething over Cain with changed heart.

Armeth threw an arm over Cain and pulled him back into the entrance room as the people fought their way towards him. The Warriors rushed back into the palace and the guards slammed shut the doors.

Darius and Ethebriel crossed the entrance room and stopped before the Warriors.

Darius eyed Cain suspiciously. "Do you see the chaos you have brought upon us? Tarsha has fought for four hundred years; Ceerocai has been nothing more than a myth to fuel our hope. We do not need it to win this war, we never have and never will.

'Now that the sword is here however, the people will do whatever it takes to end their suffering. Before the battle to come, they grow scared and uncertain. A great host marches upon us. Their brothers, husbands, sons, they may lose them in the days to come. They may lose everything if we do not win this battle. The city may fall, our people may be slaughtered. The fate of Tarsha and our very survival hangs on this battle. They want it destroyed. It should be destroyed, it has to be destroyed! We could end this war right now…we could end it all!'"

"It cannot be destroyed," Armeth answered.

"There is a way…" Malecai replied. The group turned to him curiously. "We can throw it into a volcano. Only then will it be destroyed…"

"Really?" Silas asked.

"No you shit head! How could that possibly work? The sword is fashioned of pure cerebreum! There is no known way to destroy it."

Armeth raised a brow at the extent of this stranger's knowledge. "Aye, it cannot be destroyed. At one time, we had the skills and knowledge to work with cerebreum. But until we figure out how to do that once again, we can only use it as bait to lure Abaddon into reckless action."

Darius shook his head at this. "It would be too dangerous. It should not be wielded by anyone, who knows what it may do to mortal man." Isroc nodded in agreement as the others remained stolid.

"Then what do you propose we do with it then?" Armeth retorted. "If we cannot destroy it, and we cannot use it, what then remains to us? Throw it over the wall and let the armies of Andred figure it out?"

"We should study it," Ethebriel offered, "Until we learn of a way to destroy it. We cannot do more with it, or any less. Let Cain bear it if he wills, until that day of knowledge comes. No other option remains to us." A long moment of silence followed his words.

Malecai stepped toward Cain and raised a hand in the air. "It is a powerful weapon, but in the hands of Cain Taran...it is divinity incarnate. Just as its former owner. He is the only known person who can use it to its full potential. Let him use it, and we will surely win. We do not need to destroy it. We can use Abaddon's soul against him...and defeat him in our own way." Everyone in the room looked at Malecai questioningly.

Isroc stroked his beard in thought. "What makes this time so different from any? Millions have fought this war before us. Millions have given their lives in the attempt to defeat Andred and put an end to Abaddon's genocide. What makes us so different from them?"

Malecai turned to him and smiled. "We have Cain Taran..."

"How do you know Cain can use Ceerocai?" Jiran inquired. "Ivandar wielded it in life as nothing but another sword, no mortal can wield it with any greater power, no man can call upon the soul save for Abaddon himself, and I don't think he will be so inclined to help us."

Malecai remained quiet for a moment. "I do not know," he surrendered, "it is nothing more than speculation I suppose."

Darius turned to Cain, blinking slowly as if fighting to form his next words. "I permit you to wield that…monstrosity, until we figure out a way to destroy it. You hold in your hands, Cain, the indomitable will of Abaddon. Search your soul and decide whether the power is worth the price, for Abaddon had to make that decision, and look where his soul lies now…"

**** ****

The following days were spent in endless preparation, night and day spent ever in chaos. Ships filled nearly the entire breadth of the Alar. Soldiers from across Erias poured into the city from land and sea daily. The gates of Morven lay open to a constant stream of troops that now flooded the streets like a molten sea of steel.

Smoke hung over the city as dense as any fog, the fires of hundreds of forges burning like the avid bowels of hell. Weapons, armor, and supplies carted across the city at a blinding rate. Soldiers armed for combat, and for death.

The last of the Kaanosian troops entered the city. Twenty thousand men poured off the transports, filling the docks with the emerald and russet gleam of their armor.

Days passed in a fleeting glimpse, a mere blur in time as night and day slipped from memory.

On the fifth day, a massive fleet of black ships sailed into Morven from the eastern gates. The head of the column halted before the docks of the city. Creedoc descended the gangplank of the lead ship.

Twenty five thousand men now marched as an endless wave of crimson from the decks of the ships, swelling the roads and barracks.

Two hundred thousand soldiers now stood poised for war, ready for whatever end.

**** ****

The week went by unwillingly for all. The morning sun shimmered in the windows of the palace. The Warriors began a silent meal alone in the empty guard's room. They ate quietly, each in their own withdrawn thoughts.

Heavy footfalls thudded on the wooden floor of the hall and the group turned to the archway. Creedoc appeared from the hallway, his sabatons echoing in the domed room. The Warriors turned and looked at him anxiously. "The enemy is here."

**** ****

"How long until they're here?" Darius screamed, his shout reverberating in the marbled throne room. "How much time do we have!" The Warriors watched the exchange from the side, Ethebriel and Armeth beside them, each with a vexed expression.

"How much time do we have left?" Darius shouted again.

"I know nothing more than you, brother," Creedoc replied simply. Darius yelled and threw a hand around his brother's breastplate, pulling him forcefully towards him.

"And what of your men, brother...what of the fifty thousand you promised us? You brought only half that number!"

Creedoc returned his fierce stare, their faces mere inches from the other. "I could not risk leaving my country undefended; we suffered an assault under Andred not long prior. I cannot leave my country unarmed for it would fall at the mere whim of the enemy." Darius glared at him, a scowl pulling at his lips.

"Believe me, if I could have brought them all I would have, you are a king as well, you know we must do what is best for our country before all else. You understand my circumstances."

Darius shook his head at this. "No, no I do not. You have damned us all! The entirety of Tarsha is in peril, hanging on the edge of a sword, on the very brink of destruction! And if you're too afraid to sacrifice what is required for the greater good then no...no I do not understand your circumstances."

He shoved him forcefully away. Creedoc stumbled back, gripping his maimed arm in pain. Darius sighed deeply, his shoulders heaving as he exhaled. "We must gather our forces," he continued after a tense silence, hand twitching nervously on the pommel of his sword. "The enemy is upon us, we need to be ready as soon as possible."

The King began to walk in a slow circle around the group, his arms outstretched to the skies beyond the palace walls. "The end is upon us, let us embrace it..."

**** ****

The Warriors stood at the edge of the palace court, looking over the city from their vantage point. The streets below flowed with rivers of soldiers, distant glints of armor flickering under the setting sun. The rivers flowed toward the end, toward certain death. A grave silence filled all of Tarsha.

The bitter winter's wind whipped across the courtyard. The gust lashed the Warriors, their hair thrashing about as they held their cloaks close. Not a word was spoken; they knew what lay ahead.

The last of the Citadel Guards began the long descent to the city. The column of wagons disappeared behind the bend of the road and the noise of their rasping wheels soon died in the wind. The Warriors stood frozen, watching the armies amass for war.

Adriel stepped back from the group, her footsteps shaking them from their thoughts. She caught Cain's eye and gestured for him to follow. He walked after her and together they left the others and walked across the courtyard.

"Forgive me," she murmured as they walked, finally breaking the unease between them.

"For what?"

"For everything. I…I didn't come across properly when we met," she continued, "I don't want you to think I'm something I'm not. I just want to say sorry, before anything might happen to me."

They reached the foot of the palace stairs and Adriel gently brushed her hand against the wings of a statue as Cain sat down on the marble steps.

"Something could happen to any one of us, Adriel. That is war, we stare it in the face and take our gamble, after all…we can only win or lose." They fell silent for a while and gazed out across the mountaintop to a sky painted with the blood of a dying day.

Adriel removed her hand from the statue and looked at him. "All of you fight for revenge. If that's all you fight for, then why continue?"

Cain fell quiet and gazed out over the sunset. It spread its hues fast across the clouds, filling the heavens with a deep and ominous scarlet. The clouds seemed to float atop rivers of blood. In the distance the sun sat, broiling and heavy in the cradle of the world.

Cain's unremitting anger, after so many years of harboring its lonely walls, had finally died. He struggled to fan its embers through this journey, but it festered like rot on his heart.

Since the death of his wife and son, he fought for a renewed chance at vengeance, or so he had made himself and everyone else believe. However, this was nothing more than an unspoken confession of the pain that wallowed deep within. He longed to make sense of the unjust deaths of his family, and in revenge, he had found his scapegoat.

He never really knew how he would attain his vengeance. He never really knew how he could sate the insatiable. Revenge was nothing more than a fire amid fields; nothing could quench its desire. He crawled from its destruction, eyes illuminated. He could no longer morn for his family. The time for tears has passed.

He stood up and rested a hand against the wing of a statue. The pain of his loss fell at last from his heart. The sorrow he had carried with him since the fall of Andaurel faded to memory. The loss of his family would forever weigh on him, but the pain at last surrendered its hold. In its place was an emptiness, a void that must be filled.

Tarsha needed him; the people needed him. With the discovery of Ceerocai, he finally realized his importance to the people and the hope they placed upon him. This was more than himself now, the lives of millions were on his shoulders, and he vowed to protect every last one of them, to the death if need be.

Cain gazed out over the setting sun, its orange and scarlet lights filling his eyes. With the warmth of the sun against his face, he felt also a warmth in his heart at last. The void had been filled. He turned to Adriel and stared into her eyes with such heartfelt intensity, forcing a tear to rise in her eye.

"I used to fight for revenge, vengeance for the deaths of my family, vengeance for the senseless loss of it all. That was all I had.

But now, now my eyes are open, and I see the light of these truths. I see that life itself is worth fighting for. The freedoms we have never felt, the happiness we have never had, the peace we have always sought but never known, all that is worth fighting and dying for. It has become far more than my own convictions…my selfish revenge. I fight for the hope of peace; for hope is all we have left. I fight for Tarsha and its people now. I have found peace in my heart at last…"

**** ****

The Warriors crossed the Alar; the entire river now covered in a thick layer of ice, the once still and lifeless waters now frozen by winter's unforgiving hand. They crossed the drawbridge and followed the road past the endless buildings, walking on in silence.

They eventually came to a wall of steel, armed soldiers crowding the streets and buildings over a mile away from the gates. The soldiers immediately stepped aside for the Warriors.

Men saluted earnestly as they followed the long gap to the walls. They eventually reached the gates and ascended the flight of steps beside the gatehouse to the causeways above.

The King of Erias approached them as they came out onto the causeway. "Lord Verin has not come," Darius informed them, "we must make do with the hands we have been dealt. Two hundred thousand men are now at our command. The enemy is close…now we wait." The Warriors nodded in response.

"I have other matters that require my attendance; I take my leave of you for now. I ask you to wait with my men, I will return by daybreak." With that, he turned on his heels and disappeared into the masses.

The Warriors joined the immense line of soldiers that stood shoulder to shoulder, each man peering out over the desolate plains of snow before them.

Ivory-capped mountains lined the horizons, mere silhou-ettes against clouded skies. The moon hung full ablaze in the night, its light gleaming across the streets like a mirror of stone that set all the city aglow. A chill wind blew across the causeway, caressing their skin with quivering lips.

Cain stood gazing over the beauty of possibly his last night alive, his eyes cast over the sea of shimmering snow. This would be the greatest battle any of them had ever known. He knew that any one of them could die. The last thing that had yet to be taken from them, their lives, could soon be stolen away, and they accepted this with open arms.

Isroc's voice filled his ears. He turned to see his friend staring at him with concern, his brow furled in thought. "I haven't known you for very long, my friend," he said, "but even the blind can see when you are burdened by your thoughts."

Cain laughed despite himself. "Aye…it would seem so." He leaned heavily against the cold stone of the causeway and Isroc followed suit.

"You know," Isroc continued, "after a night like this, I wouldn't mind death." Cain laughed anxiously. "Look at those stars."

They looked up to the heavens, hundreds of thousands of tiny lights flickering in an ocean of solemn beauty. "Search the heavens and you may come to find the answer to your problems."

Cain shook his head slowly, returning his gaze. "What if I am my problem?"

Isroc thought for a moment. "Aye…every man carries his own burdens. I cannot give you the answer you seek, that is for you to find. Alas, our burdens are our own." He scratched his beard in thought. "You have lost your home, your family, why add another load to your already troubled mind?" He gestured to the sword at Cain's back. "That's only a burden, that's all it is and ever will be."

Cain nodded at this and thought for a moment. "I have to bear it, for no one else will. I have to carry it, until we may destroy it. But yes, Isroc, that's all it will ever be, a burden. I know not what price I must pay to keep it, but I feel it may be a great one."

Isroc raised a brow. "Then why do you hold onto it when you know there is such a costly price to come? We need the sword, but we don't need someone giving their life to carry it."

Cain looked up at his friend, their dark eyes locked. "I finally have a purpose that I have not felt this entire journey. Finding this sword has pulled me from my shadow. I realize now that I can help put an end this cycle of suffering. If it means I must sacrifice everything I have to bring an end to Abaddon and his genocide, then so be it." Joshua, overhearing their conversation, looked away from them and wiped his eye.

Isroc pounded his fist onto the causeway. He sighed angrily and closed his eyes. "Damn it, Cain! That sword is indestructible! We cannot destroy it! This is a needless war, a war we will only lose!" The surrounding soldiers looked at him with solemn eyes.

Isroc looked to each of them and turned to Cain with a whisper. "As long as Abaddon's soul lives on inside that sword, then this war will only continue, and your sacrifices will have meant nothing!"

Cain nodded and replied, "This may be a needless war, but look where we are now." He gestured around them. "I must fight, because in the end that is all I can do...all anyone can do. It may not be much, but it's something." He smiled at his friend before finishing. "Malecai...did say there was no 'known' way to destroy the sword."

Isroc turned and looked out over the city walls, smiling softly. "Maybe there is a way...maybe we are the ones to finally end this all..."

In the Blood of the Enemy

The sun rose slowly over the east, spreading its light across the citadel of Morven. Silence ever reigned. The streets were desolate of citizens. The buildings were filled with every man, woman, and child that dare remain. Two hundred thousand armed men lined the causeways and streets below, yet not a word was spoken in the tension.

They waited for hours, silence absolute. It was surreal, a feeling none of them had ever justly felt. The fate of Tarsha rested on the sword of every man. Everything the Warriors had ever done, all of it hinged upon these next few hours. Whatever was to happen would decide their very fates.

The muted rasp of steel on stone echoed in the morning air. Soldiers polished their shields and the quiet songs of bowstrings tested sent their hushed notes across the armies.

Cain rested his bow against the wall of the causeway and shouldered his quiver. He pulled his hand from the strap and sighed anxiously. He looked around, absorbing his surroundings with the new dawn's light.

They all stood here now because of hope. They had endured Abaddon's genocide of humanity for over four hundred years, all in the name of some forgotten deity. They stood here now for the hope of peace, for the hope of atonement in the eyes of their creator and punisher. They longed for the peace they have never felt, and in the coming hours of battle, they may find the victory they seek.

Cain closed his eyes and felt the wind brush across his skin, feeling the breath pierce his lips. He felt something rest on his shoulder and he turned to see a small hand. Adriel looked at him; the sapphires of her eyes gazing into his own, a concerned countenance on her face. "Do not trouble yourself, Cain, it is the path you have chosen, is it not?"

He stared into her eyes for a moment, long after her words fell from his ears. "Aye...it is. But you Adriel, you stayed with us after all of this. After so much has happened, you still remain. I often try to make sense of it but I cannot."

Her lips pursed as she thought of an answer. "I stayed for many reasons, Cain," she replied, "yet one thing above them all showed me the value of love, of sacrifice, of a tender heart that I had forgotten long ago. It taught me to open my eyes and see. I had long closed my heart to the world, but now it is opened." She touched his arm and smiled fondly. They broke their gaze and looked to the southeast across the fields of snow.

"They are here..." Malecai whispered. Cain turned, his mouth opened to reply when a distant noise silenced him.

A faint note rippled across the wind, stirring the soldiers of the Alliance from their thoughts. The sound repeated itself, and the city strained to hear its feeble notes. The deep thrumming continued ever louder.

"They're here!" Ethebriel cried.

A thin line of black appeared on the horizon, slowly approaching with the notes of distant horns and beating drums.

Four hundred and fifty thousand Andreds marched in the formations of war, their footfalls shaking the very earth.

The Andreds stood as tall as any man, many of them mightier in size and girth. Their skin was black as coal, ebony folds drawn taught over sinew and bone. Their flesh had long since begun to rot, exposing the bone and bloody muscle beneath. Lidless eyes stared out behind thin webs of grayed hair; their pupils stained luminescent silver. Amber fangs leered from behind lipless maws and below them lay rows of human teeth, tinged with blood and rot.

From their mouths, no noise was uttered. They were forever mute, as silent as the death that once gripped them.

Over their rotten flesh were layers of tempered armor that gleamed dimly in the sunlight. They were painted black, the scarlet crests of Andred swathed along much of their armor. Beneath the plates of blackened steel were gray folds of chain mail. Spiked shields, vambraces, gauntlets and pauldrons adorned their muscled forms. In their soiled hands were massive pikes, scimitars or axes.

As the army advanced across the fields, a looming wall of Gehets followed closely behind. These were no beasts of earth; seeming from darkness they emerged. They stood fifteen feet in height and wide as the trunk of the mightiest tree.

Plates of lustrous steel covered their dark, stone-like skin. Four ebony horns adorned each grotesque face, one pair gracefully flowing up from its brow, another curving sharply down. They bore mighty axes of steel, several times the size of any man.

Their great bodies wreathed in flames. Fires bound across their flesh and spewed forth columns of rancid smoke. They walked on unharmed and unhindered, as if fed from the very fires.

The armies of Andred covered the earth before Morven for miles, an eternal black abyss that seemed to swallow all life from whence they stood. Their silence was unnerving, inhuman. They marched with utter resolve, thoughts of blood stirring in their hollow skulls. Not a sound stirred the earth save the war horns of distant Arzecs. Their dire notes echoed across the four corners of the earth, resounding and ever loathsome.

The army of the Alliance gazed out over the hordes of enemies before them; terror in their hearts. The end was upon them.

Darius drew his sword with a long rasp of steel. "Men of Tarsha!" He cried after the horns of their enemy ceased for the moment.

"This is the day your wills are tested! This is the day your hearts bleed with courage! This is a day worthy of remembrance, the day that war and peace is won! Let us meet our enemy with sword and spear, for the carrion fowl shall sing of our glory! Bleed with me on this day, bleed for your countries, bleed for the Alliance, bleed for your freedom! Stand with me men, stand and fight for our salvation!" The King of Erias thrust his sword high into the air, the two hundred thousand defenders of the Alliance following likewise. Their earsplitting battle cry rose from the city, drowning out the war horns of their enemy.

"Bows at the ready!" Darius commanded. Thousands of bows were raised into the air as arrows were notched, the rasp of wood faintly heard under the din of the enemy's approach.

"Fire!" Darius cried as he thrust his sword forward. Thousands upon thousands of arrows were unleashed; shooting past the soldiers on the causeway as they spilled over the ramparts. The cloud of arrows descended over the enemy, suspended in flight before falling into the sea of blackness.

The steel rain crashed into the shields of their targets, reaping little damage among the masses. The Andreds marched on undeterred, and as the last arrow fell from the skies, thousands of black horned bows rose from the abyss.

Barbed arrows spit forth and blotted out the sky before they arced gracefully through the air and crashed over the city. The defenders raised their shields as death sowed hell among them. Thousands of arrows recoiled against their shields but many met their mark. Soldiers tumbled from the walls above, screaming as they fell to their deaths.

The volley ceased with a dying breath and the Alliance dared venture from behind their shields. The approaching army suddenly broke from their march, a deafening thunder rising from the tempest of their charge. They burst into a fearsome sprint, a mindless haul across the vast fields before the city. Yet, the gap between city and its ruin quickly closed.

"Slow them down!" Darius screamed, "Slow them down!" The Alliance once more aimed their bows into the onrushing army and let loose a desperate volley. Arrows pelted down into the oncoming tides. Bodies tumbled to the ground, instantly swallowed in the masses.

"Fire the trebuchets!" Ethebriel commanded over the scream of their arrows. The hundred loaded trebuchets that lined the walls now pulled back their nets. With the force of mighty ropes, they released and fired their munitions over the city. Great boulders crashed into the onrushing army, sending thousands of bodies flying.

The Andreds rushed forward undaunted and slammed into the gate, engulfing the city in instant blackness. Andreds threw themselves into the walls, shaking the ancient stonework to its core. A ring of steel broke from the clamor below as the Andreds began thrashing the metal gates with their weapons, eager children of war awaiting their vocation.

The archers above now aimed at the surrounding tides below. Arrows cascaded down the ramparts and felled the Andreds like hapless insects. Barbed arrows disgorged themselves from the masses and dropped men from the causeways above.

Through the rain of death, the enemy's ranks split and gradually revealed the trunk of some unearthly tree, over one hundred feet in length and several in girth, suspended above the earth by a throng of Andreds. At its head was a cap of solid steel fashioned in the form of a strange, irate beast.

The massive battering ram soon reached the city gates and its silent wielders prepared for the first strike.

The steel beast reeled back and quickly gained momentum before slamming full force into the gates. With a tremendous shudder of the doors, flames exploded from its maw, sending forth a fell cloud of smoke and sparks.

The battering ram staggered back as its wielders gathered momentum for a second strike.

"Bring it down! Bring it down!" Darius screamed. The archers atop the causeway fired volley after volley over the ram, quickly felling the defenseless Andreds. As the wielders were shot down however, more leapt forward to take their place.

The Andreds continued undisturbed by the death around them, the bodies quickly piling at their feet as they threw the ram forward for another strike. The beast slammed into the gates, and with a raucous explosion, reeled back for a third strike.

Boulders spewed forth from the bowels of Morven and crashed down on the armies below, throwing bodies into the air and grinding flesh beneath their weight in clouds of savage gore.

The hours passed as the ram's wielders continued their attack, soon climbing a growing mountain of bodies to reach the doors. Blow after blow the doors shook, yet in the deep-seeded ballast of stone upon which they perched, they would not relent.

A powerful boom erupted from the drums of the army. Hundreds of massive bundles then ejected themselves from the masses and rocketed towards the city. The bundles descended into the city and crashed into the packed ranks of the Alliance. Soldiers were crushed under their weight, sending blood and entrails spurting across the streets. Men sailed through the air, smashed against building walls as their screams were silenced beneath the crunch of bone.

The bundles settled and the soldiers cautiously approached them. Corpses of men, women, and children lay mutilated and mangled within, limbs and heads long since severed. Trails of blood covered the streets, dead and stolid stares gone unnoticed to the fetid stench that now arose.

Soldiers screamed in horror, their countrymen now being used against them in this siege to the death.

Scores of enemy war machines released their munitions. The massive boulders crashed over the causeways, throwing up debris as they slammed into walls of defenseless soldiers, sending hundreds of men plummeting to the streets below.

The fighting continued for hours and the light of day slowly slipped behind a constant veil of arrows. The sun at last surrendered its hold and night fell over the city.

Fire filled the city and sky, their light and wrath engulfing the battlefield. Flames licked up the city walls, its gate glowing red with death. Men's cries pierced the night and bodies tumbled in endless slaughter.

Boulders continued sailing through the clouds, sowing death among both armies. One boulder met a fortunate mark and smashed into one of the gate's statues. The statue exploded apart and its upper half broke off before falling backwards over the city.

It struck the walls, obliterating the causeways and sending thousands of men flying over the city, screaming to their deaths. With an earth-shaking explosion, debris rained down over the walls and into both armies, crushing both Andred and men alike as they sought to escape

Through the ensuing chaos, the ocean of Andreds split and ten Gehets marched towards the city. Their bodies were like ominous beacons in the night, their skin ablaze with fire. The beasts marched on vehemently towards the city, tearing through the corpses of their dead.

They soon reached the city gates and walked head-on into a volley of arrows that plinked uselessly against their armor.

They thrust their mighty axes into the now decrepit gates, the doors shuddering violently from the impact. The beasts pounded the gates as the battering ram beneath continued its relentless assault. Flaming debris fell continuously around them and the gates began to flag with every strike.

The defenders behind the gates stepped back fearfully, shields and spears held desperately against what would soon pour through those gates.

As the trolls continued their battery, the armies split again to reveal a wall of Gehets marching onto the city.

However, as they reached the gates, the soldiers on the causeways above noticed a smaller shadow at the front of the procession. Below the flaming beasts a lone figure rode.

In the saddle of a white horse sat a man swathed in black. He raised an armored hand from the folds of his cloak and the Gehets stepped away from the battered gates, grunting with displeasure. The figure rode over the thousands of dead Andreds and held out his hand once more. With a gesture, the ram and wielders were tossed into the air, instantly engulfed in the raging fires.

The archers on the wall shrugged off the man's display of power and aimed their bows at him. They shot down a massive volley that swallowed him instantly in a cloud of steel. With a burst of light, the arrows exploded, shards flying harmlessly off him. He then pulled a sword from the depths of his cloak, and with a ring of steel, the sounds of battle fell silent.

He thrust his weapon forward and a column of blue light shot towards the gates. The light slammed into the doors with a deafening crunch that shook them to their very core. The man stood undaunted, snow suspended in animation around him.

The archers continued their desperate volley, anything to stem their fates. Yet against such might, their efforts were fruitless.

The man raised his sword and thrust it forward, and with a flash of wind, a brilliant light slammed full force into the gates.

The steel doors blasted off their hinges and shot into the city streets, crashing into the soldiers that filled the road. Their tightly cramped ranks were instantly eviscerated, thousands of men ripped apart and sending their mangled bodies flailing through the air.

As the gates settled over the bodies, a squall of arrows blasted through the open archway, felling hundreds of the now dispersed and terrified soldiers. Once the arrows ceased, the soldiers peered out from their shields to see the lone figure riding through the gateway. Suddenly, a wall of Gehets rushed past him, and from behind them, charged the armies of Andred.

The Alliance quickly raised their shields as the Gehets slammed into them. Their roar filled men's hearts with dread, the great pillars of fire burning swiftly through the dispersed Alliance. The beasts tore through their front lines, throwing scores of screaming men into the air and sending limbs and entrails flying with every violent swing of their blades.

From behind the Gehets, the armies of Andred rushed forward and crashed into the Alliance.

With the cries of battle, the true fighting began. Bodies tumbled to the earth by the hundreds, blood gushing across the streets as the Andreds plowed mercilessly through their enemy. Rivers of scarlet stained the air and earth below, churning at their knees as the fighting raged on with mindless ferocity.

The mere size of the enemy alone thrust the Alliance swiftly backward. The masses pushed through the city's defenders, turning the cramped streets into a rampant bloodbath.

The Warriors drew their weapons as the fighting raged below, fear setting silent on their hearts. Grim faced and heavy hearted, they bid farewell.

"This is it," Joshua said, "everything we've done has come down to this. Now who's first?"

Silas laughed and clapped his brother on the back. "Looks like you," he jested as he pushed his brother down the stairs. "Now who's last?" With a brusque salute, he turned and dove into the battle.

Isroc pulled his short swords from their sheaths and twirled them skillfully before approaching the stairs. He turned to the others. "See you on the other side." With that, he followed the other soldiers down the stairs.

Aaron shrugged to the remaining Warriors. "I feel like I should say something, anything."

"You've said and done it all," Cain replied, "by being my friend."

Aaron smiled and shook his friend's hand before sprinting over the bodies and down the stairs.

"Let's go, Cain," Adriel said, pulling on his arm. Cain started forward but Malecai jumped before him and stopped Cain in his tracks.

"What are you-"

"Your obligations have shifted now, Cain Taran. It is not about you and your friends anymore. You must begin a new course, one that you have no choice but to follow."

Cain looked at him in bewilderment. "What? Is this about the sword? You're the one who gave me the damn thing!"

Malecai shook his head at this. "I cannot explain the importance of the part you will come to play...but you and you alone must win this war. I am no longer needed."

Cain pulled his arm away from Malecai's strong grip and stepped beside Adriel. He peered at his friend through the squall of arrows that roared around them. "No longer...needed?"

Malecai nodded. "I have done my part. The winds of war are changing; it is you that must help in her transformation."

Cain passed a hand through his hair, struggling to make sense of his friend's puzzling words. "I don't understand."

Malecai returned Cain's gaze despondently. "I do not expect you to. Follow your feet, Cain, and you will find the right direction." Their eyes locked as arrows continued to whip around them. "Now," he said as he raised his sword. "Let us put an end to this war. Let us find the bastard fueling these fires."

"Find the leader?"

"Aye, we will lose this battle if it continues much longer." Malecai stepped closer and rested a hand on Cain's shoulder. "You must realize the power you now have; you must release it if we are to win this war. Let the blood on your hands fill your spirit, for in revenge you shall become the most fearsome of monsters, more wretched than your enemies and more savage in your wrath."

Adriel's hand tightened around Cain's arm as Malecai finished. "I don't like this…" She whispered. Cain glanced at her, her thin lips pursed with distress.

Cain turned to Malecai. "Let's go."

"Good." Malecai sprinted down the stairs and disappeared into the tides of black.

Cain approached the edge of the stairway and looked over his shoulder. Adriel solemnly returned his gaze. Without a word, he raised Ceerocai and rushed down the steps.

He landed among his enemies and brought the massive sword down over their heads. A dozen Andreds were cleft in two as the monstrous blade ripped through their ranks.

With every swing of the great beast, heads and limbs were ripped from their owners; and with every howling strike, death was dealt. Every effortless swing dropped several Andreds, blackened blood pouring over their killer. Cain rushed forward and carved a path through the endless tide of black that now flowed from the city gates.

The fighting continued in utter depravity, a sea of blood and death now flooding the streets. The Andreds, devoid of all former humanity, fought on silently, tirelessly, and with sheer resolve. The Alliance battled with despair, knowing full well that the end was upon them. The hours slowly drained away as the fighting raged on for the front gate.

An endless river of black surged through the open entrance, splitting the fires that now engulfed the entire south wall of Morven. The Andreds charged recklessly into their foes, hacking and cutting violently through every frightened man. Bodies littered the streets amid a sea of blood that now gushed through every inch of the city, torrents of blood and entrails tossed about the legs of the combatants.

Boulders continued to fly over the walls and crash through buildings. Homes and buildings exploded with every clash, raining rubble down on the battling armies. Undiscerning between Andred and men, hundreds of bodies were crushed beneath the debris, screams silenced on the stone below.

The overwhelmed Alliance finally wavered, and every man turned and ran from the bloodbath. Soldiers broke formation and turned their backs on the enemy, fleeing down the streets in madness.

Oceans of Arzecs burst from the throngs and washed over the retreating men, bringing them to the ground before plunging their fangs into their victims. The Andreds fought through the carnage and gave chase to their fleeing prey.

Thousands of men retreated down the market road, screams of horror filling the wartorn skies. Amid such violence, their end was certain.

The Warriors sprinted through the crowds and fought their way through the attacking Arzecs.

Joshua rushed toward a kneeling Arzec and swung his great-axe, cleaving the beast in two. He ran towards the downed soldier to help him. The man wailed in agony, clawing at the entrails that gushed from his stomach. Joshua tore his gaze from the dying man and stumbled over him.

An Arzec suddenly leapt on his back and dug its fangs into his neck. He howled with pain and spun around, swinging his axe wildly into the oncoming hordes.

Silas's Sitar shot from the masses and embedded itself in the Arzec. The creature flew from Joshua's back and Silas rushed forward and pulled his weapon from the Arzec. Together, the brothers plunged their weapons into its chest.

Joshua raised his bloody axe and swung it at a charging Arzec. The blade sliced through its stomach, and he lifted the beast from the ground, raising it above his head as blood poured down on him. With a fearsome bellow, he swung the Arzec into the masses and charged forward. Together, the two Warriors hacked through the enemy, reaping slaughter among the silent Andreds.

Silas stabbed his Sitar forward, plunging it into the face of an onrushing Andred. Using the momentum, he spun himself into the air and over the Andred. He ripped the head from the Andred and impaled his weapon through another. Like a deadly dance, he spun and weaved through the enemy, steel flashing about him in a pirouette of blood.

Aaron hacked his way through a group of Arzecs and passed Silas, screaming, "We have to get out of here! The city's overrun!"

Silas and Joshua reluctantly withdrew and turned their backs on the battle. The three men sprinted down the market road and wove their way through the vast city with thousands of Andreds close on their heels.

Adriel burst from a corner road, a group of Arzecs close on her heels. She screamed for her friends as the hordes enclosed. The men continued their retreat, unable to help her.

Suddenly a boulder crashed overhead and slammed into a tower. The building blasted apart, hurtling debris over the city. Joshua, Aaron, and Silas darted through the raining wreckage and burst out the other side as the tower's remains settled along the road.

Adriel continued forward undeterred and bound nimbly up the rubble, firing arrows into the pursuing Andreds as she climbed higher and higher. She shot a final arrow into the masses, embedding a broad head into the face of an Andred. She turned and flipped gracefully onto the other side and slid down towards her friends.

Together, the four followed the Alliance deeper into the city as the armies of Andred began to trickle through the side roads and over the rubble, soon encompassing half the city.

**** ****

Vastly outnumbered in the city's slums, Cain fought desperately against the encircling Andreds.

"Cain!" a voice called out from the chaos. Cain searched for the source of the call and found Malecai yards away, swinging his sword wildly about him. Cain fought through the Andreds and soon reached his friend.

Malecai swung his sword low, hewing the legs from an Arzec before bringing his sword down over it. He spun and swung his weapon up, cleaving the torso of an Andred in two. He lurched forward and stabbed his sword into the face of another, blood and brain exploding forth as the sword shot through its skull. He wrenched the massive blade from the body and beckoned Cain to follow. Together, the two men tore through the Andreds and up the main road.

Malecai suddenly sped up and rushed towards the back of a Gehet. He threw his sword and the blade tumbled over itself before shooting into the beast's back. The Gehet fell to its knees and Malecai rushed up its back and pulled the sword from its spine before leaping through the flames and swinging it again, breaking off two of its horns. He plunged his sword into the creature's skull, rending its helm asunder with a spurt of dark blood.

The creature crashed to the earth and Malecai grabbed the broken horns from the ground and plunged them into each of the Gehet's eyes, silencing it instantly.

"How did you do that?" Cain cried as Malecai yanked his sword from the bloody mess. Malecai simply smirked and gestured for him to follow.

The two Warriors fled the battlefield and ran for several minutes, flames and debris raining down around them. Malecai grabbed Cain and dove for the shadow of a building. The men paused for a moment and watched as a group of Andreds ran past, giving chase to several terrified men. "Come on," Malecai urged.

They turned and ran for the shadows, weaving their way through the maze of buildings and streets. The sounds of battle slowly faded into the distance as they continued through the slums. They soon came to the docks and paused to catch their breath.

"Where are they retreating to anyways?" Cain asked through haggard breaths.

"There is nowhere to run. They are retreating over the Alar to slow down the Andreds' advance and bide some time at best. The river should prove an effective deterrent for our enemies if we manage to pull the bridges up in time."

He fell quiet as the din of battle once again reached their ears. The two armies clashed on the docks, hundreds of thousands fighting to the bitter death.

"Our friends are over there!" Cain cried and rushed into the moonlight.

Malecai grabbed his hauberk as he passed. "It is not about any of you anymore! Pull your head out of your ass and listen to me!" Cain turned and gave a questioning look to his friend. "There is nothing you can do for them. We have to find their leader and put an end to this..."

Cain sighed and lowered his sword, blood dripping at his feet. "This is the end isn't it, Malecai?"

"Come on," his friend urged. They stepped back into the shadows and turned their backs on the carnage.

They followed the bank of the river, sprinting across the silent docks. After several minutes, Malecai turned and stepped out onto the river, leaving the docks and buildings behind.

"Where are we going?" Cain called out to his friend a few yards ahead.

Malecai stopped and knelt beside a decapitated soldier. The bodies of several Citadel Guards lay limp around them, staining the ice red with blood.

The sound of stirring snow reached their ears and the two men looked up at the direction of the noise. A lone figure approached.

The Spirit of Revenge

Cain and Malecai stepped forward warily, weapons poised.

"I didn't know I would have to kill so many before you would come, but I knew you would, Malecai..." A deep voice called to them through the dark.

Malecai's eyes lit up instantly. "I thought I killed you..."

The whites of his teeth appeared through the dark as the man smirked. "Kill me? I'm as hard to kill as you are."

Cain stared uneasily at the man, struggling to perceive him through the shadows.

He stood a few inches taller than either of them. A great mane of silver hair parted over his forehead and flowed over broad shoulders. He had a sharp nose and sallow lips pierced with metal rings. Black plates of scaled steel covered his large frame from chest to toe, and the crest of a scarlet serpent danced across his breastplate.

"Ten years? Has it been that long?" He pulled his head back and looked up into the brightening skies, the moonlight fleeting across his icy gray eyes. "Let us restore our communion." He held out a hand to Malecai.

"You killed her...Alanis."

Alanis shook his head. "I didn't kill her. You did. Abaddon gave me the order, and I simply followed my instructions. You were getting out of hand again. He needed you put back in place. But don't get me wrong, I enjoyed the deed." He licked his teeth at this. "You see, Malecai...you

311

killed Raven long before I did. You broke the girl's heart. I merely released her from her suffering."

"You're sick!" Cain spat.

"Insult leads to bitter company, Cain Taran!" Cain's eyes lit up at this. "Yes, I know who you are. My master is omnipotent, all knowing, blessed from the very heavens! He is divinity incarnate!" A fierce gale tore across the river as he continued.

"Why do you fight him? You cannot win against the immortal. You can only join him and hope for mercy. Don't you see? No...no you do not. You have never seen him. None of you have. You do not know him, you do not see him. All of Tarsha fights but the idea of him. You fight your own fears, nothing more. We humans are fickle things...we fear the unknown. Do you understand?" Cain remained stolid, sword raised at a moment's call.

"No," Alanis continued, "I would not expect you to. Let me put it into context for you. He sees and knows all...he has wanted you dead for many years. His wishes have gone unfulfilled, even after we destroyed your pathetic Andaurel twice. Yet here you stand before me, giving me the chance to end it all at last."

Cain stared at him for a moment, lost for words. "Because of me...Andaurel was destroyed?"

Alanis smirked. "All because of you." Cain lowered his gaze. "Only you can wield Ceerocai. Only you have the potential to release the spirit within, for in you it recognizes its master. Abaddon's soul was safe in the Tombs of Atuan, allowing him to live unhindered for nearly five hundred years. Now it is found, found by the one that will shape the future of Tarsha. You are a liability, Cain Taran, for as long as you have Ceerocai, Abaddon cannot achieve his genocide."

"What are you saying?"

Alanis brushed the hair from his eyes. "Abaddon has always known of your family's 'uniqueness.' He has spent four centuries eradicating those of the blood, until only you and your parents remained. Why else would we attack Andaurel?

'The first assault on your precious city had but one intent, to eliminate the last remaining threat to Abaddon, your family. Yet, you somehow survived the purge and for the thirty years since, we have hunted you.

'We discovered you had laid roots in your old city, so we attacked Andaurel yet again and killed your son, the last of the blood. Now only you remain."

Cain shook his head at this. "No…this can't be. Because of me Andaurel was destroyed, my family killed, thousands killed…because of me?"

"Don't fret," Alanis continued. "That's not even the half of it. You are the very cause of so much of Tarsha's suffering. Abaddon has waged this genocide in the name of the Forgotten. Long ago he would have succeeded and cleansed the world of the filth that is humanity.

'He needs you dead, Taran. You must be dead. You are the one thing that is standing between him and the Forgotten from easing Tarsha of her misery. That is why we attacked Morven. You see, Abaddon has planned this from the very beginning…

'This attack on Morven is only for you. Abaddon allowed Tarsha to know of this attack beforehand in the knowledge that you would be lured here by your superiors and your own thirst for vengeance. And here you stand…giving me the chance to end this war at last.

'Now do you understand? The attacks on Andaurel, the assault on Abraxas and Alon Heath, they were nothing more than a ruse to lure you in and kill you. Yet you always escaped. Until now. The Destroyer lured you here, giving me the honor to finish you.

'For as long as you are alive with Abaddon's soul in your hands he cannot achieve his god-given vocation. Your so called friend here knew of this; why else would he have given you the sword after so many years of searching for it?"

Cain turned and glared at Malecai. "You knew that the attack on Morven was a plot to kill me? That only I can wield this sword? Why didn't you tell me?"

Malecai looked at him solemnly. "I was going to tell you on the ship back to Morven. But I did not have the heart...you were not supposed to find out like this, Cain."

"Why me? Why me, Alanis?" Cain screamed. "I'm just a soldier! I want my wife back! I want my son! I don't want any of this! I don't understand..." Cain bowed his head in distress. "I don't understand..."

"If only you knew who you really are," Alanis replied, "if only you knew what you could become, the things you could do against the Destroyer. Alanis laughed heartily. "If only you knew, Malecai. Don't you realize the mistake you've made?" Malecai tore his gaze from the man and stared wide eyed at Cain who held Ceerocai before him, stupidly returning his gaze. "You shouldn't have given him the sword, terrible mistake. You've strived for perfection all these years...it must be dreadful to feel only human."

Alanis swung his cloak to the side and revealed a five-foot long sword. The blade was made of dark steel, emblazoned with many jewels. A hilt of twisted steel fashioned like the wings of an eagle curved over a bone handle.

"Allow me to ease your heart of pain. You may finally join your lost love," Alanis flicked his sword up at Malecai, "and maybe this time...she'll forgive you."

"I will kill you right this time!" Malecai screamed. He raised his broadsword and led Cain in a charge towards Alanis.

Malecai threw his sword forward and Alanis blocked the strike, swords clashing with a ring of steel.

Cain rushed past his friend as Alanis jumped back. Their swords met and Cain flicked his weapon back, sliding

Alanis' blade down its edge before catching it in the vicious hook.

"Ah, Ceerocai," Alanis muttered, inhaling deeply as if to smell it. Cain grimaced and spun his sword, breaking their lock. Alanis shot forward and punched Cain in the face before grabbing his arm and forcing him to his knees. With a fierce kick to the chest, Cain was thrown across the ice.

Malecai rushed at Alanis once more and their swords collided in a blur of sparks. Alanis ducked as Malecai's blade swung overhead. He grabbed Malecai by the neck as he dodged and lifted him into the air. Malecai threw a hand onto his arm and black lightning danced between them. Alanis cried out in pain and dropped him.

Malecai then jumped forward and swung his sword as his foe shook himself from the shock. The two men began a fierce exchange of steel, sparks searing across the ice.

Cain ran towards the struggle and threw himself between them. The Iscara spun, blocked his sword, and immediately deflected a blow from Malecai as the two men bore down on him.

Alanis tossed his sword between his hands, deflecting every strike with inhuman ease.

The three swords flew in a haze of gray, singing shrill with every fearsome blow.

Cain jumped back as he parried his opponent's sword and brought it around for a second strike. Alanis blocked the attack and spun his sword, sliding it down Ceerocai's edge. He swung it down and slammed Ceerocai into the ice.

Cain pulled on Ceerocai but Alanis struck him in the throat with the pommel of his weapon and sent him tumbling to the ice.

Malecai jumped over his friend as Alanis brought down his sword. The two blades struck and sent a shower of sparks over Cain.

Alanis swung his opponent's sword to the side and spun around. He thrust his arm out and a wave of wind sent

Malecai skidding across the ice as he struggled to retain his balance.

Alanis stepped back and twirled his sword with indifference. "Even after ten years," he muttered, "nothing has changed. You're still the same weak, tortured soul."

"I have changed much in ten years..."

Alanis flicked his shoulder, knocking the cloak off his back before casting it aside. "And how is that?"

"See for yourself." He suddenly lurched forward and threw his weapon at the man. Alanis jumped aside and the massive sword flew inches past his face before imbedding itself in the ice behind him. Malecai sprinted towards him and swerved to the side.

He flew at his sword and landed on its side before bounding off it. He threw down his hands as he leapt over the Knight, fire exploding from his palms. The flames blazed towards their target, and Alanis dove to avoid them.

Malecai landed and slid across the ice. He held out his palm and his weapon rose from the ice and shot toward its owner. It jumped into his hand as he skidded to a stop, smoke rising about him.

Alanis turned and charged. Malecai jumped into the air and swung his sword. The Iscara jumped as well, and the two men sailed past the other, blades caressing with a kiss of sparks. They landed and dove at each other once again, weapons dancing fiercely.

Cain stood up and shook himself of ice. He rushed towards the fight and unleashed a savage barrage over his opponent.

Alanis barely blocked each strike tossed his way, the enormous swords smashing into him with brutal, crushing blows. The two men continued forward, throwing blow after blow into the Knight, each strike sending him stumbling in desperation.

Alanis swung his sword out and the three blades met in a strident clash of steel. The men struggled against each other, fighting to bring down their opponent.

The Iscara threw his opponents' swords back and jumped away. He then thrust his hands forward and a powerful blast of wind sent the two men flying across the ice.

Alanis then grabbed his sword in both hands, and with a cry on his lips, dropped to one knee and slammed his sword into the ice. A massive web of light shot from his blade and seared across the river. The ice suddenly exploded apart, violently tossing great chunks of ice in the air with a torrent of river water.

**** ****

Night held sway over the skies, the city below cast in its dim abyss. The southern half of the city was now swarming in a black sea of Andreds.

The battle for Morven had turned to a bloodbath, a butchery of the masses. The city streets were soaked knee high in blood, and every second thousands of bodies sank beneath its depths. The battle pulsed across the docks as each side pushed back the other before slowly faltering again.

"Drop the bridge already!" Adriel cried up to the towers behind them.

"We're trying!" A soldier replied as several men wound the gears atop the towers. The chains of the drawbridge gradually lost their slack and lowered the bridge over the river. The Alliance pressed against the drawbridge, their front ranks thinning by the second.

With a great thud, the drawbridge settled at last against the opposing riverbank. The Alliance began a mad dash across the bridge, each fighting for their very lives to cram across the bridge. Hundreds sprinted across the drawbridge, their forces slowly amassing on the other side.

As the last few soldiers crossed the bridge, Darius shouted up to the towers. "Raise the bridge!" The grinding of gears sounded once again and the drawbridge lifted off the riverbank.

Several soldiers still along the bridge screamed in fear as it began to rise from the earth. Higher and higher the bridge climbed, and the men clung desperately to its planking as they were lifted far above the heads of the enemy.

Several lost their grip and slid down the bridge, falling into the beasts below with dreadful screams. The Arzecs and Andreds tore them asunder, entrails spewing and blood gushing from where bodies were only moments before.

The armies of Andred suddenly dove off the docks and charged across the river ice. A vast sea of black soon covered the entire Alar as the enemy began a reckless charge toward their escaping prey.

The ice then gave way beneath the immense weight and plunged thousands of Andreds into the icy depths. They quickly sank beneath the shattered ice, buried instantly in a watery grave.

Yet they continued undeterred, climbing over their drowning brethren and scrambling across the now exploding ice. Countless Andreds were engulfed in the chaos and gripped by the churning tides, silent death warring before the eyes of terrified men.

The Andreds stumbled through the clutches of the Alar and many soon reached the opposing bank. The Alliance held their ground, shields and swords flashing with undying ferocity. Andreds and Arzecs alike were instantly slaughtered upon reaching the north bank, blood now spilling into the Alar.

Thousands began crossing the river's gauntlet to storm the north bank. An endless tide of black soon poured across the Alar to death's embrace.

Above the rushing tide of Andreds, Isroc desperately clung to the now vertical drawbridge. He peered down into the awaiting eyes of thousands of Andreds, fear gnawing at his heart.

An arrow embedded itself near his face and he screamed as several of the beasts began shooting at him. Arrows plinked against the planking around him as he began to climb up the length of the bridge.

Soldiers around him followed his lead and began climbing to the nearby towers. But as they struggled to avoid their fates, death met their escape. Arrows plunged into their backs, sending their bodies dropping into hordes of ravenous Arzecs. Spared by fortune, Isroc continued climbing up the bridge, arrows clinking around him.

A soldier reached down for Isroc as he neared the top of the bridge. However, an arrow struck through the man's neck and he fell silent into the masses below, limbs instantly ripped from his body. Isroc cursed and reached desperately for the tower, mere inches beyond his grasp.

A Gehet burst from a side street and charged at the bridge. With one fell blow, the drawbridge blasted from its chains and hurtled over the river. Isroc clung for his life as the bridge's remains exploded into the icy Alar, crushing hundreds of Andreds beneath its weight.

The Alliance fought beneath an ever-enclosing sea of Andreds, slowly losing ground under a relentless assault. It was only a matter of time before they broke. Death ruled the night, chaos filled the skies; the end was imminent.

**** ****

The ice chunk Malecai and Cain were on suddenly lifted as all of the river's ice rose for the skies. Alanis stood on a nearby ice chunk, sword held at his side and hair dancing in the wind. He jumped for them and raised his sword to strike them down.

The Warriors leapt desperately from the ice, free falling several yards back to earth. They leapt between the ice chunks, sliding across their surfaces before bounding toward another, working their way quickly down to the river. They soon landed heavily on the river ice and looked up to the sky.

Alanis plummeted straight for them, swiftly maneuvering through the ascending ice. He swung his sword, and with a burst of light, cut through a chunk of ice, the remains of which rocketed towards Cain and Malecai.

Malecai dove over Cain and raised his hands, a wall of wind whipping over them as the ice crashed harmlessly into an unseen wall. Alanis landed before them with a great blast of water and ice.

Cain and Malecai leapt off a chunk of ice and onto another as frigid water gushed around them. The two men weaved across the river, desperate to avoid the crashing waters.

Alanis shot through the torrent and their swords clashed yet again. Ice and water smashed around them as they battled across the fracturing ice, the entire surface of the Alar falling apart around them.

They jumped between chunks of ice, balancing across their surfaces. Swords clashed and sparks flew, their wielders mere blurs among the ice as they fought without reprieve.

Cain ducked and narrowly avoided Alanis' swinging blade. He lashed at his opponent's feet and Alanis jumped, the blade slicing harmlessly beneath him. Alanis spun and deflected Malecai's sword before sending a wave of flames gushing from his palm.

Cain jumped before Malecai and threw his weapon before him, the flames bounding harmlessly off the cerebreum blade. He ran forward and twirled his sword, sending the flames returning to its sender. Alanis dove for a separate ice chunk as the flames seared past.

The two Warriors rushed at the Iscara, swords raised with a murderous cry. Malecai threw himself forward and skidded across the ice towards his opponent. He pulled his arm back and tossed his sword at Alanis again. Alanis deflected the flailing sword and sent it into the air.

Malecai flipped over the Knight and caught his weapon in mid air, spinning around as he landed to block a strike.

As their swords met, Cain rushed forward and released a fearsome barrage. Alanis fended off the roaring blade before jumping to a different hunk of ice.

He lifted his hands, and again the river's ice rose into the air. Cain jumped off as their platform rose slowly into the air. Malecai and Alanis continued dueling across the ever-rising ice, water and ice swirling around them as they ascended higher into the skies.

Alanis turned from the fight and jumped to a separate ice chunk. Malecai bound and landed beside him. The Knight jumped again and leapt between the many ice chunks, Malecai close behind. Their swords sped near a blur as they strafed back and forth, struggling to push the other off the still ascending ice.

Alanis feined right and dove forward as Malecai's blade sped past. He slammed his palm into Malecai's chest and with a flare of wind and light, blasted his opponent off the ice. He landed painfully on his back on another chunk as Alanis descended upon him. The Knight swung his sword and cleft the ice in two.

The river's ice fell swiftly back to earth and Malecai fell helplessly among them, knocked about by every slab of ice. The ice crashed into the river and Malecai disappeared in an explosion, freezing water gushing around him.

Alanis landed lightly as the water fell back to the river. Malecai groaned with pain amid a fractured platform, near buried in ice. Alanis stepped over him, a smirk on his lips at the sight of his downed opponent. Cain cried out to his friend, but separated by several yards of water; he could do nothing but watch what was to happen.

Alanis kicked Malecai's sword away, sending it sliding to a stop feet away. Malecai clenched his chest and tried to crawl toward his weapon, but every crack of his ribs forced him to stop.

"Look at me," Alanis ordered before kicking him in the side. Malecai rolled over and looked helplessly up at Alanis. The Knight brought up his sword and swung it across his ribs, throwing a spray of blood into the air. Malecai let out a feeble gasp.

"No!" Cain screamed as Malecai struggled to crawl away from his advancing opponent. A trail of blood poured from Malecai's open chest, and Alanis stepped slowly over him, bloody footsteps in his wake. Alanis grabbed Malecai's arm, and with a forceful throw, sent him rolling across the ice.

The Iscara walked forward and stepped over his dying opponent. Malecai lay in a crumpled mess atop the ice, blood gushing from his open chest. He gasped for air, struggling to fill his collapsing lungs.

Alanis rested his sword tip against Malecai's neck. He looked down his weapon at him and sneered. "Get up..." He knelt down, grabbed Malecai by the neck, and pulled him to his knees. "At last...you are human." He propped a boot against Malecai's bloodied face and pushed.

Malecai fell back through the ice and was quickly swallowed by the depths of the Alar. He reached for air, flailing above the water's surface for a few precious moments. Slowly he slipped through the ice and his body disappeared beneath the depths. The stream of air bubbles ceased and the ice caps slowly rolled back in place, sealing his watery grave.

"Malecai!" Cain screamed out in agony. "Malecai! No!"

Alanis stepped back in silence and sighed at his victory. He turned and looked over his shoulder at his last remaining opponent.

Cain stared on in disbelief, Ceerocai held limp in his shaking hands. His friend had just been murdered, swallowed up by the depths of the Alar. Cain blinked slowly and lowered his head, fighting the disbelief that swirled in his mind.

He had struggled to drown out his revenge, his blood-lust, but now it swelled within him, fighting to be freed one final time.

"Yes, Cain," Alanis muttered, "show me the animal you really are."

Cain raised Ceerocai and looked up at his friend's killer, hate pouring into his heart. The sword in his hand suddenly began to glow a bright scarlet, pulsating with every beat of its wielder's racing heart.

Alanis staggered back and eyed the glowing blade curiously, its light beating now with a life of its own. Cain closed his eyes for a moment and felt the heated steel in his hands and its bloody light flicker against his face.

He opened his eyes and charged forward, nearly a blur as he rushed toward his opponent. Cain jumped from the ice and blasted through the air, a bloodthirsty scream on his lips as he sailed the several yards toward his foe.

Alanis jumped back as the sword slammed into the ice with a shower of steam, cleaving the ice clean in half. He burst from the falling ice and shot towards his opponent, screaming in rage.

Their swords met with an explosion of sparks and they began a violent exchange of steel, flying across the ice with inhuman speed.

Under the fury of Ceerocai, Alanis relented and jumped off the ice chunk, landing lightly on another.

Cain landed beside him and spun as Alanis struck out at him, swords meeting in a lock. The two men fought across the ice for several moments, swords howling with every clash of steel. Alanis deflected a blow from his opponent and thrust his palm forward, sending Cain flying backwards through the air.

Cain quickly stabbed his sword in the ice as he rocketed through the air, and using the momentum of the blade, swung himself back to the ground. He pulled the sword from the ice and jumped backwards. The blade tore the ice apart, splitting the platform in two overhead. He landed on one of the halves and the ice crashed into Alanis, water erupting about them. Cain burst through the flood and descended upon Alanis. Ceerocai plowed into Alanis's sword and instantly shattered it.

The Iscara faltered and stared at the useless stub in his hand. Cain returned his glare, their eyes locked in the quiet of the falling snow.

Suddenly, the weapon in Cain's hands shook violently. The entire sword trembled and threw forth growing rays of scarlet across the ice.

The sword raised itself and pointed towards the heavens. A great wind shot down from the skies above. A resounding clap echoed through the air, stirring the skies and river below.

The clouds swirled and parted, and from them, a great light fell. The fiery light shot down from the heavens and crashed into the ice with a tremendous explosion.

Cain cautiously peered from behind his hand at the strange light. Slowly it faded and revealed some unearthly creature.

It stood many yards above even Gehet and many more in length. Its blood red scales shimmered dully, as if the light of day never left its flawless surface. Depthless eyes glowered down at Cain, ebony jewels amid its massive, ruby head. Seven horns adorned its head, each curving out like the prongs of a crown, and one curving out far before its face.

Above its fanged maw were two slits of nostrils. A long row of spines extended from the top of its neck to the tip of its sword-like tail that stretched as long as its body.

The beast stood on four legs as thick as the trunks of trees. Ebony claws extended from each of its colossal feet, its knife-like talons impaling the ice upon which it stood.

The animal flicked its shoulders and four bony limbs lifted from its side. They stretched out from its body for several yards, revealing four massive wings of membranous tissue.

It was surreal, grotesque, and yet strangely beautiful. The very fires of hell seemed to glow within its ribs, playing across its ruby scales with the radiance of a dawning sky.

The beast's wings shuddered and it stooped its great chest low to the earth. With a deep, bloodcurdling growl, it turned its head to Cain, a thin wisp of smoke rising from its grimacing maw.

Cain held Ceerocai unnervingly before him, the blade now flickering a fierce crimson with every pulse of light that arced along the beast's scales.

The creature lowered its head at him, the black abyss of its eyes seeming to swallow Cain by mere whim. It turned these hell-bound eyes from Cain with satisfaction before turning its attention to Alanis.

The Knight started back in fright beneath the shadow of the monster, a stump of steel gripped uselessly in his hand.

The creature threw its head up and opened its maw, its black tongue quivering in the chill air as it bellowed forth an ungodly roar. It shot out its wings and swept into the air.

Alanis let out a terrified scream and tossed the stub of his sword before sprinting across the ice, running for his life. The beast spanned the gap in an instant, its great wings carrying it effortlessly through the air.

Alanis dove for the ice and buried his head in his arms. The creature sailed overhead and flicked its wings, throwing itself higher into the sky. Alanis picked himself up and ran for his life, eyes lit with terror.

The beast hovered above, eyes locked on its prey. It suddenly plummeted to the earth and descended over him.

A great plume of ivory flames shot from its gaping maw, completely engulfing Alanis. A gut-wrenching cry filled the sky as every inch of his body was instantly incinerated.

The winged beast sailed through the flames and crashed into its prey, sending his flaming body sailing through the air. Anguish flew from his lips as Alanis crashed through the ice.

The river instantly swallowed him whole and snuffed out his smoldering remains beneath the ice. A great pillar of smoke rose from the churning waters as he flailed for his life. Slowly, his body disappeared beneath the depths. The ice caps settled back into place and the smoke faded in the winds.

Cain stood frozen in bewilderment as he watched the beast circle victoriously overhead, merely a blur in the bright dawn sky. He lowered his gaze to the sword in his hand.

The glowing light around the blade flickered before dying, and bringing with it, the light of the creature's scales. It seemed to diminish, scales, talons, wings and all. As the fires left its flesh, the creature let out a final roar. A vivid flash of scarlet lit up the skies and sent a pulse of wind rippling across the earth.

Then as swiftly as it had come, the creature vanished. The spirit of the sword returned to its ever-silent slumber, Ceerocai once again still in his hand.

Cain stared at the sword with disbelief. What was that beast? Why did it help him? Why can he alone use the sword? What makes him such a valuable target to Abaddon? All these questions and countless more swirled in his mind. He shook his head to clear his thoughts if even for a moment.

He looked down the length of the Alar to the city of Morven that lay barely visible through the snowfall. The hellish din of battle had long since ceased. An ear-splitting cry filled his ears as thousands of men screamed with victory.

The battle had been won. The armies of Andred were at last routed from their land. Peace had been bought for a few precious moments.

However, the war was still to be won, the genocide was still to be stopped. It would only grow in magnitude. A perpetual spiral of death embraced Tarsha. As long as Abaddon's soul lived on inside this wretched Ceerocai, Cain knew it would only continue.

With Malecai swept from life, it seemed Cain was now the only one who knew the truth. Death and war would hold sway over humanity eternal, an unjust punishment for some past transgressions.

The only way to end all of this lay in his hands, the indestructible key to Abaddon's soul. Fighting this war was useless, and the deaths of millions meant nothing as long as Ceerocai remained. However, what good was this knowledge if it could not be destroyed.

Despite this grave truth, Cain knew he must continue. He fought for more than a spirit of revenge; he fought for more than himself and his own petty vengeance. He was finally fighting for something now, something that mattered. He fought for hope, a white rose in the bloody tides of war.

He ran a hand through his soaked hair and gazed up into the sky. He closed his eyes and felt the cool kiss of snow on his face.

The battle for Tarsha and the rebirth of the Alliance had been won, but a strange air now brewed in the winds. A feeling of tension fell over him. War it seemed...had only just begun.

**** ****

Thus concludes Book one of
The Atonement Trilogy

Excerpt of Book two

A New Reign

The doors to the throne room burst open. A hooded figure stood in the doorframe, peering intently into the dark hall before him.

Lofty windows lined the walls and small torches flickered against their glass, filling the room with a dim, ruddy light. The man tightened his grip on the rapier in his hand and cautiously walked down the hall.

All was silent. Nothing filled the room's empty walls but the clicking of his boots. At last, he came to a stop at the foot of a dais. Sitting in a massive ebony throne at its top, was Abaddon.

The tyrant of Tarsha gazed down at the intruder through the slits of his elaborate helmet. "At last, you have returned to me..." He spoke with a cold and rasping voice, a voice that had lost all warmth long ago.

"Do not play games," the man replied, "You know why I am here."

"I do."

The man flicked his hand at this. Every torch instantly flashed a vivid blue, lighting up the entire room. He raised his rapier to Abaddon and muttered, "I have come to kill you..."

**** ****